Friction | **6**

Friction 6

Best Gay Erotic Fiction

Edited by
Jesse Grant and Austin Foxxe

alyson books
los angeles | new york

© 2003 BY ALYSON PUBLICATIONS. AUTHORS RETAIN COPYRIGHT TO THEIR INDIVIDUAL ARTI-
CLES UNLESS OTHERWISE STATED. ALL RIGHTS RESERVED.

MANUFACTURED IN THE UNITED STATES OF AMERICA.

THIS TRADE PAPERBACK ORIGINAL IS PUBLISHED BY ALYSON PUBLICATIONS,
P.O. BOX 4371, LOS ANGELES, CALIFORNIA 90078-4371.
DISTRIBUTION IN THE UNITED KINGDOM BY TURNAROUND PUBLISHER SERVICES LTD.,
UNIT 3, OLYMPIA TRADING ESTATE, COBURG ROAD, WOOD GREEN,
LONDON N22 6TZ ENGLAND.

FIRST EDITION: FEBRUARY 2003

03 04 05 06 07 a 10 9 8 7 6 5 4 3 2 1

ISBN 1-55583-768-9

LIBRARY OF CONGRESS CATALOGING-IN-PUBLICATION DATA
  FRICTION, VOLUME 6 : BEST GAY EROTIC FICTION / EDITED BY JESSE GRANT AND
  AUSTIN FOXXE.—1ST ED.
    ISBN 1-55583-768-9
    1. GAY MEN—FICTION. 2. GAY MEN'S WRITINGS, AMERICAN. 3. EROTIC STORIES,
  AMERICAN. I. TITLE: FRICTION SIX. II. GRANT, JESSE. III. FOXXE, AUSTIN.
  PS648.H57 F756 2003
  813'.008'03538—DC21   2002038564

COVER PHOTOGRAPHY BY BRAD ERICKSEN.

Contents

Preface

I love this job. Who could complain about having to choose the hottest tomatoes from the past year's bumper crop of gay erotic fiction? Certainly, you'll not hear any bitching from me. And if you do, I can point you toward a few leather daddies in these pages who'd be more than willing to teach my whiny ass a lesson!

Along with my coeditor Austin Foxxe, I invite you to sit back, unzip, and tuck in to some of the hottest scenes we've ever seen in print. You'll find glory hole action and construction site shenanigans, first-timers and gang-bangers, lighthearted fantasy and hard-core power fucks raunchy enough to make Mama clutch her pearls—though you might want to get a grip on something else.

Special thanks go to Nick Street, the latest addition to the editorial team at Alyson. It's been a pleasure breaking in the new guy.

Enjoy.

—Jesse Grant

Late Night, Summer, Behind the Garage

Duncan Frost

I finished drying the last of the dishes, then stepped out onto the back porch for a breath of fresh air. Gary, the guy I was renting a room from, waved at me as his pickup rolled down the drive. He was heading across town to spend the night with Lena, the gal he'd been carrying on with for the past couple of months.

Hell, I wished I had somebody to fool around with, but I hadn't been having much luck meeting anyone since my divorce was finalized a year before. But to tell the truth, I hadn't been making much of an effort. Maybe I was afraid of finding myself in another disastrous situation like the one I'd just left. Whatever the reason, I was bored blind and horny as hell! I figured I'd been staring for way too long at the cracks in the bedroom ceiling while jerking off, so I sauntered across the backyard and slipped behind the garage instead. There, snug between the garbage cans and the rusted hulk of an old lawn mower, I leaned back against the wall. I peeled off my sweat-soaked T-shirt and ran a hand over my belly, ruffling the long, silky hairs that trailed down the middle. I flexed my arms, which were knotted with solid muscle.

Doing heavy construction work wasn't necessarily the easiest way to stay in shape, but it did the trick well enough. Thinking about muscles reminded me that I had one particular muscle that

1

needed special attention. I popped open the button fly on my jeans and pushed them down my thighs. My cock swung free, already starting to grow. I wrapped my fingers around the fat, veiny shaft and gave it a friendly squeeze. Within seconds my hand was full of hard, hot cock. I was jerking off to beat the band, really starting to get into it, when all of a sudden I stopped dead. I could've sworn I heard some heavy breathing besides my own. I listened intently. I heard it again. It was coming from the other side of the old wooden fence that separated our backyard from the house behind us. There was a knothole right in front of me, so I crept over to it and had a look. Damn if there wasn't a guy standing buck naked on the other side. He was tall and slim, built like a swimmer. A distant streetlight cast a silvery glow on his skin and his curly pale hair. His eyes were closed, but he sure as hell wasn't napping. His fist was moving up and down like a piston, heating up his salami big time. I backed away, figuring he probably wouldn't like the idea of someone spying on him. At least I wasn't the only dude in town who was getting his rocks off solo.

Somewhat to my surprise, finding out that I wasn't alone hadn't made me any less horny. My cock was still jutting up in the air and leaking like a faulty pipe. I got a good grip on it and went back to business. I was moving in on the magic moment—kind of getting off on the thought of another dude stroking it within arm's reach—when I heard a muffled grunt from across the fence. I leaned forward and peered through the knothole just in time to see my neighbor shoot his load. Jism gushed out of him and splattered onto the ground at his feet. I pounded my prick like mad and blew my wad as well.

Afterward, I sank down on my haunches, letting the warm breeze ruffle the hairs on my chest. I didn't move till I heard the guy on the other side of the fence go back into his house.

As it turned out, that guy was a horny bastard. He was there every night for the next two weeks, whacking his wang like he'd just discovered it hanging between his legs that very day. I kind of enjoyed the company, although we never said anything. I mean, I sure as hell wasn't about to lean over the fence and exchange comments about the weather with some stranger while he was beating off.

One Saturday night it was hot as blazes and lightning was flashing way off in the distance. After I'd watched the news, I headed back to the scene of the crime. I peeled off my shirt, used it to wipe the sweat off my face and torso, then dropped it on the ground beside me. I had just popped the top button on my fly when my neighbor's head appeared above the fence.

"Evening," the guy said. "Mind if I come over?"

"Uh…I guess not," I sputtered.

"Hot tonight, isn't it?" he remarked cheerily as he vaulted over the fence.

"Uh…yeah," I said gruffly. My conversational skills had deserted me completely. I jammed my hands in my pockets and stared stonily at the fence. I wanted him to go away, but I also kind of liked having him there, standing next to me. It was weird.

"Seems like we've got a common interest," he said. I looked over at him. He glanced at my crotch, then looked down at his own. The strange situation had done nothing to shrink the lump in my pants. He was obviously suffering from the same problem.

"It appears that we're both pretty horny guys," he continued.

"I guess we are at that," I admitted. I looked at the man again. He winked at me.

"I'd sure as hell like to climb your frame, buddy."

"I'm not…I mean, I'm…" I sputtered to a stop. The situation was rapidly spinning out of control.

"I'm getting pretty damned tired of hand jobs," he said. "How about you?" Of course I was tired of jacking off, but I sure as hell wasn't going to tell him that! Who knew what might happen then? The dude was staring at my chest, like he was trying to count the hairs or something. I glanced down at my shirt, wadded up on the ground at my feet. Shit, I should've left it on.

Next thing I knew he was touching me, his fingers splayed across the expanse of my pecs. "Damn, buddy, you're fuckin' hot," he muttered. He grabbed my shoulders and started kneading the knotted muscles. Then he stroked my belly and slipped his fingers into the waistband of my jeans. I groaned when I felt the buttons popping.

"Oh, yeah," the guy murmured as he pulled my hard-on free of my jeans. "Nice cock, man. Fuckin' hot." He wrapped his fingers around the shaft and squeezed. I suddenly felt weak in the knees and leaned against the wall of the garage.

He pressed himself against me and ran his fingers through the hair on my chest. "You can touch me, buddy," he whispered. "I won't mind." I clamped my hands on his arms. His skin felt like warm silk stretched over hard muscle.

He put his mouth on my left tit and started sucking. The touch of his soft lips shot sparks of pleasure straight to my throbbing groin. He bit into the tender flesh, and his warm spit drooled down onto my belly. I tangled my fingers in his curly hair and pulled his head back. His eyes were closed. His pink tongue flickered across his upper lip. I leaned down and started kissing him. His lips parted and his tongue darted out, forcing its way deep into my mouth. We kissed for a long time.

Lightning flashed around us, followed by a loud rumble of thunder. I looked skyward as the world lit up again. This was so fucking strange: me, a 30-year-old hetero construction worker, holding some guy I'd just met so tight that he could hardly breathe and kissing him while his hard cock throbbed against my belly. It should have been a total turnoff, but it wasn't.

"Damn, you sure can kiss," the guy said, winking at me again and pinching my tits hard. "Now let's see what else you can do."

"Huh?" I stood there, looking at him dully. He shook his head, then dropped to his knees in front of me.

"Got a rubber?" he asked. I nodded. I always keep one in my wallet, just in case. I retrieved it and gave it to him. He ripped open the foil pouch, plopped it onto the end of my cock, and rolled it slowly down the shaft.

I damn near howled when his lips touched my knob. Then he was going down on me, sliding lower and lower, till my cock was buried deep in his throat. He sucked and slurped noisily, slobbering all over my hairy balls, his head bobbing up and down, his forehead smacking into my belly as regular as clockwork. It was fuckin' hot.

"Well," I rumbled, pulling him to his feet roughly. "I guess now I know what a cocksucker does." I winked at him and dropped to my knees. I'd never even thought about sucking cock until that moment, but I sure got thinking about it then! Hell, I figured all you had to do was open your mouth and slobber. I knelt there in the grass and watched him take a condom from his own pocket and bag his dick in latex. It stuck straight out from his pubes, bouncing up and down with his heartbeat. I swallowed him, and my hands cupped his sleek ass cheeks. He shuddered, and his thighs pressed tightly against my hairy chest.

I was kind of awkward at first, but after I slowed down and got into it, it seemed to come real naturally. His prick was a perfect fit for my mouth. When his pubes were tickling my nose, his knob was just nudging at my tonsils. I tried to duplicate his moves, bobbing up and down and sucking in my cheeks. Judging by his groans, I must have done OK.

I was really getting into this cocksucking stuff, squeezing his tight little ass while I slammed his hard belly against my face. I could have kept it up for hours, but he grabbed me by the hair and yanked my head away.

"I got some other things for us to try out," he gasped, leering down at me. "Stand up, buddy."

I did.

"So—what now?" I asked, humping my cock against his belly. He was a handsome little fucker: full lips, chiseled features, wideset eyes. I couldn't really tell in this light, but I suspected that they were blue. His nose looked like it had been busted a couple of times. No doubt about it, I was making it with another man—and I was liking it!

He spit in his palm, then held it out to me. I spit too. He lubed my hard-on, then spun around and braced one hand against the wall of the garage. Lightning lit up the sky again, and I felt the first drops of rain falling on my head and shoulders.

"You ready for it?" the man groaned. I stared at my swollen cock. It was so hard the shaft was arced backward like a tightly strung bow. I was ready all right! He reached around and grabbed me. I leaned into him and felt something tight and springy press against my cock knob.

The sky split open at that moment, lashing us with sheets of rain, but all I was really aware of was the incredible heat I felt as I thrust forward, penetrating him. The muscles in his shoulders jerked, and he pressed the heel of his other hand against my belly. I reached around him and gripped his stiffy. I stripped off his rubber and started pumping. Hot, slippery juice drooled across my hairy knuckles. His hand dropped from my belly, and I thrust deeper, sinking slowly into his yielding body. When I was buried to the hilt, he looked around at me.

"Fuck me," he whispered, his voice hoarse and dreamy. "Fuck me senseless." I pumped my hips tentatively. His asshole clenched around the base of my cock. The rain beat down, glistening on his shoulders, and his curly hair was plastered to his neck. "Fuck me," he cried, his voice muffled by the storm. "Fuck me!"

I braced my hands on his shoulders and fucked frantically— my nuts bounced off his every time I drove my cock home. He writhed against me, and the muscles in his ass contracted spas- modically, playing my cock like a hot, wet fist. It was like nothing I'd ever done, and I never wanted it to stop.

The rain fell in torrents, cascading down the dude's back, then running over my balls. I knew I was gonna blow any second, so I pressed him up against the wall of the garage and put one hand on his cock, the other on his balls. He twitched and squirmed against me, his ass pipe grabbing at my cock frantically. Hell, that did it. I slammed back into him and pumped my heavy load into the rubber stuffed up his tight ass. He shot too, coating the wall of the garage with glittering trails of thick white jism.

The rain stopped soon afterward, and we stayed out behind the garage all night, talking and laughing and fucking our brains out.

Around sunrise, I boosted him back over the fence. We didn't make a date or anything like that, but somehow I figured I wouldn't be facing any more solo jack-off action anytime soon.

School Queer

Bob Vickery

Saturday night is my night to shine. All the guys neck with their dates out at Bass Lake, or the drive-in over on Route 27, or maybe at Jackson Lookout. But because the girls here are all "saving themselves," they tend to get the guys wound up so tight that the poor young studs could fuck a knotty pine by the time they finally take the little virgins home. So with blue balls aching, they head to the back of the Bass Lake boathouse, where they know they'll find me, waiting. I suck the hard cocks of these Southern Baptist boys. I let them frantically fuck my face as they clamp their eyes shut and imagine its not my mouth wrapped around their stiff, urgent dicks, but *pussy.*

They groan and whimper while their full-to-bursting balls slap against my chin, and when they finally shoot, they cry out "Cindy Lou" or "Peggy Beth" as their loads splatter against the back of my throat. When they've finally got the relief they've needed all evening, the guys pull up their jeans and walk away, disappearing into the bushes without so much as a "Thanks." But before I can get too resentful, the next shadowy figure rounds the corner of the boathouse, and the ritual starts up all over again. Sometimes there are actual lines. Other times, the guys stand side by side, and I work my way down the row and tend to the stiff dicks throbbing in front of me. During the week, I'm shunned by most of the other students at the small Baptist college I attend. But on Saturday night the boys can't get enough of me. It's a lonely life, being the school queer, but I serve a useful function, so I'm tolerated.

I don't suck every dick that comes my way. And among the men I deign to suck off, I do have my favorites. At the top of the list is Bill McPherson—what a sweet, hot guy. I can tell he was raised right: well-nourished, muscular body, straight teeth, clear complexion, glossy brown hair, steady blue eyes that meet your gaze with honest conviction. And so *earnest*! That's the charm of these Baptist boys. They're so damn *wholesome*—you just want to eat them up. Bill is well-liked on campus, an unexceptional student but still a big fish in this tiny pond: captain of the wrestling team and vice-president of the Kappa Gamma Chi fraternity. He dates Becky Michaelson, this year's Azalea Princess in the school's homecoming parade. Lucky for me: She holds on to her cherry as if it were a piece of the One True Cross. More Saturdays then I can remember, Bill has come around behind the boathouse, frustrated, shy, embarrassed, dropped his pants, and offered his dick to me. And it's such a beautiful dick: thick, meaty, veined, pink and swollen, with a head that flares out like a fleshy red plum.

I love making love to Bill's dick. I suck it slowly, drag my tongue up the shaft, and finally turn my attention to the head. Then I probe into Bill's piss slit, work my lips back down the thick tube of flesh, and roll Bill's ball sac around in my mouth as I stroke him. His cock is familiar enough to me that I'm able to draw him to the brink of shooting, back off, and draw him even closer.

Bill gasps and groans, his breathing gets heavy, his body trembles under my hands as I knead and pull on his muscled torso. When he finally shoots—every time he shoots—he cries out "Sweet Jesus in Heaven!" Like he's offering his orgasm to God. When I finally climb to my feet, wiping my mouth, damn if Bill doesn't look me in the eye, shake my hand, and thank me. It's a small thing, maybe, but he's the only one who acknowledges me, which gives me just one more reason to like him.

Except for his final thanks, Bill has never spoken to me during our cocksucking sessions. So it's something of a surprise when one late-spring night, while I'm on my knees before him, he clears his throat and asks, "Do...do you ever do this to Nick Stavros?"

I take Bill's dick out of my mouth and look up at him, but his face is in shadow and I can't read his expression. I know from seeing the two of them around campus together that Bill and Nick are good friends. "Yeah," I reply. "Nick comes around here from time to time. Not nearly as much as you do."

Bill doesn't say anything, and I pick up where I left off. I twist my head as I slide my lips up Bill's cock shaft, because I know he likes that. He starts to pump his hips and slide his dick in and out of my mouth. After about a minute, Bill clears his throat again. "What's Nick's dick like?" he asks. I look up at him again, and Bill, seeing the quizzical expression on my face, laughs nervously. "Nick's always kidding me about what a ladies' man he is," he says, "and so I was just curious about how he...well, measures up to me."

"You don't have anything to worry about," I say. "Your dick is awesome." I put it back in my mouth.

"Yeah, well, OK," Bill says, "but what's Nick's dick like?"

This is weird, I think. "You really want me to describe Nick's dick?"

"Yeah," Bill says. "Do you mind?" By his tone of voice, I'm almost sure he's blushing.

"Unlike yours, it's uncut," I begin. "And a lot darker. It curves down, which makes it easier for me to suck. Though I sometimes wonder whether that makes it harder for him to actually fuck someone. It's a mouthful, but not quite as long as yours, though maybe a little thicker. His piss slit is really pronounced."

Bill listens intently, as if there's going to be an after-lecture test on all of this. I half expect him to start taking notes. When he doesn't say anything else, I return to blowing him. After another minute he clears his throat again. "And his balls, what are they like?"

OK, I think. "He's got some low-hangers," I say. "They're a couple of bull nuts. When he fucks my face, they slap against my chin. I love sucking on them, washing them with my tongue, though I can only do them one at a time. They're too big to fit in my mouth at the same time."

Bill says nothing else during the remainder of his blow job. As his dick gets harder, right before he shoots, he winds his fingers into my hair and gently tugs at it. "Sweet Jesus in Heaven" he murmurs, as usual, just before his dick pulses and floods my mouth with his load. On my knees before Bill, I hold the post for a long moment, as his dick slowly softens in my mouth. Finally, he let himself slip out of me and pulls his jeans up. As always, he shakes my hand and thanks me before disappearing into the night.

From that night on, we settle into a new routine whenever I suck Bill off. Bill peppers me with questions, asking for more details about Nick's cock, or his balls, or his ass, or how he acts when he shoots. I carefully answer every question, describing in detail just what it feels like to have Nick slide his dick in my mouth. Eventually, I tell him how Nick likes to push my face hard against his belly, to make me choke on his dick and to see my nose buried in his dense thicket of black pubes. We establish that the odor of Nick's balls is like the sweaty, pungent scent of a male animal in rut. I recount the low grunts Nick makes as his load squirts down my throat, and what that load tastes like (salty, with just a faint hint of garlic). I watch Bill's dick stiffen whenever I give him a report on my sessions with Nick, and I think how strange it is to know Bill's secret: He is queer for his best friend.

One day Bill catches up to me on the main quadrangle. I try to hide my surprise. Normally, nobody as high up on the campus pecking order as Bill would be caught dead talking in public to the school queer.

"Hey, Pete," he says. "How's it going?"

"I'm OK," I say cautiously.

We walk along the brick path in silence. The people we pass stare at us with the same astonishment I feel. "Look, Pete," Bill says, lowering his voice but keeping his eyes straight ahead. "Can you be at the boathouse tonight? Around eleven?"

I let a couple of beats go by. "It's a weekday night, Bill. I have a chemistry test tomorrow that I have to study for."

Bill stops and looks at me, and I can see the desperation in his eyes. "I'm begging you, man," he says.

This is all *very* weird. "OK," I finally say. "If it's that big a deal for you, I'll be there."

Bill looks relieved. "Thanks," he says. He turns on his heel and walks off.

The moon is nearly full tonight, and its light bounces off the lake and flickers against the boathouse walls. I sit on one of the overturned boats, smoke a cigarette, and wait. I glance at my watch: a little past eleven. There's a rustle of bushes, and Bill steps out into the light.

"Hi, Bill," I say. But Bill looks behind him, not toward me. Again the bushes rustle, and suddenly Nick steps out and stands next to Bill. He glances at me, scowls, and looks away.

Bill takes a couple of steps closer. "Nick and I were double-dating tonight," he says, "But our girls just wouldn't put out." He gives a laugh that rings as false as a tin nickel. "And, boy, do we have a nut to bust! So we just swung by here tonight on the off chance that you'd be here to help us get a little relief."

I look at Nick, but he's still staring at the ground, refusing to meet my eye. My gaze shifts back to Bill. "You guys are in luck," I say coolly. "I'm normally not here on a weekday night."

Neither Bill nor Nick says anything. After a couple of beats, I decide it's up to me to get this ball rolling. "Who wants to go first?" I ask.

"Why don't you go ahead, Nick?" Bill says, turning toward him. "I'll wait."

Nick shrugs, still taciturn. He has on a pair of cutoffs and a school T-shirt that tightly hugs his torso. Nick can be a surly bastard, and I like Bill way better, but there's no denying Nick's the more handsome of the two: intense, dark eyes, an expressive mouth, powerful arms, a muscle-packed torso, and tight hips. As always, I feel my heart racing as he unbuckles his belt. I pull his cutoffs down past his thighs, and his fleshy, half-hard dick swings heavily from side to side.

"You take care of my buddy, Pete," Bill says. "Suck him good!"

I glance at Bill. His lips are parted and there's a manic gleam in his eyes. If he were any more excited, he'd have a stroke. Because I like Bill, I decide to give him the show he so obviously wants. I look up at Nick. "Why don't you take off all your clothes?" I say quietly. "It'll be more fun that way."

Nick glares down at me fiercely. After a brief pause, he hooks his fingers under the edge of his T-shirt and pulls it over his head, to reveal his muscular torso. He kicks off his shoes and steps out of his cutoffs. "OK?" he asks sarcastically. I glance again at Bill. He marvels at Nick's naked body like a starving dog eyeing a T-bone steak.

"Yeah," I say. "That's just fine." I wrap my hand around Nick's dick and give it a squeeze. A clear drop of precome oozes out of his piss slit, and I lean forward and lap it up. I roll my tongue around his cock head and slide my lips down his shaft. I feel the thick tube of flesh harden to full stiffness in my mouth. I begin to bob my head and turn at an angle to give Bill a maximum view of the show. Nick responds by pressing his palms against both sides of my head and pumping his hips. Ever the aggressive mouth fucker, he slides his dick deep into my throat and pulls out again.

Bill moves toward us and stands next to Nick. He unzips his jeans, tugs them down, and his dick springs up, fully hard. "Now me," he says hoarsely. I look up into his face, but his eyes are trained on Nick's rigid, spit-slicked cock. Bill's the big man on campus, and I may be the queer boy with zero status, but tonight the tables are turned. It's clear that sweet Bill wants nothing more than to trade places with me: to get down on his knees and work Nick's dick like I'm doing. He wants Nick to plow his face. But it'll never happen. The closest he can let himself get to this fantasy is to have me suck his dick with the taste of Nick's dick still in my mouth. I actually pity the guy as I take his frustrated prong in my hand and slide my lips down the shaft.

While I work on Bill's dick, I reach over and start jacking off Nick. Nick pumps his hips, fucking my fist the same way he fucked my mouth a minute ago. One thrust catches him off balance, and to steady himself he reaches out and lays his hand on Bill's shoulder. Bill reacts as if Nick's touch is a jolt of high-voltage current—his body jerks suddenly, and his muscles spasm. *This poor guy wants it so bad,* I think. With my hand still around Nick's dick, I pull him closer to me until his dick is touching Bill's. I open my lips wider and take both their dicks in my mouth, feeling them rub and thrust against each other. Bill trembles at the sensation of Nick's dick against his, and Nick's breath comes out in short grunts.

I wrap my hands around their ball sacs and give them both a good tug. Bill groans, I feel his dick throb, and my mouth fills with his creamy load. "Sweet Jesus in Heaven!" he gasps. Nick thrusts hard into my throat, his breath comes faster now, and his legs begin to tremble. Suddenly, his body quivers, and his dick squirts jizz. I suck hard on the two dicks as they pulse in my mouth, their combined loads splattering against the back of my throat. I roll my tongue through the double dose in my mouth, savoring it like a gourmet.

Nick and Bill pull away. For a brief moment the three of us are frozen in our positions: me on my knees, come dribbling out of the corners of my mouth, Bill and Nick on either side of me, buck naked, their dicks half hard and sinking fast, their eyes not meeting each other.

Bill is the first to break the silence. "Damn," he says his voice low. I look to meet his gaze, and the strangest thing happens. For an instant there's a spark, a little jolt of *connection.* For that brief flicker of time, I'm not the school faggot and he's not the big man on campus: We're buddies who've shared the pleasure of Nick's flesh.

Nick pulls up his pants and breaks the spell. He picks up his T-shirt and puts it on. "Let's go," he grunts to Bill. He walks back into the bushes and vanishes without looking back at either one of us. Bill gets dressed hurriedly and rushes after him. Before he disappears into the night, he turns, gives me one last look, and plunges into the bushes after Nick.

I get up and smooth my clothes, take a comb from my back pocket, and tidy my tousled hair. I walk in the opposite direction, down to patch of gravel where my car is parked. I'm sure I'll see Bill again this Saturday night, with or without Nick. If he's alone, we'll have something to talk about. Either way, it should be fun.

Teammates

Dale Chase

W hen they called me up from Double-A ball to the Triple-A
Hornets, I was one step closer to the big leagues—every
minor leaguer's dream. You'd have thought I'd be happy about it,
but there I was, accepting slaps on the back and pats on the ass
while I eyed Denny, a pitcher who was also my roommate and,
since my first season, my lover. Like the rest of the team, life in the
bigs, or at least in Triple-A, was the dream. But until that moment,
I hadn't considered what leaving Denny would be like. Maybe I
never really thought I'd make it. Maybe I was so caught up in
Denny that I'd stopped thinking about anything else, but there it
was. It was a golden opportunity of the worst kind.

"You'll do fine," Denny told me our last night together. "You'll
meet someone."

I hated the sound of that, so I said nothing, I just crawled
down, got his fat prick into my mouth, and sucked out his come.
Next morning I caught a bus to Mackey Field, home of the Hornets.

It was a great little ballpark, and maybe if I hadn't had such
mixed feelings about being there, I would have appreciated it:
diamond groomed a rich green, infield smooth, and a clubhouse
that made Double-A look like high school. I went two-for-four in
my debut and turned double plays so spectacular you'd have
thought I'd been born a second baseman. Afterward, in the clubhouse, I was heartily pummeled and congratulated. Everyone made

me feel very much a part of the team, but I still felt hollow feel because Denny wasn't there.

I was to room with Johnny Ray Sims at an apartment house where most of the single guys lived. Johnny Ray was a down-home country-boy shortstop who spoke with an accent so thick I couldn't always catch what he was saying. He was a nice enough guy, though. We had dinner with several of the other players that first night, followed by some beers. Because we had another day game ahead, all of us crashed early.

I lay in the dark, listened to Johnny Ray's snore, and jerked my cock as I thought of Denny. Was he doing the same thing, I wondered, or had he found someone else? Maybe he'd gone after that kid who'd signed just out of high school, an 18-year-old phenom who was always half-hard in the shower. Denny and I had talked about how ripe he was. Suddenly I hated him. I forced myself to concentrate on Denny alone, recalling how I'd climb onto him, shove my cock up his ass and ride him until I unloaded big time. He'd shoot into the sheets while I did him. We'd shower afterward and do it again in there, fucking or maybe just humping front to front, all soapy, cocks sliding up between us until they started spewing cream. I was replaying the shower scene when I came. I squirted jizz all over my belly. Johnny Ray kept on snoring.

The next day we lost. By five o'clock were in the pool at the apartment complex. The guys were rowdy, pissed at losing, and full of energy. I watched Rusty, our hard-bodied left fielder, get playful and pull the swimsuit off Craig, the starting catcher. I continued to watch as things escalated between them. They were just being playful, of course, just carousing like everyone else, but I could see there was something more going on. Craig and Rusty tussled in the deep end. Craig ended up with an arm around Rusty's neck. He held on tight and yelled while Rusty thrashed his arms. To everyone else it looked like good-natured roughhousing, but I could see Craig was humping Rusty. My dick twitched at the sight. These two guys were a couple.

I knew they were roommates, but it hadn't occurred to me

there might be more. They obviously had something going on, even if no one else could see it. They bobbed in the water and Craig did a marvelous acting job, roughing up Rusty as he rode his ass. They kept at it until Craig suddenly fell silent; I knew he was coming. A few more hoots and splashes—all from Rusty—and they settled down. The swimsuit, which someone had fished out and left at the pool's edge, ended up back in Craig's hands. Once he'd put it on, Craig climbed out, announced he was tired, and went up to their apartment. Rusty stayed about five more minutes, then followed. I sat on the steps at the shallow end and pictured them in bed. Rusty would get his now, his cock up Craig's ass, or at least in his mouth. Or maybe they were in the shower, doing what Denny and I had done.

"You OK?" Johnny Ray asked as he paddled up to me.

"Yeah, just tired. I think I'll go hit the sack for a while. Maybe I'll see you later."

I climbed out of the pool and tied a towel around me to hide my erection. Up in my apartment, which was next door to Rusty and Craig, I stripped and got into the shower, soaped my swollen prong, and had a good solo session while I gave some thought to what was happening on the other side of the wall.

Two days later things began to change. After a win full of crazy plays, two home runs, and four stolen bases, the clubhouse was wild. I finally retreated to the shower, where I found Rusty. He was turned toward me, and water sprayed off his back. Soaping his nicely rounded pecs, he let his hand slide down his stomach and into his pubes, where his efforts took on a slow, sensual pace. His cock, substantial and cut, was about halfway erect. When my dick began to fill, I didn't try to hide it. I took the soap and began to wash myself, playing around with my balls while Rusty watched, a grin on his face. When I started in on my dick, he started on his. We handled each other's cock, not giving a flying fuck who might walk in.

Rusty got himself so worked up that he began to grind his hips and fuck his hand. Then he turned around and started to soap his ass and run his fingers into his crack. He worked a finger over to his hole and stuck it in. I sucked in an audible breath, which made him look back over his shoulder and smile.

After torturing me a few more seconds, he turned back around and concentrated on his cock. He applied more soap, pulled himself, and played with his balls, giving himself a thorough working-over without ever really jerking off. He stared at me as he soaped a tit, fingering it while he sustained a gentle stroke below. My restraint lasted about 10 seconds—then I got into some serious cock work. At that point, I didn't care whether anyone saw me. I started to pump my meat. Rusty raised his eyebrows in feigned shock, then started in on himself. And there we were, jerking frantically, eyes locked onto each other. Finally Rusty arched his back and let go a magnificent come shot: long creamy squirts arcing toward me. His mouth was open, tongue hanging out in ecstasy—everything unleashed yet silent. Seconds later, as he squeezed out his last, I unloaded. I clinched my jaw to muffle a cry, but I was unable to remain quiet because—the climax was so intense. Every muscle in my body went rigid as wave after wave rolled through me. I kept my eyes on Rusty the whole time.

Afterward, we stood beneath the showerheads to cool down. We shut off the water and began to towel ourselves.

"You've really made a difference here," Rusty said as he dried himself. "On the field, I mean. Best second baseman we've seen."

"Thanks," I replied.

"Craig and I like to have a few beers in our room after dinner. Want to come over?"

"Sure."

"Cool."

In the locker room Craig found Rusty. Their talk became subdued; I recognized that special interplay reserved for couples who enjoy an intimate relationship. When I finished dressing, I started past them, but Craig stopped me. "So we'll see you later," he said. I was thrilled they'd been talking about me.

"You bet," I told him.

Johnny Ray wanted to hang out after dinner—to cruise chicks at the local country-western bar—but I begged off. "Day game again tomorrow," I said. "I'm gonna crash."

Johnny Ray shook his head. I knew he was disappointed I wasn't becoming the buddy he'd hoped for, but he didn't press, and I was grateful for his acceptance. "See you later," I said when I left him and headed back to the apartment complex. I went straight to Rusty's and Craig's and knocked on the door.

"Yeah?" Rusty called.

"It's Jason," I said.

There was a brief silence, then the door swung open. I stepped into a semidarkened room, and the door slammed shut behind me. I turned to find Rusty naked, sporting an erection and a grin. Craig lay on the bed on his back. His knees were up, and he had a towel beneath him. A two-headed dildo, shiny wet, was wedged partway up his ass. "Wanna get naked?" Rusty asked.

I stripped in record time while Rusty ran his hands over me, playing with the hair on my chest and fingering my nipples. I wrapped a hand around his cock and gave it a couple of vigorous tugs. "Hey, guys, don't forget about me," Craig called.

"Not even," Rusty said with a laugh as he led me to the bed. "Craig likes a blow job while he's got a cock in him," he told me as he pulled out the dildo. "I think we can do better than this thing."

Rusty rolled a condom over his prick, lubed himself, and said to Craig, "Now you're gonna get your fuck-and-suck. Go to it, Jason."

I crawled up beside Craig. His cock, a good-sized piece of uncut meat, stood tall and wet. As Rusty got into position at Craig's hole, I leaned in. When Rusty pushed his dick into Craig, I took Craig's very wet prick into my mouth. "Shit, yeah," Craig moaned as we began to work him over.

"I always fuck Craig when we win," Rusty said matter-of-factly as he established a steady stroke.

I pulled off Craig's dick because I had to ask, "What about when we lose?"

"Craig fucks me," Rusty replied.

We shared a laugh, and I went back down for more meat. In a brief flash of clarity I realized I'd begun to get over Denny.

Craig began to buck his hips into my face. "I'm gonna…" was all he managed to say before I pulled off, grabbed him, and jerked the juice out of him. This got Rusty going in all kinds of ways.

"I'm gonna fuck your ass," he growled over and over, riding Craig hard now with a squishy fuck-slap. Rusty let out a yell when he came and grabbed Craig's feet to torque downward for the big moment. He kept pounding, even after he'd come. His rhythm subsided gradually, and finally he pulled out. He tossed the rubber, crawled up beside Craig, and fondled his lover's spent cock. "So good," he cooed as he kissed the catcher.

I worked my meat and urgently needed some attention. Without a word, I got down to the foot of the bed, pulled up Rusty's legs, and began to finger his pucker. "Let me fuck you," I ordered

"My pleasure." Rusty replied. "Condoms are in the drawer."

As I suited up and lubed myself, Rusty said, "Craig's gonna watch you do me. He likes that."

"Whatever," I said. At that point I didn't care about anything but getting into an ass and letting go. I ran a gob of lube into Rusty, and he moaned.

"Oh, yeah…give it to me, baby," he said.

He clamped his sphincter muscle and grinned as I pushed my dick into his hole. "I like a good piece of meat up there," he said with a bearing-down kind of groan. "Now fuck me, baby. Ream my ass."

Craig turned around now, facedown where the action was, but he made sure to keep his cock available to Rusty. And sure enough, after a few strokes, Rusty turned his head and sucked the soft cock into his mouth. I kept thrusting, relishing not only the sensation but also the fact I was fucking our left fielder while he had the catcher's cock in his mouth. I did my best not to come too quickly. Every time the rise began, I eased off. During these reprieves Rusty moaned and begged.

We kept at it for quite a while. Rusty had a hand on his dick, which he stroked almost absentmindedly as he gobbled Craig's sausage. And as much as I loved the scene, I really needed some release. I started to pound Rusty, who pushed his ass up at me, fucking me back. He was still sucking on Craig's cock as he pulled on his own meat. I let out a yell when I came. Seconds later Craig called out "I'm there," but he didn't pull out of Rusty's mouth. I watched as Rusty took Craig's load down his throat. Then it was Rusty's turn; he pumped jizz onto his stomach as he sucked dick. Fucking and sucking until we were empty, the three of us finally quieted, pulled out of one other, and collapsed into a pile.

"Shit, man," Rusty moaned, "that was something."

I murmured my agreement and fell asleep.

We stirred near dawn—nurturing a pile of erections. I headed for the shower and had managed to get myself awake and mostly clean when Rusty joined me. He had a grip on his stiff cock. "Help me out here, man," he said.

I soaped him, pulled him to me, and we started humping front to front—just like the old days with Denny. My old flame was really fading, unable to outshine the here and now, not nearly so hot at the feel of another cock riding my own. Rusty grabbed my ass. The two of us grunted at our labors. We kept at it until big squirts of jizz shot up between us.

Back in the bedroom we found Craig out from under the covers, lying on his side with one hand on his cock and the other at his mouth. He was sucking his thumb.

"Big fucking baby," Rusty whispered. He crawled gingerly onto the bed and carefully pulled the thumb from Craig's mouth, then stuck in his dick. Craig began to suck. The hand wrapped around his dick began to move. He lay sucking Rusty and stroking himself for about minute before he came. Through it all he never opened his eyes. Once he was done, he settled back into a deep sleep. He looked like he'd never stirred.

"He won't remember it," Rusty said. "He'll wake up and want to fuck."

We shared a quiet laugh, and I began to dress. Only then did I think about Johnny Ray. "What am I going to tell him?" I asked Rusty.

"That you met a local and went to her place for the night. You'll be his hero."

It happened just like that, except Johnny Ray wanted details. "How many times did you fuck her? Did you do it in her mouth *and* her pussy? Did she have big tits?"

He was in his underwear, seemingly oblivious to his hard-on. "I found me some girls, but none would put out," he whined. "Where'd you meet her?"

"The Taco Bell near the stadium," I said, pulling a reply out of my ass.

He grinned, shook his head, and headed for the shower. I figured he'd do himself there and consider having tacos for dinner.

The game that day seemed better than the games earlier in the week. Rusty got two singles and a sacrifice fly, and Craig slammed the ball over the left-field fence for three runs we desperately needed. I had a double and stole a base. Every time one of us came back to the dugout, the other two sought him out, charged by the game and by the promise of a randy celebration later on.

After the game Johnny Ray begged me to go with him to the Taco Bell. "Maybe you'll meet your girl again," he said.

"How about you go and meet her," I replied.

He was stunned. "You don't want to? What's wrong with her?"

"Nothing, man. I'm just not that interested. You go on down there and see what you can do."

He was all puffed up when he left, full of innocent enthusiasm—very appealing. I hoped one of the girls would see it in him.

I went to the pool, where the horseplay unfolded much as before, except this time Rusty and Craig had their hands all over me, groping and prodding. My cock got so hard that eventually I was ready to let go. And Rusty knew it.

"Make me come," I whispered to him. Obligingly, he shoved

me, and I shoved him back. We disguised our caresses with lots of splashing.

Finally, I grabbed him from behind and did to him what Craig had done—right there in front of the team; right there while they tossed around a beach ball, climbed onto each other's shoulders, then fell off; right there with guys lying poolside, sunning themselves and drinking beer. I had my dick up against Rusty's crack, humping like mad, when Craig got into the act. He splashed and hollered, giving great cover just as I started to come. I let out a hoot that vanished in the din, and jizz shot out of me in long streams. When I was done Rusty pulled back, grabbed me around the neck to continue our acting job, and released me, as if he'd won our mock battle. I paddled over to the edge and hung there to regain my composure. I looked around at the scene: Everything was unchanged, even though the second baseman had just come in the pool.

"Let's go get some dinner," Rusty said when I climbed out of the pool.

"You mean…?" I queried.

"No, I mean food," he said with a smirk. "I want a burger."

We dressed and walked down the block to a tiny café, where we settled into a booth. "Word is Jake Carson is being sent down," Rusty said as he bit into a double cheeseburger. "His average is down to .180, and they're saying he's gotta regain his swing before he can come back up."

"Jake Carson?" I was stunned.

"I know," Rusty said. "I almost cream just thinking about seeing him in the shower."

Jake Carson, 25, was a world ahead of us. He'd signed a major league contract his senior year of college, skipped the minors entirely, and his first two seasons hit .300 plus. But by his third—this one—it had all gone to hell.

"You know why, don't you?" Craig asked with an arch look.

I shook my head.

"Where you been, boy?" Rusty teased. "Oh, yeah, Double-A— the end of the world. You at least know Jake's gay, right?"

I nodded.

"OK, good. What I'm hearing is that he's been fucking Randy Jenkins, who's totally lost it as a result. I mean his curve ball is flat, his slider stinks, and his fastball is now a change-up. The man's 34, married with kids, and he's off the deep end for Jake. Management found out and they're leaning on Jake to end it, which has them both totally fucked up."

"Holy shit," I said, trying to picture them together. It was easy enough to envision Jake Carson with his cock up somebody's ass, but it was almost impossible to see Randy Jenkins taking it. He was "Mr. Clean and Proper." Then again, if anybody could get the closet door unlocked, it would be Jake: six feet tall, well-built, with a broad chest and a narrow ass—one of those solid powerhouse types.

We sat in silence. Each of us was off on his own little fuck trip with Jake. What was going to happen when he arrived? After dinner, the three of us went back to Rusty's and Craig's place, stripped, and got hard talking about what we'd like Jake Carson to do to us. And then we did it to each other.

Jake arrived the next day. He accepted our welcome but kept his distance. There was obviously a lot on his plate: the busted relationship, the shitty average, and the embarrassment he had to feel, now that management knew his business. He played hard, but off the field he was quiet, almost sullen. We gave him plenty of room, content to feast our eyes on the sight of him. Instead of taking an apartment in our building, he stayed at a motel near the stadium.

In our minds, he was the perfect man. He had that All-American look: sandy hair, blue eyes, strong jaw, white teeth, big shoulders, furry chest, washboard stomach, and a big fat dick. Cut, his cock nested in a thick bush and curved endearingly to the left when it was hard—and it was hard every time he showered. He spent extra time with it, not giving a damn whether anyone saw. He soaped slowly, took care of the rest of his body, then came back to his cock, working it until it jutted out. He washed his balls unhurriedly, while water dripped off his hard-on. It was easy to picture Randy Jenkins down there on his knees, sucking madly. Rusty, Craig, and I watched Jake's every move, delighting in the show he was giving us and certain we were being discreet. How wrong we were.

It happened one night at the Dairy Queen, after Jake had been with us about 10 days. Well, maybe it didn't happen there, but it started there. We'd come off a weeklong road trip. Rusty and Craig headed to a local bar, but I begged off, preferring to be on my own for a change. My plan was to grab a burger and go to bed, but then I saw Jake's yellow Corvette parked in the back of the lot. The door was open, and I could see a bare leg stretched out. I got a Coke and sauntered over. When I got up close, Jake said, "Hey, Jason, what's up?" He had a pint of something in his hand and his words were slightly slurred. All he had on was a pair of khaki shorts.

"Not much," I replied. "Sure glad we've got a night game tomorrow. The heat is just too much after a while."

He ran a hand slowly across his chest. I swear he paused to play with a nipple. "Wanna take a drive?" he asked. "Cool down?"

I almost laughed. *Cool down: right.* "Sure," I said, "but only if you let me drive. I've never driven a Corvette."

He thought about my proposition for a second, then agreed. He crawled over to the passenger seat. I climbed into the car, adjusting the seat for my smaller frame, and we took off. I had no idea where we were going—just out of town. It didn't take long before we were on the highway. I saw nothing but headlights, a half moon, and lots of promise.

"You really nailed the ball today," I said. "What is that, twelve doubles since you got here?"

"Doesn't mean shit," he mumbled.

OK, don't go there. I decided not to say anything more, to let him lead. He took a long pull on his pint, then said, "You and your little friends sure been gettin' an eyeful."

"Oh?" I replied coyly.

"It's OK. Only you really need to be more careful when you scope out dicks in the shower. There's guys who'll beat the shit out of you, ya know."

"Right. Sorry."

"Don't be sorry. I'm enjoying it. The attention's about the only bright spot in this God-awful place. You got something going?"

"Kinda."

He murmured his approval, drained the last of his whiskey, and said, "You know about Randy Jenkins and me, don't you?"

"Yeah, word's around."

He went silent, and I concentrated on the white line ahead. Finally, he started to really talk. "He won 20 games last year, and you know why? He was happy. He's spent his whole life not being who he is, but with me he can turn loose. And he couldn't get enough, and it was the best—just the best. You can't imagine what it's like with a guy who's been waiting his whole life to get fucked. I did him for hours, and when I didn't have my dick in him, I had my fingers or my tongue. He was so goddamned hungry, and now he's up there, starving. And his game's gone to hell right along with mine."

"Are you in love with him?"

"You don't fall in love with married guys."

"It sounds like you had something really special, though."

"Shit, yeah. He's in great shape for a 34-year-old."

He went silent again, sighed heavily, then continued. "He loves having his cock sucked. One time when I was on the bench and he got taken out in the seventh inning for a pinch hitter, I followed him into the clubhouse. We were alone; I made sure of that. He was so upset, pissed, and disappointed at the same time. I took him into a corner, got his pants down, and sucked him off. He came in a gusher and just about cried. After that, it became a kind of thing—he was having a bad time and I had just the cure." He laughed bitterly.

"Good times, I did him too—but those were long fucks in my room, celebration fucks. We only did it on the road at first—we were so careful—but we couldn't stay away from each other. We started meeting at a local motel on the edge of town, then a friend of his wife's mother saw us going in—all the way out to hell and gone, thinking we're safe. It's never safe with married guys: Remember that. So the wife finds out, raises hell, but doesn't leave him. Worse, she says he's got to stop seeing me and she tells our manager, so there's this conspiracy to keep him straight. He goes along with it, we don't see each other, and everything goes to hell as a result. He's living his life but can't pitch for shit. And I can't hit. I got sent down because I'm the problem." He laughed again. "Too bad they don't see I'm the cure."

We were far from town when Jake said he had to pee. I pulled off the road and parked near a cluster of trees. I got out as well to stretch my legs. After Jake took a long piss, he turned to me, still holding himself. "Just what you've been lookin' at," he said, pulling on his dick. "How'd you like a taste?"

I kneeled, guided his rising prong into my mouth, and heard him utter a long "Oh, yeah."

He was a real mouthful, but I gobbled all I could. I ran my tongue down his shaft and sucked him into my throat. He let me work him, began an easy thrust, then suddenly pulled out. "Hell with this. Let me fuck you," he growled. Before I could reply, he whipped a condom out of his pocket and pulled it on.

"You gonna drop 'em?" he asked. I looked around, saw nothing and no one, and took off my pants.

"Get up against the car," he said. He had a packet of lube open and began to grease his cock. When he had me bent over the hood of the car, he said, "Spread 'em."

I did, and he ran a gob of lube into me and worked it around. "Nice," he said. "Now let me show you what makes a 20-game winner."

He shoved his big piece of meat into me and started riding me rough, pumping so hard that we set the car rocking. Grunting with each thrust, Jake drilled me, but not for long. I could tell he had a big load to deliver. He dug his fingers into me, and I knew he was coming when he started growling "Shit!" and "Fuck!" I pictured that big dick shooting cream inside me.

My own cock was ready to fire; partway through his climax, I let go all over the Corvette's hood. I also let out a yelp because I was beyond ecstatic, thrilled to be shooting while getting so totally reamed by the great Jake Carson, of all people.

I was done before he was. He kept on pumping, reluctant to let the climax go. Or maybe let me go. I wondered if he'd fucked anyone since Randy. I squeezed my muscle and he groaned, then slid out.

I turned to watch him toss the rubber and zip up his pants. As I dressed he saw what I'd done to the car. "Shit, man," he cried as he got a rag and cleaned off my spunk. I was in a state of panic, knowing how some guys are about their cars, when he said, "Guess I'm gonna have to keep a come-rag in the glove compartment."

He wouldn't let me drive back to town. I worried because he'd been drinking, but he seemed sober now, as if getting off had cured him. We rode in silence; not until we were at the apartment complex did he speak. "You room with the shortstop, right?"

"Yeah," I said.

"What would he say if you didn't come home tonight?"

"He'd ask me how she was."

"And what would you tell him?"

"Great pussy."

He put the car in gear and we drove to his motel, where he took me to bed and fucked me again. And again.

The next day he went four for five, including a homer and a triple. And that night he sucked my dick for hours. He fucked me in the shower, in the bed, and on the floor. The following day I hit a home run—my first since I joined the team—which made his day. I was grateful for all the high fives and pats on the butt, but the wink he gave me in the dugout really did it for me.

We had a nine-game road trip—long hours on busses all over California and Arizona. Jake took his Corvette, but other than that, he was one of us. I knew the clock was ticking; his climbing average was a mixed blessing. He was now tearing the cover off the ball, hitting .320, ripping up the league. He got the call in Scottsdale early one morning. We had a night game. He'd be gone by then.

We took the Corvette out into the desert, found a secluded spot behind a ridge of boulders, put down a blanket, stripped naked, and went at it. His sandy hair glistened in the sun, and sweat poured down his face. I couldn't get enough of the smell of him, the feel of him pushing his cock up my rectum, the texture of his rough hands on my feet as he held my legs high and wide. He made it last, said he wanted me never to forget that fuck because he sure as hell wouldn't.

When he came, it was with a roar that shattered the desert calm—he finally emptied himself of everything he'd been holding inside. After I shot a good load up onto my belly, he pulled out, slid on top of me, and kissed me. He hadn't done that before; I almost cried. "Maybe someday I'll see you," he said. He meant maybe I'd get up to the big leagues too. I couldn't begin to imagine that now. Nothing could match where I was, what I'd known with him.

"You're the best thing that could have happened to me down here," he said, kissing me again. "You know that, don't you?"

I wrapped my arms around him and held on, trying to etch the feel of him into my memory. "Part of me wishes I didn't have to go," he added.

"All of me wishes you didn't," I told him.

When we got back to my place, Rusty and Craig saw us drive up. "You gonna tell your buddies about us?" he asked.

"Not if you don't want me to."

"What the hell, go ahead."

I smiled, told him what a pleasure it had been on and off the field. "Mostly off," I added.

He nodded. "Yeah, me too. Mostly off."

I got out of the car and stood with Rusty and Craig, who began to pester me for details. "I *knew* it," Craig said as he gave Rusty's arm a tug.

"Later guys, OK?" I said. "Right now I want to be by myself."

I avoided everyone until game time, and even then I kept my distance. Here I was again, caught once more in baseball's never-ending cycle, which amounted to a whole lot of leaving. When I took the field, I thought about Jake standing out in left field in a big-league park. Was he thinking of me, or was Randy Jenkins on the mound? Before I had a chance to make myself miserable, I heard the crack of the bat, saw a hard grounder heading toward me. I scooped it up and fired it to first, where Casey Phipps, a sweet little 19-year-old just up from Double-A, made the putout.

Tag-team
Muscle Studs

Bearmuffin

After the match, champion pro-wrestler Griff Stoner stomped toward the locker room looking for Colt Preston, one of the jobbers who took the falls.

Griff had been ringside, watching wrestling stud Mack O'Brien twist Colt into a sweaty pretzel. Griff grabbed his crotch and squeezed his throbbing boner. Fuck! He couldn't wait to wrap his lips around Colt's thick, meaty cock.

Six-foot-four Griff grinned lustily as his uncut cock bounced over his heavy balls. A shaggy mane of red hair framed his lantern jaw and deep-set emerald eyes.

His huge shoulders sloped off an awesome bull-neck. His big barrel chest glistened with golden fuzz. Rock-hard muscles ribbed his powerful midsection. His meaty, bubble-muscled ass was squeaky tight. Griff's ego was bigger than the hefty 13-incher throbbing inside his skintight Lycra trunks.

Griff licked his lips when he saw Colt's magnificent six-foot muscle-corded torso sprawled over the massage table. Scott, a brawny blond masseur, sensuously kneaded Colt's superb mega-muscles.

Griff tapped the masseur on the shoulder, winked at him, and jerked a thumb toward the door. Scott returned a conspiratorial wink and padded away.

Griff's greedy eyes roamed over the 25-year-old's magnificent body, packed with a solid 185 fat-free pounds. Brutally handsome, Colt tied his dirty-blond hair into a long ponytail. A dark tan emphasized his hirsute ruggedness. Over a pair of sensuous lips curled a bristly mustache. Colt's piercing blue eyes sparkled with self-confidence.

Colt sported jockstraps in and out of the ring. A solid-steel cock ring looped around his meat, making his cock bulge outrageously within the pouch. One look at Colt's protruding bubble-butt and waves of lust crashed over Griff.

Griff arched an eyebrow and lewdly ran his tongue along his upper lip. His heart began to beat excitedly at the stunning sight of Colt's tight jockstrapped bubbles gleaming with baby oil and fresh sweat. Griff's tongue ached to dip into those meaty muscle-buns.

Griff picked up a bottle of baby oil and flipped the cap open with his thumb. He drizzled some oil across Colt's wide back. As Griff rhythmically massaged the oil into smooth skin, his eyes widened with admiration at the young stud's thick neck blending into rugged shoulders. Colt's immense, powerful back tapered dramatically to well-muscled, compact hips.

"Oohh, Griff," Colt cooed. "That feels so fuckin' good." Griff felt Colt's muscles undulate with pleasure underneath his sweaty palms. Colt grinned. Yeah, it had to be Griff. Colt would know those big, burly hands anywhere, anytime.

"Love my cock, dontcha, stud?" Griff said.

"Yes, sir!" Colt replied. "I sure fuckin' do!" Griff smiled when he noticed some oil trickling lazily down the small of Colt's back. It pooled into a small puddle above the jobber's tempting ass-crack.

Griff's boner swelled anxiously at the sight of Colt's ass, which was exquisitely framed by the straps of his jock. "Open wide," Griff whispered huskily, as he wrenched the young wrestler's butt-cheeks open. He licked his lips and buried his face between Colt's melons, sniffing up his butt like a dog in heat. Colt moaned when he felt Griff's nose burrow inside his ass-crack.

Griff briskly shot his tongue through Colt's anal hole. "Aw, fuckin' jeez," Colt moaned. He twisted his ass sideways. Griff snorted like a pig, digging further up Colt's ass, giving it a thorough tongue-lashing.

Colt moaned, thrusting his butt higher into the air. "Please!" he moaned. "Please fuck my butt!"

Griff was only too happy to oblige. The brawny wrestler whipped off his Lycra trunks and quickly slathered some baby oil over his impatient, thick-veined 13-incher.

"Ya ready, stud?" Griff inquired.

"Yeah," Colt gasped. He clenched his eyes and grabbed the sides of the massage table to prepare for a wild fuck.

Griff slid his brutish hands under Colt's armpits. He took a moment to knead the stud's firm mounds of pecs. Colt's nips swelled, jutting against Griff's sweaty palms. Yeah! Some hot nipple-play would do the trick! A lusty shudder went through Colt's body when he felt Griff's callused fingers scrape his nips.

Colt felt Griff's lusty snorts blasting against the nape of his neck. The young stud wanted to get fucked, but his hole instinctively snapped shut at the first sign of Griff's anal assault.

"Ease up or I'll rip you wide open," Griff snorted.

"Yeeoww!" Colt howled when Griff pinched his tender nips. Sharp needles of pain racked Colt's sturdy body. His asshole suddenly yawned open. Griff slam-dunked his mammoth cock inside Colt's dilated hole.

It felt like a rusty crowbar was ripping him to shreds. "Yargh!" Colt screamed as his body writhed from the pain. His hands gripped the massage table. He hung on for dear life, bucking like a wild bronco as Griff began riding his ass.

Griff pinned Colt's wrists. "Whoa there, stud. Steady now. Gonna do me some hard riding. So relax, y'hear?" Griff snorted like a mad bull in heat, brutally thrusting his cock inside Colt's ass.

Griff felt a come-load bubbling inside his swinging bull-balls. With a hearty grunt, Griff pulled out his cock halfway and suddenly shifted gears. He changed from a smooth, steady motion to some heavy-duty piston pounding.

Colt groaned with macho pleasure. A big, bulked-up brute like Griff was the perfect top. He could feel Griff's awesome power inside him. There was nothing like 250 pounds charging up his aching hole.

Griff's expert stroking deep within Colt's asshole was transforming the pain into hot waves of pleasure that crashed through his brain. Colt gleefully thrust his ass back to meet Griff's expert cock-strokes.

Colt's slick asshole sucked greedily around Griff's pumping cock. "That's right!" Griff grunted encouragingly "Gimme that ass. Push back with your fuckin' ass!"

The pleasure sparks were electrifying, shooting all through Colt's body. He felt a familiar stirring in his groin. Yeah! His cock was hard and ripe, ready to burst. Colt felt his jizz sizzling inside his nuts. He was really enjoying the fuck now, tossing his whole heart and soul into it. His ass and Griff's cock became one.

Griff grunted hard, the width of his cock expanding to a full three inches inside Colt's hole. "Daddy's just about to shoot his sweet fuckin' load up your ass!" he hissed down at the horny jobber who clenched his eyes, shuddering with lustful anticipation. He knew that Griff was ready to splooge.

"Fuck, fuck, fuck!" Griff yowled, pulling his cock up just below the crown. A wild lust-filled smile froze on his lips. He was ready to slam into Colt for the home run.

"Here it comes, stud! Gonna shoot my fuckin' load!!!"

Suddenly, the door burst open. The baby oil fell off the table and rolled on the floor. An angry voice shot through the room. "Ya goddamn son of a bitch!" Colt looked up at the hulking figure filling the doorway.

It was Mack O'Brien! An imposing 6 foot 3, Mack was every inch a mega-stud. His vein-corded bull-neck was welded to powerful shoulders that flared wide like the hood of a cobra.

The symmetry of his V-shaped torso was stunning. Thick black fur swirled over his impeccable six-pack abs. The goatee-wearing muscle-bear had a flat top. Thick bushy brows shaded his deep-set black eyes. His horse-head rod was packed inside skintight black Lycra trunks.

Mack bounded over to the massage table. He pulled Griff off Colt. Griff's hard-on plopped out of Colt's hole with a loud squelch. Yeah, Mack was pissed as hell. Only minutes ago, Griff had bopped him on the head with a folding chair. That had just been the usual wrestling match high jinks—but Griff had taken it personally. Griff snarled disgustedly. Goddamn it! Mack *would* show up now. Just a couple more strokes and he'd have popped his rocks up Colt's sweet butt.

Mack aimed a knee at Griff's abs. Griff tried to block it but Mack connected, sending Griff crashing into a wall. Mack scrambled over Griff, straddling him between his tree-trunk thighs. Mack's angry cock jabbed into Griff's eyes. When Griff yanked down Mack's trunks, out popped Mack's mighty butt-buster. It rose up to full glory before Griff's greedy eyes. A drop of precome glistened temptingly from the tip of Mack's swollen cock. And Griff couldn't resist lapping it up.

Griff fastened his mouth over Mack's twitching cock. With rapid corkscrew motions, he began to suck on it. Mack swiveled his pelvis, forcing his cock deeper into Griff's mouth. Mack was wiggling his butt so much that Griff couldn't resist sticking three fingers inside Mack's asshole.

"Yeaw!" Mack shouted. That Griff sure knew how to play with a man's ass. Within minutes, Mack felt a wild spunk geyser rising deep within his bull-balls.

"Unngh, unngh, unngh" Mack snorted. Griff mercilessly strummed his fingers in Mack's asshole while his tongue fluttered over Mack's cock. Then he hollowed his cheeks and sucked the bruiser's bull-balls into his slobbering mouth. Mack's sweaty balls danced on his tongue.

"Aw, fuck!" Mack hollered. He was going to splooge.

Griff suddenly flipped Mack on his back, pinning his broad shoulders to the floor. Mack's legs wiggled in the air, his cock about to burst. Griff shoved his hand up Mack's butthole and counted "ONE, TWO, THREE!"

"Fuck!" Mack bellowed as he thrashed and flopped like a fish out of water, shooting his spunk. He thrashed and moaned some more as spurt after spurt of wrassler-come burst into the air. Griff laughed as he watched the come-ribbons shoot from his buddy's prick. The last spurt landed right on Colt's face.

"Yee-haw!" Griff snorted as he flexed his muscles, howling his macho triumph.

Colt stood rooted to the spot, his eyes bulging with amazement. Griff's mighty cock hovered just a mouthwatering inch from his lips. Colt watched Griff's piss slit open and close like a tiny mouth as huge drops of precome oozed from the hole.

Griff grabbed Colt by the mane, forcing his cock between the jobber's slobbering lips. Griff's plowing bull-meat made Colt choke and sputter. His chin was firmly wedged against Griff's balls. Griff bellowed his insatiable lust. "Suck that cock, faggot! Suck it!"

Colt slavishly worked his hungry tongue over Mack's pulsing meat. His tongue flew over the immense shaft. He licked and slurped until Mack's monster cock had swelled to a full mind-boggling 13 inches.

"OK, faggot!" Mack barked as he hoisted Colt up and slammed him facedown over the massage table. Colt's sweat and oil-slicked buttocks were exposed for yet another brutal anal attack.

"Yeah!" Mack bellowed. He spread Colt's trembling cheeks wide open and swiftly plunged his cock into the jobber's still-dilated hole.

"Open up, stud!" Mack howled. "Gonna fuck ya good!"

Colt grabbed the table and screamed for mercy when he felt Mack's mighty cock tear into his asshole again. When his hole was totally filled with Mack's pumping meat, he thrust his ass back and began to enjoy the ride.

By now Mack had recovered from his incredible orgasm and was watching Griff power-fuck Colt. He was mesmerized by the pumping action of Griff's hairy buttocks as they bobbed and tensed with each thrust into Colt's heaving ass. Mack licked his lips and squeezed his boner. In a flash, he was on his knees. He stuck out his rosy ravenous tongue and plopped it inside Griff's ass.

"Whoa!" Griff cried when he felt Mack's probing tongue hit his pucker. He pushed his ass back, reaching behind him to force Mack's face farther inside his ass. Mack wasted no time and began to chomp hungrily on Griff's asshole. Mack's piggy grunts echoed through the gym as he rooted around in Griff's stinking pucker.

When Griff felt Mack's tongue snaking further into his butt, he howled, "Suck my ass, motherfucker!" Get that tongue in there. Lick it clean!"

Griff couldn't believe it. Mack and Colt were servicing him like two horny, insatiable suck-slaves. Carried away with lust, Mack dropped his guard. Griff took advantage of this opportunity to knock Mack down. Griff's cock popped out of Colt's bereft fuck-hole. Not wasting a moment, Colt instantly scrambled over the dazed flat-on-his-back Griff.

Then the lusty jobber crammed his cock inside Griff's mouth and gave him a brutal face-fucking. Mack picked Griff's brawny legs up and hoisted them over his shoulders. He spat on Griff's ass-hole and then plowed right inside him.

"Yeow!" Griff screamed, his cries smothered by Colt's meaty cock. Griff began jacking his own cock as sparks of pain melted into waves of pleasure, spreading all through his body. Colt continued mercilessly to fuck Griff's face. Mack ass-fucked Griff with a tornado fury.

Soon, the three men were ready to shoot their loads. "Yeah!" Mack cried as his cock exploded inside Griff's burning asshole. Griff bucked and heaved as his own cock erupted with hot spurts of man-jizz.

Colt clenched his eyes, his lips tightened for a moment. Mack let Colt's cock slip from his mouth. He quickly wrapped his sweaty lips around Colt's come-swollen balls.

Then a lusty cry burst from Colt's mouth: "FUCK!" Colt's

mighty cock swelled and lurched up as he began to shoot his heavy load into the air. A thick, steady come-stream rained down over the three wrestlers until everybody was soaked with Colt's sizzling splooge.

Afterward, Mack popped his cock from Griff's sore butt. "Fuck!" Griff exclaimed as he licked a come-dribble from the corner of his mouth. "You know something? We three'd make a great tag team! How 'bout it?"

Mack and Colt aimed their bloated cocks at Griff's kisser. Just a few hot strokes and another round of spunk spurted all over his face.

"You're on!" Mack and Colt replied. And with shit-eating grins on their faces, the three wrestlers raced into the auditorium for their first tag-team match.

The Craving

Jay Starre

I would never have gone to that particular park on an ordinary night. I preferred the bright discos, packed with gyrating bodies. I loved choosing a sexual partner in the frenzy of a night filled with music and intoxicating liquor. But the moon was full, and I had an unusual craving.

Earlier that night I had been to the leather bar—also not one of my usual haunts. But that was where the craving—the itch—had begun. Hard eyes, shiny black leather, caps that disguised and biceps that bulged beneath snaking tattoos. I was overwhelmed by the sexual rankness of it. There was an itch in my crotch, down between my legs, where my balls snuggled against my ass crack. And there was an itch in my ass, an insistent craving that somehow had to be satisfied—and not in the usual manner.

I knew I would have to seek something new, something rougher, something more extreme. So I found myself on the path that led to the infamous place in the park where men met for more than conversation. I soon left behind the streetlights. Fortunately, the moon provided enough light to keep me from stumbling on the gravel trail. A dense thicket surrounded me, and trees loomed overhead.

"Hey, pussy boy, looking for something?" A harsh whisper growled at me from the shrubbery to my right.

There he was in shadow, only a barely visible leather cap marking him as the one I would need that night: the one who might be able to satisfy my ravenous craving.

"I'm looking for something, all right," I growled back. "But maybe you aren't man enough to give me what I need." My aggressiveness might have proved a turnoff to the mystery man, but it was an inseparable part of my longing that night. I knew what I wanted, and nothing else would suffice.

"Get over here and show me your ass," came his retort. "Then we'll see if *you* have what *I* want. Then we'll see whether I can give you what you need." The voice was gravelly, but there was nothing common about it. The edge of cunning hinted that this was someone out of the ordinary. I was intrigued—and aroused.

I moved into the thicket, shoving aside branches, until I stood in front of him. He was slightly taller than I was—over six feet—and his cap added another inch or two to his height. The moonlight offered me a glimpse of his face: aquiline nose, deep-set eyes, lush lips, a square jaw shadowed by a dark goatee. He was hot and fierce. He gripped my shoulders in his powerful hands and, before I could consider protest, he whipped me around so that my back was to him. He continued to grip my shoulder with one hand. With the other he began to grope my butt roughly.

"Nice ass," he said approvingly. "So far, so good. I take it you want some back-door action: a stiff dick up your little hole?" His voice was husky in my ear as the hands squeezed and poked at my butt. He slipped his hand into my jeans and worked his fingers into my crack. I gasped helplessly as the craving I'd felt all night bubbled to the surface under the insistent pressure of those groping paws.

"More than that," I grunted in reply. "I want more." I was a little uncertain myself of what I meant by that. *More than a simple fuck* is what I imagined.

"More?" he growled back. This time, his hands moved even more swiftly around in front of me, tearing at my buckle and zipper, yanking down my jeans to my knees. He accomplished it all in seconds. I shivered with a tantalizing shock of fear and made no attempt to move away.

His hands briefly and roughly squeezed my swelling cock, then moved back behind me. They groped my ass cheeks again—

a big paw for each cheek—and I shoved my butt back without thinking, which caused him to chuckle lightly in my ear. I could feel his hot breath on my neck. Then his hands ripped apart my underwear. He literally tore the material in half with one good yank. I was left with the waistband dangling from my hips as he ripped the shreds off my body.

I shuddered, my crotch and ass naked to the balmy night. "I've got lube," he said from behind me. "Would you like your sweet twat greased?" The hoarse whisper sent wracking waves of electricity down my spine, into the crack of my ass, and right to the quivering, expectant hole he was already searching for with one of his big thick-knuckled hands.

"Yeah, grease me up. Make me into a slick hole!" I heard myself say. Yeah, that sounded good. That entreaty sounded like it would invite the kind of attention I needed to sate my ravenous craving.

He moved like lightening. How he did it, I will never know, but suddenly there was slippery goo spilling down my open ass crack and dripping over my hole in cool puddles. I was trembling steadily and spread my legs reflexively in order to steady myself. The maneuver also helpfully opened my butt crack.

"Yeah, open up your thighs, like the slut I know you are," he commanded. "Now bend over." Before I complied, he reached around to give my stiffy a proprietary tug. My body bent into an L, and I placed my hands on my knees and closed my eyes. Waiting.

The lube turned my crack into a slick little slut rut. He stroked the length of it with his fingers, sliding around roughly, then exploring my parted cheeks with slow, firm strokes. I felt his fat fingertips graze my asshole, which clamped shut of its own accord. But then I felt it gape back open as those probing fingers settled on it. He thrummed them there, teasing the opening with little tickles and light jabs. I moaned, splaying my feet as wide apart as I could, and parted my thighs even further. I wanted to be nothing but a hole for him to fill.

"You like those fingers there?" he asked menacingly. "You want more? You want my fingers to open you up?"

I was breathing heavily and couldn't reply at first, too intent on his fingers, which by then he'd begun to rub insistently against my butt. He teased it open and lightly jabbed two, then three of his chunky fingers just inside the snapping entrance. He was driving me mad.

"Did you hear me, pussy?" he bellowed. "Answer me! Do you want my fingers up your greased hole?"

I grunted as he suddenly forced two fingers knuckle-deep into my asshole. "Yes! Yes!" I screamed as he stretched my tight little man-cunt. "Finger my butt! Shove them up there!"

He laughed. I groaned. He rammed two fingers deep, banging my prostate and loosing a flood of pain and pleasure that deluged my body with a searing heat. My face flushed and my cock, trapped between my belly and thighs, jerked and throbbed. I was shaking so violently, I was unsure I could remain standing. He solved my dilemma.

"Get down on your knees in the dirt," he commanded. "Get down on your fucking knees with your ass in the air, you little cunt!"

I dropped my knees to the muddy earth. His fingers slid from my asshole with a slick, smacking noise that set my head spinning. He was right behind me, shadowing me with his big hands and looming body. As I bent over to support my torso with my hands, he wedged himself between my ankles and went right back to work.

"Feel those big fingers?" he rasped. "There's two of them there. How many can you take?"

"More! I want more!" I grunted as he buried those two thick sausage fingers deep in my ass. My butt rim enveloped them, and the sounds of lube slopping loudly filled the quiet thicket as he frigged me roughly. For a few moments I was lost in that sound, then I felt him dribbling more lube over my ass and crack.

"Let's get your sweet butt nice and slippery," he said. "We'll grease you up like the little slick cunt you are!" With his free hand he rubbed the slippery goo all over my cheeks and up into my crack. Those two fingers kept drilling my ass all the while, the pace of his thrusts increasing with each passing moment. I grunted and shoved my ass in the air, reveling in the sensation of my butthole opening in response to his fingers, the ache becoming ever more gratifying. That's when the third finger joined the others.

"Ohhh!" I moaned, dropping my head and giving in to the assault on my poor ass. But this was just the beginning. He used three fingers to tear into my butt, lifting my ass with his pumping thrusts, stretching the rim and frigging rapidly in and out with deep steady pokes.

I shot my first load. Come rocketed out of my untouched dick. Coarse laughter reverberated in his massive chest. He was fully aware of my explosion: My body heaved and convulsed and my asshole snapped wildly over his ramming digits.

"Yeah, unload that cock," he chortled. "You got more important things to think about, like how your greased twat will feel with my whole hand up it!"

The dam within me burst and I began to weep, sobbing with a mixture of postorgasmic release and the unabated yearning of my insatiable anal slot. He had me: He knew me better than I knew myself. He would take care of me. Everything I'd held back to that point, I let go, along with the jizz that drained my balls and ran down my thighs. I completely surrendered.

He understood where he'd taken me, and he took his time after that. With one hand he held my ass cheeks apart while he crooned behind me. "What a hot little stud—nice, sweet bubble-butt and nice muscles too. You got a craving though, don't you? You want a bigger stud to open you up, to make your twat sing, to make it into a hot, wide-open gash. Well, I can do that for you. I can unfold you like I was peeling and orange. Here's something for you, sweets. Here's a fourth finger going in now."

I was blubbered, begging him to stop—at first. Then I begged him to go on, to fill me up with his big hairy-ape fingers—all of them. He cooed some more as I felt that fourth finger splitting me in two, but by then the sloppy sound of lube squishing around his writhing fingers was the only music I wanted to hear. I wanted it more than any other thing in the world. I wanted to be on my knees with a hand working its way into my ass, working its way past my gaping pucker, farther and farther, all four fingers and more. I realized he was fucking me with all four by then, and it was feeling astonishingly, insanely delicious.

"Good boy, good boy," he said soothingly. "Your twat is nice and warmed up. You can take all I have to give. Now just relax. Let your ass ride over my fist."

He had said it: fist. I was going to get fisted. That was the unspoken craving that had infected me when I walked into the leather bar earlier in the night. That was what I wanted! And he was going to give it to me. Could I handle it?

I listened to his gently encouraging words and let them sink in. Slowly I began to understand what it meant to participate in my own fuck. I began to gyrate against the fingers in my ass, working my butt over them, inching backward with small, steady humping motions.

"Yeah, like that: Ride those fingers," he coached. "My thumb is going in next. Ride it, boy. Ride my fist with your sweet little ass!"

His words did the trick. I was riding him, rising up and squatting over his fingers. Then I felt his thumb begin to slip into my anal pore, stretching me beyond my wildest imagination. I felt the ridge of his massive knuckles at the threshold of my ass. The slippery paw settled right there. I humped it as he'd taught me and, thwarted on the first try, I cried out. I wanted it! I rode it again as he held his fist still for me. Suddenly, my asshole became dark, rank chasm, and I felt his fist slide inside me.

I wept again, and I shook all over. I was up on my feet in a squatting position. With his free hand he firmly grasped my shoulder to keep me steady. That was what it took—that and my own willpower. I dropped down over his fist until I felt it inside my guts. To my amazement, I realized I'd swallowed his wrist too. I could hardly believe it was happening.

"You're getting fisted!" he exclaimed. "Your twat has a big hairy fist inside it! Now ride it! Ride it like you love it!" The thicket crackled with his raucous laughter.

With no wish to end my lesson now, I did as he instructed. On my elbows, I kneeled in the dirt again, the tatters of my underwear still clinging to my waist and my ass wide open. I humped his buried fist and a powerful growl rumbled up from deep crevice where I felt that fist had settled inside me. I growled, gasped, and moaned, like the nasty fuck beast I'd become.

"Yeah, little twat!" he goaded. "Moan like that! Yeah, show me how much you like it while I shoot my jizz all over your greased ass!"

I was intent on my own pleasure, not giving a thought to how much he must have been enjoying the scene as well. But when I felt warm come splatter my butt, I knew he was right there with me, another beast in the woods, satisfying his own craving.

I fell to my face, that big fist still planted up my throbbing rectum. He chuckled as he slowly withdrew it. I whimpered and felt my balls churn and my cock suddenly spring back to life. His hand came out, my asshole expanding around it as the knuckles slipped by. Then I was empty, wet, and warm. Lube and ass juice dribbled down my thighs.

"Feel it," he ordered. "Feel your nice wet twat." He grabbed one of my hands and twisted it behind me.

He pressed my fingers into the wet maw that was my asshole. I gasped. It was pulsing, slick, and gaping. I easily inserted three fingers. He held my wrist and fucked me with my own fingers. It was incredible. His other hand came around and began to pump my stiff cock. I writhed and grunted, listening to the squishy sounds of my asshole being pumped by my commandeered digits. I shot in the dirt with my own hand wedged up my ass.

He left me there, my clothes a wreck and my ass a slack gunny-sack. That's where the next guy found me. And that's where I got the second fist of the night up my ass. And where I got the third fist. When the light of dawn found me, I was still in the thicket

I finally limped away, my craving more than satisfied. That is, at least for one night. I wondered what I had become. Something had been unleashed that night: the beast that craved.

Hollywood Boulevard

M. Christian

This isn't one of those nice Hollywood stories. You know the kind, where the hero—usually the guy with top billing—rides off into the sunset. Not this time. Not this story.

I guess you could say it does have a happy ending, if you look at it the right way. All I ever wanted was a nice place, like one of those big houses in the hills above Hollywood Boulevard: a place with a nice big hot tub.

Well, I got it. But not the way I wanted it, of course.

There's just been a murder in one of those big Hollywood houses. The homicide squad's on its way there now, sirens wailing down the boulevard. A guy's been killed: two bullets in his back, one in his stomach, his body left soaking in one of those room-size tubs.

You should hear this story from someone who knows, before those big Hollywood columnists get their hands on it, turn it into something cheap and sleazy.

Look at me, bobbing there as my blood stains the expensively treated water. Poor dope, all I wanted was a hot tub. Unfortunately the price was just a little too high.

I was one of those journalists you don't hear about. You know the kind, the ones whose names always seem to get lost by the time the editors settle on a headline. Definitely I was not one of those columnists who get to turn tawdry into sleazy. I'd had a couple of good scores. Remember that big piece a couple of years ago: that old heartthrob that people almost forgot all about, until he got linked to that cute little high school jock? No, I didn't get the scoop, but I proofed it for the guy who did. I was that kind of journalist.

The only thing I had to my name was the cheap furniture in my cheap apartment, an ancient laptop, and my car. It wasn't much—it wasn't anything at all, but it was my life. The problem was that things were tough; my money was almost gone. I'd had to hock whatever I could, and I still didn't have enough. My landlord was a nice old queen whom I knew I could put off for at least another two months—but my car was another matter. The finance company was getting increasingly nasty. If I didn't pay, they'd come and drive it away.

Can you imagine being in L.A. without a car? It was a cruddy car, but it got me around. I was driving it that Thursday afternoon, going from one paper to another, trying to get someone to give me something on spec—I needed anything just to keep the repo man away—when the thing sputtered and died. I managed to pull into a side street off Hollywood Boulevard east of the 101, down where those big old houses hadn't been torn down to make way for cheap apartments like mine. The place was really overgrown, tangled weeds and vines covered the front gates and the tall brick walls all around it. But you could see that at one time the place had been fantastic—all glass, chrome, and style. Now the grounds were choked with dirt, dust, and weeds, but once this had all been grand.

I noticed that the huge iron gates were ajar. I don't know why I went in—just curious, I guess. It was part of '70s Hollywood, from the era of roller disco and platform shoes. I wanted to see what was left.

Inside the gates, the place was big—really big. There was a pool, empty of water but full of leaves. There was a big Cadillac in the drive, once pink and now deep red with rust, sitting on four flat tires. I was just starting to walk up to the big front door when it opened.

"You're late," he said. "He expected you hours ago."

When you're older, drag just doesn't work. It's just a man's cross to bear, I guess: Put on a wig and you're suddenly five years older. Sometimes it's pathetic, other times it's just tragic. But he—or she—was old, maybe even in his 60s, yet being in one's fifth or sixth decade worked for him. He wasn't Cher, but he could almost have been Bette Davis. He wore curls as red as that rusting Cadillac, a simple white dress, and just enough make-up so he didn't look like he'd been caught in an explosion at Max Factor. His incongruous voice was a deep rumbling bass, with a hint of a German or Hungarian accent. He made no attempt at a falsetto.

I went in. White shag, pink leather sofas, mirrors everywhere. A disco ball in the living room. A huge television occupied one wall, and on the opposite, a collection of vintage movie posters. Some I'd seen, others I hadn't—*Backroom Boys, Disco Dynamite, Roller Leather,* and the like.

"This way," Bette said, leading me toward a brass-and-marble staircase winding toward the second floor.

"Excuse me," I started to say, "but I just came to—"

Then someone from upstairs called: "Maxine! Maxine! Is that he? Bring him upstairs this instant." Bette turned, looked down at me from the first step, and said. "He is waiting for you. This way."

So I went up those stairs behind Maxine and noticed, as I ascended, that the brass had turned greenish, and the marble was deeply cracked.

He must have been a special hamster, maybe related to some famous hamster, though I couldn't think of any. He was lying there, on a velvet pillow, his little feet stiff in the air.

It took a few minutes to get it straightened out. No, I hadn't come from the vet; no, I hadn't come to take the little creature away. I was just in the neighborhood when my car broke down, and I just wanted to use the phone.

I answered his questions and tried not to stare. I knew him from somewhere. The moment Bette, or Maxine, brought me upstairs, opened the door to the big master suite, and ushered me in with a gravelly "He's here," I realized that something about the man of the house was familiar. But why?

He was handsome. There was no denying that. Standing by the huge round bed surrounded by gold-veined mirrors and floodlights, I was instantly struck by his beauty. It had faded, certainly; skin that had once been clean and smooth was now rugged and deeply tanned, and a body that had once been strong and broad-shouldered was now stooped and softer. "Well, what are you doing here then, if you're not going to take little Manuel away?" he demanded.

His voice was marvelous, deep and rich with a purr that reached down and tugged at me. It was another piece of the puzzle, another clue to this man's identity, but my mind was still not putting it all together.

"I was just in the neighborhood. My car broke down. I just came to use the phone."

"The phone?" he said, that powerful voice slipping into a glass-breaking screech that made me wince. "You came into *my* house—disturbed me—because you wanted to use the *phone?*" Without waiting for my response, he turned and bellowed to Maxine, standing in the doorway. "Show this gentleman out."

Then it hit me. As Maxine reached for my arm, I turned and blurted it straight out, without a clue in the world where it was going to lead me, what was going to become of it: "You're Norman Desmond. You used to be in porno. You used to be big."

"I *am* big," he said. His voice rang with injured pride, thundered with a vigor that defied the stooped shoulders. "It's porno that got small."

Eventually, it came out that I was a writer, and that changed everything. His blue eyes sparkling like new rhinestones; he took me by the hand and pulled me past sneering Maxine and into the hall. "Ah, a writer! Just the kind of man I need to see. Just the man—"

The hall was bedecked with more white shag, more gold-veined mirrors, and rows of tiny white lights where the mirrors met the shag. He took my hand in a firm grip and pulled me along. Our reflections multiplied into an endlessly duplicated couple striding into infinity.

Norman Desmond—there was a name that took me back. He'd been one of the greats, if not the greatest. Before Norman Desmond, queer porn was full of greasy plumbers and potbellied sailors. Loops long on cock sucking but short on plot. Sure they would get you off, but they didn't stick in the mind beyond the mechanics that happened between the plumbers and the plumbing. Then came Norman Desmond: handsome, strong, virile, but more than that: a presence. Norman Desmond filled the screen with attitude, with charisma. You didn't watch one of his flicks to see where his impressive cock would go, what he did with it, or whom he did with it; you watched him because his unmatched magnetism. He was a star.

Now I remembered those films—*Backroom Boys, Disco Dynamite, Roller Leather,* and all the others, the movies those posters downstairs advertised. They were some of his greatest: the best of the best. I was in shock, in awe.

But more than that, I was hopeful. Norman Desmond, *the* Norman Desmond—alive and well and living in that great big house full of memories and stories, right off Hollywood Boulevard. It was just what I needed. It was a story—had the makings of a kick-ass story—and he wanted to tell it to me.

The backroom looked like a set, something straight from *Hollywood Hustlers* or *I Love the Big Life*: crystal chandeliers, a big leather sofa, mirrors, mirrors, and more mirrors, and right in the middle of it all, a hot tub. Not just any hot tub, mind you, but rather *the* hot tub. Sure, some may call *Hot Water* derivative. How could you not, considering the plot was stolen from an old '40s film? But for me, it was pure Norman Desmond. I stood and stared at it as the flick played in the back of my mind. The bubbling, steaming water where Norman took Roger Biggies from behind, his muscular ass driving into Biggies till he screamed, his come mixing with the churning water in simple cinematic genius. This was the tub where he splashed with Tumescent Dan and took Dan's impressive tool into his throat in one awe-inspiring swallow. Looking at the water I felt my own cock stirring, aching for a touch, any touch.

"Here," Norman said as he retrieved a thick manuscript from a table next to the sofa. Five, six hundred pages, at least. It felt like a phone book. *Salomé: The Norman Desmond Story* was the title. I looked up at him. "You're a writer, you'll be able to help. I'm not really so good with…words. Now the pictures, those I'm good at. But this, this is something I could use some help with. I want to tell my story, to remind everyone of who Norman Desmond was. Yes, yes, to show them all that Norman Desmond is still here, just waiting for the right chance to get back up there on top, where he belongs."

I held the manuscript with both hands. "You want to make a comeback?" I asked, my voice catching somewhere between my throat and my lips.

"No. I hate that word. No, I'm going to return—that's the word—return to the thousands of people who have never forgiven me for deserting the screen."

I didn't say anything. I just stood there, weighing the heavy book in my hands. Even as an older man, there was still a power about him—something beyond the crow's feet, the thinning hair, and the gentle potbelly—something remained of the legendary Norman Desmond. I also considered my tiny apartment and my even tinier life.

I said something—probably "Yes," or "I'll do it"—but to be honest, I don't remember. All I remember is his hand on mine, his piercing blue eyes looking straight into me, filling me with some of his boundless determination, looping me into his dream of returning to the movies, and tugging at my memories of the great Norman Desmond.

So that's how it happened, the very first step. I had no idea at the time where it would lead me, or just how far it would go.

At first I only came by the grand old place on Hollywood Boulevard a couple of times a week, but quickly I realized how empty my apartment was compared to the grandeur of Norman's house. My old laptop and knockoff furniture just didn't compare to the hundreds of films, the thousands of fan letters. My place reminded me how small I was, how pathetic.

One day I was sitting at a huge steel coffee table in Norman's living room while he was upstairs watching some of his films in the tub room. Maxine puttered around, dusting the furniture and polishing the mirrors. Looking over Norman's manuscript, I guess I muttered something to myself about his fantastic life as one of the true legends of the porno screen. Maxine must have overheard, because he stopped polishing and walked over to me. "He was the greatest of them all," he said. "In one week he received 17,000 fan letters. Men bribed his hairdresser to get a lock of his hair. There was a prince who came all the way from England to get one of his jockstraps. Later he strangled himself with it! You are privileged to be here, privileged to be allowed to work on his return to the screen."

Eventually, I moved into a tiny room above the garage, where I spent most of my days working on the book. At first occasionally, then frequently, Norman came by to check on my progress.

It wasn't all toil, at least not on Desmond's part—not by a long shot. The fragile ego that was Norman Desmond required constant stroking. First, there were the fan letters that arrived every day. Maxine brought them to Norman on a silver salver, and the two of them opened and gushed over the letters for hours. "Wonderful," Norman warbled in his melodic voice (the very same voice that had demanded, "Suck my cock" in *Alley Tails* and "I'm going to fuck you long and hard" in *Beachfront Property*) as he opened them.

Then there were the movie nights. On those nights Norman escorted me upstairs to the tub room, and we sat and watched movie after movie. The steam from the water made clouds that caught stray fragments of light from the old projector. I'd seen a lot of them before, of course, but having Norman there was like a personal tour through the heyday of Hollywood queer smut. I learned all about the stars, the directors, the gossip, and the dirt. It was fascinating, and I began to look forward to those nights.

Then everything changed.

I'd been working on the book, and I'd begun to realize what a mess it was. The heart was there, the passion that was Norman Desmond the legend, but Norman had obscured his flame by filling the pages with bitterness, delusion, and outright fiction. I had to be careful, very careful, about what I cut and what I didn't. Norman screeched in a piercing falsetto—a tone that made me wonder whether the commanding Norman Desmond of *Army Brats* might indeed be gone—when I suggested any change.

Norman walked into my room. I readied myself for the usual fight over the book, but he shocked me when he put a hand on my shoulder and said in his good voice, his purr of firm masculinity, "You look tense. Why don't you come up and soak in the tub for a while?"

The tub—my mind reeled. To be honest, I never thought Norman would have any interest in me. Not that I'm a troll—I never had to look hard to find a date on Saturday night—but I simply wasn't in his league. I worked out just enough, I took care of myself just enough, but I definitely could have done more. Yet the legend of 8-mm loops, of *Backdoor Romeo,* had invited me up for a soak.

I felt was walking into a loop myself as I stood in front of that famous hot tub. It was just like the one I'd always wanted—because I'd seen it, this very tub, in his movies.

Norman stripped quickly and efficiently, as if performing some kind of magic trick he'd learned in porno school. His clothes simply vanished in the slim space between scenes. I sat on the edge of the tub, dimly aware that the bubbling, steaming water was soaking my pants and shirt. Norman Desmond was a very handsome man. Age had come a-calling: He had wrinkles, sags, that little belly, the thinning hair, a few liver spots on his arms, and a few rose marks on his chest. But time had yet to overcome his powerful determination to remain an idol, to freeze himself at the height of his career.

My cock was instantly erect—a fact which Norman acknowledged with tacit approval. He still projected in the flesh what he'd delivered so many times on the screen: a tremendous sexual presence. What's more, I was getting naked for the man who had been a key player in my sexual fantasies for as long as I could remember. Mere wrinkles couldn't diminish my enchantment; in fact, I doubted anything could.

Naked and hard, I stood in front of him. The bubbling waters of the tub behind me added to the heat that rose in my body. I was sweating, gleaming, but only partially from the steam.

He reached out and wrapped his hand around my hard cock. He held me that way for a good long time, never once looking at anything except my eyes. He slowly smiled as he looked deep into me. Then, never taking his hand from my cock, he led me into the hot, churning water.

It was good, as good if not better than I thought it would be. But there was something else—something that skated over the surface of my mind and refused to come together until much later, when I'd cooled down. He took my cock in his mouth and brought me close to tears. I touched him, amazed by the noises he made, the way he played his body like a fine instrument. He stroked me and worked my cock like a master—which he was. I felt self-conscious returning the favor, but he seemed to truly enjoy himself. When his come followed mine into the steaming water, I smiled at his deep, rumbling growls of pleasure.

We spent a long time in the water. The heat of the tub added more steam to our play. My fingers wrinkled, and my head started to swim from the heat, but we kept at it. It was like stepping into one of Norman's old reels. All the familiar details suddenly came to life: the pebbled texture on the bottom of the pool and the white translucent plastic. At one point, Norman playfully took a deep breath and vanished into the wildly boiling water to take my cock in his mouth. I looked up and caught myself and Norman reflected in the mirrors overhead. I was dazzled—no other word for it.

Finally, Norman tired and we climbed out and toweled off. I worked back into my clothes as he slipped on a big terry-cloth robe that Maxine held out for him.

As I walked the long mirrored hallway back to my room—the possibility that I might actually sleep with Norman Desmond never occurred to me—he called my name. I turned to see him at the far end of the corridor, silhouetted against the wavering light from the hot tub room. "You see," he said, his voice breaking slightly, "you see, I can still do it! I still have it! Soon it'll just be me, the cameras, and those wonderful people out there in the dark!"

A chill shot through my body. But I gave him my best smile and returned to my little room over the garage.

We quickly settled into a nice little routine. I continued to work on the book, and Maxine continued to dust and clean and deliver a new stack of fan mail every day for Norman. Each night Norman and I returned to the tub, where my awe and his insatiable need for admiration remained evergreen. It was good, at times very good, but there was also something else there: a vague feeling of menace that hovered just out of sight but never out of mind.

Sometimes when Norman sucked my cock as I stood in the burbling water and I caught him gazing off into the distance, playing for a camera—an audience that wasn't there anymore. Other times he behaved archly, or worked too hard at sucking or stroking me, still performing for the director in his mind.

His return began to obsess him more and more. The world could have burst into flame and fallen into ashes, and he'd only miss his fan mail. I began to stand in front of the window in my room, stare out at those high walls covered with dead creepers, and wonder about the world. Sure, it hadn't been a great world—at least not the part of it I'd experienced—but it was real. It was a world that revolved around the sun and not Norman Desmond.

I started to sneak out at night, rather than return to my little room over the garage. Exhausted from Norman's performance night after night, I tried to walk as far as possible, just to prove to myself that the world hadn't ceased to exist.

One night, Maxine waited for me at the door. The master was asleep, but he expected me all the same. At first I was ashamed to have abandoned the all-encompassing light that was the great Norman Desmond, but then I felt a stab of anger. "What is it, Maxine? His highness miss my adoring presence for 10 minutes?"

Maxine glowered at me through his thick black lashes and clenched his hands. "You are not worthy of him. He is Norman Desmond and you—you are just a distraction. He is great, one of the greatest that ever lived."

"Take it easy, Maxine," I said, seriously wondering for a moment whether the old drag queen might have stroke. "I just needed a breath of fresh air. No harm done."

"You do not realize how important he is. How carefully I have maintained him for the moment when he will return to his rightful place on the screen. I will not have you ruin him for that great time when he is accepted back as the legend that he is."

I'd had my fill of the "let's worship Norman" game. I had taken my walk, and I had seen that even at night in the dark there is more in the sky that the Great Norman Desmond. "He's a big boy, Maxine. He can take care of himself."

"Do you really think so?" he queried. He stepped back and started to close the door, to leave me to tramp around to the side entrance. "Then I suggest you check the handwriting on those fan letters."

The next night that uneasy feeling that had been lurking at the edges of my mind was right there in my face, obvious and more than slightly grotesque. It made its appearance after a worshipful screening of *The Plumber Rings Once,* after Maxine floated through the flickering lights of the tiny 8-mm projector to hand us our martinis. Norman stood with a flourish and intoned, "Maxine, you may go. We want to be alone."

There we were: me, Norman, the hot tub, and the precious

myth of the famous porn star—a myth that was more important, and more real, to Norman than anything else.

We got into the famous tub. Norman was in fine form; for a while, suspicion and depression kept their distance. It was just Norman and me. He kissed me, something he hadn't done before. As we stood in the hot water and as bubbles lapped at my balls and my quickly hardening cock, he gently bent forward to touch his lips to mine. His lips were soft—something I knew very well from having had them attached so often to the head of my cock—but with that kiss I realized they were almost too soft to feel. Cautiously, his tongue touched mine, and time seemed to stop. We embraced and lost ourselves in the kiss. It was good. It was just very, very good.

Soon things really started to heat up. As we kissed I gradually became aware of his cock against mine—an unconscious dick dual in the gurgling water. Then he broke the kiss and smiled at me. He was Norman: not Norman Desmond, just Norman. I thought—I wanted, really and truly—to believe I saw the real man.

Then he pushed me back against the edge of the tub. Before I could say or do anything, his lips were on my cock, and the water roiled around his emphatically tanned shoulders. If it had been good before, it was fantastic now. Yes, he was fantastic.

He worked me for what felt like hours, maybe even days. Finally, when I was ready to explode, he released me, and a thread of saliva vanished into the steam. He stood and faced me. Then he spoke, and everything fell apart: "Jerk off for me."

It took a few moments for the words to reach the part of my mind that was actually capable of thought. It was an uphill battle: I struggled through all that lust, through long minutes with my hand wrapped around my cock. I stroked myself slowly, then faster, as the water lapped like a thousand hot little tongues on my shaft and head. I was close, so close, when those words finally hit me. Not just those words, because I'd heard those words before, but rather the way he said them, the way he stood over me, the look he gave me—he was posing for the camera again. It was a reprise of *The Plumber Rings Once*: action for action, word for word, a reprise of his performance. I had been wrong. Norman wasn't there, probably had never been there; it was all Norman Desmond, the great, the legendary, Norman Desmond.

The water was cold, not hot. No, it was not hot at all. I stopped. A pearl of precome formed at the head of my cock and slowly dropped into the water. I stood motionless. Anger flared through me, and my body went rigid with fury. I climbed out of the tub. Norman might have said something as he stood there looking lost and alone in the bubbling water, but I didn't hear it.

When I finally heard his voice, he implored: "Darling, come back, darling!" I furiously thrust myself into my discarded clothes.

"No," I growled. "No, Norman, I'm going. I have to get out of here. I have to get out of this damned museum. I have to breathe real air, not this dusty celebration of who you used to be."

"No!" he screeched, "you can't leave me! I'm Norman Desmond. You have to love me, just as all my fans love me."

I stopped and held him in a furious gaze. I was angry, but seeing him, his carefully coiffed hair mussed from exertion and hot water, his face scarlet with emotion, I was also sad for him. I was sad for the lies he had spun around himself, the fantasies that had become more important to him that reality. "Do yourself a favor, Norman. Look at the handwriting on all those letters, and talk to Maxine about it." Then, and I said, "I'm sorry, Norman. I really am." And I honestly meant it.

"I'll kill myself," he screamed. His perfect blue eyes were wild with fury. "I will, you watch! You watch!" He walked over to a small table and opened a drawer. The pistol was small, like a toy in his big hands. I knew what it was and what it could do, but the sight of it in his hands only reinforced the sadness of him. I marveled at how low someone so talented had sunk.

"No, Norman, you won't. Wake up. There wouldn't be anyone to appreciate the gesture. It's just you and Maxine in this empty house."

"This isn't over," he said in a voice that recalled the thunderous command he'd exerted in those long-ago loops. "I'll be back, you'll see. I'll be back up there on the screen where I belong. I'll be back. I swear it! I'm Norman Desmond!"

"No," I said, "You used to be Norman Desmond."

Then it happened: three shots. He fired two into my back and one into my stomach. There wasn't a lot of pain, which surprised me. The bullets spun me around and slammed me facedown into that famous hot tub. My maroon blood unfurled in the bubbling water.

This is where we came in, at that famous tub, the one I always wanted. It's morning now and everyone's here: police, photographers, and those trash-talking columnists too. But don't believe them—believe me, I was there. Who are you going to believe: the latecomers or the corpse himself?

Like I said—not exactly a happy ending. I got my pool, but ultimately it brought me to a place farthest from joy.

What becomes of Norman? Norman puts on quite the show as they lead him away in handcuffs, as the flashbulbs pop and the hacks cry out for statements. He gets the best deal of all—infamous celebrity, the star of tabloids for years to come. It may be his last close-up—but he's more than ready for it.

Entangled States
David Wayne

I awaken in customary fashion, with my head nestled in the contour of Daniel's shoulder and my ears filled with the sound of his heartbeat. The room, though, is unfamiliar. It isn't until I hear again the footsteps that first roused me that I remember where I am, where we are. The footsteps are Creed's, and we are in the guest room of his family's cottage. The room is still decorated according to his elderly mother's taste and comfort.

I hear Creed puttering about the kitchen, preparing for his morning run, and I smile at how accustomed I have grown to this routine after only two days. I kiss Daniel on the temple, then slip out of bed and out of the room.

As expected, Creed is lacing his sneakers. I hang back but half hope he will catch me watching him. He is shirtless, and even though his back is to me, in my mind I see the dense hair that covers his chest, thick almost as sheep's wool and flecked with silver. His shorts are cut high, revealing muscular thighs, and as he tightens his laces, the muscles of his arms and back dance beneath his skin.

Creed stands, and I duck into the hallway in a childish game of hide-and-seek. When I peak around the corner, I am disappointed to discover that he is gone. I hear the screen door bang closed and watch from the window as he lopes up the driveway, then down toward the beach.

The thought of taking a shower is tempting, but I choose to forego it since I know we will go swimming at the lake before lunch. Instead, I tiptoe back into the guest room to retrieve a book. Daniel slumbers on. Given the extensive sexual territory that he and I have explored with Creed over the past few days, I doubt he will awaken anytime soon. Grabbing my book, I retreat to the living room.

Like the guest room, the living room has a matronly air, reminding me of boyhood visits to my great-aunt's farmhouse. I sink onto a couch, which sags in friendly accommodation. Any other seat offers a better view of the garden, but this location gives me the best angle on the road I know Creed will be running up— drenched with sweat—in half an hour.

The thought of him wrecks my concentration. Even the tawdry intricacies of 28 Barbary Lane fail to hold my attention. My eyes dart from the pages at every sound. Eventually, I realize I've reread the same passage a dozen times. At last I give up and simply stare out the window, awaiting Creed's return. My behavior, I realize, borders on addiction. I crave Creed's primal sexuality.

Daniel and I make love.

Creed fucks.

The minutes creep by, but at last Creed strides back into view. A sweaty sheen covers his body. I peer at him through the filigree of curtain as he stretches in the sunlight, then trots toward the rear of the house. By the time the kitchen door opens, I have settled deeper into the couch, my back to the kitchen. I hear water splashing in the sink, followed by thirsty gulps. The sound of footsteps follows, but these halt at the end of the linoleum. I know that Creed is appraising the situation: me alone on the couch and Daniel asleep in the next room. His gaze is hot on my flesh. I sense his decisiveness, and I am so attuned to his presence that I can actually feel his approach, the heat rolling from his body in waves.

Creed rests his hands on my shoulders.

"Would you like some coffee?" he asks, knowing I never drink the stuff.

I run a hand up his thigh, slipping it beneath the nylon of his shorts.

"Not coffee," I reply, tilting my head backward to look up into his eyes. He smiles, and creases form at his eyes and mouth. I roll my head across his groin, and he presses his hips forward, his eyes glazing. Through the fabric, I can feel the blunt stab of his stiffening prick. He lifts his hands from my shoulders, allowing his fingertips to trace the curve of my neck, before he buries them in my sleep-tangled hair. I respond by pushing harder against him and allowing my hands to range freely over his thighs. I find the waistband from the inside and tug. Creed rewards me with an encouraging sigh. I pull his shorts down a few inches before they snag at the root of his erection. Releasing my hair, he snaps his shorts out and down below his balls.

I take this opportunity to turn around and kneel on the couch, my eyes level with the nipples protruding from his sculpted pecs. I grab a tit between my teeth. It is thick and rubbery, and only years hence will I learn that I could have been much, much rougher. Still, my gentle gnawing elicits a satisfied groan. I tweak his right nipple with my fingers as I lick the left one. His hips jut forward, thrusting his cock against the plane of my belly. It is difficult to continue working his nipples when such temptation rubs against my abdomen, and eventually I succumb to it. My tongue draws me downward as I relish the briny taste of his skin. Creed's divine musk rises from his crotch. I burrow my nose into the damp curls, enjoying the warm pressure of his cock beneath my chin.

Creed worms his fingers back into my hair as his other hand grips the shaft of his erection, directing it into my mouth. It is thick, the head blunt, and already semen leaks from the end. I would savor its taste, but Creed pushes forward, burying the full length in my throat. It goes down easily—I've had ample practice these past few days.

Creed batters the back of my throat for a few moments, then pulls out to let me catch my breath. He leans forward, licking his semen from my lips. As our tongues tangle, Creed's hands slip inside my shorts to find the cleft of my ass. As soon as he begins to spread my cheeks, we both know how this is going to end. The world reduces to simply me, Creed, and our mutual need. He rubs his stubble-covered jaw against my smooth cheek until his lips are at my ear.

"Do you want to move to a very squeaky bed?" he asks, chuckling.

"Yes," I say, before I have time to reconsider.

We stand and pull up our shorts, erections brimming over our waistbands. As we creep past the guest room I peek at Daniel, then follow Creed into the other bedroom, leaving our door ajar—an open secret.

The room is still a boy's room. The headboard of the twin bed is painted fire engine red, as are the shelves and the window casings. A bright blue night stand sits against the wall, and I imagine forgotten comic books and baseball cards still haunt its drawers. I drop my shorts to the floor and climb naked into the rumpled sheets. The bed squeaks noisily, as promised.

Creed pauses, his hands poised on his hips.

"We've never done this without Daniel," he says. "He won't mind, will he?"

"No, of course not," I answer, and it's not a lie—just a misjudgment. I grip his cock, pulling him toward me as he sheds his shorts and socks. Surrendering to my tugging, Creed pounces onto the bed with a leap that has me giggling until I note the urgency in his eyes. He kisses with a ferocity sufficient to roll me backward, and I become so intent on the play of our tongues and lips that I am only dimly aware that his left hand has slid to the drawer of the night stand. He retrieves lubricant and condoms, dropping them by my side with practiced ease. When I spread my legs, he sinks into the valley of my thighs, his cock dropping below my balls to poke at my asshole. I squirm against him, begging him with my body rather than with words.

The lube bottle opens with a snap, then Creed's cupped hand descends over my thighs, through my crotch, and down to my ass. His palms the fluid into my skin, and I arch my back in time to his strokes. I feel a finger poised against my asshole, and I freeze in expectation. He smiles, then slowly and painlessly drives his finger home. Simultaneously, he grips my cock, tugging in rhythm with his internal stroking. I'm nearly lost in the gentle explorations of his fingers, until the foreplay becomes almost torturous.

I find the condoms at my side. As I tear one from its wrapper, Creed leans forward. I drape the rubber over the tip of his erection, then unroll it down the length of the shaft. Creed rubs lube along the length of his cock. When I sense he is ready to proceed, I swing my legs up onto his shoulders. He needs no further encouragement. Gripping his cock, he rests it against my asshole, then leans forward and gently pushes into me.

There is pain, but it is a familiar. And I've begun to crave it. The muscles of my ass futilely clamp around his cock, but finally surrender. Creed pushes further, tilting me up onto my shoulders, then using the leverage to drive himself even deeper. He grinds his hips, then withdraws. I feel the head of his cock raking against that magic button buried inside me. He lingers there, then presses forward again. I grasp his hips and writhe against him, drawing him in further. We pause until the last vestiges of pain melt away, leaving only a sense of fullness and an itching desire.

"You ready?" Creed whispers.

I squeeze his hips in reply. Beneath my fingers, I feel his muscles coil. Creed lowers his head to kiss me and simultaneously pulls his hips backward, only to slam into me half a moment later. Pain blossoms, then fades, replaced by an ecstasy that billows through my entire body. After a brief hesitation, Creed withdraws and thrusts again, faster, then again and again until there are no more pauses. Our mouths weld together. We exchange ragged breaths until my lungs burn. I drop my head backward, gasping in time to his thrusts. His lips move to my throat, and when he begins biting and licking the flesh along my neck, my self-control boils away. I become a wild thing, bucking against him, trying to find purchase against skin slick with perspiration. Dimly, I become aware of the syncopated banging of the headboard against the wall, but the din is no more meaningful to me than the animal cries emerging from my throat. All that matters is Creed's mouth at my throat, Creed's cock in my ass, and the divine friction of Creed's body against my cock.

It is impossible to say how long this goes on. Creed, nearly 20 years my senior, fucks with the abandon of a teenager. All too soon, though, I feel the climax building. Creed's rhythm falters, becoming more frenzied, until at last a roar emerges from his throat. He collapses on top of me, his hips still pumping. My perception of the universe condenses to the slide of my cock against Creed's sweating flesh and the building pressure in my groin. A final thrust from Creed finishes me. Hot semen erupts from my cock, filling the gap between our bodies and rolling down my sides. We kiss again, tongues and saliva intermingling, and we continue kissing long after Creed's cock has slipped out of me.

Creed rolls off me, spent. As the sweat and semen dry on our skin, we talk intimately—like lovers—for quite some time.

Except, of course, that we're not. We're friends, good friends, but this isn't love, and no amount of sex, no matter how spectacular, will change that. Love is having spent five years with Daniel, who is still asleep in the next room. Love is staying together through a cross-country move, through funerals, through the almost insufferable familial complexity that is the holiday season. Love is going to the drugstore at midnight for cough syrup. Love is coupon clipping and grocery lists. Love is arguing over the vacation plans and directions, but knowing we'll reach our destination regardless. Love is all of Daniel's foibles and features bound into a knot that I wouldn't unravel if I could.

And that's not what I feel for Creed.

That's not what I've felt for anyone else.

"I'm surprised we didn't wake Daniel," Creed says, disturbing my reverie.

"Me too," I say, the first stab of doubt lancing my conscience. "Maybe he won't notice," I add.

Creed looks at me for a moment.

"You shouldn't keep secrets from him," he says with certainty, and from his expression I understand he has learned that lesson the hard way.

We get up and walk together down the hall. Creed kisses me one last time, then vanishes into the bathroom; I continue toward the guest room. Daniel lies in a tangle of bedclothes. True to form, he has stolen my pillow. His petty larceny causes affection to well up within me. I climb into bed and burrow into his armpit.

Daniel stirs.

"What have you been up to?" he murmurs, his voice thick with sleep.

A dozen half-truths vie for my tongue, but at last I simply say, "I'll tell you later. I promise."

And we both drift back to sleep.

Wendy Fries One Wish

Don't wake up dead. The experience has little to recommend it.

I had everything to live for too: My first book was six weeks from publication, my agent reported nibbles from producers interested in a movie treatment, and one spectacular day followed another in the middle of an Atlanta autumn. Things were looking good.

Then I took the evening off to see *Gabriel,* Alan Currier's new movie. I'd expected another of Currier's "I'll hurt you so good," bad-guy roles. I was all set to lust over that hot body and beautiful English accent, come home happy and horny, and get to work.

Instead, I left the theater in a daze, my head aching and my sinuses blocked from crying.

Go see the movie; you'll believe in earthbound angels stripped of their wings. But don't walk away from the experience too distracted, as I did. You don't want to be so unfocused that you do a little hip-check on a speeding car. The car won't mind, but you will. Believe me.

"Dead, dead, dead," someone clucked.

Flat on my back on a sticky downtown sidewalk, I looked up. A round woman with stubby wings poking out of her back hovered a few feet above me. She wedged a pinky into her ear and scratched vigorously.

"Come on, time's wasting," she said. She reached down and dragged me off the cement. She pulled me along and talked fast:

"My name's Dixie, I'm an angel, you're dead, and before I can cart you off to the big pearlies, you get one final wish." She interrupted my shocked silence to exhale: "And don't even try with the world peace crap. I can handle Beatles reunions, calorie-free chocolate, and Technicolor sunsets. Keep it simple, sweet meat, and we'll be home before you know it."

"I'm dea—" I started to ask, when a man, obviously oblivious to our presence, walked through my chest and out my back.

"Yes," Dixie said with an impatient sigh. "And believe me, it's better this way. Now come on. If we hurry, I can have you in wings before morning."

I stopped short. "What the flying fuck are you talking about?" I asked.

Ms. Pugnacious stopped dead in traffic. As a phalanx of pedestrians walked through her, she said, "One wish. You get one wish before we," she pointed skyward, "take the elevator up."

"Eh?" I mumbled.

She arched an eyebrow and looked at a clueless purple-haired teenager beside her. "Why do they ask why?" she mused aloud. "What's so hard to understand? I caught on. You look bright," she said to the kid. "You'll catch on. But these"—she gestured at me—"the writer-types, the actors: I think it's a congenital problem."

"I love old restaurants," Dixie said.

We were in a dark joint, full of ancient smells and prime rib. It was cocktail hour.

We weren't sitting, mind you, and we certainly hadn't ordered anything. We strolled between the tables as waiters scurried by with food. I didn't understand why we were in the place until a serving tray laden with potatoes and steak passed through my shoulder. "Whoa!" I exclaimed.

Dixie trailed after the waiter and let the hot platters of food go through her twice. She floated back my way. "I love food," she said dreamily. "I married my husband because of his cream puffs."

"Is that why we're here?" I asked.

Dixie threw herself into a plush booth. I followed her lead.

"Of course it is," she replied. "I gotta eat don't I? So are you ready to make a wish yet?" She eyed a slab of birthday cake on an approaching tray. She leaned into the aisle. The cake-and waiter-passed through her head. She sighed contentedly, then burped.

"Go for it," she said. "Make a wish. What were you thinking about just before you died?"

"Ha!" I laughed, "*You* try getting run over by a car and tell me what *you* were—" An odd sensation stopped me mid sentence. Bright as a feature film, my last thoughts blossomed in my skull. I turned scarlet and murmured, "Oh."

"What?" Dixie queried.

I let my six-foot frame slump farther into the leather seat.

"What?" she asked again as she "gulped" a whiskey on its way to another table. "What? What? *What?*"

Between my legs a certain body part was a-stirring. I squeaked, "Nothing."

Dixie helped herself to a Bloody Mary. "I ask out of courtesy, mind you," she said. "I can see what you see, clear as day. Wishing will make it so. Let's go." She moved to leave.

"No!" I exclaimed as I sat bolt upright. "That's not my wish! That's just what I was thinking about before I—"

She settled back, ran spit along a feather until it looked lacquered. "I've set the wheels in motion already, my snooker-doodle. It's a good wish, so be happy with it."

"But what about a Pulitzer?" I protested. "An Oscar—"

"Ah, please. You want to bring a cold statue with you to eternity, or do you want the moist recollections of some sweaty lovemaking?"

"But—"

"It's more fun for me this way," she said testily. "The squealing and grunting is the best part."

Without even thinking I reached out as a waitress went by. I got a swig of gin and tonic through my palm. I enjoyed the drink more than I ever had when I was alive.

Dixie closed her eyes and took a deep breath. "Even the smells are great when you're dead. *Everything* is." She wiggled her eyebrows at me. "*Everything.*"

Although my hormones made me sigh reverently, I wasn't happy.

But by the time we got to the Virginia Highlands section of the city, I was ready.

"I'm gonna tie him up and make him beg," I said as I gave Dixie a determined look. "Did you ever see *Etched in Glass*? It was his third movie. This woman ties him up because, well, I forget. But he spends the whole movie begging her to let him go. Toward the end he's just begging. And it was"—Dixie was busy making us pop in and out of trains and buses (I didn't get why we had to travel on public transit like everyone else if we could appear and disappear at will)—"an incredibly sexy film, even though not a stitch of clothing came off anyone. You'd have to see it to understand."

"I'm sure," she said as she dragged me off a bus and onto the sidewalk. She pointed at something.

I looked up. THE BERSHING HOTEL, a gilded sign proclaimed. Five stories of brown brick oozed old-world sophistication and rarified charm. This was where the rich, the wonderfully famous, and the temporarily out-of-grace holed up.

Dixie gestured skyward. "There, top floor. Suite 58."

"Well, what—" I began.

Pop. Dixie was gone. And I found myself in a long corridor, standing before a door marked 58.

Now what? I wondered.

Indecision marched up my shoulder blades and sat on my neck. Obviously, I couldn't go in there; I didn't even know this guy. Maybe that sort of thing didn't matter anymore.

Well, Dixie had already firmly impressed upon me that I was d-e-a-d *and* that I wasn't going to have the chance to make a thank-you speech to a room full of literate admirers. No, all I was getting was this: the chance to have sex with a British movie star.

There are worse fates.

I passed through the door into the suite, which was dark, though it was only midafternoon. In the half-light I had another attack of the kind of anxiety common among the recently dead: I was in someone's private space, *haunting* it. Was this really the only way I could move on to the next world?

I heard a little groan. The pull of lust and curiosity were irresistible.

I skirted an en-suite kitchen, a sitting room with a long white couch, a cavernous bathroom, then...oh, Lord.

In the bedroom were shadow-light, silence, and a sleeping, naked man. He was beautiful.

Seconds of shock ticked by. Without thinking, I crept into the room, stood at the foot of his bed, and stared.

Oh, my yes. Sure enough and hallelujah. It was he: Alan Currier, passed out, dead to the world. His long blond hair was in tangles around his face. He had flung both arms over his head, and his hairless chest was a dance floor just waiting for my tongue. I watched his flat belly gently rise and fall with every breath. Then I let my gaze follow the precious "Hairway to Heaven" down, down, down to his crotch. I stood drooling like a village idiot.

If you've spent enough time fantasizing about someone, you start to feel like you really know him. Trust me on this. You imagine you're quite familiar with his predilections and every precious inch of his body. I licked my lips, crawled onto the bed, and in one hungry motion engulfed the man's cock with my mouth.

He was salty, warm, and half-hard. I ran my hands along the soft skin inside his thighs and then spread his legs wide. He didn't even shift in his sleep.

Oh, you delicious slut, I thought.

Long ago—when I was still alive and well—I had a boyfriend who used to open his legs astonishingly wide when I went down on him. He'd had a lot of practice with that maneuver. Somehow the idea that he was easy, that he reflexively spread 'em like that to get it, always turned me on. Because I regularly worked him over with an almost religious fervor, he swore that each orgasm was better than the one before.

It wasn't quite like that with Alan.

He stayed half-hard, but *just* half-hard.

I gave him my all too. I pumped his British banger like a pro. But he didn't move, he didn't moan, and he certainly didn't dance the "I'm coming now" tango. He just snored softly: a definite spirit dampener.

I kneeled on the bed, looked down at that long, achingly gorgeous amusement park of flesh and muttered, "Now what?"

Pop.

"Were you digging for fossils or something?" Dixie wanted to know. We were behind the hotel's main desk. "How about some grace? Maybe charm? Or don't they teach that in writer school?" Dixie peered over the shoulder of the hotel's desk clerk. "Oh," she cooed. "Johnny Depp's here. Now there's someone worth doing. He makes good movies. Hardly any explosions."

I tried to kick a potted plant. "Look," I whined, "who asked *you?* This is *my* wish, right?"

Dixie scratched at her ear with her pinky. "Yeah, but *I'm* not getting any fun out of it either. All I'm saying—" She stopped and squealed, "Ben Daniels is here! Do *him.* I like him even more. Hey, do both of 'em and—"

"Gah!" I said, full of infinite grace and lots of fucking charm.

My angel sighed and said, "OK, *fine.* Do whomever you like."

Pop.

I was back in Suite 58 at the foot of Alan's bed. What was the big deal?

Dixie had irked me all to hell and I figured, *Screw it. I'll just go to heaven or purgatory, or the eternal Wal-Mart in the sky, and I'll just skip right over the last-wish thing, OK?*

Then Alan tossed fitfully in his bed, kicked off the last bit of sheet, and turned onto his belly.

My little dead heart started to sing.

There it was—his glorious behind, rising up like a beautiful fuckable mountain.

"I bet he's an ass man," I sighed reverently. And, oh, what an ass. Round, smooth, so damned inviting, it might as well have sent out invitations.

I knelt on the foot of the bed in a prayerful post and looked at my prey. I took hold of his ankles and gently spread his legs.

"Come to papa," I suggested, wriggling up between his thighs and resting a hot hand on each butt cheek. "Come *for* papa," I amended, and bowed my head.

I plugged my tongue between those plump orbs with the abandon of a man certain he's having the world's safest sex. The first time a boyfriend did this to me I woke up already coming. It wasn't the actual tongue work so much as the thrill of waking to an X-rated program already in progress. So I plunged, lapped, and waited smugly for an appreciative moan, and arch of his back, a throaty little exclamation of "Oh, God, *yes!*"

Instead, I heard a decidedly unpromising rumble in his lower intestine. I needed no more prompting to levitated away from the object of my desire.

Looking down at those plump little mountains I whined, "What *is* this?"

Pop.

Suddenly we were behind the counter of a coffee shop.

"Nothing's happening!" I howled. "Snores, some gas: These are the responses of my hot love-machine? I mean, he could not *be* less interested, Dixie. If I don't get to wish for a Nobel or a Tony, if I have to go for a little grunt-and-push, then can we make sure everyone's, you know, *awake* for it? Or is this one of those monkey's paw wishes where I find out he's actually a zombie, or I'm a giraffe, or we're both on *Ricki Lake?*"

Dixie hovered over the cappuccino machine, drawing in snootfuls of steam. "God, I love cappuccinos." She cooed. She flicked at one with her tongue, then cast a glare at me. "You know, for a writer, you have the imagination of a mollusk." She pumped her stumpy little wings mightily until she hovered. "Stop treating him like a side of cinematic beef. Treat him like a human being."

I looked at her, about to retort smartly, when she went *pop* and disappeared.

For the next three hours I sat on the cappuccino machine, sucked steam, and moped.

Inside Suite 58 the light was gray and misty, like the sky outside. Though my eyes didn't need to adjust, I stood in the middle of the living room and soaked in the chilly darkness. The rainy walk from the coffee shop did wonders for my mood. Dixie was right: Everything felt better than it did when I was alive. The rain was like a cool caress, calming my overheated imagination.

As I gave myself over to the peace of my surroundings, small sounds began to creep through the suite. I couldn't quite make them out.

Tiptoeing, even though I was quieter than a cat, I began to search the room. My dead little mind was mercifully empty.

It didn't take long to find him.

He hunched on the couch in the sitting room, eyes squeezed tight and knees clasped to his chest, and rocked back and forth like a child. Somehow I remembered—perhaps Dixie whispered it to my subconscious—that Alan suffered from debilitating migraines. That explained the dark room in the middle of the day and his utter unconsciousness before. He'd doped himself to try to sleep through the pain.

It was obvious he'd woken too soon: my doing, no doubt.

As he rocked and moaned, I finally saw him not as dashing Gabriel or sexually sinister Anthony Milton. I saw, at last, a human being.

I moved toward him. Instinctually I put my hands went on his brow and began to stroke gently. My caress was soft, even for a ghost, but as soon as I touched him his feeble moans subsided. I massaged his temples, feeling his bones beneath my hands. Subtle changes in his breathing told me he wasn't hurting anymore.

He stretched out on the couch, and I lost track of time as I continued my ministrations. I tended him long enough for his brow to unknot and for his breathing to become a clock in my head. And long enough for one other thing.

"Oh, there you are," he said softly.

I looked down at him. He was looking up at me.

Try being invisible for a half-dozen hours. When someone finally looks straight at you, all blond lashes and unblinking blue eyes, it's quite a shocker. I thought I'd climax right there. Of course, at that point, I didn't know whether such a thing was technically possible.

"Here I am," I said, my heart in my throat. What else could I say? He didn't seem surprised, so I didn't act surprised. "Better?"

The tips of his fingers brushed across the back of my hand, zinging electricity straight to my cock. "Much," he said. "Thank you."

I ran my hands along his forehead and into his hair. He twisted a little and closed his eyes. I thought he had fallen asleep. But he opened his eyes, looked at me, and whispered, "Will you wash my hair?"

My eyebrows crested in surprise, but I didn't laugh. I knew he'd just dropped every barrier between us. In his own way he had asked me to make love to him.

"Yes," I said, as I caressed his jaw and a day's worth of sandy stubble.

He rubbed his cheek against my hand and smiled. My mind traveled to the darkened theater where I'd watched him smile dozens of times—a villain's smirk, a self-effacing hero's grin. I always wanted him to smile for me, and now he was smiling.

I pulled a chair over to the big silver sink in the suite's kitchen. "Come," I said, holding my hand out to him, "Let's get wet."

He gave me a lopsided grin. As he walked toward me, he crossed his arms and tugged off his polo shirt. Underneath he wore nothing but soft skin and sleek muscle.

"Oh, mother of God and half of Miami," I said softly.

I was a spook, specter, spirit, or shade. But I *felt* blood surge through me, flush my skin, and raise my cock.

He sat languidly in the chair and looked up at me with those bright blue eyes.

I pulled out the phallic little dish hose and blasted water into the sink until it grew warm. I reduced the pressure and angled the spray toward his head. When the water touched him, he moaned.

Oh, that moan was a revelation.

Relief bubbled up within him like molten glass, and I also sensed desire, permission, and trust. He knew I couldn't hurt him.

Baby, if only you knew.

I ran my free hand through his hair and combed it out with my fingers. He moaned again, and his eyes flicked closed in pleasure. His mouth gently gaped open and I heard that relief again: a soft, continuous sigh that drained the hurt from him.

Ghosts can get hard—a fact I'm sure is missing from all the supernatural literature. I felt my erection in a way I never had when I was alive: I was keenly aware of the blood engorging me, the skin stretching.

"Do you know how many nerve endings are in the human scalp, love? Ten million," he sighed, "or so I've heard."

He was nothing like the characters he portrayed in his movies. He displayed no fury, no attitude, and no meanness anywhere. I'd never touched anyone as gently as I touched him.

"I think," he said softly, "I hear my soul singing."

That was it. I sold the ranch, moved lock, stock, and barrel from wanting to fuck to that sweet place of needing to make love.

That was when his hand wrapped around the back of my leg and slowly crept along my thigh to my ass. I was so—shall we say—*moved* that I accidentally hosed water down his chest.

He didn't even open his eyes as the stream sluiced down the flat wonderland that was his belly and into the waist of his jeans. Instead, he lifted his free hand and skimmed his hard, wet nipples with his palm. When he was sure I was good and interested, he pushed his hand into his jeans and moaned like you wouldn't believe: sharp, breathy, like he was already coming.

It's a miracle I didn't hose down azaleas three blocks away.

He started masturbating right there in the kitchen. At first he just moved his hand inside his jeans, but then he started pumping his hips. He moaned steadily and—here's the crazy-sexy part—so quietly. I had goose bumps from my ears to my balls.

I stopped washing his hair. The hand inside his jeans grew still.

In the next moment I fired up my fingers and so did he, unbuttoning and unzipping his jeans. He began to fuck his fist—if you'll pardon my French—for all he was worth. For a moment, I forgot to breathe. Then I sucked in air and just watched as he kept pumping those hips. *Come, God, just come.*

But he didn't. Instead he turned his face toward me and bit my prick through my jeans. Oh, mama! Dead men can get so hard it hurts.

I took one hand away from his head long enough to unbutton and unzip. How I could be a walk-through-walls ghost in one minute and solid enough to have an erection dripping precome the next? Did I really care?

"Harder," he moaned. At first I thought he meant me, then comprehension dawned and I massaged that man's cranium for all I was worth. He responded by sliding his finger in and out of his mouth suggestively—I was dripping like crazy now. Then he pushed his finger into my ass.

I heard angels sing.

He stopped masturbating, turned in his chair, and clamped his hot mouth around my cock. Then he wedged another probing finger into my ass.

A damn *choir* let loose in my head.

"Oh, good God," I remarked as I frantically humped that gorgeous tough-guy face. "Oh, great, good God," I amended as I thrust deep enough to feel his throat close in around me.

How I stayed focused enough to keep my fingers kneading his scalp, I don't know. It probably had a lot to do with the vague worry that everything might come to a screeching halt if I stopped. So long as my fingers probed his aching head, he sucked me hard

and finger-fucked me deep. There's nothing else like positive rein-
forcement to keep you on task.

"Alan, God, yes! I'm gonna come—for a week!" I said through
a series of groans. I wasn't stingy with my own supportive encouragement.

It helped that I wasn't joking. My ghost-guy senses magnified
everything; I believed I was having a religious experience. His teeth
grazing the head of my cock, the goose bumps marching across my
shoulders, and those fingers digging away inside my ass were about
to bring on the rapture. It was celestial, and I could have gone on
like that forever. But Alan wasn't like me; he was a hot and horny
human who wanted a mouthful of my spunk.

So I dug my fingers into that dripping blond hair and held on.
I closed my eyes the better to see what I was feeling and started
pumping harder and deeper into his eager mouth until I thought my
body was on fire.

I know you've heard the term "full-body orgasm," but I think
you've got to be dead to really appreciate the experience. The knee-
melting, nipple-hardening, ass-clenching, full-whammy effect can
not be adequately described. If I didn't come for a week—down his
throat and all over that beautiful face—it sure as hell felt as if I did.

I felt so reverently grateful for the experience that after the last
thread of sensation left me, I had to go directly to my hands and
knees to offer.

He was on me quicker than that Dixie chick can pop in and out
of a filet mignon.

After priming with saliva what needed no priming, he pushed
himself inside me. That initial sensation was worth a hymn itself. I
think he composed one on the spot: a sweet little number in the
key of moan.

"Fuck me," I requested sweetly, "Hard."

He needed no further prompting.

Maybe judiciously measuring out glimpses of sublimated sexuality had allowed Alan to conjure those mean-guy performances
from his sweet self. After only a few words of encouragement from

me, he went for the gold medal in ass pounding. I hadn't had a man's balls hit me that hard in a lifetime of happy bottoming.

I'm not complaining, of course. I had another half-dozen religious moments as he speared me righteously. When he finally went silent and still and started coming in beautiful hot spurts, I *knew* I'd died and gone to heaven.

And I had, and I did.

Amen.

Escorts

Bob Vickery

The phone on the nightstand next to me suddenly rings, and I damn near have a heart attack. "Hello, Roger?" a baritone voice asks.

"Yes?" I reply.

"This is Doug. I'm stuck in traffic and I'll be about 15 minutes late. Is that OK?"

I take a deep breath. "Yeah, sure. No problem."

"Room 326, right?"

"Yeah, that's right."

"Great, see you in a little while." Doug hangs up.

I glance at the clock on the nightstand. It's a quarter to 10. The zero hour is now pushed back 30 minutes. I still can't believe I'm doing this. During the sales seminar today, all I thought about was getting together with Doug tonight. I mean, hell, I don't even know what the protocol is for something like this. Do we make conversation first? Do I just tell Doug what I want him to do? Do I pay him up front or afterward? When I finally hear a knock on the door, I seriously consider not answering it. But my Midwestern politeness wins out. I put my head between my knees, take a deep breath, get up, and open the door. My heart beats hard enough to wake the dead.

Doug stands framed in the doorway. He's dressed in jeans and a light blue tank top that hugs his torso like a second skin. He doesn't look real. In fact, he looks a lot like a Macy's Thanksgiving Day balloon: biceps pumped up like cannonballs, pecs that threaten to rip his shirt open, shoulders you could build a fucking condominium on. I have never in my life seen a man so muscular. He regards me with calm blue eyes.

"Hi, Roger," he says, holding out his hand.

"Hi," I say back. We shake hands. Doug's grip is firm but cautious, as if he knows he could squeeze my hand to pulp and is making a painstaking effort not to do so. He walks into the room and looks around. He has the air of returning to familiar surroundings.

"You've been in this room before?" I ask.

Doug smiles. "A couple of times."

OK, I think. Doug has the corn-yellow hair and broad face of the Swedish farmers I see back in Green Bay. His hands are the size of dinner plates. He sits in a chair and crosses his right ankle over his left knee. I sit opposite him. We look at each other.

"So, Roger," he says. "What brings you to L.A.?"

I clear my throat. "A sales seminar. I work for a publishing firm in Wisconsin. We do inspirational books, like *Be a Winner, Not a Whiner.* That was a big seller. Maybe you heard of it?"

Doug smiles blandly and shakes his head. "Sorry," he says. Silence lies between us like a dead flounder. "You ever been in L.A. before?" he asks.

"No. In fact, I've never been out of Wisconsin before." I clear my throat. "I've never done this either. You know…"

"Hire an escort?" Doug gives a slow, lazy smile.

"Yeah." I let a beat go by. "I can't believe I'm doing this." Doug just sits there, looking at me calmly. "I flew in last night"—I continue, speaking faster now—"and I picked up this gay paper at a bar across from the hotel. And there were all these *ads* in the back. All these hot guys for sale. I never saw anything like it!" I glance at Doug. "It was just a spur-of-the-moment thing. Here I was, loose in this city, and I just wanted to do something I'd never done before. Something crazy."

"Cool," Doug says. He looks bored.

"I'm sorry to talk so much. I'm kind of nervous."

"Don't sweat it," Doug says. He stands up and nods to the bed. "Shall we get started?"

"Yeah, sure," I say. I hesitate. "But, could you…"

"Yeah?" Doug asks.

I swallow. "Could you put on a strip show for me? Just let me watch you as you take everything off?"

Doug grins. "Yeah, Roger. Sure." He hooks his thumbs under his tank top and slowly peels it off. His torso is amazingly cut—every sinew is on display. I have to remember to breathe. His nipples stand out like little pink fireplugs. He kicks off his shoes and pulls his socks off. He unbuckles his belt, pulls down his zipper, and slides his jeans down thighs as solid as tree trunks. He's wearing white cotton briefs underneath. The bulge in them lives up to the promise of his huge hands.

He steps toward me. "OK, Roger," he says, stopping in front of me. "You do the rest." He stands so close to me that I can feel the heat rising from his body. After a couple of beats, I hook my fingers under the elastic band of Doug's briefs and slowly pull them down, past his dark-blond, neatly clipped pubes, past the plump tip of his cock, past inch after inch of the fat pink shaft that follows. Fascinated, I trace the course of a vein until I get to the ridge of Doug's cock head. Free of the confining fabric, Doug's half-hard dick springs up and sways slowly in front of my face.

"Jesus," I mutter.

Doug's dick is fat, spongy, and candy pink, with blue veins snaking up the shaft. His cock head flares out into a rubbery, red fist of flesh, the piss slit deep and pronounced. He shakes his hips to make his cock swing from side to side in a slow, pendulous motion. His ball sac hangs low. It's furred by a light dusting of blond hair, and the right nut hangs lower than the left.

"You like it?" Doug asks.

I look up into his wide, blue eyes. "Hell, yeah."

Doug turns and walks back to his chair. His high, firm ass is the color of pale cream, the crack a thin, tight line. He sits down and spreads his legs apart. His balls hang so low they cover the crack of his ass. "Come here," he says gruffly.

I slide out of my chair and crawl across the carpeted floor to Doug. He sits still, with his eyes fixed on me. I reach up and run my hands up his thighs, feeling the hard muscled flesh under my fingertips. "Yeah," Doug breathes, "that's right, go for it." I lean forward and bury my nose in the soft fleshiness of Doug's ball sac and inhale deeply. A scent of musk and fresh sweat fills my nostrils and flows down into my lungs. The scent is strong and heady; if the evening consisted of nothing but my sniffing Doug's balls, I'd be content. I press my lips against the loose folds of the fleshy pouch and tongue it, sucking on one ball and then another as Doug rubs his cock over my face.

Doug raises his legs and exposes the pink pucker of his asshole to me. I tongue that too, something I've never done before. I slide my tongue past his balls and up the thick shaft, as I reach up and squeeze Doug's nipples. Doug's body squirms under me. "You can squeeze harder," Doug murmurs, and I increase the pressure of my fingers. I push my tongue into Doug's piss slit, tasting the drop of precome that dribbles out, and slide his cock into my mouth, nibbling down the shaft until my chin presses against his balls.

Doug lays his hands on either side of my head and proceeds to fuck my mouth with long, deep strokes. His dick widens at the base, and each time it slides down my throat, I can feel my lips pull back. I look up across the expanse of muscled flesh into Doug's light-blue eyes. Doug regards me calmly as he pushes his hips up to fuck my face. *This is just another day in the office for him,* I think. *How fucking strange!*

I pull his cock out of my mouth. "I would love for you to suck my dick," I say, without any real hope that Doug will do so. But Doug pushes himself out of the chair and stands up, pulling me up with him. He undoes my belt, pulls down my fly and tugs my pants down past my hips. He kisses me lightly on the mouth and kneels in front of me, wrapping his huge hand around my dick, stroking it slowly. He bends his head down and I feel his lips work their way down the length of my shaft. Doug bobs his head faster, jacking me with his hand as his mouth slides up and down the shaft. I run my hands through his thick yellow hair.

"Fu-u-uckkkk," I groan. Doug gives great head. He presses his lips tightly around my shaft and twists his head from side to side, sucking me off with genuine enthusiasm. I arch my back, my eyes shut tight, and I feel him draw me closer to orgasm. I push him away just before I shoot.

"Not yet!" I gasp.

Doug looks up at me, his eyes bright. "Let me fuck you," he growls.

"Sure," I say, laughing.

It just takes a minute for Doug to sheathe himself and grease up. I pull him on top of me onto the bed. and he slings my legs around his torso as I guide his dick to my asshole.

He slides his dick in all the way, until I feel his balls press against me. He starts to pump his hips, slowly at first, then with increasing tempo. There's a mirror that runs across the length of the wall next to the bed, and I watch Doug's reflection fuck mine. His dimpled ass pumps up and down and his dick slides in and out of my asshole. Doug's face is inches above mine, and I turn and meet his gaze, looking deep into his eyes. Doug fucks me with a hard, driving energy, his balls slap loudly against my ass, but his eyes keep that same deep, level calm as they peer into mine. I crane my neck upward to kiss him, and Doug slides his tongue into my mouth. I stroke my dick in time with Doug's thrusts and bring myself to the brink of shooting, but hold back to wait for him. Sweat trickles down his face and drips down on me. His eyes are hard and deadly serious now; his lips pull back into a soundless snarl.

"I want to watch you squirt your load," I pant, and Doug nods. After a few more thrusts he quickly pulls out of me.

"Here it comes," he growls as he yanks the condom off his dick. He straddles my chest squirts his load hard against my face, one blast after another. I open my mouth as the thick gobs rain down onto my cheeks, chin, and eager tongue. A few strokes release my own orgasm, and I cry out as my load pulses out and splatters against Doug's back.

Doug looks down at me, grinning. When the last spasm passes through me, he rolls off onto his side and kisses me lightly.

"Well," he says. "Did you have fun?"

I just laugh, without saying anything.

I have one more night in L.A. before the seminar is over. The next morning, while the others students learn about marketing strategies for midsize publishing companies, I sit in the back and pore over the escort ads in the gay newspaper, hidden away in my course manual. I'm in the grip of some crazy wild energy; it's like I'm possessed.

I make a phone call during the class break, and that night I'm visited by Carlos, who describes himself in his ad as "a punk with attitude." Carlos is short, muscular, and theatrically contemptuous, with dark eyes that burn with a bright cynicism in his handsome face. He wears a gold cross around his neck. On his left biceps is a tattoo showing a buxom naked lady riding a crescent moon; on his right is Our Lady of Guadalupe.

Carlos fucks me mercilessly, spewing out a steady torrent of abuse. "You like that, cocksucker?" he growls as he thrusts deep into my ass. "That feel good, you pussy bitch?" He's like a goddamn force of nature: His hands roam all over me, his cock-thrusts deep and sure, and his liquid dark eyes glare down into mine. When I finally come, groaning loudly, Carlos startles me when he covers my mouth with his and tongues me fiercely. My orgasm sweeps over me like a swelling breaker and slams me down hard against the mattress. When Carlos shoots his own load into the condom up my ass, he thrashes wildly in the bed, tearing at the blankets and crying out in Spanish. He leaves 15 minutes later with my money stuffed in the back pocket of his jeans. He slams the door on his way out; his last dramatic touch makes me laugh lightheartedly.

The following Monday, my boss, Jerry, walks into my office. He asks, "How was the seminar, Roger? Did you learn anything useful?"

"Yeah," I say. "It was very productive." I slide a brochure lying on my desk toward him. "In fact, there's going to be another, more advanced training seminar a couple of months from now. It might be a good idea for me to go."

"We'll see," Jerry says, looking at the brochure. He's being cagey, but Jerry's a sucker for these seminars, and I'm pretty sure he'll bite. After he leaves, I pull the gay newspaper from my briefcase and turn back to the escort ads, already fantasizing about the boys I'll pick next time around.

Angels Don't Fall in Love

Todd Gregory

"Angel—"

I wake up in the middle of the night whispering his name. When my alarm goes off at seven in the morning, for a brief instant I imagine he's here with me in bed, that he never left, that his warm body lies next to me. When I awaken, his round liquid-brown eyes will look into mine with that curious, sexy mixture of innocence and awareness.

But my eyes open, as they do every morning, to find the other side of the bed empty: a vast desolate waste of cotton sheets and woolen blankets. My heart sinks into the darkness of despair, loneliness, and missed opportunity. For I have known love, passion, and joy.

And lost them all.

I first lay eyes on Angel one night as I wandered home from the bars at about two in the morning. I'd had more than my fair share of drinks that night and had given up and decided to go home. Staying out no longer held the promise that I might meet the man of my dreams, or even just a warm body with a forgettable name for the night. Late nights promised only more alcohol, more disappointment. I'd begun to stand alone in a corner of the bar, not approaching anyone—and nobody approaching me.

Before I left home that night I promised myself I'd break the cycle. I would not stay out ordering more drinks and thinking that maybe in five minutes the right guy would walk in. The drinks only clouded my judgment and distorted the way guys looked, making them seem far more attractive than they would appear in the cold light of morning, when I would ask myself, *What were you thinking?* It was a tired old game, and one I didn't feel like playing anymore.

He was standing—leaning, really—against one of the old gaslight lampposts on Royal Street in the French Quarter, just a block from my apartment. A cigarette dangled from his lower lip.

His dark black hair gleamed blue under the streetlight. He sported a mustache and goatee, and he wore a clingy white ribbed tank top. His jeans were several sizes too big and swagged low across his hip to reveal black boxer shorts. There was a tattoo on his right arm: a cross in outline with beams of light radiating from it. In the flickering gaslight lamp he seemed large, but when I got closer I saw he was maybe 5 foot 5, maybe 5 foot 6. His eyes were amazing: wide pools of liquid brown flecked with gold, like the sad eyes of a Madonna in a Renaissance painting. His long, curling lashes looked dewy in the flickering light.

"Hey," he said as I walked past him.

"Hey," I said, nodding. I stopped when I saw him cast his eyes down at the broken sidewalk as a shy smile sharpened the corners of his mouth. The smile struck sparks behind his eyes; he was radiant. "How ya doing?" I ventured.

He shrugged, though the smile was undimmed. "On my last cigarette," he said matter-of-factly. He took one last drag and tossed the butt into the street.

"That's a drag," I said.

"Ain't it though?"

I wanted to touch his brown arms, wiry with lean muscles. I wanted to taste his full red lips. *He's probably a hustler,* I thought in a bright flash of clarity: *a hustler looking for a drunk trick to rob.* But his eyes, those amazing eyes: I couldn't be right. Even if he were out to roll an unsuspecting john, he was welcome to the $20 in my wallet. I smoked; I wanted to offer him a cigarette to replace the one he just finished. How to ask him to come back to my apartment? How to initiate the seduction of this beautiful apparition? I wanted to speak, but I was afraid no sound would come out of me. "My name's Mark," I said slowly and stuck out my hand.

"Angel," he said as he took my hand. When we touched I felt electricity pulse through my body. I suddenly felt clear and alert—unencumbered by the effects of my excessive drinking. My cock stirred to life inside my pants. I wondered whether he felt the same too. He must have; this had to be a shared experience. How could I have felt like I did if we weren't really connected by this circuit?

He cast his eyes down again, the looked up at me through those dewy lashes. "You live nearby?" he asked. He had a slight accent I couldn't place.

"Uh-huh."

"Can we go there?" He reached out, touched my arm, and sent chills down my spine. He smiled at me.

"Um, sure." I smiled hesitantly at him and wondered whether I was about to do something very stupid. I'd never picked up someone on the street before. Then I laughed at myself. Like you can't pick up someone dangerous in a bar? But in truth the possibility of danger—the chance this pretty boy might be rougher than he seemed—made the scene even hotter, more intense, more erotic.

My grew fully erect and began to throb. "It's just up the street a little ways," I said weakly. I started walking.

He fell into step beside me, reached out, and took my hand. His skin was warm and soft. I felt that electric charge again, not quite as intensely but still palpable. The little hairs on the back of my neck stood up. My nipples hardened and chaffed again the fabric of my T-shirt.

I slipped my key into the door, opened it, and reached in to turn on the overhead light and the ceiling fan. I stood aside to let my Angel in. He smiled at me. "Beautiful place," he said.

"Thanks," I said. I felt fear again in the pit of my stomach. *Am I about to be robbed? Beaten? Murdered?* But he was smaller than I was. He turned those innocent eyes toward me again, and I banished my fearful thoughts once and for all.

He stepped toward me almost shyly, hesitantly, and bit his lower lip. I leaned down and gently pressed my lips against his. They were soft but firm, tender but strong. He tasted of stale smoke and spearmint. He brought his arms up and around my back and pulled me closer. I slid my arms around him and down his back. I put my hands on his ass. It was round and hard, solid. I longed to see it bare, freed from his clothes.

"You seem very sad," he whispered as he brushed his lips against my neck.

I shook my head. "No, not now."

"It's still there." He tilted his head back and held me in his steady gaze. "In your eyes."

Again, I shook my head. What was there to tell? My lover had left me a few months earlier, breaking my heart on his way out the door. I'd spent countless nights at the bars, hoping to meet someone and drinking myself into a stupor. The few times I thought I'd made a connection with someone, I'd awakened the next morning to cruel disappointment. The past was a nightmare I didn't care to revisit; I wanted to be awake in an unexpected luminous moment. I kissed his neck and flicked my tongue across his salty skin.

"*Madre de dios.*" He whispered. "That's so nice."

I slid my tongue to the spot where his neck met his shoulders. I kissed the hollow of his throat and squeezed his ass harder. He arched his back.

He pulled his head away and smiled at me. "Do you want to fuck me, *Papi?*"

"Very much," I replied and kissed his lips again. I smelled his cologne—Escape by Calvin Klein—and luxuriated in the velvety smoothness of his skin. He moaned a little as I continued to kiss his neck and squeeze his hard ass with both hands.

He reached up and pulled on my tender nipples. I slid my arms around him and lifted him up, and he wrapped his legs around my waist. Through his jeans I felt his erection: hard, insistent, and urgent. He bit one of my nipples through my T-shirt, just hard enough to send another jolt of arousal through my body.

We stood like that for an eternity, it seemed.He gently grazed my nipples with his teeth and lips, and my cock become harder and harder. He slid down off me at last and loosely gripped my cock through my jeans. I let out my breath explosively.

I reached down, undid his belt, and unfastened his baggy jeans, which fell easily to his ankles. He stepped back from me and sat down on the couch. He took off his clunky boots—his socks were white—stood up, and stepped out of his pants. His legs were muscular, covered with wiry black hair. He reached down and pulled his tank top up and over his head in one motion. There was a trail of black hair from his navel down to the waistband of his boxer briefs. A few straggly hairs curled around his dark nipples. There was another tattoo on his left chest: a halo. He smiled at me.

As I kicked off my shoes, he dropped to his knees in front of me and slowly unhitched my belt and slid my pants down my legs. I lifted one foot, then the other, as he pulled my pants off me. He leaned forward and put his mouth on my cock through my cotton underwear. I closed my eyes and tilted my head back.

"You like that?" he asked softly, barely audible over the sound of the air-conditioning pushing a cool breeze through the vents.

"Yes, Angel, I like that."

He slid his thumbs beneath the waistband of my underwear and jerked it down. My cock slapped against my lower belly. I felt my underwear slide slowly down my legs as he ran his tongue along the underside of my cock. He licked it, stopping just before his tongue reached the head of my cock, then started back down the shaft. He took my balls into his mouth and applied gentle pressure, just enough to make me moan but not enough to cause pain. My balls slid around inside his mouth, brushing up against his teeth, as his tongue nudged them from side to side.

He moved his mouth to my inner thighs. He softly kissed and bit the delicate skin from my crotch to just inside my knee. Then he worked his way back up the other leg. I moaned gratefully. Sex had never felt like this before. No one had ever taken the time.

His tongue slid back to the base of my cock and then toward the head, which he slipped into his mouth. He started to suck gently on the head, swirling his tongue around it, into the slit and then back to the outside. Goose bumps rose on my skin and I began to tremble a little bit. Then he took my entire cock into his mouth.

I began to grind my hips back and forth. I put my hands on his head. My cock slid slowly, gently, in and out of his mouth. He gagged once, and I felt his body react to the reflex: His stomach clenched and his shoulders lurched forward. I moved back, but he grabbed my ass and pulled me back toward him, down into his throat.

"You wanna fuck me, *Papi?*" he asked again, smiling up at me as he stroked my wet cock with one hand.

"Yes," I replied in a whisper. The word barely escaped my mouth.

He stood up and stepped out of his boxer briefs. His own cock was swollen and hard. I reached for it and kneeled to take it into my mouth. He moaned as I licked the head for a few moments and slid my tongue along his piss slit. Then I swallowed his shaft until I reached his shaved balls. I reached up and took a nipple in each hand, pinched them gently, and pulled on them.

A gasp escaped his lips, and his body went rigid. He stepped away from me, turned, and got down on the floor on all fours.

There was a pair of matching tattoos on his back, one each shoulder blade: mirror images of each other. They were wings, outlined in blue ink but tinged with red, green, and yellow. They were the most beautiful tattoos I'd ever seen—the work of a real master. I stared at them as he arched his back and lifted his breathtakingly hard ass into the air.

"Fuck me, please," he whispered. "Please."

I got down to my knees, pulled a condom from my pant pocket, and tore the package with my teeth. I slid the condom over my cock, spit into my hand, and ran the wetness over my shaft.

He gasped when he felt the pressure of my cock head against his asshole. His body went rigid for an instance, then he relaxed and my cock slowly started to slide into him. Even as he relaxed and opened up for the fuck, I saw the muscles in his back and shoulders tense with anticipation. I reached down kneaded his shoulders, digging my fingers gently into his flesh and moving them with slightly increasing pressure. He moaned and gasped again as I moved deeper inside of him. I stopped when he cried out; my cock was only about halfway in. I moved my hips backward and slowly slid out of him. His entire body was rigid. I stopped when only the head of my cock remained inside of him, and began to press forward again. To try to loosen him up a bit I began to move my hips in a circular motion. He moaned and balled his hands into fists. "You like that, Angel?" I whispered.

"Oh, yes, *Papi,* I like that," he said breathlessly.

Once again, I was a little more than halfway inside of him when I met resistance. I leaned down and kissed the back of his neck.

"Oooooooh…" he sighed.

I pulled back a little, then slid forward again, a little farther this time. I pulled back again, and finally, he opened up for me completely. My cock slid all the way in, and my balls lightly slapped against him. I grabbed his shoulders and pulled him back. He moaned gratefully. For several moments I sat still, fully inside him, holding him, until he began to move his ass back and forth. I released his shoulders, pulled back, and slid almost completely out. He began to gasp. I moved slowly and began to enjoy the feeling of his ass tightening around my cock and gripping it as I gently pumped in and out.

My eyes closed briefly, and then I opened them to see those angel wings shimmering on his back. They seemed alive as they moved with the rippling of the muscles of his back. They wanted to unfold and spread their brilliantly colored feathers, which glinted in the light from the chandelier overhead.

He began to press his ass back toward me as I slid into him, slowly at first, then faster, as he tried to drive me deeper inside him. I teased him with my cock: I pulled it out, leaving just the head inside, and waited for him to shove his hips backward to draw me back inside. Beads of sweat glistened on his wings.

Finally, I had enough of teasing his ass, and I started moving faster to match the rhythm he created. I drove deeper into him, trying to reach his core, the center of his very being. My cock grew harder, thicker, and longer as I fucked him. The feathers of his tattoo sparkled beneath the sheen of sweat on his back. I began to sweat too: it trickled from my hairline and gathered at my bangs, which grew damp, and the hair under my arms became slick. Beads of my sweat dripped onto his beautiful back.

This was how it was meant to be.

My balls ached for release, but I wasn't ready. I wanted to keep fucking him, to keep pounding away on his beautiful ass while his wings sprang to life and lifted us into the air, far above the twinkling lights of the French Quarter.

He grunted, gasped, and his body shuddered as he came.

My entire body arched and went rigid as the condom filled with my come. I convulsed as my cock emptied itself and my skin twitched and tingled.

Afterward, we stayed in our embrace for a few moments. My cock softened inside him as we returned to earth.

He slid away from my cock and turned to face me. His face and hair were damp with sweat. He smiled, and his heaven-deep gaze enveloped me.

I stood and took his hand, kissed it, and led him back to the bedroom, indifferent to the puddle of his come on the hardwood floor. We didn't speak as I gently pushed him onto the bed, lay down beside him, curled my arms around him, and pulled him to me. We kissed once, tenderly, without passion—a sweet kiss, like one shared by two teenagers who have just discovered their bodies are capable of experiencing ecstasy.

Holding him felt so right.

"I love you, *Papi*," he whispered as he brushed his lips against my throat.

"I love you, my Angel," I whispered back, pulling him closer.

I woke alone in my bed to daylight streaming through my window. I called for him, walked the length of my house, and hoped he would still be there. But he was gone. He'd even cleaned up the puddle he'd left on the living room floor. It was as though he'd never been there. I sat down on my couch, naked, and hugged myself. I felt more alone than I ever had in my life. Tears came to my eyes. "Damn you, Angel," I said aloud, though truthfully, at the moment our hands had first touched under gaslight, I'd known I'd never see him again. Nevertheless, it was too, too cruel.

There was a note on the coffee table. *Papi, I cannot stay here with you, much as I would like to. It is forbidden. But thank you for giving me such joy. You won't always be sad. Angel.*

"Forbidden?" I said aloud.

That's when I saw it—lying underneath the coffee table. I reached down, picked it up, held it up to the light, and smiled to myself. It was all I had left of him, my Angel, and I vowed to keep it forever: a long green feather flecked with hints of gold and red.

The Ice Cream Man Cometh

J. Hitman

On hot summer Saturdays I sometimes drive into downtown Boston, park my car, and head over to the Charles River Esplanade. I like to sit under a tree on the bank of the river—more often than not dressed casually in a T-shirt, shorts, and slides (no underwear)—and do some work at my leisure while watching the boats and the world drift by. I usually get a lot of writing done, and the guys Rollerblading, rowing, jogging, or just walking past makes for much better scenery than I could enjoy sitting at home.

I met Freddie on one such Saturday afternoon late last summer. I didn't know his name was Freddie when I drove past his battered old ice cream truck on my way into the city, or that he'd end up playing such a significant part in my life. All I was aware of at the time was that he was undeniably one of the most handsome guys I'd ever seen.

Because the truck had no driver's side door, his whole body was visible as he sat behind the wheel. But I had to lean over to get a look at his face."Whoa!" I gasped when his astonishing visage came into view. This ice cream man was a young stallion. He looked like he was a couple of years younger than I—19 or 20, but no older. His black hair was short and neat, and there was a trace of a scruffy goatee on his chin. Tan cargo pants, white socks and sneakers, and a white T-shirt covered his trim, perfect body. The pits of his shirt were slightly damp, and I could see the fullness of a nicely packed crotch at the center of his pants. His most dazzling feature was the infectious smile he flashed when he noticed me noticing him. It took my breath away.

I gave him a flirtatious grin and fanned myself. He replied with a thumbs-up, then turned on his truck's calliope music. We gestured back and forth a few times—a wink from him, a blown kiss from me—before we reached the exit for the waterfront. As I turned off, I waved goodbye to him, seemingly for the last time. Still dazed by the encounter, I parked my car, slung my backpack over my shoulder and set off for a day of peace and quiet work under a maple tree in a remote corner of the Esplanade.

A few hours later I was out of mineral water and had edited a good 20 pages of work. When the sound of an ice cream truck reached my ears, I figured it was time for a break. I packed up my stuff, dusted off my butt, and trudged to a bend in the road where a handful of adults and their kids flocked to buy something cold. I didn't recall my morning encounter until I saw that the ice cream truck had no driver's side door. Then I realized that the same handsome young man I'd flirted with on the highway was doling out cold drinks and ice cream to the crowd. Up close, he was even more handsome.

As the crowd thinned, the ice cream man looked around and recognized me.

"Amigo!" he exclaimed playfully as he flashed that beautiful smile.

"You talking to me?" I countered.

"If that was you riding my tail out there on the highway, then yeah. Come here," he said, waving me over. "I got something special for you."

I strutted over, folding my arms. "What could you possibly have in there for me?"

"Something cold," he said, handing me a frozen Rocket Pop. "On me."

"If it was *on* you, it would be melting," I said with a chuckle. Then, grinning as widely as he was, I accepted his gift.

The ice cream man ignored my comment. "It's just a little thank-you."

I licked the tip of the Rocket Pop seductively. "You're thanking me? For what?"

"For making me feel like a macho hombre." He pumped his arms, and his smooth, tanned biceps bulged out of his damp T-shirt. I licked my ice cream faster and marveled as a single drop of sweat trickled down his forehead onto his nose, then from his nose to the counter.

"Damn, dude," I sighed.

The ice cream man relaxed and leaned down to face me, locking his eyes on mine. "Do you usually come on to strangers like this?"

"Only if they're really cute," I answered simply. "And you, amigo, are the cutest."

The ice cream man glanced around to make sure we were still alone and then declared, "I'm not gay."

The impact of that statement was as painful as the ice cream headache that set in after I accidentally swallowed a mouthful of cold slush.

"What are you?" I managed to ask after I recovered from the temporary trauma.

"Curious, I guess," he said, extending a hand. "My name's Frederico, but my friends call me Freddie. You?"

"Jake," I replied, studying his long, strong fingers for a moment before taking his hand in mine. His grip was warm and firm.

"So, Jake," Freddie sighed in a lower voice, "you ever do it in an ice cream truck?"

I was so surprised by the question that I lost my grip and dropped the last of the melting Rocket Pop on the pavement.

"I thought you weren't gay?"

"I said I was curious," Freddie growled under his breath. His expression suddenly seemed very serious. "And you're really cute."

A wave of embarrassment rushed through me, heating me up and driving out the last of the iciness inside me. "Now I need to do something to thank you."

"Yup," Freddie replied, his infectious grin returning. "So why don't you come on up here in the truck?"

I started to argue about not being such an easy catch, to tell him that I truly, honestly was looking for something a little deeper than a onetime fuck with a curious straight dude—despite the fact that I'd been so flirtatious with him out on the highway. But before I could utter a single word, Freddie tipped his head toward the missing front door.

"Don't worry," he said. "The back closes up. We'll be alone in here, just you and me."

It hit me that he was serious. I looked around, shocked. As remote as our shady spot on the Esplanade was, it was still broad daylight in the heart of a busy city.

"Are you nuts?"

Freddie reached down and grabbed the full, obvious bulge in his cargo pants. "Maybe a little," he laughed. "Aren't you up for a little adventurous sexperimentation?"

I hesitated a moment longer, then tossed my backpack through the open window. "Maybe," I said, my insides twisting into knots in anticipation of having sex with such a gorgeous guy. "Yeah, just maybe."

I stepped through the driver's side door and, from there, into the refrigerated rear of the truck where Freddie waited. It was a tight fit, but the air—a mix of cold from the freezers and warmth from Freddie's body—proved to be intoxicating. Freddie quickly closed the vendor's window and pulled a curtain across the rear of the truck, effectively cutting us off from the eyes of the outside world.

"So now what?" he asked. "I'm new at this, remember?"

"How about we start with the basics?" I said playfully.

"Like kissing?" he asked with a slightly nervous quiver in his voice.

I took one of his hands in mine. He squeezed it before bringing it to his lips. "Yeah," I said, reaching for his shoulders and pulling him closer to me. "Kissing…"

Freddie wrapped his arms around me and backed me against the nearest freezer, roughly crushing his lips against mine. His movements were frantic and awkward at first, but the longer we kissed, the softer and gentler he became.

"That's it, Freddie," I sighed between kisses, running my hand through his hair. His arms, at first clasped around me in a death grip, slowly relaxed. He slid one hand under my shirt to explore my chest. The other slipped down the back of my shorts to squeeze my hard runner's butt.

I opened my lips wider to accept Freddie's tongue into my mouth. We pressed our bodies together, and I realized we were both rock-hard. As the handsome boy ground his cock against mine, I swept my hand across his chest and the taunt expanse of his six-pack abs. Freddie yanked off his T-shirt, and his warm, sweet scent filled my nostrils.

Taking my hand in his, Freddie guided it down the front of his cargo pants into the tangle of crisp, black curls beneath the waistband—and then to the prize just a little farther.

"Yes-s-s," he huffed. His Adam's apple slid up and down in his throat as he swallowed. I cupped the straining bulge in his pants and gave his goods a firm squeeze. Looking down, I saw a small circle of precome spreading across the tent between Freddie's legs. "Do it, amigo," he begged in a deep, breathless growl. "Go down on my *verga*!"

I sank to my knees as I unzipped Freddie's pants. Like me, he was free-balling since it was a hot summer day. I had an unobstructed view of his manhood.

"Fuck," I sighed.

As I'd expected, Freddie's respectable tool was uncut, capped by a crimped hood of foreskin. Two meaty nuts dangled below it in a loose sac covered with curly black hair. I gripped Freddie's cock and pushed back its hood, forcing the moist pink head from the folds of musky skin. Leaning in, I took a tentative lick. A bittersweet taste tingled on my tongue.

"Yeah," Freddie groaned. "Suck it!"

I glanced up at his face—he looked almost deliriously happy. Reaching around, I gripped one of his hard butt cheeks in each hand, then pulled him forward and drew his cock between my lips. The salty tang of his foreskin and precome exploded in my mouth. I swallowed him until my nose was buried deep in his pubic patch and his low-hanging nuts were bouncing against my chin.

As I knelt at Freddie's feet, slurping his uncut prong, I worked my shorts partway down my thighs and began grinding my boner against his leg. After a while he pulled his tool out of my mouth and replaced it with his balls.

"Lick my nuts, amigo," he commanded.

I lapped at his sweaty bag while he rubbed his drooling cock against my cheek. As I got ready to gobble his rod some more, Freddie reached a hand between my legs and pulled me up to my feet by my dick.

I wasn't sure whether he planned to suck on my pole or just jack me off. He yanked down my shorts and stood there in front of me, admiring what he saw: another man's cock and nuts. Giving in to his curiosity, Freddie toyed with my bag and rubbed our cocks together, teasing both our knobs with his spit-soaked foreskin. Instead of taking me in his mouth, he made it clear that he had something completely different in mind.

"Turn around and bend over," he growled. "I want to fuck that hole!"

I was more than willing to give up my ass, but only if we played safely. I pulled a condom out of my backpack and rolled it over Freddie's cock. I applied a bit of lube from a small tube I had with me, then turned around to await his assault on my ass. To my surprise, he lowered his head and stuck his tongue in my crack to get a taste of my funk. Bent over the ice cream freezer, I ground myself against his face. The tickle of his goatee on my most sensitive flesh drove me right to the edge of shooting my load.

"Fuck," I heard him say as he exhaled. His warm breath teased my pucker.

I reached around and stroked his sweaty mop of hair. "What is it, man?"

"I never thought a guy's ass would taste so sweet," he groaned. He plunged his face back into my crack and tunneled his tongue deep into my hole one more time. Then he stood up and prepared to mount me. Breathing heavily, Freddie lined up his sheathed cock with my freshly tongued hole. A swell of anticipation rushed through me when I felt the tip of his dick poking at the outer ring of my pucker.

"Yeah," I moaned.

Freddie leaned forward as he pushed into me, pressing me down on the freezer until he was flush on top of me and his mouth was right at my ear. The pressure of his firm, strong body against mine, the smell of his breath, and the sensation of the cool metal of the freezer beneath me made every square inch of my flesh tingle. In my excitement I flexed my sphincter around the cock nudging its way into me. Freddie inhaled sharply and pushed in farther. When he was all the way in, his nut sac banged against mine.

"Oh, man," I sighed. "Do it, Freddie. Fuck me!"

Freddie shuddered and eased out of me just enough to tease my prostate with the head of his cock before shoving it all the way in again.

"I can't believe how fuckin' tight you are," he huffed between gasps. "Your stuff is way tighter than any chick's!"

Freddie fucked me passionate abandon. Locked together with my chest pressed against the cold metal and his hot body grinding against me, we grunted and sweated until the action sent us both over the edge.

Freddie shot into the rubber up my ass, and I blew one of the biggest wads of my life right there on the floor. He was still stiff inside me when the sound of a fist banging against the outside of the ice cream truck brought us out of our reverie.

As Freddie pulled himself together and went to take care of

his customer, I quietly savored what we'd just shared. I knew it was a one-in-a-million chance, but I was hoping we'd made more than just a physical connection. As it turned out, we had.

Almost a year has passed since Freddie and I met. He is no longer just curious. In fact, he's become something of an expert when it comes to making love to another man. On Saturdays in summertime, I still head down to the Esplanade to write. But now I usually ride shotgun in the ice cream truck, right next to the greatest guy alive, my Freddie.

Touché

Lars-Peter Ingemann

Damn! Damn, damn, damn! I thought as I narrowly dodged the long blade coming at me. *Too close, I need to—shit!*

I had been successfully blocking my opponent's blows with my own weapon. But thinking too much and reacting too slowly, I misjudged his change of rhythm. He feinted to one side, then swung his sword around mine and drove the tip sharply into my chest.

Overhead, a light came on and a buzzer sounded, triggered by my *lamé,* an electrically wired vest worn to determine hits in fencing. I swore quietly under the heavy mesh of my protective mask. I was frustrated more than hurt. Roger had nailed me right in the sternum, but the padded practice jackets under our *lamés* softened even the hardest jabs.

"Left touch and bout," declared Gavin, the fencer directing our session. "Alec, are you OK? I thought I heard you yelp when Roger scored the touch."

I lifted my mask. "Yeah. I'm just annoyed I didn't see that one coming."

Gavin chuckled. "That'll come with time. You're doing fine." He glanced over at the clock. It was 9 P.M. and the training area was beginning to empty out. "I guess we can call it a night."

As Roger joined the stream of students heading to the locker room, I turned to Gavin and said in a low voice, "Are we still on for that late dinner?" I'd asked him out earlier in the week, but he hadn't given me a definite yes. To my relief, he nodded.

"Sure. I just need to clean up and lock up." I'd already gathered as much. Maggie, the head coach and owner of the *salle*—the fencing club—was away for a weekend tournament. All of the assistant coaches had gone as well, leaving Gavin, the most senior club member, to manage the *salle* this Friday evening. "You don't mind, do you?" he asked.

"Not at all. Do you want help?"

"That'd be great, actually." He smiled demurely, and I felt myself swoon just a bit. Gavin was a formidable swordsman, but he seemed very reticent away from the *salle*. That didn't matter to me. I'd had a tremendous crush on him from the get-go, and his shyness only made him more endearing.

At 26, Gavin was three years younger than I was. He had honey-blond hair cut in a short preppy style, pale green eyes that captivated you if he didn't look away too quickly, and the lean body of a lifelong fencer. I, on the other hand, had only taken up the sport in the last month by way of adding variety to my mundane weight-training regimen. If my three-inch height advantage didn't exactly enable me to tower over Gavin, we were still a study in contrasts: He was a slender, fair-haired pretty boy, and I was a brawny, raven-haired rugby jock.

Normally, I trained with Maggie, but that hadn't stopped me from chatting up Gavin at every opportunity. I did most of the flirting, but he sent enough signals to tell me he was interested. That's where the fencing uniform was something of a mixed blessing. Both the practice jacket and the *lamé* cover the wearer's pelvis, which prevented me from sneaking peeks at Gavin's crotch. But at the same time, they helped conceal the telltale hard-ons I always sprouted when I was near him.

As I helped Gavin organize the storage closet, he made small talk about dueling with the advanced students that evening. The image of him skillfully parrying and thrusting with his foil was fueling my filthy imagination, so it was disappointing when he switched gears to discuss my performance.

"You know, I hope you're not discouraged that Roger beat you in both bouts I directed," he said amiably. "He started weeks ahead of you, but you're catching up to him really quickly. I never would've guessed you two started so far apart if I hadn't seen your first lesson with Maggie."

I grinned naughtily at him. "So you were watching, huh?"

Gavin blushed. "Hmm…a little," he confessed, and I left it at that. We stowed the last of the loaner equipment and shut the closet just as the few remaining students came out of the locker room. He bade them good night and locked the front door behind them, then followed me into the changing area.

Fencing in full gear, I had discovered, was like doing aerobics while wrapped in a heavy quilt, so I eagerly peeled off my *lamé* jacket and sweat-soaked T-shirt while Gavin opened his locker. "So, where do you want to eat?" I asked, kicking off my sneakers. I hadn't yet bought proper fencing shoes, but regular athletic ones were fine for a beginner.

Gavin took a long swig from a bottle of water, then undid his *lamé*. "Well, there's that new Italian place up the street that I've been wanting to try."

"Sounds good." Perfect, in fact—I'd already eaten there, and not only was the food excellent, the restaurant was cozy and very romantic. *Hmm, is that why he picked it?* I asked myself. *I wonder…*

That train of thought distracted me from the hefty erection that began to stir under my uniform when we entered the locker room. As I absentmindedly stripped off my boxers with my knickers, my seven-inch boner popped out and up, like the blade of a fencer saluting his opponent. I snapped out of my reverie when I saw Gavin's startled expression.

"What…? Oh, shit! Oops!" I quickly grabbed a towel from my gym bag and wrapped it around my waist as best I could. "Uh…sorry," I stammered.

Gavin exhaled. "Um, it's OK. We, er, all have moments like that."

He seemed more amused than embarrassed, but I was mortified that I hadn't had the sense to turn the other way first. I broke the awkward silence. "Gavin…"

"It's OK," he interrupted. "Really."

"Gavin, I really like you...obviously."

That made him laugh. "I'm flattered, Alec. I like you too." Fidgeting, he glanced away nervously before looking me in the eye and adding, "I mean, a *lot*."

That was all the invitation I needed. I moved closer, drawing him to me, and kissed him very lightly. My heart leaped when he responded warmly, putting his hands on my face and returning the gesture. He traced my lips slowly with his and welcomed my tongue with what felt like the softest, most sensual mouth I'd ever encountered. Gavin's kiss would have engorged my dick if it hadn't been rigid to begin with.

I removed his uniform, unzipping his jacket and using my teeth to slip off his damp headband. My hands caressed his taut, lithe torso, which was smooth except for thin lines of hair between his pecs and below his navel. I drank in his taste and scent. The sour tang of his dried sweat made me ache with lust.

I slid my hands over his hips and into his knickers, pushing them down with his briefs. Right then he tensed. *Uh-oh,* I thought, *I can't possibly be moving too fast at this point!*

I looked down. His cock was jutting straight out at me. Fully hard, it was decidedly on the petite side of five inches. As I studied it, Gavin said, "Before you ask: Yes, that's as big as mine gets."

"I wasn't going to ask."

"Some guys do."

"I'm not one of them." *Is this why he's so shy?* I mused. *Ah, psychoanalyze later.*

Gavin looked as though he were waiting for me to lower the boom on him. Instead, I dropped my towel, revealing my unflagging hard-on once again. Putting one arm around his waist and using my other hand to reach for his, I pecked him on the cheek and smiled. "Anyway..." I began.

He relaxed slightly. "So it's not a problem?"

"What?"

"Um, my size."

I sighed, then squeezed his hand fondly. "You've been watching too many porn movies, Gav. Does it *feel* like it matters to me?"

I took hold of his wrist and guided his hand to my erection. The head was drenched in precome, which I cheerfully smeared all over his open palm.

Gavin was visibly stunned by my boldness. "Alec…"

I couldn't verbalize a response. Having his hand on my cock pushed me over the brink, and raw horniness was starting to eat my stomach from the inside out. I sat down on the nearest bench and pulled Gavin to me with a gentle tug on his dick. I leaned over and gave the circumcised tip a tender, lingering kiss just like the one I'd placed on his lips. Then I opened wide and sucked him down to his pubes in one easy glide.

Gavin quivered in delight as my tongue lolled over his glans. As I sucked faster, he started humping my face. His hesitancy evaporated in the heat of my mouth, and he was already in the throes of a man who'd been pent-up for too long. *Atta boy,* I thought. *You know you want it as much as I do.*

I squeezed his peach-fuzzed ass with both hands. All those fencing lunges had paid off handsomely: His delectable little bubble butt was solid muscle. Working my finger into his crack to tease his sphincter actually required some effort.

That little tickle was all it took to finish Gavin off. He abruptly withdrew from my mouth, twisting his body so his come volleyed over my shoulder rather than erupt in my face. It was an impressive wad, each spurt slapping wetly on the locker doors behind me. *Nice to know I've got him as worked up as he has me! And speaking of my needs…*

I reached for my gym bag and fished around in it until I located a condom and lube packet. Needing no prompting from me, Gavin kicked off his shoes and knickers while I moved to the floor, my back against the wall. As soon as I'd applied the condom and lube to my throbbing saber, Gavin was standing completely naked before me. Without a word, he grabbed my shoulders, squatted over my hips, and casually lowered himself onto me. He grunted as his pucker swallowed my dick whole, but I was surprised he took me so easily—he felt so tight, I would have expected more of a struggle.

"You've got the most amazing ass," I said, tipping my head back blissfully.

"Yeah?" Gavin replied. He smiled sweetly at me. Then he clenched.

I whimpered involuntarily, and he took that as his cue to begin bouncing on my cock. An ecstatic spasm ran the length of my body, and everything but my dick immediately went limp. I felt pinned and helpless under Gavin, twitching uncontrollably in the uncanny grip of his ass. He was doing all the work, but that was fine by me. Having my fantasy literally land in my lap like this meant it was taking all of my willpower not to lose my load then and there.

I managed to last for a few minutes. Then Gavin sped up his writhing and my cock surrendered, exploding so forcefully that I thought the condom surely would burst. But it didn't, and Gavin somehow rode my orgasm so perfectly that he even gasped when I did. After he'd milked me dry, he slumped into my embrace, my scimitar still snug in his sheath.

We might have dozed off contentedly, had we been in a more comfortable position. Instead, we disentangled, staggered to our feet, and headed for one of the shower stalls to wash off the fresh sweat we'd worked up.

As the steam cleared our heads, Gavin's coyness resurfaced, causing him to edge away from me a bit. So I proceeded to give him a brisk rubdown under the warm spray of the shower, cuddling him and nipping at his neck and shoulders. All the attentive fussing soon dissolved his resistance, melting his knotted muscles and turning his short, uneasy breaths into yielding murmurs.

I turned off the water and went down on my knees in front of him. Hugging his magnificent fencer's thighs, I hungrily licked and sucked his cock until it was hard again, savoring the way his nub of flesh swelled to its full size in my gullet. "Gavin," I cooed, "wanna fuck me?"

That caught him off-guard. "Really?"

"Of course. I'm a versatile boy. Did you think I'm strictly a top or something?"

"Well…yeah, actually."

"Why? Are you strictly a bottom?"

"Um…kind of, yeah. Because I'm not, you know…" His voice trailed off.

I ran my tongue over his scrotum and along the underside of his hard-on, ending with a twirl around the tip. He shuddered in anticipation. "More?" I asked.

"Yes!"

"You'll have to fuck me, then." I cupped his dick in both hands and kissed the head. My fingers stroked his thick dark-golden pubes, and my thumbs massaged his shaft, bringing forth a bead of precome from the slit. I dabbed at the crystalline droplet with one finger and spread it down the length of his erection. "Sounds good, doesn't it?"

Gavin's breathing quickened. "Y-e-e-es…"

"Good. I've got more condoms and lube in the inner pocket of my bag," I told him. "Off you go," I added, giving his ass a friendly smack.

Gavin left the shower room, returning momentarily with the supplies in hand. We sat on the floor, and I kissed and fondled him while I assisted in his preparations. Now that the frantic getting-acquainted sex was out of the way, I figured we could afford the time to enjoy each other more thoroughly.

I lay on my back and brought my knees to my chest, my ass primed for the taking. Gavin placed his hands on the back of my thighs and slid his cock into me with a soft little moan. A tingle bristled up my spine, as if he had suddenly completed a secret circuit of pleasure in my brain.

Gavin pumped his hips with a slow, even rhythm. Gazing up at him, I was transfixed by his celadon-green eyes looking back at me. In them I saw the same winsomeness as ever, but there was something new as well: Affection? Trust? More? We had clicked almost from the time we'd met, even had our own little "moments" while chatting and flirting. But this was different: Warmer. Deeper.

Apparently, Gavin read the same thing in my eyes, because right then he leaned in and kissed me harder and more passionately than before. When he came up for air, it was only to pound me faster, going from steady pile-driving to merciless jackhammering. I roared in tandem with him but didn't complain. The boy had made a new discovery and was understandably making up for lost time.

Gavin finished with a loud cry, his orgasm clearly as intense as mine had been. Panting, he pulled out and tugged off the jism-filled condom. I sat up and caught him before he collapsed, and he nuzzled against my shoulder gratefully. At that instant everything I wanted to say to him slipped from my mind, so I simply cradled him while he got his wind back. His long eyelashes fluttered against my lips, and my fingers curled around his as if by reflex.

After several quiet minutes, I finally spoke up. "You know, this wasn't exactly what I had planned—I thought I'd at least take you to a nice candlelit dinner before trying to seduce you."

Gavin smirked at me. "You can still take me out, Alec. I'm starved."

"Only if you let me follow through and seduce you again afterward." Suddenly, I remembered that he had yet to suck me off, and the very idea of my cock stuffed into his velvety mouth made it stiffen once more. A better sword-swallower I'd never find.

His smirk became a wicked grin. "Maybe I'll seduce *you* this time."

Laughing, I playfully pushed him onto his back on the tiled floor. Lowering myself into his arms, I pressed my nose to his and whispered, *"Touché."*

Pretty Little Pup

Thom Wolf

"The first thing I ever put inside my ass," Frank said in a relaxed and dreamy voice, "was my finger."

"How old were you?" I asked, kissing the smooth skin of his inner thigh.

"Fifteen. I stole some lip balm from my mom's vanity case and used it as lube. It had a really sweet smell. Cherry. I used my allowance the next week to buy a proper bottle of lube."

I trailed my tongue along the underside of his hairless balls. He squirmed, spreading his legs wider. "What else did you put up there?"

"Carrots. Zucchini. Then I started using eggplant," he giggled. "I haven't looked back since."

I probed his nuts with the tip of my tongue. They spread in their sac, drooping on either side. Frank sighed, arching his back slightly. He rolled his head on the pillow, turning to Victor. They kissed, their mouths making wet appreciative noises. Out of the corner of my eye I saw Victor's fingers tweaking the young guy's nipple ring.

"Eggplant can get pretty big," I said, moving my lips around the base of his modest cock.

"Yeah. I spend ages at the grocery store, picking out the biggest."

I reached for the head of his pink cock. Frank's dick was around six inches thick. It was in perfect proportion with his compact body, but the real treasure of the piece was his foreskin. He had a nice juicy fold that hung over the tip by a half an inch or so. I sucked it softly between my lips, draining his sticky precome.

"What else do you like to do?" Victor asked, kissing his neck.

"You guys already know what I like. I love any kind of attention to my butt."

We lifted him up and turned him onto his stomach. He ground his dick into the mattress. I moved my mouth over his buttocks, kissing and nibbling the cheeks. Frank's ass was beautiful, smooth and creamy, with just the slightest powdering of soft brown hair. I parted his highly arched buns and slipped my tongue down the seam. He let out a little moan into the pillows. I found his tiny hole, flicked it gently, wetting it. I could taste soap and a gentle hint of sweat.

Victor paid attention to the young guy's top half, kissing his tanned shoulders, his neck, and his small ears. "What fantasies get you hot?" he asked.

His asshole flowered around my tongue—access was easy. I moved my lips around his rim, pressing, probing, and kissing. He moved his hips in little circles, pushing back. Controlling his ass was easy; I knew all the tricks to get him hot. I lubed my hands and gently finger-fucked him, one digit at a time. He responded, lifting his ass back onto my hand, rotating, thrusting. I eased in deeper, following the soft incline of his rectum, massaging the miracle zone inside.

"Oh, that's nice," he gasped. "Sometimes, when I'm fucking myself, I imagine I'm lying on a table and this huge guy is fucking me. His dick is massive. It hurts a little, but if I really concentrate I can take it. I push my ass against him so I can take it all. A whole bunch of other guys are lining up behind him, waiting to take their turn with me when the first guy is finished."

"You dream of a gang bang," Victor murmured, his face pressed into the crook of Frank's neck.

"Yeah. That would make me really horny: all those cocks lining up to fuck me. All those men wanting to come inside me. That's my favorite fantasy."

Suited up and lubed, I lay across his back and positioned my cock against his asshole. I wrapped one arm around his hard body and used my other hand to ease my cock into him. His sphincter popped. I waited, giving him a moment to relax, before pressing in to the hilt. The best thing about fucking Frank is the tightness of his ass. Velvety muscles held me in their grasp. He turned his face toward me, mouth open, and I kissed his soft lips. Victor moved in closer and we shared a three-way kiss, tongues darting between lips. I licked a film of sweat from Frank's plump upper lip.

He hitched his ass back against my cock. He was relaxed and ready for it. I moved back and forth, giving him a long, slow stroke. The entire length of my cock tingled with the most extreme sensations. I rocked my hips gently against his, sometimes sliding my cock all the way out. I loved this guy's spry, nubile ass. I wrapped both arms around him, caressing his taut but slightly underdeveloped chest, and kissed his neck and shoulders.

Although by his own admission Frank had been stuffing things up his ass since he was 15, I suspected he had been a late developer. Even now in his early 20s his body was firm but unmuscled. I predicted that Frank was one of those guys who wouldn't grow into his body until he was nearer 30. And when he did he was destined to be the hottest guy in town. He was well on his way already.

We fucked his ass all afternoon: lifting him, spreading him wider, and moving him around. He took our dicks with glorious enthusiasm. Victor lowered him to the floor and banged him doggy-style until he came. I sat on the edge of the bed with Frank bouncing on my cock, his strong legs wrapped around my waist. My lips were sensitive and raw from so much passionate kissing. I looked into his large green eyes and groaned, reaching the pinnacle. He bore his ass down on my cock and I shot, filling the rubber with ropy wads of white-hot spunk.

I grabbed his cock and jerked him off, supporting his ass with my other hand. He threw back his head, his face twisted, his hips bouncing on my still-hard dick. His come struck the underside of my face. His expression crumbled in relief. He spurted again and again, hitting the incline between my pecs, splashing his own flat belly.

When he was done, I lifted him onto the bed and we lay down

on either side of him. Victor and I were the couple, both in our late 20s; Frank was our regular fuck-pup. He had been coming round to our apartment on Sunday afternoons ever since he'd made the first move on me at a book signing six months earlier. He was a voracious bottom. Not interested in fucking either of us one at a time, he wanted our dicks in him all the time.

"So you have a gang-bang fantasy?" I asked, stroking his legs.

"Yeah. I think about that kind of thing all the time when I'm jacking off. Have you ever done that?"

"Jerked off? Every day since I was 11."

"No," he laughed. "Have you ever had a gang bang?"

"No," I said, giving his butt a playful slap. "We've been to plenty of orgies, sex parties. But those are different from being on the receiving end in a gang bang."

"How?"

"No one's going to hurt you at a party. All the guys will fuck your brains out if that's what you want. But they'll also stop when you tell them to. Reality isn't always as exciting as your fantasies and you don't want that kind of thing to get out of hand."

"Mmmm...I think I'd like to try it all the same. I used to dream about threesomes, and my experiences so far haven't disappointed me."

He related more of his fantasy to us. "I'd like to get fucked by a whole bunch of guys—big guys, strong and meaty. The bigger and fatter their cocks, the better."

"Size queen," Victor laughed.

"I'm not a size queen. This is my ideal fantasy. I don't take a tape measure to the real men I fuck. There's something different about a really big cock, though. My insides seem to shift when I'm full of dick. Image what a challenge it would be to take on four or five big guys. Just knowing that they weren't gonna stop pounding my ass until they'd emptied their nuts."

Paul and John were another two of our regular fuck buddies. They were in their mid 30s and had been together for 10 years or more. They were fit and good-looking. Paul was a fitness instructor with a beefy body and dark hair. John, a police officer, was muscular and blond.

Victor and I got together with the guys on a regular basis. I had quite a fondness for Paul—he was a tough, versatile lover who could take it as hard as he gave it. I called him one night later that week and explained Frank's desire to live out his fantasy in a safe, trusting environment.

"Do you want to help him out?" I asked.

"How could I refuse? Are you sure the little guy is up to it?"

"He insists he is. He's been shoving things up his ass since he was 15, so he's had some practice. If not, then we'll take some of the pressure off him."

The following Sunday, Victor and I drove Frank to Paul and John's fashionable apartment. I had done my best to reassure Frank that we'd look after him, but I still expected the little guy to have second thoughts about the party. I was wrong. He was less anxious about taking part in an orgy than I was. He sat in the backseat, chatting excitedly for the entirety of the 20-minute drive.

When we arrived, Paul and John were waiting in the living room with a man called Adrian. I hadn't met Adrian before, but my first impression of him looked more than good. He was English, probably in his mid 30s, with a very handsome, angular face. His short black hair was flecked with traces of gray. He was one sexy bastard.

We shook hands as Paul introduced us.

A porn movie played on the wide-screen television—a Kristen Bjorn orgy scene involving a large group of men—come shots galore. John gave us each a glass of red wine, and we sat around for a while talking, watching the movie and becoming increasingly aroused.

"Frank," I said. "I've been telling the guys what a good cocksucker you are. Why don't you show then all what I've been talking about?"

He grinned, his green eyes twinkling. His tongue flickered

across his plump lips. John was the first to his feet. He unfastened his jeans and pulled out his meat. Frank got down on his knees and polished off the fat head with his tongue. Paul and Adrian were quick to rise and stand on either side of John, cocks in hand. Frank divided his attention three ways—using both his hands and his mouth, he made sure that none of their dicks missed out.

Victor and I undressed. I took off everything except my white vest, which I knew to be part of Frank's fantasy. Instead of removing it, I hiked the garment over my chest and hooked it behind my head to form a frame for my pecs.

Frank was really into what he was doing, slobbering over three mature cocks. His lips bulged, and he breathed loudly through his nostrils. His hands were full too, jerking and stroking. Adrian had a foreskin and, being a guy of similar endowment, Frank knew exactly how to play with it. I could see from the blissful expression on their faces that my friends were impressed with Frank's technique.

"Damn, that's good," Paul exclaimed.

Frank grinned, his tongue fluttering round the head of Paul's cock, probing the slit.

Victor stood behind me, his arms around my waist, his cock nudging my ass. "This is hot! Look at the little guy go."

"Yeah," I said tugging my nuts. "Let's get some ass."

Five of us undressed Frank. We stripped him of everything but his white jockstrap, another element in his fantasy. He had stained the front of the cup with precome. The view of his creamy ass in a jock was breathtaking.

We picked him up and carried him like a doll into the dining room, where we lay him on the dining table. Previous experience had taught us that Paul's table was exactly the right height to fuck on. Victor grabbed Frank's legs and spun him around until his ass hung just over the edge of the table.

I worked on his ass while the other guys suited up.

"Are you ready for this?" I asked, kissing his tight pucker. The rim fluttered against my lips, as though trying to return the kiss.

"Yes," he said, eyes bright.

I squeezed a massive blob of lube onto my fingers and started applying it to his hole. He was going to need all the lubrication he could get. His asshole chewed on my fingers when I pushed them inside him. He opened his legs wider. I kissed his inner thigh.

"Tell the guys you want it."

"I want it."

"Beg them, pup. Beg them to fuck you."

"Please. Please fuck me. I want you. I want you all."

"How bad do you want it?" Victor teased, fisting lube over his cock.

"I want it so bad. Please, guys—come on and fuck me. I want you in my ass so bad. Gimme some cock. I fucking need your dicks inside me."

Adrian was the first to enter him. He edged up to the table and lifted Frank's ankles onto his shoulders. The rest of us gathered round to watch.

"Oh man," Frank exclaimed as the big piece of English meat broke his sphincter.

I watched Adrian's dick slide into Frank's ass and saw the smile it generated. Frank lifted his head from the table to watch. I opened a bottle of poppers and held it beneath each of his nostrils; he inhaled slowly. As the amyl took effect, his face became flushed and he hitched his ass higher.

Adrian grabbed Frank's hips in both hands and started pumping his butt, quickly building a long and fast rhythm. He alternated his strokes, teasing Frank's first ass with short jabs, then filling it with long strokes. Adrian soon passed the point where he could control his rhythm. He bucked Frank's ass with a purpose, not holding back. Frank looked into Adrian's face as he fucked him, taking his cock with determination.

We stood around the table, watching. The room was thick with raw heat and the sound of sex—skin slapping against skin, hands sliding over cocks.

Adrian shot his load in Frank's hole and withdrew. John was

the next to fuck him. His big dick had no problem entering the fuck-loosened orifice. Adrian ripped off his condom and stood back to watch. John put his hands on Frank's thighs, spreading them wider, then fucking him harder. It was incredible to watch. John's a very knowing top: He senses just what to do with his cock to drive his bottoms wild. Frank's eyes were glazing over in ecstasy.

"Oh, yeah," John roared enthusiastically, emptying his balls.

I moved into position next, sliding deep into his hot ass. I tugged Frank's jock aside, releasing his cock. I stroked his meat while I fucked him. He looked directly into my eyes and smiled. I fucked him, satisfied that this reality was living up to his fantasy.

Paul was behind me, his big dick impatient for some action. I felt the pressure of his hand on my back, pushing me forward. "Bend over, Thom. I want some of your ass."

I leaned across Frank, resting my elbows on either side of his shoulders. I moved closer to him. His breath was hot and fast on my face. I licked the sweat from his mouth, following the lean line of his jaw. Paul's fingers were in my ass, preparing the way. Then I felt his cock slide between my cheeks. Victor offered the open bottle of poppers. Frank and I took a hit. The rush was instant. My desire to be fucked intensified. Paul shoved his cock into me, spreading my ass while I speared young Frank's.

"Oh, yeah," I moaned. "That's fucking awesome."

I buried my cock as deeply in Frank's ass as I could. Paul matched the stroke, filling me entirely. His thick black bush tickled the cheeks of my ass. He took control of the rhythm, pulling back and forth. I went with the flow, allowing his cock to propel my own. Frank raised his head from the table, his mouth open, wanting to kiss me. Paul's lips moved over the back of my neck as he pounded my ass.

My cock started tingling, and my ass tightened. "Oh, God, I'm coming."

I erupted inside him. I buried my face against his shoulder. My dick squirted stream after stream of spunk into his ass. My cock head throbbed with the intensity of the sensation. My orgasm acted as a catalyst, and I saw Frank's eyes glaze over and felt the wet heat of his spunk spurting across our stomachs. The spasms of my ass muscles during orgasm were enough for Paul. I felt his cock jerk, and he pumped his load into my gratified ass.

The party lasted until late that night. The six of us lay around, kissing and stroking. We opened more bottles of wine and watched a couple of new porn DVDs Adrian had brought over from Europe. Frank took each of our dicks again: in his ass and in his mouth. The young pup's appetite for cock was insatiable.

When we took him home that night ,he kissed us both on the lips. "Thanks, guys," he said. "That was incredible. Next time I jerk off, I can reminisce about today rather than just fantasize."

"You could always come up with another scene," I suggested.

"I think I'd like to explore this one some more first," he said with a cheeky grin. "Good night, guys. See you next week."

Money

Dale Chase

"It's not about money," Johnny says. But, of course, it is. How could it not be? We both know we're driving into a neighborhood well beyond our means.

Johnny had met Cyril at a party, during which Cyril invited Johnny to a small gathering at his home. "Intimate," Cyril said. "Bring a friend if you like."

"I just want to see his place," Johnny says as we turn onto Mulholland.

"Yeah, right," I reply.

"I mean it."

I don't press. Johnny is my best friend, a cute little number who wants to find a daddy to take care of him.

"What's he look like?" I ask.

"Cyril? Tall, slim, elegant, English-looking. You know, like old movies. Silver hair."

I know what happened at that first party because I know Johnny. I wasn't there, but I can easily imagine the scene: Johnny trolling not for action but for promise. If Cyril is attractive, so much the better for all concerned. But Johnny will never convince me it's about anything but security. "Money buys freedom," he has said more times than I have fingers and toes to count.

I go along now out of curiosity. And because I'm on the lookout too—not for a daddy, just some good sex. I have no illusions about permanence; it's not on my agenda, which tends to give me the upper hand, in a way. We're both eager in our respective quests. But Johnny has a sad air of quiet desperation.

Cyril's house is a hilltop aerie with an incredible view. The spread is all chrome and glass: sleek, like the young men lolling around the pool. I recall Cyril's calling the gathering intimate. Obviously he didn't mean we'd have his undivided attention; there's quite a crowd, both inside and out.

It's a late-October night; the air is hot and dry from the Santa Ana breeze that has been blowing all day. Guys glide through the pool or lounge at its edge. Most are naked. Cyril is clad in a white Speedo to highlight his deep tan and holds court near the shallow end. He immediately sweeps Johnny into his arms, and they exchange little whispers.

When the two of them end their clutch, Johnny introduces me. Cyril takes my hand in his and squeezes as he offers a welcome. "It's so hot. Why don't you get out of those clothes and make yourself comfortable?" he suggests. He keeps his eyes on me as he says this, and I see what Johnny means. The man is not merely attractive; he exudes sensuality on a grand scale. His profligate gaze promises much more than money.

Johnny and I undress in a spare bedroom littered with clothes. A basket of swim suits sits nearby, but we choose to remain naked. We stand side by side before a mirrored wall, making sure we look our best. "Isn't he something?" Johnny says as he runs his fingers through his thick blond hair.

"He certainly is," I reply flatly.

Since the party was in full swing when we arrived, there's already plenty of action in progress. One couple fucks on the steps of the pool, another on a mat near the deep end. Some lounge and watch the show, lazily stroking their own dicks or those of others. A couple of blow jobs are also in progress. From the corner of my eye, I catch a glimpse of a fellow getting his ass eaten out. Apart from the usual distractions of an orgy, the event is a delicious parade of bodies. As Johnny and I enter the scene, we enjoy the appreciative gazes that follow our movement. Johnny heads toward Cyril.

After I get a drink at the bar I turn toward my audience to display my rising cock.

Seconds later, a gorgeous little thing sidles up next to me, gets a drink, and lets his bare ass brush my cock. He wiggles back into me and asks, "How do you know Cyril?"

"I don't," I reply. "My friend does."

"So you're on your own."

"Totally."

"Why don't we find ourselves a quiet corner?" he suggests. I follow him to a patch of lawn off to one side of the house.

He stretches out, then rolls onto his side. He pulls one leg over the other to showcase his firm little ass.

I lie down behind him, slide my dick up against his cheeks, and begin to hump him gently. He murmurs his approval and hands me a condom. This makes me laugh. He is stark naked but still well-provisioned. I roll the rubber over my prick, lube myself with spit, and ease into him. We lie on the lawn fucking while others splash in the pool.

Soon he begins to ride my dick, pushing back into me as he strokes himself. This does me in; I start to come, pumping juice into him. He lets go as well. We jerk and fuck, and when we're done we discover another naked guy has been watching us.

I roll over on my back, pull off the rubber, and look up at him. His dick is big and hard. "Nice show," he says. My partner scrambles to his knees and sucks the guy's cock into his mouth. I head back to the bar for another drink.

At the pool, I don't see Johnny or Cyril. I assume they've sought some privacy for themselves. Shyness strikes me as an amusing thing to want in the middle of an orgy. But maybe the host likes to watch, but not to be watched. I take my drink to the pool and slide into the shallow end, where I lounge on the steps and get pleasantly drunk.

After a while a furry guy swims over to me, smiles, looks down at my dick, sucks in a breath, and submerges himself. I enjoy a brief underwater blow job. The bear surfaces and gasps for air. He has me hard again. "Why don't you get out of the water?" he suggests.

"Not just yet," I reply, whereupon he swims away. I see Johnny emerge from the house without Cyril. A hot number quickly moves in and Johnny, much to my surprise, doesn't resist. They move to a poolside mat and start to kiss and to play with each other. I wonder whether Cyril is watching.

Curious, I go into the house. I have to pee anyway and once I'm done, I explore a little. I find the library and begin to scan the bookshelves when I hear Cyril's voice. "Are you a reader?" he asks.

"Not really," I reply. "More of a movie buff." I turn to find him naked. I'm impressed: His cock is big, uncut, and on the rise. He moves in.

"Bret, wasn't it?"

I nod.

"I have some wonderful volumes of pornography I'd like to show you," he tells me as he reaches past me to finger the books. "Videos as well." He slides a hand down onto my ass, runs a finger into my crack, finds my hole, and prods. "Of course, the real thing is so much better, don't you think?"

I spread my legs as I tell him yes, and he eases a finger into me. He begins to work it a bit. "Why don't I show you my bedroom?" he says. I begin to ride his palm; I haven't had anything up there in a while, and his attention feels damn good. I follow him down the hall to a spacious bedroom with a huge bed.

The painting over the bed catches my eye: a jumble of lines that seem to converge into an orgy scene the longer I study the image. Much is left to imagination, but further concentration banishes my doubts.

"Isn't it wonderful?" Cyril asks as he gets behind me and pushes his stiff dick between my legs. "The painter is an absolute genius," he continues. "A few brushstrokes and suddenly everyone's fucking."

I close my thighs around his dick, and he begins to thrust gently. His cock head is wet. His hands move from my hips to my prick and he begins to play with me, pulling at me and squeezing my balls. As he nuzzles my neck, he whispers, "I want you to fuck me."

I reach down to explore his cock, and he says, "Johnny's told you about me, hasn't he?"

"Yes," I reply.

"Well, Johnny doesn't quite know everything. Sometimes..." he stops and pulls me around to face him. "Sometimes, I just need a good fucking. From the moment I saw your magnificent cock, I wanted it in me."

I slide my hands onto his ass and squeeze his cheeks, then run a finger into his crack. He murmurs his approval and squirms in eagerness. When I prod his pucker, he bears down and I push in. "Oh, yes," he says, "all the way." He thrusts his ass back until my finger is buried in his ass. "Wonderful," he moans, "but let's do the real thing, shall we? Get your cock up there."

He pulls away and climbs onto the bed. He pulls at his dick while he rolls onto his side to present me with his eager ass. I can't believe this is Johnny's potential Daddy. I pull a condom from the bedside bowl, grease myself with one of the assorted lubes, move behind him, and guide my prick into his ass. He groans and rides my dick as if he were doing the fucking—and not me. I establish a steady rhythm and reach around for his prick. It's dripping wet. Just as I take hold, I hear Johnny's voice behind me. "Lookin' good," he says.

I don't turn. I keep fucking Cyril, and I feel Johnny climb onto the bed behind me. "Want some company?" he asks.

"How about it, Cyril?" I ask as I tug at his dick and keep pumping his ass. "Johnny wants you."

Cyril's delight is irrepressible. "Darling boy," he gushes as we disengage. "By all means."

Cyril quickly dons a rubber and makes a production of lubing Johnny's ass. I lean back on my haunches and watch Cyril psyche himself into a sexual frenzy. He maneuvers Johnny into position: He rests Johnny's head on a pillow with his legs tucked under him and his ass high. Then Cyril plunges in, letting out a long, gratified moan, but doesn't start to fuck. "Now, Bret," he says.

Though he's buried in Johnny's ass he still manages to lean forward and to part his cheeks. "Fuck me," he says, flexing his muscle. I glance at the winking hole and get behind him again. I've never done this before; I've never been party to an honest-to-God fuck chain. As I push into Cyril I get an incredible rush.

Cyril lets out a cry and continues to vocalize loudly. I can't say I blame him. Fucking and being fucked: He's got the best of both worlds. He has embarked on quite a trip.

When I begin to thrust, he quickly matches my pace. Soon we establish a perfect rhythm. It's not long before the three of us are completely wet and slippery; runny lube dribbles from assholes and covers our balls. My familiar fuck-slap finds an echo, and I have to remark, "Listen to that: the sweetest sound there is."

Cyril goes silent, and for a while there is only fucking. "Hey, Johnny," I finally say, making him laugh. "I'm fucking Cyril's ass. How do you like it?"

"Dick city, man," Johnny chortles. "Go for it."

Cyril loves the banter and starts to come. "Fuck me, Bret," he cries. "Come inside me now!"

I pick up the pace and feel my own spunk rise. "I'm gonna fill your ass," I growl at him. He repeats the line to Johnny as he unloads.

He slams into Johnny and I continue to pound him relentlessly. I dig my fingers into his hips as I ride out an incredible climax. Cyril lets out a howl as I spend my load. I fill his ass with the power of my orgasm as his own energy roars into Johnny.

We keep at it for some time, reluctant to break our fuck chain until the last drop of jizz works its way out of us. Even then, the three of us cling together: Cyril's arms encircle Johnny, and mine encircle Cyril. "That was so good," Johnny finally manages to whimper.

"Hear, hear," Cyril says between gasps.

I pull out of Cyril, who pulls out of Johnny. We discard our condoms. The three of us lie side by side, with Cyril in the middle.

When Cyril begins to snore, Johnny and I leave him there to go to the kitchen for water. As I drain half a bottle, it occurs to me that our three-way may not have been as spontaneous as it appeared. I consider saying something to Johnny, then decide against it. If the price of his entrance into Cyril's life is bringing along a partner, so be it. I had a good time and, after all, it's not about the money.

The Greener Grasses

M. Christian

When I got home, Terry was in the kitchen, working his magic in a pan. It was a Thursday, so I knew the steaming mixture was rice, shrimp, tomatoes, onions, and all the rest that went into Terry's magical paella. It was wonderful: spicy without being too spicy, full of elegant flavors—and it was always on Thursday.

"Hi, honey, how was your day?" he said as I walked in. Terry's glasses were off, lying on the kitchen counter so they wouldn't steam up. I could have been bleeding from the eyes, and he wouldn't have seen, wouldn't have changed the routine of my walking in the door, Thursday or not.

"Fine," I said, struggling to keep the teeth out of my words. My lover, my husband—or wife, depending on how he was acting—labored in our kitchen to make me a wonderful dinner. But I really wanted him to throw me down on our Spanish tiled floor, undo my belt, zip down my fly, fish out my cock, and suck me hard, right then and there.

"That's good," he said as he added something sharp and flavorful to the mixture. We'd been together for five years, and I still didn't understand what went into that pan, just that it was good. Always had been good and always would be good. "Mr. Lawrence behaving himself?"

Mr. Lawrence was my boss. He'd been in Paris for a month and wouldn't be back for another one. I'd told Terry that at least a dozen times. "He's fine too."

I got a beer out of the fridge and watched him cook for a minute. *Tell me to suck your cock—order me to suck your cock. Fuck me till I bleed. Make me stand naked in the rain. Make me jack off into your mouth. Shave me. Cut me. Mix my come with my blood and drink it down.* "That's good. I'm glad," Terry said, never taking his eyes off his pan. "I love you, sweetheart."

"I love you too," I mumbled as I finished the rest of my beer. *Pierce my nipples. Put your fist up my ass. Carve your initials in my back. Whip me.*

Then he did something nasty. He put the pan aside, wiped his hands on his Kiss the Chief apron, got his glasses from the counter, and walked over to me. Kissed me. Not deep, not hot, not hard, not viscous—just his soft lips to mine. Then he did something worse: "I'm so glad you're here," he said, when our lips parted.

Restrain me, wrap my cock and balls in fishing line, make my dick hard and blue. Maybe needles; maybe a current and voltage; maybe a single quick touch of a smoldering cigarette— maybe a lot of things, but surprise me, shock me. "I-I am too," I stammered.

He went back to his cooking. I got another beer. I usually only have one, but he didn't notice. I loved Terry—loved him with all my heart—but I also hated him like I'd never hated anyone before.

"Dinner will be ready in just a sec," he said as he stirred and stirred. The steam from the pan obscured his head.

"I can't wait," I said and then walked away.

Dinner was good—as it always was on Thursday nights. We talked as we ate, though we said nothing really important, nothing different. They say that domesticity isn't pretty. Well, what we had was a serious form of ugly.

"You're seeing Robert tomorrow, right?" Terry asked, sipping a glass of red wine.

"Yeah," I replied as I pushed rice, shrimp, tomatoes, and onions around on my plate. Robert: Mister Robert—not Master, not Sir, just Mister. Mister Robert had made me scream, cry, bleed, and come too many times to count.

"Give him my best," Terry said, smiling.

"I'll do that," I said, smiling back, my face painful from tension. Terry was a sweetheart, a treasure, and a prize—he understood that sometimes you need more in a relationship than just one person, one way of doing something. If he weren't so understanding—if instead he threw things and screamed—I'd have been much happier.

After dinner we watched *Buffy*. Terry laughed and smiled the whole way through. I wasn't paying attention. *Cover my eyes. Tie me up, make my wrists and ankles burn when I pull against them. Light a candle; fill my nose with the smell of hot sulfur. One burning dot, then two, then three—wax splashing on my rigid body, making me scream, making me hard...so hard.*

We went to bed and had Thursday sex. Paella sex: spicy without being too spicy, full of elegant gestures. Just like every Thursday. Good sex. The problem was, I wanted great. I wanted fantastic.

Terry faded into sleep, but I couldn't. Wide awake, I looked out our bedroom window at the bright moon that shone on our carefully manicured garden, and at the silhouettes of distant trees waving gently back and forth. I'd done it before: I'd let my discontent blaze for a few hours until it cooled to a glowing ember I could manage for another week. But that night, that Thursday paella night, I balled my hands into fists until my palms throbbed.

On Saturday afternoon I took Terry to Valentino's. It was unexpected, different. Saturday lunch was usually something we grabbed from the kitchen, or snacked on as we did whatever chores we had to do that day. Valentino's was special, but also unexpected. Even though he smiled as I drove us across the city, we both felt the tension in the air.

After we ordered our meals we made small talk. I felt like screaming. I felt like crying. Then Terry said the one thing he never should have said: "What's the matter?"

I want out, I want out, I want Mister Robert. I want Mister Robert all the time. I don't want a happy home; I want to be property, 24/7. I want to feel what I feel with him all the time.

"I—this isn't working," I finally croaked out.

"What do you mean?"

"I think I need to leave, Terry. I want out. I'm sorry."

He was quiet for a long time. "Can you at least tell me why?"

"I'm not too sure," I said, looking down at my meatless lunch. *I want to be thrown down and fucked. I want a knife at my throat. I want to wake up in ropes. I don't just want to be loved; I want to be owned.*

"We've been together for five years. I think you owe me at least that."

Whip me, beat me, cut me, tie me up. Tell me what I am; show me what I am. I don't want to love, then hate, then love—I don't want complexity, compromise. I want to be an object. That's safe—this isn't.
"It's complicated."

"Life's complicated. I didn't hear you complaining before."

Mister Robert isn't complicated. There the world is just the two of us: a possession and the possessor. "I just want out, OK—don't make this harder than is has to be."

"Five years together is not going to make this easier," he swirled whatever was on his plate, hypnotized for a minute by the colors. "I think I know what this is all about."

Anger tensed my spine, flushed my face. "What?" I spat. I knew he didn't understand, that he never could—that he thought he did made me angrier, cheapened what I felt.

"It's Robert, isn't it?" He watched my face, and his blue eyes stared through me. "It's better with him—easier." He saw something shift in me and added, "I thought so. I was worried about that. What we had was special—don't tell me otherwise—but that's scary, isn't it? I love you, you love—or loved—me. But it's not like being a plaything is it? It's not easy—"

"Go on, Terry," I said bitterly, "tell me what I'm feeling. You've got it all figured out."

His hand reached out toward mine, but I pulled back. His face darkened. "Go on, play your games with 'Mister' Robert. With him you don't have to pay the bills, do the laundry, listen when he talks about his day, or hurt when he hurts. Go on. I'm sure it's better for you—and that's sad. That's really fucking sad."

I didn't say anything. Terry never swore. I knew he was angry, knew that he was hurt, but that one word shocked me. I was about to say I was sorry—and mean it.

"Fine," he interjected, "we'll break up. If that's what you want. I'm going to miss you, but I certainly don't want you around if you're not going to be happy."

"OK," I managed to squeeze out. We sat and stared at each other for a long time, until the check came.

As I paid for our lunch (it was my turn), I wanted to say something, anything, either to make it better between us or to let out the fury that churned my stomach, but no words came. We drove home in silence, to coldly work out the logistics of turning two into a pair of ones.

Hand on the knob, I took a deep breath. I resisted checking my watch again, not wanting to show, even just to myself, how nervous I was. Rules formed the world, framed it, and defined it. The door would only be unlocked from 1:15 to 1:25 in the afternoon. After that he would throw the bolt, and I'd have to come back next week—to a frightening punishment for having been late.

I turned the knob; the door was open. I stepped in and closed it carefully. Japanese. I felt Japanese—or at least what I imagined it might be like—a member of a rigid world, where punishment for transgression was certain and terrifying. But I knew one thing for certain: I belonged to Mister Robert.

Down the hall and through the door at the end was the room— the room where I lived, where I existed. Black carpeting covered the floor and walls, even the door. The bare wooden ceiling was rough: bare beams flaked with old white paint, track lighting with three high-intensity spots. One wall had a board bolted to it, and to the board Mister Robert had attached a line of cheap coat hooks. On the hooks hung his collection of dark leather toys. Another board with two big eyebolts adorned the opposite wall. In one corner stood the sawhorse. I wished never to leave this room.

I got undressed and carefully folded my clothes in a corner. I waited. Ten minutes, exactly. Then the door opened.

I didn't turn. To turn would be to break a rule. I was Property; I belonged to Mister Robert. Property wasn't a man with desires. Nevertheless, I was happy.

Eyes straight ahead, Mister Robert walked into view—and I momentarily held my breath. Every time I saw him I tried to absorb more details, for afterward: tall and broad, strong and smooth—not a hair on his body, his head, or his face. He was skin, muscle, and skill—that completed the inventory of Mr. Robert. Except for his voice. He had a voice like a sledgehammer breaking rocks.

"Are you ready, Property?" he asked, eyeing me like a connoisseur. Pride made me tilt my head back. "Yes, Mister Robert." I felt my cock stir.

"Good. Today you'll need to be ready." He walked over to the row of toys, ran his fingers through the hanging leather, feeling one, then another—weighing them for some unknown, terrifying quality. He hesitated over one and carefully unhooked it. I glanced toward the toy, but I couldn't see what it was, which made my fear and excitement even greater. "The sawhorse," he said, not bothering to gesture. I knew what to do.

The sawhorse: wood, nails, and a piece of thick leather. Mister Robert: muscles, skin, bone, and will. I wanted to cry as I walked over to the horse, bent over it, and exposed my bare ass to my owner.

A tough hand ran over my ass cheeks, examined my skin for some kind of elusive quality, and found it. "You're breaking in nicely, Property. Very nicely indeed."

I felt a tear well and fall. "Thank you," I said very softly.

Though I had not spoken softly enough. Property doesn't speak unless spoken to. Pain splashed against my ass, shot through me, and forced a short, sharp gasp through my clenched teeth—

which gave Mister Robert no choice but to swing the whip again. This time I kept my teeth together and captured the offensive sound before it escaped my throat.

"You learn well, Property," Mister Robert said as he caressed my ass with the strands of leather. "It is always a pleasure to use you."

This was the world I wanted to inhabit all the time. I wanted to be the cherished property of Mister Robert, his favorite plaything. There was nothing better.

The whip fell anew: a beginning stroke. He wasn't punishing me, just warming up. The individual blows from his whip began to blend together into waves of something not exactly like mindless pain and not exactly like empty pleasure. The waves of abuse increased in frequency and modulation, as did my breathing and the thumping of my heart. I tried not to make a sound, tried to keep it in—to please him who owned me. But some noise escaped: a deep bass sound that bounced off the floor in front of my face, a human accompaniment to the sound of the whip on my bare skin.

Then it broke—not the toy, nor my ass, but the feeling lodged deep inside me. A roar emanated from a spot down below my soul.

The whip stopped, and I felt tears again: fear that I had broken a rule, and fear that I hadn't, but he was going to stop anyway. "On your feet, Property," he commanded. "Face me."

I complied. Despite the tears I had wasted, I was still the property of Mister Robert, and my cock was hard.

He put his big hand around my cock and wrapped his fingers around my balls as well. His grip was steel, iron, unbreakable—and I didn't want to break it. "Handsome Property," he said. "You may speak."

"Thank you, Mister Robert."

"Now you may not speak. One word, one sound, and I stop. And you get dressed and leave."

I had been ordered not to speak, so I didn't. Not even to say I understood—after all, if I spoke, I would no longer be worthy of the name "Property."

He smiled, sly and quick—which told me he also understood. Then, still smiling, Mister Robert started to squeeze.

At first his grip was a just a firm handshake around my cock and balls, but it grew in force and intensity until my breathing became quick and ragged. He squeezed my cock and balls in a merciless flesh and bone vice. The pressure on my dick didn't hurt nearly as much at the throbbing ache of my balls. Despite my will and training, I felt myself begin to curl toward the cruel tug of his hand around me. I straightened, even though doing so meant even more pain as my stomach muscles pulled against the reflex to shield my balls. I started to breathe so fast that the air whistled through my clinched teeth.

He didn't stop, or even hesitate. Little by little, he continued to tighten his grip. Suddenly, I was overcome with fear—fear that he would crush me, crack my eggs, and destroy my cock. But still I held my tongue, didn't open my mouth, except to wheeze and softly moan. I was his property, and I would do anything he asked, even offer up my cock and balls to the will of Mister Robert. In pain, I was never happier.

Then there was nothing. He stopped, pulled his hand away from the agony of my cock and balls, and I screamed. I bellowed like an animal as blood rushed into my empty veins and arteries. Despite my training, I doubled over and pressed my face into his smooth skin. My breath mixed with his rutting, heavy, masculine scent.

"You're hard," he said in a tone of voice I had never heard before, a tone almost tender, almost proud. I pulled away, a thank-you unspoken on my lips, to see that he was right: My cock was hard, very hard.

He extended a hand, palm up, just under the bobbing head. "Come in my hand," he commanded. "Now."

My cock was slick with sweat, and a pearl of precome glistened at the tip. One stroke, two—I matched my rhythm to the strike of my owner's whip against my thighs until I felt the come start to push its way out of me. Then my jizz erupted in long spurts into my owner's open hand.

Then he spoke, and all was right with the world: "Thank you, Property. You did good. Now clean yourself up and get dressed, but do not leave—not yet."

I did as I was told; I quickly donned my underwear, socks, shirt, pants, and shoes. But I wasn't aware of anything except my owner's voice, my owner's praise. This place was where I belonged: here and nowhere else. To be the property of Mister Robert was my life's wish.

I had just finished tying my shoes when he walked back in. "Come with me into the kitchen for a minute. I need to talk to you."

I didn't know what to say or do. But my training took over, and I did as I was told. In the years I had been Mister Robert's, I had never been anywhere except for the hall and the playroom. I didn't want to go anywhere else—but he was Mister Robert.

It was a simple kitchen, and smelled faintly of gas and cat food. He sat at a '50s Formica table decorated with sickly yellow flowers. The kitchen was lined with rough wooden shelves on which were perched rows of spices.

"Sit down, please," he said. He'd also gotten dressed: jeans, work boots, and a white T-shirt. He didn't look like Mister Roberts; he looked like someone you'd pass on the street. I didn't know where to look.

"We've had a wonderful time all these years, haven't we?" he asked. "Lots of great sessions. Lots of great afternoons. But I have to tell you something. This is going to be our last time together."

I couldn't say anything. Even if I had known what to say, I was still Property—and Property didn't speak, didn't question, and didn't argue.

"It's nothing you've done, or even something you haven't done. I…I've just reached a point in my life where I need to have something else in a relationship. This is great, what we have, but I need something deeper, more meaningful." For the first time he actually looked uncomfortable. "I need to be in love with someone, I guess: someone to pay the bills with, to really connect with. It's a hard decision, but one I really need to make to be really happy."

I hung my head. The world—the only world that mattered to me—had fallen apart. Yeah, Property shouldn't speak, but suddenly I wasn't Property—I'd never again be the Property of Mister Robert. I still didn't know what to say.

"I hope you'll understand," was the last thing he said to me, before he shook my hand and led me outside.

Uncle Ted's Big Send-off

Bob Vickery

By the time the third joint is passed around, I'm floating in a warm blissed-out fog, no body part touching ground. It's such a bitching day: the sky like a pure-blue bowl, the sunlight sparkling on the Pacific. I close my eyes as a breeze passes over me and let myself drift. One of the guys sits off to the side and beats on one of those small East Indian drums, and the drumbeats thread through my skull like fuzzy worms. Around me float snatches of conversation among Uncle Ted's old friends. I don't really know anybody here well, except for Uncle Ted, of course, or what's left of him. His ashes are firmly sealed in the Folger's coffee can that occupies a place of honor in the middle of a blanket spread out on the beach.

Two of the guys (I think their names are Mark and Al) talk heatedly off to the side. They keep their voices low, but since I'm at the edge of the group, I hear every word.

"Are you sure you gave him the right directions?" Mark asks.

"Yeah, I'm sure," Al says. "Will you just relax? He'll be here."

"He fucking better. Without him the whole ceremony will be ruined."

"Jesus, will you calm down? This guy's very reliable. I've worked with him before."

"Yeah," Mark snorts. "I just bet you have." He rejoins the

group, intercepts the circulating joint and takes a hit.

"Look," Al says, pointing behind us, "What did I tell you?"

Sure enough, we see the shape of a man crest the nearest sand dune.

"Hey, Clancy," Al shouts, waving. "Over here!"

Clancy turns toward the sound of Al's voice and waves back. Mark visibly relaxes.

The sun is behind Clancy's back, so all I see is his silhouette: broad shoulders, the V of a well-muscled torso, the bulge of biceps, narrow hips. Everyone else also draws a bead on Clancy, and the mood of the group noticeably shifts; suddenly, we're all alert. Clancy reaches us, and Al puts his hand on his shoulder to pull him into the circle of friends.

"Everybody," Al says, "this is Clancy." All of us pretend not to feast our eyes on Clancy. The words "golden boy" flit through my mind: His smooth skin is honey gold, as is his shaggy sun-bleached hair. He flashes the easy smile of a man who drifts nonchalantly through life because an accident of fate has made him heartbreakingly handsome. He wears a tie-dyed tank top and board shorts; it's impossible to imagine him in any environment other than a California beach on a warm summer's day.

"Hey, guys," Clancy says, regarding each of us with friendly blue eyes.

"Did Al explain the…ceremony we had in mind?" Mark asks.

Clancy shrugs. "Sure. Piece of cake."

Mark glances around at all of us. "Let's get in a circle," he says. We all comply, except for the guy with the drum. He continues to beat out a steady tattoo. Mark reaches down to pick up the coffee can and peels off its plastic lid. "Hold out your hands," he instructs us, and we obey. Mark slowly walks around the inner perimeter of the circle, stops in front of each of us, and pours a handful of ash into our outstretched cupped hands—all except for Clancy, who stands in the center of the circle, arms at his side, watching us. Mark reaches me last and turns the coffee can completely upside down, thumping it lightly on the bottom. A pile of fine ash forms a heap in my hands. I stare at it, trying to grasp that I'm holding Uncle Ted.

Mark nods to Clancy, who lazily hooks his thumbs under the hem of his tank top and pulls it over his head, revealing a torso packed with muscle. His nipples are two wide brown circles set on tawny flesh. Clancy yanks open the Velcro fly on his shorts and lets them drop to his ankles. He steps out of them, kicks them aside, and stands naked in the center of our circle. Sunlight pours over his body, and his skin gleams with a film sweat. I'm still totally stoned from the killer weed we've all been smoking, and there's a steady buzz in my ears that mingles with the soft whoosh of the waves behind me and the rapid beat of the drum. None of this seems real.

"OK, guys," Mark says. "You all know what Ted's last wish was, how he wanted his ashes scattered. Let's get to it." His voice is matter-of-fact, but there are tears in his eyes. He steps forward and sprinkles ash on Clancy's body. It clings to Clancy's sweaty skin and quickly forms a gray paste.

Al steps forward and the others join him. Soon we are all smearing Uncle Ted's ashes over Clancy's naked skin, across the mounds of his pecs, the rounded curves of his biceps, down the hard, chiseled stretch of belly, over the smooth, twin globes of Clancy's perfect ass. Clancy is our canvas, Uncle Ted the medium. I take my own handful of ashes and fling them against Clancy's torso, then slide my hands down his belly. All the stroking is clearly arousing Clancy. His dick slowly lengthens and thickens, and the head pushes out from the uncut foreskin. I wrap my sooty hand around his shaft and stroke it slowly, then tug on Clancy's low-hanging balls, coating them with ash as well. I cup them in my hand and roll them around. Clancy watches me calmly and our gazes meet. Stoned as I am, I fall into those liquid-blue eyes. I reach behind him, slide my hand into the crack of Clancy's ass, and massage his asshole. I push a finger inside, and Clancy's dick twitches in response to my probing.

We all step back to regard our handiwork. Clancy's body is no longer golden-brown, but dull gray. Long dark smears follow the contours of his torso and face, and ashy clots cling to his hair. His dick juts out thick and hard, pointing up toward the sky. His eyes are closed, and his mouth curves up in a lazy smile. I sway, trying not to lose my balance. I am so fucking stoned. Mark pulls a piece of paper from his back pocket and starts reading a poem by Rumi, Uncle Ted's favorite poet. We all stand still and listen to the soft drone of his voice.

When he's done, there's a moment of silence, broken only by the waves and beating drum. Clancy opens his eyes and looks around. When his gaze meets mine, he winks. The circle breaks, leaving an opening that leads out toward the softly crashing waves. Clancy calmly walks toward the sea. A wave breaks on the beach, and water swirls around his ankles. He wades deeper into the Pacific. When he's thigh-deep, he plunges headfirst into the next swell of the wave and swims out using strong, sure strokes. He circles around, comes back toward us, and staggers out of the waves that pull his legs. The water is reluctant to release him. He looks like a sea god emerging from the ocean depths. His skin gleams gold again, and what's left of Uncle Ted now rides the current into the open ocean.

Clancy walks up to us. "Well," he says. "Is that the end of it?"

Mark's eyes are still moist. He nods, saying nothing. Clancy bends down to pick up his clothes, and the sense of ritual is suddenly gone. When Clancy's done dressing, Mark takes him aside and discreetly slips some folded bills into his hand. Clancy slips the money into his back pocket without counting it. He shakes Mark's hand, waves at us, climbs the dune, and disappears behind its crest.

Al stands next to me. "Where did you find Clancy?" I ask him.

Al turns his head and regards me for a couple of beats. "On an escort Web site," he finally says. He walks over to Mark and puts his arm around Mark's shoulder. There's nothing else for me to do here. I pick up my stuff and head back to the lot where my car is parked.

I pull out onto the main road that flanks the beach. At a bus stop a couple of hundred feet down the road, Clancy stands, waiting.

I pull up next to him. "You need a ride?" I ask.

Clancy smiles his easy smile. "Sure," he says. "If you don't mind. I live over on Haight Street."

"No problem," I reply. I lean over to unlock the door, and Clancy climbs in.

We cruise down the Great Highway. On our left, the Pacific spreads out like a plane of sheet metal. "What a bitching day," Clancy says.

"Yeah," I agree. I glance at Clancy. "That thing we did with Uncle Ted's ashes didn't creep you out?"

"Naw," Clancy says. He stretches, looks out toward the ocean, then back at me. He's grinning. "Bizarre requests come with the territory in my line of work." We ride together in silence. "So, were you pretty tight with your uncle?" he finally asks.

"Yeah," I say. "I didn't see him all that often, but we had a bond—you know, the only gay members in the family: that kind of thing." I turn onto Geary Avenue. "He was a good guy. I'm going to miss him."

We don't say anything else for the rest of the ride. Clancy's got his knees spread apart, and my hand brushes his thigh whenever I shift gears. The first couple of times are accidental. After that, I make a point of sliding my knuckles against the length of his thigh each time I shift. The memory of Clancy's hard, ash-coated dick flashes through my mind. I recall how it felt in my hand when I stroked it, and I feel my own dick stir. Clancy makes no effort to pull away when my hand touches his leg. This is turning into a very strange day.

We pull up to Clancy's apartment. "Well," I say lamely. "It was nice meeting you."

"Look," Clancy says. "Would you like to come up for a while?"

"Fuck, yeah," I say.

Clancy's place is a small studio on the third floor. It faces west, and the early afternoon sunlight pours in through the one window. The furnishing is sparse, and the only decoration on the wall is a surfing poster. Clancy puts a CD on the player and sitar music fills the room. He goes into the kitchen, returns with two Coronas, and hands me one. We sit on Clancy's threadbare couch. I clink my bottle against his. "To sex and death," I say.

"Well, you can't get any more basic than that," Clancy grins. He holds up his bottle. "Sex and death," he says and takes a swig. We sit together for a moment. I still have a buzz on, and the sitar music makes my brain tingle like a low voltage current is passing through it. Clancy hooks a hand around my neck and pulls me toward him. He kisses me softly, and his tongue snakes into my mouth. I wrap my arms around him, pull him down onto the couch, and squeeze him tightly. Our kisses become hungry, our hands slip under each other's clothes, and we begin to fumble with buttons and zippers. Clancy pulls away. "Let's get naked," he says.

We strip quickly. Clancy pushes me down, straddles me, and wraps his hand around both our dicks. He gives them a good squeeze, and a bead of precome leaks out of my piss slit. I look down at our dicks pressed together, his fat and pink, the head a rubbery dome of flesh, mine dark and veined. "Fucking beautiful," I growl. I reach up and twist Clancy's nipples, not gently, and Clancy laughs. I drag my tongue across his belly and taste the salt from the ocean.

"Slide up," I say hoarsely. "And let me work that dick of yours."

Clancy happily complies. Propping himself up on his arms, Clancy thrusts his dick completely into my mouth. We hold the pose for a moment: my mouth full of cock, Clancy's heavy balls against my chin, and my hands on Clancy's hips for support. Clancy begins to pump his hips, and his dick pushes against the back of my mouth. I suck hungrily on the fleshy tube, twist my head from side to side, and wrap my tongue around the shaft.

Clancy twists around and takes my dick into his mouth. We fuck each other's mouths, eat each other's dicks, and our bodies squirm together. I slide my tongue down the shaft of his cock and start sucking on his ball sac and rolling my tongue around it as I jack Clancy off with a spit-slicked hand. Clancy groans softly. I bury my face inside his ass crack. "Yeah, that's right," Clancy gasps. "Keep doing that." I worm a finger into Clancy's asshole and twist it slowly. Clancy groans again, loudly. I start to finger-fuck Clancy and work his dick with my mouth.

"You gonna let me fuck that sweet asshole?" I growl.

"Yeah," Clancy gasps. "Go for it." He opens a drawer in his nightstand, pulls out lube and a condom, and hands them to me. I tube and lube up as Clancy watches, stroking his dick. I wrap my hands around Clancy's calves and pull him toward me. He arches his back to expose the pucker of his asshole and keeps his eyes trained hard on me. I slowly impale him. Clancy pulls me down and plants his mouth on mine as I slide into him.

When my dick is completely in, I stare down into Clancy's eyes. "You like that, fucker?" I growl. "You like being filled with cock?"

"Fuck, yeah," Clancy says. He kisses me again, tweaking my nipples hard, and I start pumping my hips. Clancy pushes up and squeezes his ass muscles tight. He wraps his arms around me, and I feel his body strain against mine as his smooth chest slides against me. Clancy gives a sudden push, and we topple off the couch onto the rug. He's on top of me now, and he rides me like a bronco he's trying to break. He snakes his fingers through my hair and gives my head a good tug. We lock gazes—Clancy's eyes bore into mine. Sweat trickles down his face and splashes into my open mouth. I pump my hips faster now, pounding away at Clancy's ass with hard, vicious thrusts. I can feel the orgasm rising up in me, heading for release.

"I'm getting close," I gasp.

"Go for it!" Clancy growls. He reaches behind and gives my balls a good tug.

I close my eyes, and suddenly, unexpectedly, a picture flashes into my mind of Clancy's naked body smeared with Uncle Ted's ashes. I arch my back and cry out as the orgasm sweeps over me. My dick pulses, pumping out its load into the condom up Clancy's ass. Clancy holds on as I thrash around and finally collapse onto the floor, panting.

I look up at Clancy. "Drop your balls in my mouth," I say. "I want to be sucking them when you squirt your load."

Clancy scoots up and obliges me, filling my mouth with his fleshy ball sac as he strokes his wanker. "Oh, yeah," he groans, and his load squirts out, splattering against my face, coating my cheeks and forehead. Clancy rolls off and collapses onto the floor beside me. He bends over and slowly licks his load off me. After a couple of minutes I get up, get dressed, kiss Clancy one last time, and leave.

Instead of going home, I drive through Golden Gate Park, past the green meadows and flower beds, until I'm back on the Great Highway again. I pull into the Ocean Beach parking lot, get out of my car and sit on the sea wall. I stay there a long time, staring out at the Pacific. *Uncle Ted's out there,* I think. *He must be halfway to Hawaii by now.* I watch the kids playing Frisbee, the lovers, the old men and women soaking up what heat they can. I don't leave until the sun dips below the horizon and the lights that flank the Great Highway blink on.

Body Sports

Jay Maxwell

The opposing team was good. They were young, and they were a college team, but they were keen. I played water polo with a master's group that had team members ranging in age from 25 to 55. I was one of the younger ones, just 28 that year. And I was good too.

I picked my man, moving through the water to shadow him as his team attempted to score. He was cute beneath his white water-polo cap, even though his cheeks were puffed out and his eyes crazed from exertion. He had a small nose, soft brown eyes, and a tanned complexion. He was almost elfin: This cutie was already driving me to distraction. To make matters worse (or better), water polo is a very physical game. You have to maintain physical contact with your man, keeping your body against his constantly.

His body was tight and hard. I shadowed him closely, pressing against him so he could not elude me and get free to receive the ball. He was irritated by my dogged determination and elbowed me under the water. I laughed at his temper; I'm experienced and rarely loose my cool. I merely moved in closer. One of my pumping legs pressed right up against his ass, then between his spread thighs from behind. Wow! His rounded bubble butt had me getting hard right there in the water.

Hoots and shouts from spectators and the other players filled the air. The water roiled around my man and me as we thrashed together and he attempted to get free. One of his hands flailed around behind him and connected with my crotch as he tried to push me away. Without meaning to, he pressed his palm against the full length of my stiffening dick.

He whipped his head around and locked his eyes on mine. A crooked half-smile bent the corners of his mouth—he had dimples too! I nearly swooned. Before I could come back to earth, he grabbed my dick and balls in a vise-hold and squeezed. My mouth dropped open, and I almost squealed in pain. But his ploy had worked: He slipped away from me, and before I knew it, the ball was in his hands and he had lobbed it into the net. The bastard had scored off my boner!

Of course, grabbing an opponent's balls is illegal in water polo—even if the referees don't catch it. I could have complained to our coach, and he would have protested. But that would have meant cutie would be kicked out of the game. My competitive zeal couldn't quell the sudden case of the hots I'd developed for this cocky young kid. I held my tongue.

Which isn't to say I didn't begin plotting my revenge! For the remainder of the game he was mine: I never let him out of my reach. His frustration was matched by his determination, and he almost scored another time. Over the course of the game, I felt almost every inch of his lush young body against my skin. I was certain he was enjoying this foreplay as much as I was—he often let his floating limbs brush against mine in a near caress. We made a beautiful kind of lover, flailing, swimming, float-ing, and hollering, now and again locked together in an intense watery embrace.

When the game ended, I was flush with exertion and sexual arousal. We had won, but just barely. As we passed by the other team to shake hands, I finally met him face-to-face. When our hands touched, I squeezed with extra pressure to signal my interest. I smiled and looked right into his eyes.

"I'm Marc," he blurted out, a blush spreading across his cheeks beneath the tan.

I nodded and held his hand a moment longer than I needed to. "I'm Jay," I said. "See you in the locker room."

I hoped I'd made my meaning clear. Although our teams changed in different locker rooms, I lingered in the shower while my teammates finished up and headed home. Would he show up? So horny was I from the game and the memory of his hard young body, I was tempted to whack off right then and there.

"Uh, hi, Jay," I heard a voice say from the entrance to the shower room.

There he was. And there I was! I had my hard soapy dick in my hand beneath the spray of the showerhead. His eyes were riveted to my crotch. He was obviously impressed with my sizable piece, with its big mushroom head that reared up out of my fist like a battering ram. Smirking, I pumped it a few times and laughed out loud. What the hell: A hard dick is only natural. If he was frightened, then let him leave.

"Can I join you in the shower?" he asked in a shaky voice. God, he was such a sweet young thing! I was sure he was a freshman, probably just 18. Even though he was thin, his body was lean and beautifully proportioned. His ass was high and round beneath the skimpy trunks he was still wearing

"Sure," I replied, letting a teasing tone slip into my voice. "You mean you haven't showered already?" All the while I kept moving my body under the spray from the showerhead and boldly continued to gently squeeze and stroke my hard meat right in front of him.

"I swam a few laps to cool down," he said, smiling shyly. Then, suddenly, he was in the shower next to me, quickly discarding his trunks in a wad on the floor. He was buck naked! His dick bobbed out in front of him, growing rapidly.

I sighed with pleasure. I wasn't sure what we could accomplish here in the shower—anyone might walk in on us. But just getting such a close look at his naked body was a treat in itself. His dick was nice—long and pointed. His balls were smallish and almost completely hairless. In fact, he was sleek all over, not a wisp or curl anywhere but around the base of his dick and on his head.

My dick wasn't getting any softer as I checked him out shamelessly. Suddenly, I realized his eyes were following mine as I made my visual inventory of his assets. It was time to make my move. I glanced through the shower room doorway into the outer dressing room, which was empty. Then I looked back at him and pulled him into the spray of my shower.

"Jay! What if someone comes in!" he squealed as I wrapped my arms around him from behind and reached down to grab his boner.

"Watch the door," I breathed in his ear. If he wanted to escape, I would release him. But he didn't make a move away from me. I nuzzled and licked the backs of his ears.

Then I did what I'd wanted to do that first moment in the pool when our bodies began to bump together. I let my hands roam freely over his satiny-smooth flesh, prodding, pinching, and caressing. I inspected every inch of his torso: his tight pecs and pert nipples, his flat stomach and throbbing prong, his tender little nuts, the lean muscles of his sleek thighs. He leaned into my embrace, his breath catching in his throat every few moments, his body shaking.

I moved away slightly and began to run my hands over his back. His wide shoulders were gracefully muscled. His back tapered to a gorgeous V at his narrow waist. Then those plump white mounds jutted out, alabaster against the tan of the rest of his body. They gleamed like sexual beacons. I ran my hands right down to them, slowly moving past his waist and then over the rounded flesh of the outer mounds.

"That feels so good, Jay," he murmured, bending slightly forward.

His body language suddenly changed, and I almost creamed myself. At the touch of my hands on his ass, he moved his thighs apart. As his cheeks opened up, he leaned farther forward and his breathing became rapid. Then when one of my hands slid over a silky cheek and slipped into the parted crack of his hairless ass, he moaned out loud.

"You like that? You like my fingers in your crack?" I teased. I ran my fingers up and down the deep crevice, searching for and finding the small tight hole, clenched and palpitating. Like the rest of him, it was hairless and sleek. It was sexy as hell.

"Yes, I do," he replied simply, his voice quavering with nervousness and lust. I quickly reached around his waist and found his hard dick again. By now it was pulsing with need. God, he was so hot! While I continued to fondle his ass with my other hand, I began to slowly pump his hard bone. He gasped and his thighs moved farther apart. My heart and my cock leaped up when his crack opened wider and I caught sight of his sweet little asshole.

I looked down at his crinkled and quivering hole. It looked so fuckable—I could have plowed it right then and there. But alas, we had no condoms. No matter: For the moment, I was happy just getting acquainted with it. I rubbed two big fingers roughly up and down his crack, pressing into his hole each time I passed over it. He moaned and thrust his butt back to meet my hand. With my other hand I continued to work his boner steadily. He caught my rhythm and began grinding his hips to amplify the sensations in his cock and ass. The scene was getting so hot, my dick was practically drooling with excitement.

Then I turned my attention to his hole and began to play with it. "Oh, God—oh, man, that is so good!" he gurgled, his eyes half shut. I glanced at the doorway again. Marc obviously wasn't checking to see whether we'd attracted an audience, and I was too far gone to care at that point. I pressed more firmly against his tight little hole and began to tease open those taut ass lips.

"Oh, yeah…oh, yeah…" he moaned, his body bucking and quaking.

I was electrified. I reached for some soap and rubbed it up into his crack while he moaned and humped my slippery fingers. I went back to work on that tight slot and began to prod it open. He grunted and dropped his head, then gasped when one of my fingers slid into the entrance, soap coating its length as I pressed in deeply. His hot little box folded around my digging digit. He flexed and relaxed his plump ass cheeks and let out a high-pitched moan—almost a squeal. I dug as deep as I could and worked my finger around, feeling the quivering walls of his rectum, silky, warm, and inviting. I frigged in and out while he humped backward and moaned more deeply and steadily.

I felt his dick leap, then suddenly erupt. A fountain of jizz splattered onto the tile floor between our legs. His asshole clenched and writhed over my penetrating finger. It was too much for me: I shot a load on his thigh, where my own hard dick had been rubbing against his smooth young flesh.

He was shaking as he stood up. So was I. I wondered whether he was embarrassed, whether that would be the end of it. "Can we go to your place or something?" he asked as our eyes met.

An hour later he was sprawled over my sofa with pillows under his stomach and his delectable young ass high in the air. We had driven to my apartment, stripped as bumped through the front door, sending clothes flying everywhere. After kissing me hungrily for a few hot moments, he had squirmed out of my embrace and dropped to the sofa to pick up where we'd left off.

"Fuck me, Jay," he said as he held me steadily in his gaze, on fire with desire. "I want your big dick where your fingers were earlier." His soft amber eyes melted into mine.

"How old are you?" I had to ask. He looked so young, tender, and innocent.

"I'm 18 and a half!" he said proudly, wiggling his ass to entice me (as if I needed enticing).

"I'll go get some condoms and lube," I muttered breathlessly. "Don't move."

"I'm not going anywhere until you fuck my ass." He grinned saucily.

I was back in a flash with the goods. God, just looking at him splayed across my couch was the sweetest sight I could possibly imagine. He was so sexy—so alive—and his tanned athletic body was so beautiful and expectant. His creamy white butt twitched with eagerness and arched toward me as I flicked open the bottle of lube. He spread his thighs wide again, exposing that sleek hairless crack.

I dived right in. Once again, my hands moved all over his body. I caressed him roughly with my stout fingers, from the top of his head, where I fondled his short-cropped auburn curls, to the soles of his small feet. He quivered under my touch, squirming and moaning continually. I could tell he was rubbing his hard dick against the pillows beneath him. My hands finally settled on that hairless ass crack. I pulled it wide open and fingered the naked hole. I played with it, unveiling the puckered opening that fluttered wide as I teased him mercilessly. I squirted a generous amount of lube over the pliant entrance and worked it in. He grunted and raised his hips. The squishy sounds of my fingers beginning to work their way into his tight slot had us both gasping in anticipation.

"That feels so good, so good," he purred, urging me on. He craned his head around to watch me as I took him. He locked his eyes on mine.

"Ever been fucked?" I had to ask.

"No, not really, I just had my own fingers up there a few times and had my cock sucked twice." He laughed nervously, his face flaming red with embarrassment.

Then I managed to insert two fingers into his throbbing anus, and he abandoned his effort to speak coherently. His groans were deep and guttural. From my own experience, I knew he was pretty close to ecstasy at that moment! I felt him from the inside, working my fingers in circles, delving deep, opening him up for the inevitable fuck. He was compliant, rising up to meet me, instinctively relaxing his sphincter muscles. I felt his anal walls widening and his asshole stretching. It was time.

I withdrew and stared down at the slippery, pulsing little hole. It was ready all right. He was squirming on the couch, moaning steadily. I quickly rolled a condom over my hard dick.

"You are so hot, getting fucked by a big stud like you is a dream come true," he blurted out as I hovered over him, my hard meat in hand. "Put it in me—I can take it!"

I took him at his word. I crawled up on the couch to straddle him. I lowered my body onto his, pointing my stiff boner at the lubed hole I had just given such a thorough fingering. It beckoned to me, and my dick ached to be inside it. I lay over him and rubbed my meat into his crack, feeling with the head for the wet slot. I found it and pressed against it. He squirmed under me as my body covered his completely. I kissed his neck and then pushed.

"YEAH!" he bellowed.

My dick slid into him. Heat surrounded my shaft as I buried it to the hilt in his slippery rectum—right to the balls. I lay over him and held my breath. It was awesome. His lush young body quivered beneath me. His asshole closed around my invading dick. I began to fuck him, pulling half way out and then sliding all the way back in.

"Oh, yes, yes, that feels so good," he grunted. "Stick it in deep as it'll go."

It felt damn good, no question about that. I fucked him slowly, pulling nearly all the way out and then gliding all the way back in. I draped myself over him and unfolded him in my arms, holding his writhing body tightly. He humped up to meet me and wiggled in circles while I maintained a steady rhythm that I knew was driving him crazy. We were in heaven, and neither of us was in a hurry to go anywhere else.

Finally, he relaxed and let me have my way. His entire body went slack, and he spread his thighs even wider. His asshole gaped open for me. He moaned nonstop as I drilled him with a quickening pace. It was the best fuck I'd ever had.

I began to ride him to orgasm. My tempo increased dramatically as my excitement crested. There was no stopping now. He moved with me, his ass rising and falling, his hard body glistening with sweat from his exertion.

"Yeah, fuck me till I come!" he pleaded hoarsely. "Please, Jay, fuck me faster till I shoot!"

I pounded his sweet young ass. We rose and fell on the couch in a frenzied dance. Friction burned my dick, his asshole a slick channel of fire.

It felt like my cock nearly exploded with the force of my eruption.

"I'm shooting up your ass!" I shouted.

"Yeah, shoot it, Jay, shoot it!" He laughed madly.

Through the haze of my orgasm I realized that his asshole had clamped over my spewing dick. He was coming too.

I pulled out and rolled him over, holding his sweaty body as his young dick pulsed and creamed all over his tanned belly. What a sight!

We cuddled all night on the sofa and fucked again in the morning. It had been one great day, winning at water polo and fucking a sweet young ass. Not a bad combo!

Anything He Wants

Christopher Pierce

There are many hot three-word combinations.

"I love you" is one of them.

"Please fuck me" is another.

But my personal favorite is "Anything he wants."

Let me tell you why.

Daryl Grant was an account representative from a sister company, scheduled to visit our metropolis for a few days. Because his account was quite important to our firm, my boss wanted me to make sure his stay here was as pleasant as possible. As senior executive assistant, I usually wasn't asked to handle anything as mundane as travel arrangements.

But this time was different, the boss said. This man was different.

He was the key to a merger that had been six years in the making, and this visit was all about showing the rep how accommodating we could be. If suitably impressed, he would give the go-ahead to his superiors, and the deal would be closed.

So I made the travel arrangements for Daryl Grant as instructed. It was a simple matter; I'd done it many times before, back when I was a junior assistant.

I even agreed to meet him at the airport and drive him to his hotel. At first I thought that was a little much, but no one asked for my opinion. But I thought, *What the hell?* At least it got me out of work early.

"Take good care of Daryl Grant," my boss said as I was leaving. "Make sure he gets anything he wants."

"No problem," I said, "He'll get it."

A few days later, at the airport, I stood near the gate where Mr. Grant's flight would arrive. I held a sign with his name on it so he could identify me. Within moments the plane had arrived, and the passengers were disembarking.

I searched the eyes of every well-dressed man in his early to mid 30s, wondering which one Mr. Grant would be. The last few passengers walked out, and for a second I wondered if I was at the wrong gate. Where was Daryl Grant?

Then one last person appeared—and he was gorgeous!

Tall, at least 6 foot 1, and handsome with dark-brown hair and a clean-shaven face: He wasn't buffed out, but he inhabited his expensive suit with confidence. His body looked lean and toned in his snugly fitting clothes. His eyebrows were dark above his even darker eyes.

My mind was whirling: Was it he? No, it couldn't be! But it had to be! The man turned toward me, read my sign, and gave me a big smile full of bright white teeth.

"You must be Chris," he said.

"It's nice to meet you, Mr. Grant," I answered. "We've been expecting you."

We shook hands, and his grip was firm and warm—just like the special something between my legs that began harden just being this close to such an attractive man.

"When your boss said his secretary would meet me at the gate," Mr. Grant said as he reluctantly released my hand, "I imagined a mousy woman in her 50s, certainly not…you."

Was he coming on to me? I wasn't sure—yet.

"I'm glad you're pleased, Mr. Grant." I said. "I'm here to escort you to your hotel and to make sure all your needs are taken care of."

He gave me that award-winning smile again.

"Well, they've thought of everything, haven't they?" he asked.

"Yes, Sir," I answered with a smile of my own. "I suppose they have. If you'll come with me, please?"

"I'll be right behind you," he said.

I hope so, I thought but did not say. As I led him toward the terminal exit, I imagined being on my stomach, naked on top of a bed, with him behind me, on top of me, fucking my tight ass with his stiff cock.

Anything he wants, my boss had said. Anything he wants.

I led Mr. Grant through the crowded airport, fully aware of his eyes roaming up and down my slender 5-foot-9 form. I knew my ass cheeks were clearly visible beneath my tight slacks. I hoped he was pleased with what he saw. I was almost sure he was. I know I'm hot. I try not to have a big ego about it, but it serves me well— like this time with Daryl Grant.

I noticed he hadn't asked me to call him by his first name, and I liked it. My experience was that when I've met someone new and they ask me to use their first name, it's usually a gesture of false familiarity, implying an intimacy that doesn't exist. I hated it when people did that. But not this time—this man was Mr. Grant, the visiting executive, and I was just Chris, the subservient secretary. For some reason, I thought the distance and formality was impor-tant and needed to be maintained.

Since Mr. Grant only had a carry-on bag and no checked lug-gage, we walked out the doors leading to the parking lot. I wanted to look at his crotch but knew that would be inappropriate, at least at this point. So I contented myself with imagining his large cock nestled tightly in the briefs I pictured him wearing, the organ shift-ing slightly as he walked.

We reached the idling Town Car, where our driver had been waiting patiently for our return. Unlike me, the driver (a young guy in his 20s) was being paid by the hour, so he didn't care how long it took us. He got out and started to open the passenger door for Mr. Grant.

"That's OK," I said, "I'll do it."

"Sure thing," said the driver as he got back in the car.

I opened the door for the executive, and he grinned at me.

"Thank you, Chris," he said as he slid into the backseat of the town car. "Where are you going to sit?"

I tried not to smile.

"Where would you like me?" I asked innocently.

"If you sit back here with me, we can talk about the deal," he said.

"Great," I answered. I walked around to the other side of the car and got in, sliding next to Mr. Grant on the comfortable seat.

After reminding the driver of the hotel where Mr. Grant was booked to stay, I also said we needed some privacy. I pressed the button that raised a pane of darkened glass to separate the front seat from the back. But just before the driver disappeared on the other side of the partition, had he thrown me a knowing wink through the rear-view mirror?

I settled back in my seat. It was quite a large space, but I didn't care about all that extra room—this was one man with whom I wouldn't have minded sharing very tight quarters. He smelled nice: a combination of expensive soap and a tiny hint of flattering cologne.

"Mr. Grant," I said expectantly.

"Chris," he answered without hesitation.

There was a moment of silence when we just looked at each other, savoring each other's appearance and presence.

"You wanted to talk about the deal," I reminded him finally.

"Right!" he said suddenly. "Well, if this deal works out, I think both our firms will benefit greatly."

"My superiors certainly think so," I said.

"Do you think so?" he asked me.

"Me?" I said, surprised. "I'm just a secretary, Mr. Grant."

"Don't underestimate yourself, Chris," he said. "You've got a brain, a sharp one I'd guess. What do you think about the deal?"

I suddenly realized he had moved closer to me, sliding across the leather seat until his knee almost touched mine. Between my legs, my cock, which had softened during the walk to the car, began to reawaken. The visiting executive's heady presence was turning me on greatly. I tried to focus my attention—what had he said? He had asked me what I thought about the deal. That was it.

"I think the basic idea is good," I said, not believing that I was talking about a business deal with a visiting client who was so hot I could hardly concentrate. "But some of the details could be finessed. There's more to be gained here than my bosses seem to realize."

"Be specific," Mr. Grant said, as his hand moved to my leg and rested there. Feeling his touch was wonderful, even through a layer of fabric. I told him my ideas about the deal, and as I did, I gently took his hand in mine and brought it to my crotch. His fingers brushed against my erect cock, which was straining inside my boxers, begging for attention.

"Those are fantastic ideas," he said, "and you haven't told your boss any of them?"

"No, of course not," I said as Mr. Grant stroked my dick through my pants. It was surreal to be discussing one thing and doing something entirely different, like loosening his tie and unbuttoning the top few buttons of his shirt. "I'm just a secretary."

The executive tenderly caressed my face with the hand that wasn't between my legs. "I'm sure you're much more than that, Chris," he said. Then kissed me. His mouth was firm and strong, his tongue soft but insistent. I was on fire with desire. I pulled his shirt from his pants and slid my hands beneath it to feel the hairless planes of his chest.

The kiss ended much too soon, and we just sat there for a moment, exploring each other with our hands, looking into the other's eyes.

"So you're here to take care of my needs?" he finally asked.

"That's right," I said. "I've been instructed to give you anything you want."

There was a pause.

Then he said: "You know what I want, Chris?"

"What, Mr. Grant?"

"I want you to suck my cock," he said.

"It will be my pleasure, sir," I answered immediately.

The sexy executive leaned back against the seat and unfastened his belt. A few seconds later I had his expensive pants unzipped and pulled to his knees. His dick sharply tented the briefs beneath his pants.

First, I touched it through his underwear, feeling the hard, hot meat inside. Then I slid my fingers under the waistband and pulled it out and away from his body.

"Ah," I moaned at the sight of his beautiful uncut penis. Even though Mr. Grant's cock was hard, it hadn't yet fully emerged from its foreskin. Its pink head looked delicious, and I took it in my mouth. The executive let out a moan of pleasure as I gently massaged his cock head with my tongue. I swirled it around the knob of hard, warm flesh, wanting to make Mr. Grant feel as wonderful as he made me feel, as hot and sexy and desirable.

I wondered briefly whether the driver had figured out what we were doing back there. It didn't matter. I moved my head downward, taking more of his thick shaft into my throat until the head hit the back of my mouth.

Then I started sucking his cock, moving my head up and down so he would feel my lips and tongue caressing him in that most intimate of places.

"Mmmm," the executive murmured, letting me know he was enjoying every second of it. As I gave him the best blow job I could, he put one hand on my head, as if holding me there, not wanting me to stop. I had no intention of stopping, of course. I found it all incredibly exciting—sucking a handsome man's dick behind darkened glass in the back of a car winding through city traffic.

Mr. Grant groaned with bliss as I pleasured his dick. It was thick and long and felt fantastic in my mouth and down my throat.

With the hand that wasn't holding me up, I reached between my legs and felt my own hot man-meat. I wanted to jerk myself off until I came, but I forced myself to wait—it wasn't the time: not yet.

Pretty soon the sexy executive's breathing sped up, and I knew he was close.

"I'm gonna shoot!" he said breathlessly, and I took my mouth off him. Then I lifted his shirt up and away from his body so that when he came he wouldn't stain his expensive clothes. "Oh, yeah, man," Mr. Grant said, and shot a nice load up above his groin. He threw his head back in ecstasy, moaning out one long "Yeeeaaahhh" as the orgasm rocked his body. I watched him as he slowly recovered. He opened his eyes with a look of great satisfaction.

"Very nice," he said finally.

Mr. Grant reached up into a ceiling compartment and brought out a hand towel. I glanced out the window while he cleaned himself up and got his pants back on. It had gotten dark already.

"We're just about there," I said, and moments later we pulled into the driveway of a very nice hotel. It was the place my company always provided for visiting clients and executives, much more expensive than I could afford.

As soon as our driver stopped the car, young sexy boys employed by the hotel stepped forward to greet us—opening the doors for us, taking Mr. Grant's bag.

"Would you accompany me to my room?" the executive asked me.

"I'd be delighted," I replied.

I thanked our driver and told him he was done for the night. He gave me a knowing grin and thanked me, too.

Mr. Grant and I checked in, and the hotel boy carrying his bag led us up to a penthouse suite overlooking the city. It was a gorgeous room, beautiful and comfortable, with only one bed. The executive tipped the boy—very generously, to judge by the grin on the boy's face—and ushered him out, closing the door behind him.

I walked out to the balcony and looked out at the shining cityscape.

"Nice view," Mr. Grant said from behind me.

"Yes," I agreed, "the city's really pretty at night."

"I meant you, not the city," he said, joining me on the balcony.

"Thank you," I said, surprised. We stood there for a few minutes watching the view.

"Anything I want?" Mr. Grant asked finally.

"Anything you want," I answered.

"I want to get rimmed while I look at the city."

"My pleasure," I said as I reached for his belt buckle. I unfastened it and unzipped his pants, letting them drop to the floor. I removed his shoes and socks and put them neatly by the bed. His pants I folded and hung in the closet on a hanger.

When I turned back to the balcony, I saw the most beautiful ass I'd ever seen waiting for me. I joined Mr. Grant and knelt down behind him, feeling his butt with my hands. The double moons of his cheeks were firm and strong mounds of flesh, yet the skin that covered them was smooth and soft. I kneaded them with my fingers, gently caressing them. The executive exhaled with pleasure: "Aahhh…"

Then I pulled his cheeks apart and smelled him. His asshole was fragrant, rich with musk and light sweat. I brought my face close, flaring my nostrils as I inhaled his odors deeply.

Wetting my lips with my tongue, I pushed in deeper, actually between the cheeks. Then I licked his asshole, running my tongue up its entire length and then down. Mr. Grant murmured with bliss and approval. I continued licking him, every few seconds pushing my puckering lips against his hole. I wanted him to experience not just pleasure but different pleasures, a variety of sensual delights for him to savor.

When his hole was sufficiently moistened, I pushed my tongue against his asshole, gently seeking entrance. The ring of muscle that surrounded his hole was tight, but after a few minutes it began to give way, just a bit. I was patient—the night was long.

Little by little I worked my tongue until I could push it inside him, inside his butt. It was a sublime feeling. I made love to the man's asshole, using my tongue to fuck him gently but insistently. I know Mr. Grant liked it because he pushed his butt back toward me, as if wanting more and more of me inside him. Actually, *like* isn't strong enough a word: I think he loved it!

"Oh, man," he said, "This is living—a gorgeous view to look at, and a gorgeous man to give me anything I want." I stopped rimming him long enough to ask, "How has your trip been so far, Mr. Grant?"

"Pretty damn fantastic so far, Chris," he immediately replied. "You better stop. I don't want to come again yet." I obeyed, leaving his beautiful ass reluctantly, and stood up. The handsome man took me in his arms and kissed my lips. I could feel his excited breathing.

"I want you to make love to me," he whispered in my ear.

"Yes, sir," I said happily. "I've been hoping you would."

I took him to the bed and asked him to lie down on his back. I quickly stripped off my clothes and left them in a pile on the floor. Then I joined the hunky man on top of the bed and lay next to him, kissing his arms and shoulders with tenderly puckered lips.

Mr. Grant rubbed his leg against my hard cock, making it even more anxious and excited. "I love the feeling of your mouth on my body," he said as I continued to kiss him. With my lips I worked my way up to his neck, which I licked as if I were a thirsty dog. Soon enough, I was at his chin, and then I kissed him properly on the lips. The visiting executive sighed with pleasure as I pushed my tongue gently into his mouth. His own tongue found mine, and they started to dance together, exploring each other tentatively at first, then more forcefully.

Mr. Grant pulled me on top of him. My cock seemed to stretch even longer, as if being this close to the other man's asshole was making it hungrier than ever.

"Lie on me," he said when he realized I was still supporting myself on my hands at his sides. "I want to feel your whole weight on me." I obeyed, letting my body gently settle onto his hard,. toned chest and abdomen, which felt wonderful beneath me.

"Make love to me, Chris," he whispered huskily, "I want you inside me."

I needed no more convincing. I slid back to the edge of the bed and reached down for my pants. When I found them, I pulled the condoms and tiny bottle of lube I'd brought out of my pocket. Kneeling back on the bed, I opened one of the square foil packets and pulled out the latex sheath.

I gently unrolled the condom over my hard dick, and I was

ready for action! Crawling back over on top of the executive, I split his legs apart and pulled him to me until my cock was at his asshole. Squirting some lube into my hand, I used it to slick my dick. I lifted the hot man's legs into the air and rested them on my shoulders.

"Are you ready, sir?" I asked him.

"Yes, Chris," he said. "Do it."

I pushed my dick into his asshole, and he closed his eyes.

"Yeah, that's it," he said. "Fuck me!"

Mr. Grant wanted to be fucked, and it was my job to make sure he got everything he wanted. It was fantastic to make love to him this way, sliding my cock in and then pulling back, then going in again. He breathed deeply and sighed beneath me, overcome with passion. It felt so wonderful, for both of us I guess, but that level of intensity was impossible to maintain for very long.

The executive grabbed his cock in one hand and started jacking himself off. My own delicious friction inside was building up to takeoff very quickly.

"I'm coming, Chris!" Mr. Grant said.

"Me too!" I answered as I pulled out of his ass. Yanking the condom off, I jerked myself the rest of the way—together, the executive and I climaxed and shot loads of hot semen all over his chest. Our yells of ecstasy and release mingled, then slowly died as the bursts of pleasure faded into blissful afterglow. We looked at each other, still panting and trying to catch our breaths. Then I got off him and lay down next to him.

"I want you to hold me while I sleep," Daryl Grant said.

"Anything you want," I whispered in his ear as I wrapped my arms around him. "Anything you want."

Pump It, Punk

Jay Starre

D ave had turned 18 only a few months earlier. He had started the job on a construction crew as an inexperienced laborer, which won him the worst job of all: pump boy. The excavation for the skyscraper was deep, and with the rains of autumn, there was a continual need for pumps to clear any water from the hole being carved beneath the city streets. Dave manned those pumps throughout his shift, ankle deep in mud.

Greg was one of the carpenters, loud and aggressive and too good-looking for his own ego. Dave was the object of his attentions, and he suffered the brunt of Greg's ceaseless mocking banter. In truth, Greg thought the youngster was cute as hell, with short blond hair and a slim but taut body, not to mention his hot pair of buns and the sweet lips below his button nose. But Greg wasn't about to express those feelings openly.

"Hey, Pump Boy, get your feet out of the muck and get your ass in gear!" Greg bellowed at the innocent lad. "Those pumps need priming! Move that lazy ass, move it!" The lad's response was to obey with alacrity, hoping to impress the foreman with his performance (and to retain his job).

Greg loved the way the teen responded to his words. He got a big hard-on beneath his work jeans as he watched Dave splash screening through the mud, bending over to prime the pumps, and straining to haul the heavy hoses from puddle to puddle. Greg had to admit the kid was a hardworking little bitch.

A week into Dave's stint at the jobsite, Greg discovered the comely youth behind a bin in the alley, where he was relieving himself, blanketing the filthy stones with a stream of piss. Greg quickly sidled up to the young man,whipped out his own meat, and began to add more golden flow to the rill already rushing down the gutter.

Dave's pretty blue eyes batted in nervous wonder as he sneaked a glance at the enormous girth of the older laborer's spraying prong. It was huge! After that first peek, Dave couldn't take his eyes off it. His own stalk grew in his hands the longer he stared. All at once he was standing there in the alley with a hard-on at full attention, his gaze riveted to the other man's cock.

Greg leaned in and growled in Dave's ear, "See something you like, Pump Boy? Perhaps something you'd like to have pumping up your sweet ass?" The shocked young man took a step back: His astonishment at Greg's prodigious prong had been the only thing on his mind.

"Sorry, man!" he blurted out as he stuffed his lonely boner into his jeans and scurried off. Greg's harsh laughter tailed him, ringing in his ears.

Greg watched that pretty little can pumping double-time as the young laborer rushed back to his job in the pit. He resolved then and there to have that ass before the day was out. He managed to spend a few minutes down in the muddy hole several times over the course of the rainy afternoon, always quick to offer Dave a word or two.

"Hey, Pump Boy, work those hoses like I know you can!" Greg growled to Dave as he passed by, hard at work dragging hoses.

"Pump Boy, you look good—bent over with your ass in the air and your face in the mud!" he chortled another time, when Dave was bent over a pump, trying to get it working as water sprayed everywhere.

It was quitting time and getting dark when Greg made his move. "Hey, Pump Boy, get your butt up here," he ordered. "We gotta clean up this fucking mess before you can go home!" he called down to the mud-splattered young blond.

Though he was tired from work and wanted to go home, Dave

was eager to please and willing to comply. He looked like an excited puppy when he arrived at the wood-strewn construction site where Greg was waiting for him.

No one else was there. Darkness hovered over the two of them as they piled broken boards and discarded metal. Dave was bent over his task when Greg went for him. His grin was feral as he took in the sight of that perky ass beneath tight jeans bent over in front of him. Greg pulled up his shirt to expose his brawny chest, which glistened with sweat in the dim light. Then it was nothing for Greg to reach out and clasp the young man by the shoulders, hauling him up from behind in a heavy bear hug.

"What's going on?" Dave managed to gasp, shaking in fear as he felt the brawny arms of the older laborer lock around him. And he shuddered when he felt Greg's hard shaft poking between his spread butt cheeks.

"How about an end-of-the-day pump?" Greg growled in Dave's ear. "You know what I mean, Pump Boy!" His big hands slid down Dave's lean torso and into the front of his jeans, feeling for and finding a semi-stiff and rapidly growing piece of man meat.

"I don't know what you're talking about!" Dave squealed breathlessly as Greg's big, callused hands gripped his boner and sent quivers of desire coursing through his entire body. He was still protesting when Greg spun him around. The young man suddenly found his mouth buried in a massive hairy chest. Greg released Dave's cock and gripped the back of the cute blond's head, forcing his mouth directly over his pec and one brown nipple.

Dave mumbled incoherently as his mouth was pressed to the hard flesh of Greg's manly chest. The crinkled hair tasted strongly of sweat and male odor. The warm nipple Greg forced between his lips was incredibly pliable. Amazingly, it was growing larger as he reflexively began to suck on it while continuing to mutter feeble, half-hearted protests.

"Take it like a man—you know you love it!" Greg chortled heartily as he ripped open Dave's fly and shoved his pants down to his knees. Only white boxers shielded Dave's tender privates from

Greg's brutal assault. Greg was still chortling as he reached behind the young man and shoved his beefy hand right down into those boxers. His hand found Dave's deep ass crevice and wedged its way between the hard cheeks, inexorably searching out the small, palpitating butthole hiding there. Greg finally discovered the little pucker with one of his thick, filthy fingers. Then, without a moment's pause, he rammed his digit past Dave's defeated sphincter and into the spongy warmth beyond.

Dave squealed like a stuck pig, but once more his protest was muffled by Greg's hairy chest and the taut brown nipple shoved between his lips. He mewled with a mixture of agony and intense pleasure as Greg's finger dug deep into him, frigging in and out, teasing his prostate and the sensitive rim of his butthole in a feverish rhythm that left him breathless.

"Nice butthole, Pump Boy!" Greg said approvingly. "Nice and tight, but it has possibilities. It's already opening up like a warm little twat should! But I know my big dick ain't gonna fit up there without some kind of lube, so get down on your knees and polish my knob before it goes up your sweet slot!"

Dave was aghast at what he had heard. The mammoth cock he had seen earlier in the day up his cherry asshole—that was impossible! But something in his guts, warm with yearning, was taking control of his will. He could have broken away from the brawny construction worker: he was agile and tough. But the nipple in his mouth tasted wonderful, and that rutting finger up his butthole caused delicious sensations throughout his entire lower body. His own cock was rock-hard, putting the lie to any thoughts he may have entertained about not wanting this encounter.

Greg had no qualms at all. He loved having his finger up the younger man's snug asshole. The thought of reaming out that tight ass with his hard cock was far too enticing to pass up. The sweet young thing was putty in his hands, for all his mumbled protests. Dave's sweet lips were sucking away on his nipple while his asshole was quivering delightfully around Greg's fat finger. He was sure the kid was going to love every minute of the royal fucking Greg was going to give him. With that agreeable thought in mind, Greg shoved Dave to his knees, amused at Dave's stunned expression as he tore open his own fly and whipped out his giant bone.

"Wrap your lips around this!" Greg instructed. "Get it nice and sloppy wet. Remember: It's gotta slide up your tight asshole, so make it real slippery, Pump Boy!" Greg laughed down at Dave's wide-eyed face.

Dave shuddered, but was drawn to the purple pole wagging in his face. When a hand gripped the short curls of his blond hair and pulled him forward, his words of protest were laughable. "Please, no, I can't lick that big thing," he begged. But then his tongue tasted the bulbous head and he began to purr with pleasure as the giant cock slid into his gaping mouth. Dave managed not to gag as Greg pressed that prong into the back of his mouth, but he nearly fainted from the taste and smell of hot male flesh. Hairy nuts banged against his chin, and the funk of Greg's sweaty crotch suffused his nostrils. That giant pole inside his mouth was hot and hard, and he had to admit he liked having it there.

Then there was the thought of the thing going up his tender asshole, the sweet little pucker quivering between his kneeling thighs. Dave moaned with surrender. Realizing he was going to get it, he decided he had best get Greg's fence post good and slick so it wouldn't tear apart his sweet cherry bum. He started sucking that shlong like there was no tomorrow.

"That's a good man!" Greg murmured encouragingly. "Slick it up real good! Get it ready to pump your butt! This hose is gonna fill your guts, and you're gonna love it!" Greg huffed with the awesome pleasure induced by those sweet lips and the twirling tongue working his hard knob and shaft.

Greg yanked Dave back to his feet by his hair, all the while laughing at the young man's whimpers and faint cries of dismay. His blue eyes flashed wildly as Greg lifted one of his legs and yanked his pants off over his filthy boots, leaving them to dangle from his other leg. Greg embraced Dave again, this time from the front, planting a sloppy kiss on his wet mouth and holding one thigh up between

Dave's legs so that the boy's exposed asshole gaped open. Dan was at the mercy of any assault Greg cared to make—and Greg cared to make one! Greg's free hand was behind Dave's back, and it moved swiftly toward its target. Fingers found the spread butt crack and zeroed in on the small, puckered ass opening. Greg rammed two of his chunk digits into the tender hole—deaf to Dave's muffled cry and heedless of the tight aperture's snapping resistance.

Greg broke their lip-lock long enough to shove the fingers that had just been up Dave's butt into the boys pleading mouth. "Get them wet so I can pump your ass with them!" Greg ordered hoarsely.

Dave swallowed the two fingers, sloppily kissing and licking them, and deposited copious amounts of slick spit all over them. He wanted them very wet when they invaded his aching butt again. The violation had hurt like hell, but it had sent him to heaven. He knew he wanted those two fingers back inside him. And he began to hope for more.

"Good, little Pump Boy. Now you got the idea!" Greg laughed, removing his fingers from the sucking mouth and promptly moving them behind Dave's back and right up into his quivering crack. Wet with spit, they slid easily into the eager boy's snug pussy. Both men gasped as the digits sunk to the knuckle, lifting Dave slightly off the floor in the process.

Greg toyed with Dave's hole for a few minutes, kissing the moaning young man. Then he abruptly released him, steeped back, and dropped his own jeans. He was grinned fiercely as he commanded the younger man to bend to his will.

"Bend over, Pump Boy. Spread your cheeks and get ready for the pump of your life!" He held his giant meat in one brawny hand, the purple flesh erect and dangerous.

Dave knew he should be running for his life, but instead he whimpered piteously and turned to obey. His face was aflame with lust and embarrassment as he spread his own thighs, bent over, and placed his hands on his knees. He was shaking with terror and excitement as he waited for Greg's next move. He wasn't going to be disappointed.

Hairy legs moved up between Dave's parted smooth ones. Hard muscle enveloped him from behind, and big brawny hands gripped his shoulders. A large knob of burning flesh pressed into his slick ass crack. Wet and slippery, the missile found its target, settling at the spongy entrance to his asshole. Dave held his breath, expecting the worst, but at the same time realizing he wanted it more than anything he had ever wanted before.

Greg stared down at his eager little ass-lackey. Dave's rump shone a pristine white in the faint light from the surrounding buildings. Greg admired the shadow cast by his own colossal cock: In silhouette, he looked like a baseball player up to bat! The compliant position of Dave's body was a total turn-on. For all his moaning, the pump boy wanted to get fucked—and fucked he was going to get! In the midst of this woolgathering, Greg suddenly felt he was in no hurry, knowing full well how big his cock was and how much effort it would require of anyone who attempted to take it up his ass, especially a tight young virgin like Dave.

He left off his musing to return to the task at hand. Grinning broadly, he began to press lightly, then pulled back and pressed forward again in short lunges. He felt Dave's body responding, and was delighted to hear the boy's little gasps and mewls of pleasure as his sensitive butt rim struggled to accommodate the plump cock head. The tapered knob began to dip past the first sphincter, spreading Dave's pussy wide. Spit eased the penetration as it began. When half the crowned knob was inside, Dave suddenly clamped his asshole over it in a spasm of fear and eagerness. They both shouted out their agony and pleasure before Greg made his move and rammed his hips forward.

"Take that, Pump Boy!" he cried as he buried the entire head of his cock in Dave's virgin anal passage. Dave gasped and wiggled, which pulled another inch of Greg's cock into his tight fuck tunnel. Greg took over at that point, sliding the spit-slathered pole deeper, then pulling it out slightly before shoving another inch inside.

Dave's butt pit was fiery hot and tight as a vise. Satiny butt flesh and quivering anal muscle enveloped Greg's invading pole. Both men focused all their attention on the juncture of their bodies—

cock and asshole—and before they knew it, they were moving back and forth in a pumping rhythm of pleasure. The scene developed into an all-out fuck, their bodies slamming together with a frantic pounding that had them both screaming.

"Yeah, feel that fat hose up your hole, Pump Boy!" Greg shouted, not caring that anyone in the surrounding buildings might hear them.

Dave had also become crazed. He shouted back at the brawny construction worker, "Pump my butt! Pump Boy wants his ass filled to the max with big fat cock! Pump me good!"

Greg would have laughed at that if he had the breath for it. As it was, he was gasping for air as he pummeled the young man with all he had. He was amazed to see Dave return every thrust with equal force. The friction around his burning cock was amazing. He could not last.

"I'm hosing you good! Feel my spunk up your cherry hole!" Greg grunted, sweat flying from his forehead, and he gripped Dave's shoulders to keep his balance while he sprayed jism deep inside Dave's squirming butthole.

Dave reveled in the sensation of that pumping cock up his guts. The feeling of power he experienced as he milked Greg's come right out of him was enough to get his own stiff cock ready to erupt. With a quick swipe of a spit-swabbed hand, he worked out a load of his own as Greg rammed him deep and filled him with man juice.

They both fell to the filthy floor in a heap of tangled limbs. Greg's cock still pumped spunk into Dave's twitching twat while Dave's cock leaked come over his bare thighs and onto the floor beneath. They lay together gasping for breath.

Finally, it was Dave who spoke. "All pumped out?" he asked, giggling, as he turned his head to kiss the older man full on the lips.

Greg had to laugh. The kid was a good sport—and his ass was heaven-sent. Greg vowed he would have to sample it again very soon. *Definitely sooner rather than later,* he thought as his cock began to swell where it was still buried: deep in Dave's tender ass.

The Wrestling Match

Cage Crawford

Billy Campbell threw open the door to the refrigerator, peered inside, and smiled. "Bingo!" he announced as he reached inside to grab two cans of beer left over from one of his parent's card games. "Look what I found."

"No way!" Digger McCandless cheered. "Are you gonna get into trouble for taking these?"

"Shit," Billy said, kicking the door closed with his foot, "they won't even remember these were in here in the first place. Come on, let's go up to my room."

The boys raced up the stairs two at a time. When they reached the top, Digger lingered to check out the family portrait. "Man," he said, "your sister is one hot bitch."

Billy frowned. "She would cut your dick off if she heard you call her that," he said, then grinned. "But she *is* a bitch. Try living with her."

"I'd love to," Digger said slyly. "Man, I got a rock in my pants just thinkin' about it, dude."

"Man, that's sick. She's my sister."

Billy led Digger into his room, a standard-looking hangout for a 18-year-old. There were trophies from all the sports Billy had played at one time or another as well posters for NASCAR drivers and one of Brady Anderson of the Baltimore Orioles. Digger eyed the poster of Anderson and smirked.

"Did you hear he was a fag?" he asked.

"Fuck you," Billy said as he set his beer can down on his desk. "He's not a fag."

"Oh, yeah? That's not what I heard. I hear that he likes to take it up the ass. They say he likes it rough."

"You wish," Billy said, looking over at the poster of his hero. He felt warm all of a sudden, and tried to break the moment. "You wanna hear some music?"

"What ya got?" Digger asked, eyeing the CD collection in a corner.

"Whatever. All kinds of shit. Pick something out."

"Madonna?" Digger questioned as he scanned the alphabetized collection.

"What? She's hot."

Digger looked over his shoulder at his buddy. "I don't know about you, Campbell. Brady Anderson on your wall and Madonna in your music collection—you sure you don't like show tunes too?"

"Suck my dick, McCandless," Billy snapped defensively. He grabbed his package for effect—and to hide the embarrassment he suddenly felt.

"You'd like that, wouldn't you?" Digger retorted. He wiggled his ass teasingly at his buddy.

Billy snorted and turned away. "I think you're the one who'd like it, fag."

"Don't start, Campbell. Or I'll have to take you down."

Billy let out a loud cackle. "Yeah right. Just try it, tough guy."

"That sounds like an invitation," Digger taunted. "Don't tempt me, big guy."

"Whatever," Billy said, turning to put in the Dave Matthews CD his buddy had chosen. Digger looked around the room.

"So, when do you expect the parental units to be home?" he asked.

Billy shrugged. "Not until late. They went to one of my Dad's company's dinner parties. They never get home until after midnight."

"So—we got the place all to ourselves, then?"

"Yeah," Billy said, intrigued by his friend's mischievous tone. For some reason, it sent a chill down his spine. In fact, he almost shuddered. "Um… Beth's staying with Cindy Brimfield, so it's just you and me." He considered for a moment, then quickly added, "Cowboy."

Digger looked at him for a moment, then replied, "How cozy." He lifted his arm over his head and sniffed his armpit. "Damn! That's rank. Hey, you mind if I get a shower soon, dude? I smell."

"Yeah, you do," Billy said, laughing. "Go ahead."

Digger pulled his shirt over his head. His chest was taut and muscular from playing on the team, and Billy stole a few quick glances at his friend's physique. And though he didn't let on, Digger noticed that Billy noticed. When he shucked his pants off and stood only in his briefs, he caught Billy's eye. "Quit staring at my dick, queer."

"Whatever," Billy said, blowing it off. "I've already seen your shit in the shower anyway. And trust me, it's *no* big deal."

"You wish! I got you beat any day of the week, toothpick dick." To prove his boast, he grabbed his own package and squeezed it.

"Whatever," Billy said. He couldn't quite put his finger on it, but there was something in the way Digger was fucking with him that was making his heart beat a little faster—and making his hands shake. As he watched Digger scout around for a towel, Billy slipped his own shirt over his head. He thought for a moment, then reached down to unsnap his jeans. Noticing the look on Digger's face, he quickly explained. "I'll get a shower after you."

On his way to the bathroom, Digger noticed a stack of magazines beside the bed. "Hey, what's this?" On closer inspection, he realized what had caught his eye. On top of the pile was a copy of *Hustler.* "Shit, where'd you get this?"

"From my dad," Billy said. "I snuck it out of his room."

"Shit," Digger said, flipped straight to the centerfold. "Damn, she's hot."

"If you like fake tits and platinum-blond hair," Billy said. Digger looked at him quizzically for a moment, then returned to the magazine. He turned the page.

"This is hot," he said.

"Thought you were gonna get a shower."

"In a minute. Fuckin A! Look at this guy's dick, man. Did you see this, dude?"

"Yeah," Billy said. "Huge, isn't it?"

"Betcha that thing is about nine inches, man. Look how big around it is. That shit is fat!"

Billy stood next to Digger, and when he glanced down at the other boy's crotch, he saw that Digger's bulge had grown to full size. His prick was clearly visible beneath his tighty-whities. Digger let his free hand drop between his legs and absentmindedly began to pull at his fly. Billy cocked an eye. "Yeah," he said, "I thought you would like that."

Digger looked at him for a moment, then suddenly tossed the magazine aside and jumped on top of Billy.

"Them's fightin' words, Campbell," he said, wrestling Billy to the floor, surprising his friend with his speed. He pinned Billy's arms above his head and smiled down at his buddy. "Take it back," he leered without much conviction. "Take it back, or else I'm gonna hurt your pretty white ass."

"Promises, promises," Billy said as he brought his knee up between Digger's legs with just enough force to send his buddy off him.

"Yeoooow," Digger cried. He clamped his hands to his nuts.

"You think you can take me, big guy?" Billy said, egging on the other boy. "Take your best shot then."

Digger looked up from his balls—which were fine—and paused for a moment. "Fuck it," he said with a shrug. He moved to get up.

"Chickenshit," Billy said under his breath, hoping Digger would take the bait.

And like any 18-year-old boy only too eager to prove his manhood, Digger did just that. He lunged at Billy again and brought him down to the floor. Billy quickly snaked his free arm around Digger's and pulled the other boy's hand out from under him, bringing Digger down to the floor and on top of him. Billy slid out from under Digger, grabbed him from behind, and pinned one arm behind the other boy's back. Digger brought one of his legs up and quickly pushed Billy aside. Then he reached out to grab the boy's waist but could only manage to hook his fingers onto Billy's briefs. Digger pulled down hard, bringing the underwear down to the other boy's thighs and causing Billy to fall over.

"Get off me, fag," Billy said through his laughter. But Digger was quick and yanked the briefs down and over Billy's ankles, then held them up in the air, dangling them like a worm on a hook.

"You lookin' for these, kiddo?" Digger asked.

Billy turned around—sporting a pretty obvious boner. Digger eyed it for a moment. Billy thought he saw Digger lick his lips, and he was sure his own face had gone red.

Digger looked into his buddy's face. "You care to explain that thing?"

"It was the magazine, that's all," Billy shrugged, then lunged for his briefs. Digger was faster and pulled his arm back. Billy landed on the floor with a thud. Digger chuckled, then snapped the briefs against Billy's smooth white ass.

"Ouch!" Billy yelped. He turned over quickly and made another lunge for his underwear. This time he managed to grab Digger and brought himself down on top of his buddy. He tried not to attend to the sensations that shot through his erection as it smashed against his friend's hairy leg—but the sensations were too good to ignore. He snatched his briefs from Digger's hand and brought the crotch of them down hard on the other boy's face. "Here," he growled through his heavy breathing. "Sniff it, you fuckin' punk! Smell my balls. Isn't that what you wanted?" As he held his briefs over Digger's nose, Billy pushed up against the other boy again, causing a drop of precome to ooze out of the end of his prick.

"Foomck yoooooou," Digger mumbled as he struggled under

the pungent Calvins stretched across his face. He reached up and jerked Billy's arm away, took a breath, then pushed Billy back against the bed. As Digger tried to get up, Billy reached for him and in one swift jerk brought Digger's briefs down hard.

"Dickwad!" Digger shouted, looking down at the trail of Billy's precome on his leg and hip.

Billy laughed as he pointed at the sticky goo oozing out of Digger's cock as well. "Dickwad is right!"

"That's it," Digger said, wiping the cock snot off with his hands. "You're over now."

Before Billy knew it, Digger was on top of him. The boys wrestled and pressed their bodies together as their throbbing rods leaked steadily. Billy caught a whiff of the sweat they were working up; despite his efforts to ignore his arousal, the aroma caused his dick to twitch even more enthusiastically. Then Digger rolled on top of Billy, and both boys gasped as their cocks slid together. The erotic contact sent shivers through their bodies.

There was a moment of silence, except for the heavy rasp of their breathing. Neither boy moved as they stared into each other's eyes. Digger looked down between them. Their hard cocks pressed firmly together, and spider webs of precome glistened in the light from Billy's desk lamp. He smiled, then looked again into Billy's eyes.

"Looks like we both got a little carried away there," he said in a barely audible voice.

Billy listened to their breathing, not knowing what to say. He loved the way his cock felt as it rubbed against Digger's, and he didn't want the feeling to end. Despite himself, he squeezed out a quiet "Yeah."

"That magazine got me all turned on too," Digger replied. He paused for a moment, then said, "I should probably take care of this." With that, he reached down, wrapped his hand around his cock, and began to gently stroke it. Billy looked down between them and stared at his friend's pumping hand as it brushed back and forth across his own stone-hard boner.

After a moment of this, Digger spoke again. "Might as well take care of yours while I'm down there." He grabbed Billy's rod and pressed it firmly against his own. Billy drew in a deep breath and closed his eyes. The feeling was incredible. Digger chuckled nervously and began to move his hand slowly up and down the length of both their rock-hard shafts. He rested his head in the nape of Billy's neck. His mouth was only inches from his buddy's ear.

"Jesus," Billy whispered. He was amazed how much he loved the friction their cocks created.

"No, just Digger."

Billy laughed, then asked, "You sure you know what you're doing?"

"Shit," Digger said as he continued to pump. "I do this at least twice a day. Sometimes three, when I'm real horned up. I damn well better know by now, don't ya think?"

"I didn't mean that. I meant—I don't know. This feels weird, you jerking us off like that. I mean—"

Digger cut him off. "Shhhhh. You don't tell anyone, I don't either. It's as simple as that, got it? It's just two guys getting off with each other. Anyway, doesn't mean anything."

"Uh, yeah," Billy said. At that moment he would have agreed to just about anything, even though everything in his body told him there was more between them than Digger allowed.

Digger lifted his head, looked down at his friend, and studied the slight smile on Billy's lips. He swallowed, then said, "You ever kiss another dude?"

Billy opened his eyes to look up at Digger. "No. Why? Have you?"

"Once, " Digger said. "My cousin Brett. He was staying with us one time, and he was talking about how he kissed the girls he was dating. I was, like, 12 years old. He started talking about what it was like, and I was pretty curious, asked all kinds of questions, until he just said he would show me. And he did."

Billy blinked as he digested the words. He was almost afraid to ask, but he was too curious not to. "What did you think?"

"It was weird. He hadn't shaved for a day or so, and I could feel the stubble on his chin and above his lip, but it was—nice, I guess. He was pretty good at it."

Digger gazed at Billy and started to lean forward. Something in Billy's stomach fell, as if he were on a roller coaster that had just gone down a huge drop. Digger brought his lips down gently on top of his, and Billy didn't have time to think about it. Instead, he found himself kissing his friend back softly until Digger pulled away. Digger sought Billy's eyes again.

"Better than your cousin?" Billy asked.

"I don't know. That was just a taste."

They leaned into each other. Suddenly, the two friends were kissing passionately. Their mouths pressed firmly together, as they each began to explore the other's body in their passionate embrace. Billy sucked Digger's lower lip into his mouth, and Digger sighed audibly. Their tongues snaked into each other's mouths. Billy couldn't recall a time when he'd felt more alive.

Digger stopped stroking them off and began to hump his cock against Billy's. They kissed with increasing intensity. Billy's fingertips and toes tingled with sensations he'd never felt before. The scent of their adolescent sweat began to drive him as crazy. It had a similar effect on Digger.

"Man," Digger said, pulling back. "You *are* better than my cousin. A whole lot better. And…" He stopped for a moment, as if unsure of himself. "And better than any of my girlfriends too."

"Thanks," Billy said. "I like this, too—"

Digger crushed Billy's last words as he pressed his lips against Billy's for another go-round. After a few moments of kissing Billy's mouth, Digger began to blaze a trail of kisses to the side of the other boy's face. He kissed Billy's cheek, his neck, and sucked his earlobe into his mouth. Billy moaned and pulled Digger's head closer to his. Digger slipped his tongue into Billy's ear. It was clean and pleasant, and Digger nibbled on the lobe some more. He opened his mouth wide and sucked the entire ear into his mouth. Billy moaned from underneath him.

"Fuck," Billy cried out. He was suddenly overcome with the desire to have his mouth all over his friend's body. "Come here!"

"Huh?"

"I said, come here!" He yanked on Digger's arm, pulling the other boy back to his mouth. Billy spat into his hand and reached down between their legs to find their dripping rods. He wrapped his slick hand around their tools and began to move it up and down. Digger squirmed against him. Billy kissed his buddy as deeply as he could while he massaged their boners with his wet hand.

"Now," he said, pulling away again, "I want to taste something else." He kissed his way down Digger's chin, his neck, his chest, pausing to suck one of Digger's pink nipples into his mouth. Digger cried out, and Billy brought his teeth gently together around the nipple.

"Shit!" Digger howled.

Billy continued to feast on Digger's chest. He licked one nipple, then the other. Digger grabbed his head and pressed Billy's face harder against his sternum. "Yeah. Eat my chest. Come on!"

Billy slid further down Digger's body until he stared down the barrel of Digger's unbelievably hard prick. He looked up at his best friend.

"Seven inches of manhood," Digger joked. "Come on, dude. Suck it. I dare you."

Instead, Billy stuck his tongue out and lapped up the drop of precome pooling in Digger's piss slit. He licked his way down the pole as if it was an ice-cream cone. Digger squirmed from beneath him, and Billy took it as his cue to put the other boy's cock into his mouth. As the head slid into his mouth, Billy thought about how odd it felt—rubbery and slick, but hot at the same time, like it was supposed to be there or something. As he slid Digger's cock farther into his virgin mouth, he closed his eyes and began to savor his first blow job. He swirled his tongue around the rigid pole and swallowed the steady ooze leaking from the tip of Digger's tool. With astonishment, he realized he liked the taste. He wondered what a whole mouthful of spunk would taste like.

"Oh, shit, man," Digger moaned from above. "Damn, that is soooo good, bro."

Billy really got into it as the scene heated up. He found he could bring Digger close to coming—a couple of times he felt his buddy's balls retract and his back arch—then pull away just in time so that Digger had to wait a while.

"I can't take much more of that," Digger said finally. "You're killing me. My balls have got to be bluer than a Smurf's."

Billy laughed at the joke. "They do look rather purplish. But I like them." To prove his point, he sucked one into his mouth. Digger arched his back and pulled down on Billy's head.

"Yeah," he cried. "Lick my nuts, man. That's hot."

"You smell good," Billy said. "Like sweat and—I guess like balls. I like it."

"Yeah? I always thought it was a weird smell. Let me sniff you."

Billy brought himself around so that his cock pointed straight at Digger's eye. Digger looked at it for a moment, then wrapped his hand around the shaft and gave it a hearty tug. He lifted it down toward him and moved his head in to get a whiff of his buddy's pubes. He took a big sniff. The heady odor shot through his nose and filled his head. *Boy sweat,* Digger thought, surprised by how much it turned him on.

He pulled away and peered at the dick in his hand, trying to decide whether he could go through with sucking it. "Don't shoot in my mouth," he warned. Then he opened his mouth and sucked Billy into him.

"Christ!" Billy squealed. He'd never been with anyone before—man or woman, and his session with Digger was driving him up the wall. He couldn't believe how much he was getting off on being with Digger, who'd been his friend for as long as he could remember. They'd virtually grown up together, and now they were sucking each other's cocks. *If this doesn't make us queer,* Billy thought as he slid his mouth around Digger's cock again, *I don't know what does.*

Digger was thinking the same thing as he wrestled with Billy's cock in his mouth. He wasn't sure why he liked it so much, but as he felt it slide deeper and deeper into his mouth, he found himself turned on by the hardness of it, by the way his lips were pressed against it, the way it felt sliding in and out of his mouth.

"Oh, man," Billy said as he came up for air. He knew he couldn't hold out much longer. "Digger, you gotta stop now. Do you hear me? Shit, man, I'm gonna shoot my wad."

Digger heard the words, but they sounded far away. He was engrossed in giving head to his buddy—and in the fan-fucking-tastic friction of another boy's cock in his mouth. For an instant, he considered whether he should stop sucking Billy's rod, but just as quickly as the thought entered his mind, it was gone. He clamped his lips even more tightly around the base of Billy's prick and sniffed some more of the heady aroma of his friend's balls. He swallowed the dick in his mouth whole.

"Dude, that's it!" Billy exclaimed. He tried to hold back, but an orgasm began to overpower him. He slammed his hips against Digger's mouth, shoving his cock far down his friend's throat, and unleashed the biggest load of his life into the warm, wet cavern that engulfed his throbbing cock.

At first, the flood of warm spunk jolted Digger out of his sucking reverie, and he almost gagged on it. But when he realized what was happening, he relaxed his throat and swallowed the first blast. He pulled back just enough to catch the second load as it spewed onto his tongue, then swallowed it down as well. He suddenly felt his own nuts swelling and moaned as he reached down to jerk off his cock.

Billy caught on quickly and swatted Digger's hand away. He pulled Digger's throbbing member into his mouth just in time to catch the first blast.

"Mmmmmmmmmph!" Digger moaned as he swallowed the last drop of Billy's potent load. Then he shot his own wad into Billy's mouth with five forceful spurts.

Billy tried to swallow all of it, but it was just too much. Some of it ran out of the sides of his mouth, but he did his best and managed to get most of it. It was bitter and sweet at the same time—

like nothing he'd ever tasted before. He wasn't sure he liked it at first, but after the last bit of it shot into his mouth, he decided it was not that bad.

Each boy was reluctant to relinquish the other's cock at first. Instead, they kept sucking as their erections subsided, then they lay panting beside each other on the floor. Digger lay his hand on Billy's chest, ran his fingers over Billy's sweaty flesh, and pinched a nipple between his fingertips.

Neither boy spoke at first. Each was afraid words might destroy the moment, might bring them back to the real world. Both of them wanted to stay in the moment as long as possible. They wondered whether they would feel guilty if they spoke about what they had just done.

Billy took the initiative.

"Digger—" he said, his words trailing off. "That was too fucking amazing. I have to tell you that."

"I know," Digger agreed. "I can't believe it either. I want to do it again. And again."

Billy smiled, and relief washed over him. "Me too!"

Digger lay his arm over Billy's chest. Billy reached up and started to massage Digger's muscles. He kissed Bigger's biceps and slid his tongue into the other boy's armpit to taste the sweat that lingered there. Digger pulled back, giggling. "You like that?" he asked, slightly appalled.

"I don't know yet," Billy answered. "I just wanted to try it. I like the way you smell there right now. Can I have some more?"

"Sure," Digger said, "but don't tickle me so much."

Billy slid his tongue back and forth across Digger's pit, and his nose filled with the sweet smell of fresh, clean sweat. He pressed his mouth against the flesh and the hairs that grew there, and his cock started to rise again. He grabbed Digger's hand and brought it to his crotch. Digger smiled.

"Dude," he said. "I can't believe this. I want you bad. I'm having weird thoughts.—like how much I want to fuck you right now."

"Fuck me?" Billy replied, a bit startled by the thought.

"Yeah," Digger said. "I really want to put my dick up inside you. I'm usually not hard again this fast after shooting off, but I can't help it, man. Just thinking about sliding into you has me all worked up. Can I try it?"

"I don't know—I don't want it to hurt."

"If it hurts too much, just tell me, and I'll take it out. I promise."

Billy thought for a moment. "All right, but just go real easy on me, OK?"

"Sure thing," Digger said. "Get on your hands and knees, OK?"

Billy bent over like a dog and felt a tingle shoot up his spine when Digger started to handle his ass, prying his cheeks apart.

"Damn," Digger said. "This is hot, dude. In fact…" His words trailed off. Billy felt something warm and wet slide up against his knotted pucker, and he almost pulled away. But as the thing snaked into his hole, he found himself pushing backward onto it.

"Are you licking my asshole?" Billy asked breathlessly.

Digger responded by sliding his tongue firmly over Billy's hole again, and Billy shuddered as arousal pulsed through his body. "Shit, man. Oh, damn, that's hot."

Digger came up for air and tried to focus his eyes on something. His entire body was buzzing with adolescent desire. He grabbed hold of his dick and guided it quickly to the pink hole that awaited his attention.

"Oh!" Billy yelped as he felt the head slide into him. "Careful, dude! Go slow!"

Digger was careless, too wrapped up in his own pleasure, and he pushed forward without hearing Billy's words.

"Owwww! Holy shit, take it out!" Billy hollered, and Digger quickly pulled back.

"I'm sorry, man, " Digger said. "Oh, man, really, I am."

"Jesus," Billy said. "Just let me sit for a moment. Were you trying to split me in two?"

"I just got carried away. I promise I'll go slower this time. Can I try again?"

Billy looked over his shoulder and melted when he looked into

Digger's soulful eyes. "Just go easy, OK? I've never had anything up there before, and you're kind of big."

"OK." This time Digger rubbed the head of his prick over Billy's asshole several times to work his friend into a groove. Both boys became incredibly turned on.

Suddenly, Billy reached behind him and grabbed Digger's hand. "Do it," he said. "Now."

Digger pushed into Billy again; this time, his cock head slid in easily. Billy gave a short yelp but caught his breath.

"You sure?" Digger asked.

"Yes! Slide it in me."

Digger pushed forward a little more and was surprised at how smoothly he slid into his friend's virgin hole. Billy felt pain course through his body, but he bit down hard on his lower lip and tried not to focus on it. As his friend probed deeper inside him, Billy tried to relax. When Digger crushed his pubes against Billy's ass, Billy howled.

"Stop!"

Digger started to pull out. "No!" Billy said, reaching back to stop him. "Just hold it there for a moment. Let me get used to it."

Digger did as he was told; he was eager to stay inside Billy's tight cavern. It was unlike anything he'd felt before, better than any jerk-off session with the Vaseline, better than fucking Stacey Myers, even. When Billy whispered that it was OK to move again, Digger pushed himself in as deep as he could go, then started to grind his hips against his buddy's ass.

"Mmmmm," he moaned. "You're tight."

"No shit," Billy said though clenched teeth.

"I'm gonna fuck you now," Digger said. He pulled out so that his cock head was all that was left inside Billy's ass. Billy moaned as the cock left his chute, and Digger pushed back inside him quickly.

"Fuuuuuuuck," Billy cried as Digger's cock entered him again and pushed up against his prostate. Suddenly, Billy was overtaken by an intense feeling of pleasure that welled up from deep inside his body.

"Yeah!" he cried out. "Do that again. Oh, God, right there. Yes!"

Digger had barely entered Billy twice, but knew he wouldn't be able to last long. Billy's ass sucked him inside, and he began to fuck his friend hard and fast, building to a quick climax. "I can't hold out, Billy—it's too hot!"

Billy was right there with him and reached down to take his cock into his hand. "Then do it, man. Shoot it up inside me!"

"Yeah!" Digger said as he slammed his hips against Billy's ass one last time before he jettisoned a second load deep inside Billy.

Billy, in turn, fired off his second load, which landed on the floor beneath him with a *splat!*

Later, the two friends lay in bed together, their arms wrapped tightly around each other. They listened to the sounds of their beating hearts and tried to make sense of what had just passed between them. Despite their muddled thoughts, neither had been happier than he was at that moment.

"So…" Billy said after a long silence. "What did you think of that?"

"It sure was something else, that's for sure," Digger replied. He nestled his head closer to his friend's neck.

"Do you feel weird about it?"

"A little. But I don't know. I kinda liked it. Did you?"

"Yeah, it was a little weird." Billy turned to face Digger, then kissed his friend softly on the lips. "But I liked it too."

There was another moment of silence between them. Then:

"So—" Digger said. "You wanna wrestle again?"

"Boy, do I!" Billy replied. He smiled broadly as he pinned Digger's hands above his head.

And the rematch began.

A Duplicitous Summer Night

L.M. Ross

The first touch vacuumed Ty away from the reality of a New York cab ride. His head spun. *Face Depina is touching my dong!* There was always a certain strain of wildness, a fearlessness in Face, and maybe Ty had forgotten that too. *Yo! Mr. Taxi Driver! Do you see this? He's stroking me off, man!* Heat was baking every atom in Ty's body. *Oh, my damn!* It was a mighty bumpy, bouncy ride through the streets of Gotham. Tyrone wanted to grab a shock of Depina's hair and drive his beautiful lips there, to that percolating place. *Does he give head too?* He could only imagine the wet warmth of Face's mouth and lips going down on him. But *this,* this was cool too, because Depina's manipulations were making him drool. Ooh! He had skills in those hands! Ty was moaning low, and he hoped the cabby couldn't hear him.

When that monumental moment came, Ty pushed Face away swiftly, and he sprayed in a thrust on the floor and the seats and his jeans. He was breathing harder than a long-distance runner. *Look at me! I'm a fuckin' mess, but I don't care!*

"That's act 1, baby. Tonight's your lucky night. Let's swing by Mirage," Face whispered.

Tyrone and his shocked penis consented.

A few minutes later, they'd checked their clothes down to their jocks and hiking boots. Ty was in deep lust with Face's physique. His eyes perused the lean almond-hued sweep of him. Face's outstretched supporter loomed abundant with an unseen butter-pecan treat. The club songs began to pump, and they hit the crowded floor. Seemed like every hot, horny cat in Manhattan was out cattin' that night.

Ty and Face moved in a screw of hips, writhing in their jocks, on fire with rhythm. *Damn!* thought Ty. *Even his dancing has improved!*

It was too loud to talk, to think of anything other than sex, so they let their grinding bodies speak for them. In mid–nasty groove, Depina grabbed Tyrone's neck, pulling his face into his. They stared and breathed, and then they kissed, long and hot, daring and wet. Ty's fast heartbeat was a bass line. In a heated tremor, Face clutched Ty's ass, pushing his writhing body forth. All Tyrone could feel was that long slab of meat lengthening under a damp jock.

Ty planted sucking kisses all across the taut, savory man-scape of Face. He lacquered Depina's neck and sweat-glazed shoulders, licked the dense wires of Face's pits, and nibbled those delectable tits.

"Wanna fuck around some?" Depina howled so boldly, so straight out with his shit. Tyrone and his dick answered, "Hell, yeah!"

Depina looked around, then slowly peeled down the front of his jock, and motherfuck! A very long and still elongating tan joint took Ty's breath.

"Diz-zaamn!" was all he could say. From his view in the audi-ence, Tyrone knew Face was blessed. He'd expected a big, firm, Urban Legend–type boner, but *this!* Diz-zaamn! Close to 10-inches of lean, uncut, tapered, pecan-colored tube reached out for Tyrone, willing him to do something hot with it.

But then Depina tucked his prize away.

Sufficiently excited, they left the dance floor in a quest for privacy. Their pricks stabbed a path through the dancing, romanc-ing mayhem, en route to the back room. Which was jammed. The high reek of sex was everywhere. Moaning, groaning men coupled in every freaking corner. No way two tall, erect ethnics would fit comfortably in that serpentine mix. Strangers would be all over them like bacon on greens, hot peppers on salsa.

"I used to DJ here," Face said. "There's this old booth upstairs, real private." Depina gestured in that direction. Ty nodded, and Face led the way. In the darkened glass booth, he switched on a red lamp. Face looked even hotter bathed in red light. There was an old turntable, a leather chair, and a gang of vintage disco albums. A small army of spent condoms littered the floor like defeated latex soldiers. Face dropped his jock. His meat torqued upward—tall, tan, and lovely as its owner. He sat in the chair, and led Ty's head, down, down... "Suck me off, if you can," challenged Face Fine-ass Depina.

Ty was hypnotized. Yes, *naked* was Depina's color. Still, there was that *shadiness* about him. Ty didn't know where the hell he and his elegant pecan prick had been. So he reached for his wallet and pulled out a Trojan.

"What the hell is *that* for?" Face asked, all indignant.

"Safety. I'm not down with the DNA Slurpee. All kinds of diseases out there. Gotta suit up if you wanna play with *me*. Besides, you don't know where I been either."

"No glove, no love, huh?" Face smirked. *Fuckin' punk!* Ty thought. *What's wrong with him? I'm clean, and he's lucky I'm payin' attention to his fortunate ass!* But Depina didn't say anything as Tyrone rolled the rubber down his lengthy span. Then, in a New York minute Depina grabbed Ty's chin and fed him warm raging knob and shaft, then more shaft. Damn, how much shaft did he have! And with more shaft came more vibration. Rising from the chair, Depina and his pinga bucked and struck the back of Ty's throat. Ty choked it back, then lapped to the sound and beat of the bass at his feet. As sexy, sweaty men flaunted and strutted and freaked below, Ty ingested the tip and shaft of a dream. Was it *real*? Was he *really* gagging on a spit and red-lit *dream*?

"I *knew* you dug me back in school. I could tell," Face said with hubris, as he stood, pushing Ty against the desk. Then, all at once, his moist lips locked on Ty's naked shlong.

Wait! Wait! Don't you want me to put a rubber on?

But Depina didn't care. Like some reckless predator, he was all over Ty, smacking his ass, twisting his tits, throttling that mounting piece with lips, mouth, tongue, and throat. Ty never imagined one man could be so sexual. Face was a rattler, licking, hissing through Ty's prickly bush. He was rough, full of slobber and rushing breaths, but a suck-sore Ty was surprised at just how much he *liked* it.

Then, he switched turntables, mixed it up, scratched it, and surprised Ty with a brand new beat. "You know," he began, "I done a coupla men before. They just love to sit on this long hot motherfucka and ride!" His voice wore a tough-guy catch when he said that. He smacked his lovely against Tyrone's thigh. "And I just love to hear 'em squealin' like first-time faggots!"

Is this your seduction rap, Face? Because as good as you look, that shit could use some work.

"I got that fuckin' part down cold," Face said. "Now I need to know the rest."

"The rest?" Ty asked, not quite feeling his flow.

"Yeah. The rest." His hands sailed down Tyrone's belly. He grabbed Ty's limb and jerked it into a long, strong, wicked hardness. "Get up. I think I want you to hit it."

It had been a night thick with surprises. But Tyrone couldn't quite *believe* this one.

Face, his long straight bone beautifully erect, lay face-up, his back on the table.

But looking at Face Depina head-on would've made Ty come too quickly—so he ordered, "Turn around."

Face did, and Ty slowly massaged the red-lit slopes of a perfectly glazed rump. He could smell the excitement in the air. Tyrone, who never left home without his rubbers, slid one on. Depina tensed, teasing the hell out of Ty, who was now one hard and juicin' brotha.

It was show time for Tyrone and the Face. And Ty was primed and ready for his close-up.

Crouching, he divided Depina's cheeks. Then he slowly let his crest, his shaft submerge inside that leather-knotted Cheerio. The clasp, oh, the clasp was so maddening.

"Aw! Oh. Shit!" Depina groaned that groan of anguished pleasure.

Ty eased in and out, giving Face more and more of his measure. "Aw! Shit!"

Ty pierced him in one impatient thrust. Face grunted hard against the slice and slide. A warm tightness enclosed Tyrone. Like a deep and magnetic furnace, it seemed to will him, pull him deeper into its heat. Being inside Depina was like plunging one's dick into the eye of a crushing, twisting cyclone.

Flipping himself over, Depina glared defiantly at Ty. "Come on! Hit it! Damn it! More! Harder! Harder, damn it!" he demanded.

So Tyrone hit him rougher. Applying more muscle, his hips drove harder, his body plunged deeper.

"Come on! That all you got? Fuck!"

Ty set a meaner rhythm, squeezing Depina's cheeks, sending his cock forcefully through him.

Depina rose up, devilishly winked, and gnashed his teeth against Ty's nipple.

"Aw! Face, man! That shit hurts!" he complained as Depina rolled the other nip between his strong, menacing fingers. This, coupled with his long history of curiosity about Face and the intensity of actually being inside him, sent Tyrone to that spacey edge. He could feel his whole body flooding, pulsating against the rub, the groove, the smoothest friction. He had maybe three strokes left, and that was it. He lunged and instantly felt his shudder. Slipping into that strange *shiver-place,* he grabbed Depina's long, rigid dick and pistoned it quicker. A vibrant charge rumbled through Depina's bone, and its quivering set Ty *off*!

Depina heaved as wild skeets ripped forth, blasting, one after the next. Fisting him wet, Ty pulled back, slammed, shook, and fired great glistening gobs of electric fire. *I can't believe it. I can't believe I just did Face fucking Depina!*

"Man!" Face sighed. "That was wild, baby. Real *wile.* But don't go fallin' in love or anything cause I ain't like you. I ain't gay. So keep this shit between us. All right?" His green eyes were weighted in seriousness. "This was just one of them experiments—you know, like a actin' exercise."

Tyrone heard him. He watched those lying eyes. But it was all sort of dream-like, or more like *waking up* from a dream, where everything sits in its own quiet haze and nothing is quite yet real.

"I mean, it felt all right. Can't say I was *really* into it. But—"

"What? Come on, Face! Don't bullshit me with this whole illusory, veiled, mysterioso trip. You give head, and you take it up the ass. Last time I checked, that's gay!" Tyrone fumed.

"See, the old Face would be kickin' yo ass right about now. But I'll just call that shit a compliment. You're all hung-up on labels. Ain't you heard Tina Turner's new cut: "What's Love Got to Do With It?" Well, what's *gay* gotta do with it, huh? I ain't like you, Ty. Hey, you ain't gotta believe me. You can ask any one of my *many* chicks. See, I'm up for this role as a gay athlete, and I'm supposed to know what the Hell I'm doin', right? Besides, shit man, I went to P.A.—I was *surrounded* by you guys. And down here, dealin' with the artsy farts, I'm *always* bein' hit on. I've been around, man. Not much turns me off anymore. See, this part, it ain't no buck-wild dick-swingin' porn. But I'm supposed to be a young queer cat. I have to *get* being queer. I mean, what's it like to kiss? Did that. You close your eyes, and it's like kissin' your damn arm. But I had to go deeper than that. I needed to know what it feels like to *be* with another man. Now I know. See. I'm in this for real. I'm tryna be an artist, not some fly-by-night. I'm dead serious about my craft."

Tyrone stared back at this *Actor,* this supposed Thespian, and for the first time, Face didn't seem so damn pretty. Who was he, really? Maybe Ty should've felt clowned again. But the laugh, this time, was on Depina. Tyrone wanted Face to know he *knew* for sure now that Pascal Ornette "Face" Depina was *not* legit.

"Acting?" Ty said. "Nah. Trust me, you were *never* that good. Sucking dick once might be an experiment. Sucking it twice, then taking it to the rim and demanding *more* just makes you another deluded faggot! You think you played me? No bruh. Ya played yourself!"

Ty began his shrivel process. The eight-inch thing that let him know how it felt to be black, gay, and *alive* was descending into a little brown sliver of pissed-off twine.

"Come on, Ty! I picked you outta all the guys I coulda picked, cause I knew you'd keep it quiet. So don't feel used. You *enjoyed* it. I *know* you did!" Face blustered, as Ty walked away. "Yo! Just keep it between us, and don't be all mad at a brotha! Hey! Ain't you ever heard of the Method?"

"Whatever's clever, Sista! You played yourself, but whatever's clever," he said, heading back to the room filled with men who knew, acknowledged, and embraced what they were.

The Glorious Fourth
Simon Sheppard

W ell, sir, Independence Day rolls around, the mines are shut
   down for the day, and damn near every man in Bodie is
drunk as a hillbilly at a rooster fight, not to mention Father
Kowalski. And the talk of the whole damn inebriated town is the
arm-wrestling contest to be held that night at the Bella Union
Gambling Hall.

Now, men have rode in from miles around for the Fourth of
July in Bodie, amongst them a great grizzly of a man, Josiah Britt by
name, who, rumor has it, has killed more than one man barehanded
by the simple snapping of the poor feller's spine. Well over 6½ feet
tall, Britt has been strutting around shirtless all day, the sweat on
the matted black hair of his chest and belly asparkle in the warm
light of Helios. And unsurprisingly, Hiram, already in his cups, has
been seen lurking around the big man, hands in his pockets,
stroking on a hard-on that's lasted for nigh on the whole afternoon.

"I figure I can beat any man around," says Britt, cocky as the
king of spades. And in demonstration he holds up his right arm
and makes a giant muscle, all impressive as fuck, though the smell
from his sweat-soaked armpit damn near knocks the bunch of us flat.

"I would be most willing to wager," says pale, handsome Lars,
the Standard Mine owner's son, "a substantial sum on your doing
just that." Lars usually ain't much of a gambling man, but face-to-
face with Britt he's got a twinkle in his eye, which gets a mite
stronger as his gaze slides south of Britt's belt.

The Bella Union has dug a big barbecue pit out in front, where for a silver dollar a man can eat and drink until he's ready to puke, and many a man has been doing that very thing. The hot sun sets, and big blasts of dynamite ricochet in the hills above town—Bodie's own version of patriotic fireworks. The noise gets me to being a tad thoughtful, remembering back to the cave-in last spring that took the life of Texas Joe. But the melancholy passes fast, it being unwise to dwell upon the Big Jump. For we miners, each and every man among us, know that what puts grub on our table is risky as walking in quicksand over hell, and what happened to Joe could have happened to me—and no hallelujah to that.

I'm painting my tonsils with another drink when Sy Tolliver, the proprietor of the joint, steps to the front door and announces in a booming voice to be heard above the sound of drunken arguments, "Gentlemen, the arm wrassling contest is about to commence."

Over in the alley between the Bella Union and Van Dine's Barbershop, Hiram looks up from where he's been sucking on the swelled-up penis of Big Owen, the town blacksmith. Hiram sees Josiah Britt heading into the Bella Union and, without a word, gets up off his knees and follows him, leaving Big Owen standing there leaning against the wall, his long, wet prong now unattended to. I, unwilling to let a pretty thing like that go to waste, walk on over and slide Owen's prodigious foreskin back and forth, frigging him faster and faster until his knees sort of buckle and, with a low-pitched moan, he spends his jissom in big, wild spurts. Some of his spunk lands to my dismay on my dungarees, which, on account of it being a holiday, are my best pair—and were just recently laundered at the Wo Fat Laundry, to boot. I rub some of the muck off with the palm of my hand, and Owen grasps my wrist, pulls my hand to his mouth, and licks his own seed down; when he lets me pull my hand away, his bushy beard is smeared with it.

The Bella Union is packed to the rafters with odoriferous drunken men. Sy Tolliver is standing before a chalkboard on which he's written the names of the contestants, all 16 of them. The combatants themselves are in the center of the room, seated two to a table, mostly stripped down to their waists, it being one hell of a hot night. And while Josiah Britt's barrel chest is maybe the most impressive of the lot, many another fellow has a muscular, well-formed body that holds the promise of a hard-fought contest ahead.

All the men are present—all, that is, excepting Big Owen, who's still recovering from the pump-draining I just provided him, I reckon.

"Gentlemen," says Tolliver, "we shall get started now. And it looks as though there's already a forfeit on the part of—" and he looks at the chalkboard, back at the men, back at the board, and calls out Big Owen's name.

"Not so fast!" comes a shout from the doorway. It's Owen, his swagger a trifle undone by the fact he's plumb forgotten to button up his pants.

"Owen," says Tolliver, "it's about fucking time, and that's a fact. You're over there, across from Duncan McCutcheon." Big Owen goes and sits.

There's a judge standing at each table. As the prize for the competition is $100 in gold, a certain amount of attempted dishonesty is only to be expected in a hellhole like Bodie.

Tolliver is explaining the rules when another voice is heard.

"Is it too late to join on in?"

We all look around to see who spoke. It's a stranger in town. His hair's as blond as Lars's hair. But whereas Lars is willowy and handsome, this fellow is quite the opposite: thickly built, with the neck of a mastiff and real big shoulders and chest. He's got the beginnings of a double chin, though he's only maybe 20 years old, and his blue eyes have a slightly crazy, determined glare. To tell the truth, there's something about him that draws my excited notice and makes my britches stir.

"Well, sir, it is indeed too late. These other men have signed up days ago for this competition," says Tolliver with a glare.

The big blond looks like he's disappointed enough to smash in Sy Tolliver's head.

"C'mon, Sy," I hear myself say. "Allow the feller to enter the tournament." A few others say the same as well.

"All right," says Tolliver, "if none of you objects, he's in, but as there's now an odd number of men, you—" and he looks straight at me "—can be this man's first match. What's your name, newcomer?"

"Will Shively," says the blond man, stripping off his shirt and heading in my direction. Quite naturally, the approach of such a prepossessing man makes my prong as stiff as a pine tree.

"Only one thing," says Tolliver. "We are short one judge now, being on account of there's an additional matchup." At which Lars speaks up and volunteers to judge our match. Though it's widely known that Lars and I are well-acquainted (and indeed many a man knows that Hiram and I have tied Lars up and plowed him on a schedule near-regular as Wells Fargo's) such is the Norwegian's reputation for rectitude that not one man objects.

Shively and I head over to the one empty table amidst the throng of spectators, and as we do, the miners make additional wagers. Most all of them, I reckon, back the big blond.

At the touch of Will Shively's strong, callused hand, I'm near overcome by desire, and I know then for damn well certain that I shan't be winning the arm-wrestling crown. Still, it was at my initiative that the new man was included in the contest, so I am well resolved to do my utmost, or at least nearly so.

Lars is standing beside our table, ready to adjudicate our struggle. My muscles tense up and become nearly as hard as my throbbing member. Then Tolliver speaks out, all stentorian, "Gentlemen, the first round of the Bodie Independence Day Arm Wrestling Championships is about to commence." A half-drunken hush sets over the room. "On your mark...get set...wrassle!"

Well, this Will Shively isn't as strong as he looks. No, sir—he's *twice* as strong, and it takes every ounce of my will not to just let him have his powerful way and have done with it. As the crowd cheers on their favorites, Shively applies his considerable leverage against me. I look into his steely blue eyes, and they gaze back implacably. Then I make my fatal error: I allow my eyes to trail downward. The sight of Will Shively's broad chest, nipples erect in a thicket of blond fur, sinews straining, sweat coursing down his bare flesh—Jesus Lord, it's quite disconcerting. For one fraction of a second, all I want is to be overpowered by this handsome man, and in that split second he senses my weakness and slams my arm to the rough tabletop.

"Winner over here," Lars calls out, even-voiced as can be, and that settles that. Only it's with some hesitation that Shively loosens his now-painful grasp on my hand, and the lingering of his strong touch upon me makes my defeat seem of no import whatsoever.

Whatever chagrin I might feel vanishes when I look around me and see that most all the other matches are likewise concluded. Big Owen has beaten McCutcheon, Britt has won his matchup, and only two of the contests are still ongoing. Scrappy Juan Hernandez is grunting with agony, his eyes a-pop with the strain of battling Bill Logue, and Easy Averill and liquored-up Penn Cobb are also still in battle, locked in a sweaty standoff. But inch by inch, Hernandez pushes Logue's arm to the wood, and then Cobb defeats Averill, and it's the end of Round 1.

Hiram comes over and he says to me "Good try," but he's looking at Shively while he says it and claps his hand on the victor's muscled shoulder. I wonder if there's ever a time when Hiram isn't hankering to drop his drawers.

The late addition of Shively to the contest has left an odd number of men for Tolliver to divvy up for the next round—nine, to be exact. But Sy Tolliver's quandary is solved when the inebriated Cobb leans over and hurls his guts onto the floor. That alone might not be official grounds for disqualification, but Cobb mutters something and makes for the door as one of Tolliver's bar backs sluices away the reeking mess and pours a pile of sawdust onto the wet floor.

"In Penn Cobb's honor," calls out Tolliver with a grin, "the next round of neck oil is on the house!" And every man cheers loud.

The second round sees Britt pinning Frank O'Rourke in less than a minute flat. Hernandez wins his matchup too, as does Big Owen, and Will Shively damn near busts poor Abel Asch's arm.

Meanwhile, Lars, no longer needed as a referee, comes up to me and asks, "Who do you make for the winner?"

"I would have said Britt till this Shively showed up," I reply, "but now I ain't so sure."

"Me neither," says my bosom friend Lars, "and it has me a bit worried, for I've laid a considerable wager on the fortunes of Josiah Britt."

"Lars!" say I, most surprised. "I never knew you to be a gambling man!"

"That's usually the case," says he, "but, oh heck, it's the Fourth of July."

The four remaining contestants, Britt against Hernandez and Big Owen paired up with Shively, make ready for their battles.

There's much to be said for the matching up of man against man, testing muscle and mettle one against the other, and not the least of them is the smell that arises from the brutes. Standing near the remaining combatants—each of them stripped to the waist and now covered with the sheen of sweat—I catch a whiff of the animal reek that rises from their bodies. If my interest had ever flagged, this odor serves as a restorative tonic.

At Tolliver's say-so the matches begin.

As Britt bears down on Hernandez, it's clear the two are mismatched. Though the Mexican's arm bulges with muscle, Britt's biceps is twice as big, and from the first the advantage is his.

"Sweet Jesus fuck Mary fuck Mother of God!" curses Hernandez, who then lapses into something Spanish that is no doubt at least as obscene. Hernandez does his best to arrest his arm on its downward path, but it's plum obvious that Josiah Britt has got the upper hand. Britt bares his teeth as he gets Hernandez's hand just inches from the table, and though Hernandez stalls it there for a bit, the effort takes a terrible toll, and with one final loud "Fuck!" the Mexican lets his hand touch wood.

Meanwhile, Lars is touching wood, as well, after a fashion, for his hand is now down the front of my pants, and if anyone anywhere in Bodie might ever have objections, the drunken night of

Independence Day is nowhere near the time. The delicate fingers of the mining engineer, well-schooled in the lessons Hiram and I have taught, work my prong into a raging lather, wherefore my crotch is damn near sopping wet.

Meantime, Owen and Britt have been struggling mightily, hand to callused hand. Their hairy forearms bulging with tension, they seem evenly matched, first one gaining advantage, then the other. But Britt gets a real funny look on his face and steadily forces the blacksmith's hand further and further down till Owen's arm is pinned, and a cheer goes up from the slavering crowd.

I look over in the corner, and there's Juan Hernandez, salving his defeat; he's opened his fly and is stroking on his big brown dick, pulling the long foreskin back and forth over his swelling penis head. And danged if Penn Cobb doesn't weave back into the Bella Union and head over to Juan. They stand there glaring at each other for one long minute, and I figure they're maybe going to fight. But then Cobb reaches out for the Mexican's organ and starts to frig it. Hernandez relaxes and grins and leans against the wall, and Penn Cobb drops to his knees and with alacrity takes the other fellow's stiff penis into his mouth.

It's down to the final contest now. Will Shively and Josiah Britt, their naked torsos streaked with sweat, are seated across from one another, ready to tangle it up. Wagered money's been changing hands throughout, and it's fair to say a quite sizable amount of cash is riding on the result.

"And now, ladies and gentlemen..." Tolliver looks around and starts again. "And now commences, gentlemen, the final round of the Bella Union's first Independence Day Arm Wrestling Championship. Will Shively here tests his mettle against Josiah Britt, and may the best man win. On your marks, get set—"

Just then the bar room air is rent by a piercing "Ya-hoo!" from Juan Hernandez, who's loudly shooting his seed down Penn Cobb's throat. And though Tolliver has yet to officially start the match, Britt jumps the gun, and strains away, forcing Shively's arm, inch by laborious inch, down toward defeat.

Tolliver tries to sputter out his instructions, but the match has started without his say-so, and he realizes it's too late to do any different. Meanwhile, big blond Will Shively refuses to let his opponent gain more ground, and their linked arms are stalled midair in an even-matched show of strength.

"Jesus," says my bosom pal   hope to holy hell that this new fellow doesn't win, for at Lars's urging I've laid a sizable sum on Josiah Britt's victory."

Now, this concerns me, for Lars comes from money, and his wealthy father can always bail him out of a jam. But Cal has worked hard for his poke of gold and doesn't have any to spare. Meanwhile, Shively is gaining the upper hand. He has muscled his opponent's arm partway down to the table's surface, and Shively's handsome face is all screwed up from the strain. Just watching the struggle makes my penis good and hard, and I'm not the only one, it seems, for here and there throughout the Bella Union half-dressed miners paw at one another. Indeed, tipsy Penn Cobb, having drunk deep of Hernandez's sperm, is now sprawled facedown across one of the tables, trousers around his ankles, his fundament spread wide, his hungry hole exposed and up for grabs. Noticing this, Easy Averill lumbers over, his short, fat prong poking out of his fly, and dang if he doesn't spit on Cobb's butt and commence to plug him right there in the midst of the tumult.

"Fuck! The newcomer's winning, and there goes the two months' wages I gave to Lars to bet!" Cal sounds frantic now.

Indeed, Will Shively's concentration is nothing short of amazing—his blue eyes drill into Britt—and it seems that nothing short of a major distraction can divert him from certain victory.

At which point I get an idea.

Now, it's true that the judge of this contest is the sheriff, but I've done him a favor or two in my time, and he's liquored up to boot, so I figure he won't stop me. I elbow my way through the crowd over to the table where the two men are locked in combat. Then I drop to my knees and scoot under the table, positioning myself between Shively's massive, sturdy legs. I unbutton the fly of his pants and reach inside, pulling out his soft root. Opening wide, I take the thing into my mouth, inhaling the high smell of his crotch, tonguing his foreskin, and hoping like hell I can distract Shively just enough to make him to flinch.

Within a matter of moments, the prick has gone from soft to stiff, and I'm sucking away with thorough enthusiasm. I was afraid that Shively would try to kick me away, but instead he kind of grabs me between his muddy boots. So I take him all the way down my throat; I'm almost gagging as Shively shoves himself into my hungry mouth. Though the shouts of the crowd have gone from a tumult to a full-on ruckus, above it all I hear Cal Callahan bellow to me: "That's the ticket! SHIVELY'S GIVING WAY!"

So I suckle on the meaty piece some more, then slide myself back a bit and use a hand to stroke it, squeezing Shively's copious precome from his big piss slit. I quickly swallow him down again, wrap my arms around his tree-trunk legs, and suck so hard that I feel his calves tense up and start to quiver. My throat milks his cock head most vigorously, and soon Will Shively can take it no longer. His whole body goes rigid, which causes my head to bang up against the table. He shivers and shouts as he pumps load after load of sweet cream onto my tonsils. Which is when I hear the loud thwack of one man's arm pinning the other's—the sound of Shively's defeat, I'm certain—and I feel a flush of pride at having helped my buddy Cal out of a jam and that's for sure.

It's not till I've gulped down the very last of Shively's jissom that I perceive the roar of the crowd, which is full-out deafening now: a huge human cry of horny, jubilant men. I back off the now-deflating penis and, out of sheer politeness, stuff it back into Will Shively's pants.

I slide from beneath the table and rise to my feet. It's then that I see what's happened, for the two men are still sitting there stock-still, a stunned kind of look on Josiah Britt's bearded face. His competitor has pinned his arm to the table, and beneath Will Shively's control it remains. It's just the opposite of the ambition I'd labored so mightily to realize.

"Tarnation!" I say to Cal Callahan. "I'm sure dreadful sorry! What in blazes happened?"

"It was a nice try you gave it," says Cal mournfully, "and Britt nearly did have Will Shively pinned. But at the moment he spent his spunk, Shively of a sudden gets all rigid, his arm having a mind of its own, and he just plain pushes Britt's hand straight down to the tabletop."

Britt and Shively relax their death-grip and stand up from their table. As all the onlookers cheer, winners and losers both, they wrap each other in a big manly hug, bare torso to naked, sweaty chest. Then Shively reaches down to Josiah's crotch, and he roars out, "Why the fuck should I be the one who's havin' all the fun?" And he unbuttons Britt's fly and adroitly pulls out the victor's swelling cock.

Which is when Lars comes up to us and says to Cal, "Well, I have a confession. I'm afraid that I just thoroughly forgot to wager that money you gave me. Comes to that, I suppose it all ended up for the best, as you otherwise would have lost it. And if you fellows would come to my hotel room tonight—" and here he smiles that most pretty grin of his, "I'll be most happy to return it to you then."

I have no way of knowing whether Lars is telling the actual truth. For though the handsome young man values verity, he values friendship more. And if it comes to that, he knows full well that he shan't receive more diligent attention than what Cal and I have given his naked, tied-up body all those nights in his room at the Grand Central Hotel.

Well now, watching the arm-wrestling matches has gotten me all lathered up; and sucking Shively's erection, even more so. I look over and see that Averill has finished drilling Penn Cobb's butt, but half-conscious Cobb is still slung over the table. Cobb's hairy ass is spread, his shiny hole inviting the next visitor, so I mosey over before anyone else can get there first, pull out my bone, and slide it up inside Penn Cobb's wide-open hole.

As I'm pumping away, and a bunch of the boys commence singing "The Whorehouse Bells Were Ringing," I feel a hand on my shoulder.

"Thanks," says Cal, "for tryin' to help me out."

"Shit," I say, not missing a stroke into Cobb, "ain't that what friends are for, buddy?"

He leans over and kisses me gentle on the cheek. "See you a bit later at the Grand Central," he says, and goes off to get another whiskey.

And I, for my part, pump ever harder, slipping damn near out of Cobb, then pounding my way back in, all to his groaning delight. Meantime, a bellow rises above the crowd, and when I look over, there's Josiah Britt, hands behind his head, sweat pouring from his furry pits, his big hard dick pumping out gob after gob of thick sperm upon Will Shively's grinning face. And after a minute or two more, I myself can hold back no longer and shoot off my sperm like it was big-city fireworks, all over the slick walls of Penn Cobb's guts, a most truly fitting end to one hot Independence Day in Helldorado—and God bless America.

Sweet Country Butt

Danny Smith

I had gone up to the Ozarks in northwestern Arkansas to visit a couple of friends who owned a cabin by a large lake there. It was early summer, and already hot and humid. My pals and I were from New York City, and we were used to the high life there, hitting the bars and clubs on a regular basis. This quiet wilderness was a welcome reprieve.

The cherry ass of a lifetime awaited me. That ass belonged to a neighbor, an 18-year-old yokel who had met my pals the year before on one of their excursions. Henry was his name. I first saw him when we were down by the water in a secluded spot. No one was around, and we city boys had shucked it all to go skinny-dipping like kids in the tepid water. He had come upon us—just for a visit, he claimed—but had torn off his clothes off and joined us at our first encouraging shouts.

He was slim and tall with short sandy-blond hair. His baby-blue eyes met mine as he came up out of the water, dripping wet beside me. "Howdy, I'm Henry," he drawled. "How 'bout ya'll?" His sweet grin melting my heart instantly.

"I'm Danny." I grinned back.

"You sure do have some fine muscles for a city dude," he said, chuckling. He stood so close we nearly touched.

My cock rose instantly. Fortunately, we were belly-deep in the murky green water, and I didn't think my arousal was visible. But something about the way I gazed intently into the young guy's eyes must have given me away. To my total astonishment, I felt a hand under the water graze my boner, then return to cop a quick feel before sliding away. I gasped.

"There's an old barn in the woods. Meet me there," he said laughing, his face flushed. He turned and scampered out of the water just like that, sweetly embarrassed by his boldness. He was just a randy teen with nothing to lose by teasing a gay dude from the city.

I got a good look at his plump butt as he splashed out of the lake, water dripping from two graceful mounds that pumped and glistened wetly as he ran into the trees. He had grabbed his clothing, but he was still naked when he bounded into the trees.

What could I do? Unfazed by the hooting jeers of the friends I was leaving behind, I followed. Grabbing my own shorts and shoes, I raced after Henry. In moments I was in the deep pine forest, the quiet surrounding me like a muffling veil. I caught a glimpse of a slim, naked body trotting ahead, and I followed, huffing for breath, my cock hard and bouncing in the air in front of me. He was following a deer path or an overgrown trail that a casual observer's gaze would have overlooked. I caught up with him in a clearing only a few minutes into the chase.

I halted at the edge of the clearing, gawking at the thrilling vision I beheld. There he was, the country teen, climbing an old rickety wooden ladder that leaned against the side of an abandoned barn. I inhaled sharply, awed by the sight of that lean young body, entirely naked, ascending those old wooden rungs. I was only a dozen yards away, and I moved closer at once, peering upward into the dappled light. God! His ass was awesome, the cheeks jiggling slightly as he moved upward, the crack parted, offering me a glimpse of a puckered hole, hairless and no doubt very tight. My cock twitched, and I shivered with anticipation. Was he going to let me into that tight butt?

"Like what you see, Mister? Like my cherry butt? It's all yours if you can catch me!" He laughed down at me, catching me ogling his sweet ass.

I wanted nothing more than to scamper up that ladder and to bury my face between those delectable buns right then and there. But of course that wouldn't be safe sex, and besides he was quick, beating me to the top and disappearing into an opening in the loft.

I followed, still huffing for breath. Once I reached the top, I peered inside and tried to penetrate the deep shadows with my sun-dazzled gaze. When my eyes grew accustomed to the light, I saw a scene as exciting as anything I'd ever beheld. Henry was sprawled across the hay on his belly, that fine ass in the air, beckoning me. He had thrown his clothes on an old pile of loose hay and was spread-eagled over them, waiting.

"Do what you want to me. I can see you got a big boner. I do too." His voice was a husky whisper in the shadowy light. His head was craned around and he was staring at me: his blue eyes nearly invisible, they were so pale.

I moved right in and crouched between his parted thighs. Wasting not another moment, I reached out and grabbed those two big cheeks. Plump and taut, they were incredible. I squeezed them, pulled them apart and stared down at the wrinkled slot I had exposed. It looked very tight.

"You're cherry, boy?" I drawled, imitating his sexy accent, grinning at him, finally tearing my eyes away from that beautiful butt for an instant.

"Yep, I never done it. I'm only 18 this year, and no one in these parts took my fancy—until I seen you today. I want you to be the one. Fuck my butt: I want to know how it feels to have your cock up there!" He was bold, for a callow country lad.

All the while I'd been toying with his ass, working it in circles, and at his words of encouragement, I moved my fingers into his crack, sliding them along the silky surface until they connected with the butthole to which I turned my full attention.

It quivered, snapped, and shuddered as I teased it with light strokes. He let out a long sigh and raised his buns to meet my probing hands. I could hardly believe my good fortune! Not only was it the sweetest butt I had ever seen, it was cherry—mine to bust for the first time. That thought prompted me to pause, to consider how to go about things properly. I wanted him to remember this afternoon. It would be his first time.

"Go ahead, I got some rubbers too. I ain't stupid, Mister," he blurted out, his ass rolling in my hands, his gasps encouraging my teasing fingers. I poked a finger tip into the crinkled anal opening, working it open dry, reveling in the way Henry responded, shoving his hips toward me in an obvious appeal for more of the same.

"Got any lube, Henry?" I asked, amazed at how calm my voice sounded, especially since my heart was galloping in my chest as fast as a racehorse—I was so turned on.

"Yep. I ain't stupid, Mister," he repeated.

"My name's Danny," I told him for the second time. Right about then I managed to insert my finger to the knuckle up his quivering hole. It was tight, silky, and blistering hot. I felt scorched by the throbbing little slot the enveloped my poking finger. I imagined my big hard cock sliding in there, and I let out a sigh of my own to echo Henry's grateful sighs and moans.

"That feels good. Poke me with that finger," he grunted, his butt raised up in the air.

I kept my finger in there, working it around a bit, while I slid my other hand around and under his belly. I found his stiff cock there. He groaned when I wrapped my hand around it, and I pumped it a few times while I kept prodding his butthole with my finger.

"Oh, man…oh, Mister, that feels so good! I can't wait to feel your big cock up there!" He groaned.

He had no idea! My finger was nothing compared to the fat shaft of my cock. He would find out soon enough, I reasoned, but first I needed to open him up some. I didn't want to hurt him, I wanted him to love it. I only wanted to hear screams of ecstasy from him.

"Where's the lube, Henry?"

He fumbled around in his shorts, which were wadded beneath him, and produced a packet of condoms and a vial of lube. A good little Boy Scout, he was indeed prepared. No doubt, he knew the fags from the city were coming again and hoped to get some action. Well, he was going to get just that.

I had to release his throbbing boner so I could squirt some lube into his butt crack. It was transparent stuff, something he had bought at the local drug store perhaps. But it was slick, and it would do the trick. It ran down his ass cleft and pooled in his pucker, where my finger was still firmly planted. I immediately slid my finger out and then back in. Henry rewarded me with a deep sigh. He was enjoying this.

"Ever had a finger up the ass before, Henry?" I asked, looking up to see his baby blues intent on me and on my hands on his ass.

"Just my own a few times," he replied with a grunt.

I shoved my finger deeper, the lube easing the entrance. "Pretending it was a big cock, were you?" I asked, shoving deeper, giving him a taste of what was to come.

"Yeah! Oh, yeah, I like that!" he groaned as he thrust his ass higher. His little slot snapped around my probing finger so tightly, I wondered how the hell I was going to get my fat cock up there.

I frigged his hole and gazed down at him. Dappled with shadows and sunlight, his body was incredible. Dusty tan except for the cheeks of his ass, his body was lean and muscular. His waist was slim, his hips gracefully blossoming into the plush bottom I was working over. His thighs were nicely muscled and covered with a light-blond down; his ball sac hung between his parted thighs. The sac was also covered with silky, nearly invisible down. His cute face, with a button nose and pursed lips, stared back at me with a yearning expression that made my cock twitch in anticipation. I simply had to ream his plump ass!

I began to fuck him vigorously with my finger, adding more lube until it was sliding quickly in and out. His asshole responded slowly but eagerly, opening up slightly. It was enough to embolden me to press a second finger against the taut entrance. "Get ready for two fingers!" I warned him.

"I can take it! It feels great, Danny!" he replied enthusiastically, his butt writing against my hands. He wanted it, the horny little bastard! I pushed, and the spongy entrance resisted for a moment, but the lube and his excitement were enough to allow me to drive inward. He whimpered and his ass cheeks jiggled enticingly as I slipped my two blunt fingertips past his sphincter and into the heated depths beyond.

"Now relax while I open you up. Imagine what my fat rod will feel like!"

He shoved his thighs wider apart and buried his head in his hands. That helped. I took my other hand and used it to spread his crack and hole apart. That too helped. Then I began to work my fingers deeper still, twisting and poking, pulling out then shoving in again. His steady groans, his quivering butt cheeks, and his writhing hips told me how much he loved it. He would love my cock—I just knew it!

I moved my free hand around his waist and under his belly again, finding his boner and squeezing it. That had him gasping. I fucked his tight hole with the fingers of one hand while I pumped his stiff cock with the other. He was a moaning mass of heated flesh between my hands. I knew I could work him into an orgasm right there and then. But we both wanted more. We both needed more. I pulled my fingers out and gazed down at his spongy, quivering, oozing hole. I squeezed the last dollop of lube from the tube and set to work.

I released his cock and scooted up between his thighs. While he waited expectantly with his head in his arms, I rolled a condom over my throbbing meat. I was harder than I'd ever been, so incredibly excited was I. My cock was so full it was purple. Next to his ivory cheeks it looked wicked, dangerous. I almost had second thoughts. Then I recalled how much I loved having a good cock up my ass. I knew Henry was going to love it too.

"Fuck me, Danny!" He moaned, waving his ass in the air.

I stared down at it and marveled again as the shadowy light played across his hairless mounds. They were sweaty now, and lube glistened along the length of his slick crack. His pouting hole trembled and twitched with eagerness. I aimed the mushroom head of my wrapped boner at the entrance to his manhole and held it there.

"Relax, just let it slide in. Your ass will take it if you don't resist," I said soothingly.

He was trembling all over. I ran my hands tenderly over his back and butt as I pressed my cock against his lubed crack. He was shaking so hard, I had to grip his ass to hold him still. I held my cock in place, pressing lightly. Suddenly, I felt his anal rim give way, and then I was sinking into him.

"Oh, yeah, let me into that cherry ass!" I sighed, shivering nearly as much as Henry.

He turned his head and held me in a gaze that took my breath away. His eyes were liquid, full of emotion. His sweet mouth opened lusciously as he licked his sweaty lips. H gasped as he felt the flared head of my cock opening him up, penetrating him. I thrust forward with my hips, just enough to get the head past the rim and into the fuck tunnel beyond. Heavens above! It felt as if my cock head had been swaddled in hot wet silk. Henry's ass quivered, pulsed, and throbbed. With a groan, I pressed deeper.

"Oh, Gawd—oh, man, yes—fill me up with that big cock! Fuck me!" He begged. He raised himself to his knees and shoved his ass back to swallow more of me than I had already offered. He was taking it and wanted more! I lunged, impaling him to the root.

"JEEZ!" He shouted, his voice echoing in the rafters.

I held my cock all the way up his ass, relishing his soft flesh against my thighs, his plump can against my balls. He dropped his head and squirmed beneath me. He wanted me to fuck him, so I did. I began to thrust in and out, slowly but forcefully. Every prod eliciting a little whimper that was music to my ears. His asshole was still a tight vise around my cock, but the lube allowed me to slide in and out without a hitch. I began to stroke him a little faster. The intensity of his moans increased.

I stared down at his sweaty butt heaving beneath me and pumped him full of cock He was taking it admirably. My hands had been on his back and ass, but I moved them beneath him, this time exploring his lean chest. I found his pecs, respectably full and firm. When my fingers grazed his nipples he whimpered and shuddered from head to toe. I had found another erogenous zone and decided to take advantage of my discovery. While I fucked his ass, I teased his pert little nipples with light pinches and tugs. He was a mass of whimpering lust beneath me. He returned every thrust of my hard cock with a perfectly matched pump of his ivory ass.

We went on for a long time. He was moaning and whimpering so much, and his body was shuddering so much, I didn't realize he had already jizzed himself. I only became aware of the fact when I dropped a hand from his nipple to his cock. It was still hard, but it was covered in gooey spunk. Obviously, he had more loads on the way. He continued to thrust backward to meet my pounding cock with hearty, grunting enthusiasm.

I returned my hands to his nipples and worked them both hard while I leaned into him to drill his cherry butt. It had loosened up considerably by then—a good 20 minutes of reaming from a fat cock tends to do that. I let out all the stops and really rammed him. He kept pace with me, urging me to fuck him good, his drawling voice a high-pitched moan by then.

My balls roiled, and my cock was on fire. His pulsing asshole wrung my meat mercilessly. Sweat flew from my forehead, and I bellowed as I began to blow my wad.

"I'm coming up your sweet ass!" I screamed.

"I love it! Unload up my butt!" He answered, writhing beneath me.

He came for the second time. His asshole snapped and convulsed, and the muscles across his country boy's back tensed and arched. We rode it out together. Finally, I fell on top of him, and he dropped to the hay in a sweaty heap beneath me.

We rolled around and faced each other. He lay his head on my shoulder and then turned his face to mine. He gave me a tentative kiss on the lips, and I responded by opening wide and shoving my tongue deep into his warm mouth. He gurgled and thrust his body against mine. My hands moved back down to cop that sweet bubble butt. It wasn't cherry anymore, but it was just as hot.

"Do me again," he said with a twinkle in his eye.

I was happy to oblige.

Fantasies of Hoss

Mel Smith

When I was a kid, *Bonanza* was my favorite show. My friends and I dreamed of being Little Joe, riding the range and killing the bad guys. Unlike the other boys, though, I didn't dream of walking away with the pretty girl at the end of the episode. I dreamed of lying by a campfire with big brother Hoss fucking the shit out of my teeny little ass.

When I suggested this to my own big brother, he beat the crap out of me. I kept my fantasies to myself after that, but they never went away.

As a teenager, I actually looked a bit like Little Joe. I had curly brown hair, almost girlish features and a tiny round ass that barely held up a gun belt. My image of the ideal man didn't change much, either. The men in my dreams were mountain-sized, with gentle hearts and wide smiles.

After the beating from my brother, I grew distant from my family. Or they grew distant from me. I slowly lost most of my friends too, so I turned to the outdoors for entertainment. I made my own adventures and taught myself all I could about trees and wildflowers and animals.

In 1975, it was time for me to start my life. Being a park ranger seemed like a natural choice. I did temporary and fill-in positions for two years before I got a full-time live-in ranger job. I was assigned to a park in Northern California. The park had one live-in ranger already, but the job was becoming too big for one person.

I arrived at the park two days before I was scheduled to start. I knocked on the door of the veteran ranger's cabin, a cheerful yet professional smile plastered on my face.

The door opened and I found myself staring at a chest the size of a Volkswagen Bug. The chest was naked. And hairy. Did I mention it was naked?

I have no idea how long I stared at that chest, but 12 years' worth of J.O. fantasies flashed through my head in about 90 seconds.

I heard a sound like the rumble of distant thunder. It was the voice that belonged to the chest, and it said, "You must be the new ranger."

I looked up, amazed that there could be more body to go with that magnificent expanse of torso.

Framed by sandy-blond lashes and spattering of faint freckles, a pair of gray-blue eyes smiled down at me. Under a pug nose grew a sandy-blond moustache dotted by dimples at both ends. The mustache hid his upper lip, but his plump lower lip looked like a wedge just sliced from a plum—moist, rosy, and mouthwatering.

I heard the thunder again. "I said, 'You must be the new ranger.'"

Dumbstruck, I managed a nod.

We stared at each other while my fantasy reel rewound and started to play again.

He looked amused. He gripped my whole head in one enormous paw and pulled me inside the cabin.

"Do you speak, or am I going to have to learn sign language?"

I nodded again, then shook my head. "What?"

He laughed. His laughter matched his rumbling voice.

Suddenly, it occurred to me to look below his waist to see whether he might be naked down there too.

Anticipation made my tongue hang out of my mouth like a puppy's, but with a glance southward I saw he was wearing jeans. Nevertheless, I realized, as I checked him out, that if his chest were a Volkswagen Bug, there in his pants was the stick shift. Five-speed, from the looks of it.

"Your name is Busby, right? Harold Busby?"

I nodded. I was still looking at his crotch. Then he lifted my chin with one of those bear-paw hands and held me in his smiling gaze.

"I think I need to fuck you, Harold Busby," he said. "Then we can get on with the introductions."

I tried to say "OK," but the sound that came out of my mouth sounded more like "eeek".

He laughed again and, in one seamless motion, hefted me over his shoulder and carried me to his bedroom. He laid me on a down comforter awash in his scent. I was embarrassed to realize how close I was to a swoon.

He peeled off his jeans, and the "Hallelujah Chorus" from *The Messiah* filled the room. Well, it was probably just in my head. He was furry and beefy, and I felt certain he could swallow me whole. I knew I'd found heaven.

His ran his paws over every part of me as he undressed me. I grinned like a madman and my cock twitched goofily, splattering precome in Jackson Pollack patterns across the comforter.

He stood at the end of the bed, hands on hips, shaking his head and chuckling. "Why do they always send me the whack jobs?"

I grabbed my toes and held them next to my ears. I couldn't stop smiling. "I'm waiting," I said in a singsong voice.

His dimples, his moustache, and his succulent lip danced and twisted as he worked up a good wad of spit in his mouth. With a sound like Velcro coming undone, he let loose with a glob that landed smack on my asshole. I let out a moan long as a freight train as his slobber ran down my crack and along my spine.

He probed my hole with a chunky finger and said, "Throw me some lube. It's under the pillow."

I fished under the pillow between my moans and my "Oh, Gods" until I found a tube. I tossed it to him.

His corkscrewed his lubed finger into my ass and rooted around until he found a spot that made cock stand up in salute and my back arch like a sapling in a stiff breeze. I tried to act cool, like

I'd been there, been done. But I'd started to grunt like a boar, and I'd locked my legs around his waist. "Oh-my-God! Oh-my-God!" ran through my head, but the only sound I could make was "Grrrkkk!"

"You're a tight one, Harold. You ever been fucked before?"

"Grrrkkk!"

"I'll take that as a 'no.'"

He greased up his cock with his free hand and worked a second finger into my asshole. I flopped about like one of the little plastic jointed dolls that dance a twitchy dance when you push the button underneath.

"I'm not hurting you, am I, Harold?"

"Grrrkkk!"

"Just checking."

He kneeled at the end of the bed and pulled my ass onto his lap. I pulled folds of the comforter around my head—it was like floating among the clouds!—while his cock poked at my hole.

"By the way, Harold, I'm Bruce Harris. But everybody calls me Smokey."

Then Smokey was inside me, and I came. I flopped around some more like the little twitchy dancing toy. The "Hallelujah Chorus" grew deafening. He slammed the breath out of me, and I saw stars whizzing around the room. I was having a little trouble with the whole breathing thing: My breath didn't seem to want to return to my body. I needed to make sounds, but nothing would come out. I became a little worried.

Finally, the air settled back into my body. I let out a screech that rattled the windows. I clawed at the comforter and panted and rocked, and my cock was still completely hard.

Smokey put a hand between my shoulder blades to keep me perched on his cock. With his other hand he stroked my face, neck, chest, and stomach. He made deep soothing sounds, and I realized I was crying.

When I calmed down, Smokey smiled gently and said, "You ready for me to fuck you now?"

"Yes, please."

He started out slow. It was like riding a rocking horse, only this tickling, tingling electric charge raced back and forth from my balls to my cock head. A steady supply of fluids bubbled out of my piss slit, and I began chanting my very own marvelous mantra: "Hoss is fucking my ass. Hoss is fucking my ass."

Smokey picked up the pace, and I threw my body into his rhythm. He slowed, then stopped, smiling at me as I impaled myself on his cock. I became a kamikaze fucker, holding back nothing.

My grunting was savage and crazed, but Smokey's voice was soft and honey-sweet. "Go for it, Harold. Fuck me, little man. Fuck my cock with your tight little ass."

I grabbed the back of his knees, and I fucked and bucked and twisted my hole on his cock. My back arched so dramatically, I was looking at the world upside down. My shoulders squirmed and ground themselves into the bed.

Smokey laughed and folded his hands behind his head while he watched. His biceps were boulders, and the sight of them sent me over the moon.

Smokey closed his eyes and his face was in pain and at peace at the same time. He whispered in that distant, thunderous voice, "Damn, little man. You sure fuck good."

I didn't want to stop. I wanted to feel him inside me and see him above me until the world ended, but I knew that might be a bit too much to ask. So I fucked even harder.

He caressed my thighs and stomach whenever we got too close to climaxing, so I slowed down. Then he leaned back with his hands behind his head and smile contentedly while I returned to my feverish rutting.

For hours we returned and retreated from the brink. When I finally wore myself out, Smokey took over. He pushed my ass high, forcing my knees to the sides of my head. Not once did he slip out of my hole. He towered above me—sort of kneeling, not quite standing—and drove his cock straight down into me. I felt his maypole rearranging my innards and synchronizing my heartbeat with the fierce tempo of his pounding. The two became indistinguishable—his piston cock and my galloping heart.

My head filled with exquisite visions, and my body thrummed with ecstatic pleasure, but I could bear this feral fucking no longer. Smokey covered my chest with one huge paw and held my cock with the other. He looked me in the eyes and his face grew tight.

"Now," he whispered and I came by the bucket, thrashing against his cock and his hands. I felt him filling me, his cock swelling and exploding, while a roar like an earthquake rumbled from deep within him.

I cried between gulps of air and I felt a little afraid again, but Smokey held me tight with his big hands and soothed me with his breathless sighs and gentle kisses. I knew I would survive when he lay back on the bed and pulled me atop that wondrous chest.

I felt I'd awakened with one foot still in some sublime dreamland; I was exhausted, groggy, and peaceful. I nuzzled into Smokey's fur, found firm nipple, and latched on to it. Smokey locked his legs around my ass and we lay together, our spent dicks bonded by drying come.

I snuggled deeper into the furry warmth of his body. His breath tickled my ear when he whispered, "Nice to meet you, Harold. Glad we're going to be living together."

I fell into a deep, blissful sleep.

The first thing I heard the next morning was the slow bass beat of Smokey's heart. The first thing I felt was his thick, soft fur against my cheek. And the first thing I saw were his gray eyes smiling at me. The first smell was last night's sex, and the first taste was a kiss from his soft, ripe lips.

"Morning, little man. I wasn't sure you would ever wake up." He kissed me again. "Ready for some breakfast?"

"Huh-hmm." I slid down his body and took his hard cock into my mouth. It grew larger and filled my throat.

"Damn, boy, you're going to be a cheap one to feed."

I didn't know what I was doing, since I had never done it before, but I didn't really care. His cock was my long-awaited, much-deserved reward, and I wanted to explore it in my own way.

I kept it deep in my throat for quite a while. Drool dribbled out around it. My nose pressed into the soft, ginger-colored hair at the base of his cock. Last night's spunk mixed with this morning's sweat. The heady smell made me light-headed.

The crown of his cock tapped at the back of my throat. His flavor was slightly hickory-smoked, and memories of those frontier campfire fantasies made me start to hump him.

"You're quite a slut, Harold. I like that in a man." His fingers combed through my hair and I purred.

I slid my face off his cock, and I held it by the base. I licked it like a lollipop. I approached it from different angles and experimented with various tongue strokes. Broad strokes over his piss slit made Smokey purr like a lion. Flicks of my tongue-tip under his crown made him growl. And when I used his balls for jawbreakers, he howled and his legs quivered powerfully.

He pulled on my hair with both hands, forcing me deeper into his crotch. I burrowed my nose behind his balls, and my tongue found his asshole. It tasted sweaty and soapy, not at all shitty, like I thought it might.

I nuzzled it, then pressed my lips against it and sucked. It puckered and pinched my lips and my tongue.

I rose, smiling, from between Smokey's legs. His eyes twinkled as he watched me. He was smiling too.

"I think your asshole likes me. It just gave me a kiss."

"It's got good taste, Harold, but it hates a man who talks too much."

I dived back in. We had a regular affair, Smokey's asshole and I. I snuggled, kissed, sucked, licked, and bit it. It kissed back a lot, but didn't do much else, which was fine with me.

I loved the feel of it as much as I loved the taste. It was firm and dense with wrinkles, but the skin was tender and delicate. It was slick with my spit and some of Smokey's flavorful secretions. I melted into another world, forgetting there was anything other than this tiny star-shaped universe I was worshipping, when the most amazing thing happened. It opened up. Actually, it was more like a blossom. Smokey's asshole blossomed, and the texture was suddenly rubbery: silky smooth, slick and rubbery. And a miniscule porthole appeared, teasing my tongue with possibilities.

I poked the tip of my tongue in, and the porthole closed around it. Smokey's body jerked, and he heaved a sigh like a gale.

He sat up and grabbed my head. "Whoa, now, little buddy. You're going where no man has gone before."

"But I was invited."

Smokey studied my eager face. "Well, to tell you the truth, I have had a yen to try it for a couple of years now. The problem is, most men who are interested in me are pig-bottomed whores— pretty much like you. I can't get them off my cock long enough for us to try anything else."

I practically bounced with excitement. "Ooh, let me try. Let me try."

Smokey shook his head in wonder. "I do believe I'm going to have trouble getting any work done with you around, Harold."

I shoved him and pushed him while he talked, trying to get him to roll onto his stomach.

"All right, all right." He got on his hands and knees. He looked down between his arms and said, "Stick that fucker in there, Harold. I got me a cherry that needs picking."

I mounted Smokey, took aim, and plunged in. If being fucked by him conjured a chorus of angels, then having my cock in Smokey's prime-beef ass made me hear Johnny Weissmuller doing his Tarzan yell. I felt like an M-A-N: the biggest, baddest, butchest stud ever to draw a breath. Granted, I probably looked like a Chihuahua humping a Saint Bernard. But, God, did I feel like a Titan!

Smokey grunted and groaned. He slammed back hard to meet every forward thrust I gave him. With all our banging, crashing, and whooshing, we sounded like icebergs calving from a glacier.

Droplets of sweat flew through the air and rained back down on us. I lost my grip more than once, and my cock dangled from his ass until I could regain my hold.

I wanted to satisfy him—I needed to hold out—but the longer

we went on, the more worried I became. What if Smokey was just too much man for me?

Then his arms gave out, and he buried his face in the pillow. He fired off obscenities like bullets, calling my name between them.

When Smokey wrapped his arms around his head and begged for mercy, my balls retracted into my body. His insides collapsed around my cock and I heard his come splattering against the sheet. Something rumbled at the base of my cock.

When I realized I'd been man enough to earn Smokey's virginity and give him an unassisted orgasm to boot, both my balls and exploded, and come barreled up my shaft, coating Smokey's bowels with thick wads of dick debris.

I could barely breathe. I couldn't think. I could not stop my hips from pumping. Smokey's head was still buried under his arms and he whined, deep and plaintive.

I thought I was recovering when our juices backed up out of Smokey's hole, dripping off my balls and onto his. I lost it again and unloaded a second series of blasts into Smokey's ass. We prayed in unison: "Oh, God. Oh, God. Oh, God."

I collapsed onto Smokey's back and he fell onto his side. I wrapped my limbs around him and bit into his shoulder, anchoring myself to him. I feared I might float away. Smokey crushed my arms to his body, seemingly concerned about the same possibility.

Much later, when I felt it might be safe to let him out of my grasp, I kissed the teeth marks I'd left in Smokey's flesh, and he rolled over to face me. He purred that big cat purr and we kissed.

As I drifted off into a sex-induced reverie, Smokey whispered in my ear.

"Harold?"

"Hmmm?"

"Invited or not, little bear, you're welcome in my ass anytime."

And I fell asleep, knowing I would no longer need my fantasies of Hoss.

Flawless

Thom Wolf

Dancing in a disco, shirt off, arms aloft, made me feel 10 years younger. I was a teenager again, shaking my ass to the beat. The dance floor was packed. Whichever way I moved, I found myself sliding and grinding against hard, sweaty bodies to a monster house rhythm. The scent in itself—a mix of sweat, amyl, and dry ice—was inebriating enough, without the large vodka tonics I'd been knocking back since before midnight.

My lover's hands caressed my ass, his fingers dipping beneath the baggy waist of my jeans. I trailed a finger across his lean chest, licked my lips as I circled his nipples. Marc threw back his head, his laughter unheard beneath the pounding beats. He reached in my back pocket and scooped out the bottle of poppers. We took a hit, and in seconds the scene had intensified. We began to move faster, the music filling us. I moved closer to him, grabbing his ass. We started kissing, passionately, right there in the middle of a crowded floor.

Marc's cock was as hard as my own. We rubbed against each other. His arms moved around my neck, pulling me into a deeper kiss. His cock leaped against my hip. We dry-humped each other. Suddenly, he spun around, pressing his wet back against me. The cleft of his ass moved around my cock. I licked the salt from his neck, holding his tight belly, drawing him nearer.

"I'm horny," he gasped as I licked sweat from his clean jaw.

"I know," I laughed, giving his cock a gentle squeeze. "Want to go upstairs?"

Upstairs there was a dark room. It would be packed by now. Fucking guys that I couldn't see wasn't my thing, but we would often slip in there for a quick blow job on the nights when we couldn't wait to get home.

He moved his ass up and down my cock through my jeans, and I ground against it, getting harder by the second. "I'm not in the mood for that tonight," he said.

"Do you want to go home then?"

He spun around again, cock to cock, face to face. His lips moved softly over mine. "Let's pick someone up," he said. "I fancy some ass."

"Got anyone in mind?"

He nodded over my shoulder, a mischievous glint in his blue eyes. "The disco bunny on the podium."

I turned to look. "Oh, yeah," I gasped. "Good choice."

The guy on the podium was in his early 20s, maybe 22 or 23. He was dancing up there for everyone to see, totally uninhibited. He was topless—his T-shirt was tucked down the back of his tight pants. The white cotton was damp and clung to his pert, shapely butt. Under the flashing lights his briefs were almost transparent, the cotton riding up his tight crack. His hair, from what I could tell, was blond. It stuck to his forehead in dark sweaty strands. He had a beautiful face and body; his muscles were lean but not over-developed. He stood out as a runner or a swimmer among this multitude of Muscle Marys.

He exuded confidence when he danced; he would *have* to be confident to get up there.

As soon as I saw him I wanted him. But so did everyone else in this place.

"He's gorgeous," I said, "but I don't think we stand a chance."

He laughed. "Wanna put money on that?"

Marc took my hand and pulled me through the crowd toward the podium. It was tight going; more than once I felt a stray hand wander to my ass. Marc told me to wait while he climbed onto the podium. I admired his confidence—at times like this he was fearless.

I stood back and waited. He whispered something in the boy's ear. He stopped dancing and they both turned to look at me. I stroked my nipple ring, returning the boy's smoldering stare.

The next few seconds seemed to last forever. I was convinced he was going to tell Marc to fuck off. I waited, already embarrassed. I looked around the room, convinced that everyone there was watching us make fools of ourselves for a piece of blond ass. I dared a glance back to the podium.

The blond was nodding. He was smiling.

My God, Marc had done it. I don't know what it was he said to guys in moments like this, but his success rate was incredible. Guys that I wouldn't ever dare talk to, Marc could win over in seconds.

A moment later they jumped off the podium and came toward me. Marc had his arms around the boy's waist. They were smiling.

"This is Dan," he said, introducing us.

"Hello," Dan said, sliding his arm around my waist and kissing me on the lips. He tasted of sweat and beer. I detected a European accent that I couldn't quite place, maybe German. Up close he was even more handsome. He had a straight nose with slightly flared nostrils. There was a cute beauty spot on his right cheeks, close to the line of his lean jaw. His mouth was wide and narrow, filled with even white teeth. He wore a gold earring in the left lobe.

"Dan wants to come back to our place," Marc grinned.

"I'd like that very much," he said in his sexy-as-fuck accent.

"Let's go, then."

We left the club together, pausing for a moment in the doorway to pull on our shirts—4:30 in the morning is no time to be wandering around with your top off. The club wouldn't close for a couple of hours yet, so we had no problem catching a cab outside. The three of us climbed into the backseat. The driver didn't seem to mind, having probably seen a whole lot more working the night shift.

Dan sat between Marc and me. We were all over him, kissing, stroking, and caressing. His body was incredibly taut and toned. He gasped, opening his mouth receptively to our kisses. His hand was on my neck, turning my head to his mouth, and his tongue licked my lips. I kissed him more, savoring his sweet mouth.

Marc unfastened Dan's jeans. I saw his head go down, quickly followed by the sounds of a cock being sucked. Dan gasped, kissing me furiously. My lips tingled while I kneaded his chest, my fingers toying with his tiny nipples. Through the corners of my half-lidded eyes, I saw Marc's head bobbing up and down in his lap.

I glanced toward the driver. He was watching us in his mirror, but showed no sign of outrage.

Dan's sighs evolved into guttural grunts and became increasingly erratic. His body bucked on the seat. Marc's stifled moans told me that our new friend had just come. Marc lifted his head and licked his lips. Dan grabbed him and kissed him passionately. I joined them for a three-way kiss, tasting Dan's potent spunk on Marc's lips. Dan's passion showed no sign of waning following his climax.

We arrived at our building, quickly paid the driver, and hurried inside. In the elevator, there were more kisses and hot groping. Dan grabbed my cock, tugging it through my jeans. I tugged down the back of his briefs and caressed his hard butt as we walked down the hall. Marc went ahead of us and unlocked the door.

"This is nice," Dan commented.

I moved around the apartment, turning on lamps but keeping the light soft. Dan was breathtaking in the warm light.

"Can I get you a drink?" I asked. "Anything: wine, spirits, a Coke?"

"Whatever you guys are having. I don't mind."

Marc led Dan through to the bedroom while I went in the kitchen in search of drinks. On the countertop we had a rack fully stocked with red wine, but red didn't seem appropriate. I opened the fridge to a selection of white wines and a bottle of vodka. I was just about to pick a bottle of chardonnay when I spotted the champagne we had been saving for nothing in particular. *Mmm,* I thought, *that might be just what we need to turn this night into something really special.*

I opened the bottle, set it up in a bucket of ice, took three flutes out of the cupboard, and carried it all into the bedroom on a silver tray. Marc was lying on top of the bed in his white briefs. Dan was admiring the view from our window. I set the tray on the bedside table and filled the three glasses.

We sat down on the bed together and drank. The champagne was cold and dry, delicious. I had the sudden urge to drink it off Dan's body. Three pairs of hands explored a tangle of bodies, caressing thighs, searching groins. It wasn't long before we were all naked.

Dan and Marc lay on the bed. Marc was on his back with Dan above him in a sixty-nine position. I drank my champagne and watched them devouring each other's cocks. The view was incredible: Dan's thighs spread on either side on Marc's head, his beautiful ass exposed, the crack an open V that revealed everything. His balls splayed across Marc's face, his dick buried inside his mouth. I knew Marc was enjoying himself—he loved to suck cock.

Dan's ass was flawless. It was firm and golden-skinned, with a little brown bud surrounded by swirls of soft blond hair. His crack and his pretty hole glistened in the soft light. I stood over him with the bottle of champagne and slowly tipped the bottle over his buttocks. He gave a little grunt as the cold liquid coursed over his hot butt. The champagne fizzed and then converged like a river to gush down the crack. I shoved my face into his butt, mouth open to drink from his ass, chasing the bubbles.

I licked him clean, from the base of his spine to his balls. Then I poured more champagne over his ass. He treated me to another muffled grunt. Mouth wide, tongue out, I worked his ass, kissing and tasting him. I sucked softly at his anus. He moved his hips up and down, fucking my lover's face.

I looked at his asshole, tight and wet, and knew that I had to be in there. While the two guys continued sucking their cocks, I pulled on a rubber and lubed up. I worked a handful of lube over my fingers and smeared it around Dan's asshole. His anus was soft when I pressed into him, first with one, then two fingers. He was ready for it. I stood over him, holding his hips for support, and pushed my dick down into his crack. My cock head targeted to his hole, I pushed in. Some guys are difficult to penetrate, but Dan's asshole opened effortlessly around me. I moved into him slowly, careful not to hurt him, but I needn't have worried. He could take it.

When I was in deep, I stood for a moment, holding his hips and savoring the warm tingling sensations in my cock. His hot ass gripped me, chewed me softly. I eased myself back, just letting the head remain inside him before driving it to the hilt. I exhaled appreciation and continued, maintaining the slow, intense pace. Holding his ass wide, I watched my dick move in and out of his bud, which was now stretched and bulging.

When Marc rolled out from under Dan, I suddenly had him all to myself. With one hand on Dan's hip, the other on his shoulder, I fucked him harder. Soon I was pounding, watching his buttocks tremble each time my pelvis slammed into him. Dan turned his head over his shoulder, watching me fuck him. He pouted and moaned, sometimes licking his lips and throwing his head back in ecstasy.

I came in spasms, jerking violently into him and yelling with each twitch of my cock. I withdrew and disposed of the heavy condom, my cock softening only slightly. Marc and Dan began to kiss again, jerking each other. I lay back on the pillows to watch them.

Marc reached into the condom bag and handed Dan a rubber. He turned to me with a tube of lube.

"Open up," he grinned. "It's Dan's turn to fuck you."

I lay back and spread my legs, tilting my ass upward. Marc lubed his fingers and gave my asshole a little, stinging slap, before shoving the lube into me. He worked two fingers in deep, taking time to relax and stretch me. Marc knew that my asshole had a tendency to tense after I've come; he wanted to make sure I was loose and lubed enough to take Dan's cock. Dan had a condom on, and he played with himself slowly while watching Marc finger-fuck me.

"You ready?" Marc asked.

I nodded, grabbing the back of my thighs and tilting my ass higher.

Dan moved on top of me, resting his elbows by my shoulders. He dropped his head to kiss me. I lifted my head from the pillows, and our tongues flicked around playfully. The grace with which Dan's cock nudged my asshole and then slipped inside amazed me. I let go of my thighs and wrapped my legs around his back. My ass was upturned and open, and he filled it thoroughly. Kissing me all the while, Dan began to move, building a fast, intense rhythm. I held his head, thrusting my fingers into his tousled blond hair as he fucked me harder. Soon he was fucking like a rabbit, jabbing my ass hard and fast. I clung to him, moaning.

He built himself up, heightening the tension. He gave one final gasp. I felt a huge twitch in my asshole as he started to come. I watched his face, flooding with relief. He pouted, groaned, and closed his eyes. His body went limp in my arms.

Then I felt wetness on my face. I looked up. Marc was standing above us, jerking off in a spectacular climax. Long ropes of spunk rained down on us, across Dan's shoulders, in his hair and over my face.

No one made any attempt to clean up afterward. Dan withdrew, got rid of the condom, then lay down on the bed between Marc and me on the damp, spunky. I poured us each another glass of champagne and we lay together, laughing and talking. It was dawn outside—Sunday. None of us had anything planned other than a few hours' sleep.

We huddled under the covers looking forward to a lazy Sunday afternoon of ass exploration.

"Do you have any toys?" Dan asked.

It was afternoon. We'd been awake a few minutes, just long enough to get up, take a piss, and down a glass of orange juice. Then we were back in bed. Dan was lying between us, an impressive morning hard-on nudging his belly button. I worshiped his balls, turning them over in my fingers. I loved the softness of his scrotum and the way that it sprung back into shape after I tugged it. He groaned and opened his legs a little wider.

"Not many," Marc said, opening the bedside cabinet. He produced a couple of butt plugs, a nine-inch vibrator, and a fat 10-inch dildo. The dildo was my favorite. Marc had bought it for me in a sex shop in Amsterdam. We had slipped straight into the adjoining cinema, where he fucked me with it on the come-stained chairs. Most of the men jerking off in the theater were watching us rather than the movie. Once, in an adventurous mood, I'd managed to take the dildo as well as Marc's cock at the same time. I saw stars that night.

Dan turned over, lifting his ass. "Play with me," he said.

His asshole pouted, typical enough for it being so soon after sex. I emptied a tube of lube into him. His hole fluttered, and I watched the clear liquid ooze back out. He wiggled his butt like a playful puppy. I wriggled a finger into him, feeling him squeeze.

"I love ass play," he confessed. "I used to have a friend who played with me a lot. He would put everything into me. Whatever he could find. Toys, fruit, vegetables. I even had a pool ball in there one time."

"Where are you from?" Marc asked him.

"Cologne."

So I was right about the accent. He was German.

We started with a butt plug. Not too large: two inches in diameter. Marc introduced it to Dan's ass, popping his ring. Dan popped the plug right back out, shooting it across the bed. More lube dribbled out of his hole.

"Bigger," he demanded.

The biggest plug we had was four inches in diameter. I slid my hand beneath his hips to caress his oily cock while Marc pressed the larger toy into him. His cock sprang to attention.

"Oh, that's much better," he gasped.

Marc shoved it all the way, resting his palm flat against Dan's asshole. He let go, and we stared at the squat base protruding from the boy's creamy ass. With a deft thrust he fired the toy out of him, shooting halfway across the bed. "Again," he cried. Marc picked up the toy and shoved it back in. Dan held it for a moment before shooting it straight back out. It was an incredible game to watch: Marc shoving it in, then Dan shooting it out.

I laughed. "Give him the big one—the dildo."

I opened more lube, shoving more of it into Dan's talented hole and soaking the 10-inch piece of rubber. With greasy hands I spread his golden buttocks wide. His asshole stretched and glistened. Marc pressed the blunt rubber head into Dan's taut orifice. It disappeared a slow half inch at a time. Dan groaned, taking it steadily deeper. I watched the thick, veined toy disappear into his soft insides.

I rolled down, scurrying underneath Dan. I wanted to kiss him. His brow was furrowed and beaded with sweat. I licked a film of sweat off his top lip. His cock twitched against my belly as Marc bludgeoned his ass with the dildo. Dan writhed, groaning, pressing his tongue into my mouth. He was oozing precome all over my cock and balls. I held his head, shoving my fingers into damp hair, and devoured his kisses.

I reached over for a condom. Marc shoved deeper with the toy, and Dan grunted. His breath caressed my face in short bursts. I opened the packet and rolled the rubber over Dan's drippy prick. Wanting him inside me, I stuffed a pillow under my hips, getting myself into a good position. I fingered some lube into my hole. I wasn't too tight.

"Oh, yeah," Dan groaned as he thrust his dick into me. I opened my legs, hitching my ass higher and wider, taking him deep inside me. Marc was still fucking Dan with the dildo, and the pressure sent his cock further into me. My sloppy ass swallowed him. The weight of Dan's chest pressed down on my own. His skin was hot and wet. I watched Marc's grinning face over his shoulder.

"Fuck him," I mouthed.

Marc nodded, suiting up and lubing himself. I watched him work a wet fist over his engorged cock. I loved the way it twitched when he touched the head. He gave Dan's butt a little slap.

"Pop that toy out, son. It's time for the real thing."

Dan's brow furrowed and I heard a squelch followed by the soft thud of the dildo on the bed.

"Good boy," Marc said, climbing into position. He pressed on Dan's back, pushing his weight more heavily on top of me. The boy groaned, sandwiched between us. I stroked his hair and licked sweat from the lean line of his jaw. He was smiling.

"I like this," he said. He closed his eyes. Marc shoved into him, and I felt the impact deep inside my own ass, forcing Dan's cock right up there. The breath was pushed out of my lungs each time Marc thrust. Sizzling sweat dripped off Dan's face onto mine. My muscles sucked around his cock like a greedy mouth. Marc was really going strong, fucking the hell out of Dan's ass, the shock waves reverberating in my own.

"Fuck him," I screamed, starting a chant. "Fuck him, fuck him, fuck him. Give him the fucking works."

Marc was gripping his waist, banging like a mad man. Dan's tight belly squashed my cock with each forward lunge. Words flew from between his sweaty lips: "I can take this."

Marc's speed increased. Dan's face was set in a taut grimace. "I'm coming! I'm coming!" He slammed his hips into my ass and emptied a ball load into me. I grabbed at his mouth, kissing while firing my own come shot onto the ridges of his stomach.

Marc pulled out and stood over us: his favorite position—he loves to see me covered in his come. He jerked out one of his spectacular high-arching shots. I held Dan tight, turning our faces to Marc's cock to let his come pour over us.

Construction Hank

Jay Starre

G rant watched the sun sink below the horizon from the framed but glass-less 15th-floor window. The city spread out before him in all its glory: huge, sprawling, and sparkling after a spring rainstorm. The apartments would have breathtaking views when they were completed. Grant stretched and sighed. His body ached after a 12-hour workday. He had been at it since seven this morning, and now it was just about to get dark. Overtime was great for the pocketbook but hard on the body.

"All tuckered out, kid?" He heard a rumbling voice behind him. He turned to face his foreman, Hank. There were only the two workers left in the unfinished skyscraper. Grant felt his stomach churn: He had decided he was going to make his move tonight—no more putting it off.

The two of them had been performing a dance of not-so-accidental physical contact and not-so-innocent innuendo for the past several months. Grant had been working with a constant hard-on. Every one of spare thoughts seemed to involve the hunk of a bear standing in front of him.

Their eyes met. Hank's soft blue gaze was wide and steady. Grant was shaking just from being alone with the man. He stared at the foreman, as the reddish light of the sunset cast a fiery glow around his head. The yellow hard hat framed his square face. He had strong cheekbones accented by a carefully trimmed goatee that surrounded his lush mouth. Grant could only stare, frozen and mute, as Hank grinned.

"What's gotten into you, Grant?" Hank said teasingly. "You look like you think I'm about to fire you or something." Hank moved toward the younger man with the rolling gait of someone with powerful thighs and an equally confident personality.

Grant shrank back toward the open window, attempting to quell the trembling in his limbs and the tightness in his throat. He had sworn to himself that he would tell Hank how much he wanted him, once he knew they were alone. But he found he couldn't speak—he simply couldn't get a word out.

Suddenly, Hank had a hand on his arm, a beefy palm that wrapped around Grant's bare biceps like a warm, firm vice. They were so close Grant could feel the heat of Hank's massive body, smell the odor of a hardworking construction man.

Their eyes were still locked, though Hank's smile had faded, a quizzical expression replacing it. Grant tried to speak but only managed to emit a strange croak that instantly left him feeling totally humiliated. Frightened by his own desire and by the possibility that Hank might reject him, he was just about to break away and make a run for it.

Then he felt Hank's other hand on his body. Hank had slid an arm around him without any warning and clutched one of his ass cheeks. The foreman held Grant firmly in his gloved hand and pulled the wild-eyed youngster against his big burly body. "I think you need some help expressing yourself." Hank said slowly. "You want to fuck?"

Grant couldn't believe his ears. And he was electrified by the sensation of that gloved hand on his ass, kneading cheeks and pressing their pelvises together. The foreman's giant chest rubbed against his. Hank's thick, hard nipples poked through the thin cotton of their T-shirts and into Grant's trembling flesh.

Grant thought he would either faint or come. It seemed those were the only two alternatives. Speaking was well beyond his abilities at that moment. No matter: A second later, Hank lowered his face and crushed his lips against Grant's lips, thrusting a fat tongue deep into the younger man's mouth.

Grant began to give into the idea that he was about to be ravaged. The gloved hand groping his ass, the bare hand kneading his arm, and the hot nipples sliding against his chest, became a blur of exquisite sensation. He moaned from deep inside his body. The sound seemed to come from the base of his cock, from his roiling nut sac, from the twitching pucker of his butthole. He was on fire with lust. He flung his arms around the foreman, grabbing his broad, muscular back. then grabbing his beefy ass and pulling him even closer. He wrapped his own body around Hank's, as if he wanted to fuck the man with his whole being.

Hank pulled back, his tongue sliding out of Grant's mewling mouth. "Whoa, buddy!" he exclaimed. "You're on fire, aren't you? Let's take our time now that we know what we want! Strip down for me. I want to see your hot body in the buff before I fuck you good."

Hank's gruff voice sent sparks of electricity shooting through Grant's body. The promise of a rough fucking from this giant stud had his asshole throbbing with anticipation.

He stared up into the big man's soft eyes, and with trembling hands he began to obey the foreman's command to strip. After months of daydreaming about Hank, Grant could hardly believe this was happening. He was afraid to close his eyes, fearing it might all prove to be just a bizarre dream.

Hank stepped back, but only a foot or two. Grant could still smell him, that heady masculine funk that had his nostrils on fire. Grant heard his sharp breathing as he drank deep draughts of Hank's scent, reveling in the odor enveloping his body.

Grant peeled off his shirt and began to fumble with the zipper on his jeans. "Nice chest," Hank said appraisingly. "Hairless and smooth, to match your sweet baby face!" Hank laughed, the rumble of his voice so exciting that Grant couldn't finish unzipping his fly.

"Too nervous?" Hank laughed again as he watched Grant struggle with his zipper. Two large hands reached out and calmly completed the task.

Grant moaned again when he felt Hank's paws on him. One gloved hand reached into his pants to pull them down, while the other hand, glove-less, deftly managed his zipper. Goose bumps crawled up Grant's spine as he felt Hank's hands on his naked flesh. Hank held Grant in his gaze as he shoved down the younger man's jeans and underwear all at once. Grant turned bright red when his hard cock popped out into the open air.

"Nice rod there, boy!" Hank said, beaming with approval. "I've seen it stiff against your fly for about the last three months. About time we took it out for a walk." Hank slipped his bare hand over Grant's shaft and stroked it lightly as he leaned over and finished shoving Grant's pants down to his ankles.

"Oh, man—man, oh, man, that feels so fucking good!" Grant finally managed to say, though the words spilled out of him in a rush of barely intelligible syllables.

"Get on your knees, Grant," Hank grunted. "And open your mouth."

Those words sent a chill chasing the goose bumps up Grant's spine. He dropped to his knees, reaching out and grasping Hank's hips as he did. Hank chuckled lightly as he unzipped his own fly and fished out a giant slab of dick meat. He rubbed the head and shaft all over Grant's face with one hand while holding the back of Grant's head with the other.

"What a sweet, handsome stud you are," Hank crooned as he stroked Grant's cheeks with his hard dick. Grant stared up at the foreman with wide eyes and opened up his mouth, offering it to the man with a pleading moan.

"Yeah, open wide!" Hank said with a lion's purr as he slid the head of his dick into the heat of Grant's gaping maw. Grant had to stretch his lips to accommodate the girth of the large member. He took it into his throat with more mewls and gurgling sighs.

This was not the first dick to fuck Grant's mouth, but it was the dick he had wanted so badly. Now he was sucking it, wrapping his tongue around the oozing head, massaging the shaft with his eager lips. Grant pulled Hank forward, a hand on each big butt cheek, feeling the power of the man's hips through his tight jeans. He snuffled and gagged and sucked the dick deep into his throat. After a few moments his excitement allowed him to open right up without any problem.

"God, yes!" Hank groaned. He let go of Grant's head and pulled down his own pants. Grant let go of the man's big ass long enough for his pants and underwear to slide down over it, then he eagerly clutched the giant slabs of butt once more.

Grant sucked on the big dick with increased enthusiasm as he ran his hands over the foreman's hairy ass cheeks. They were hard, but huge, covered with silky fur, sleek and soft and hot. Grant's fingers went crazy, grabbing, exploring, searching deep into Hank's crack, where he found a hot, moist butthole waiting for him. He rammed a finger into the palpitating slot and shoved deeper, driving Hank's dick farther into his throat. Hank's tight pucker eagerly responded to Grant's fingering, quivering and opening as he crammed another finger into it.

"A hot little fucker, aren't you!" Hank laughed from somewhere above him. Grant was glanced up from his cock-work to give Hank a smoldering stare.

Hank suddenly pulled his dick out of Grant's mouth. He was grinning as he stroked the flesh in front of Grant and stared down at him. "This thing is going up your ass!" he exclaimed.

Grant had no time to contemplate this prospect. Hank swiftly laid Grant on his back, handling him not roughly, but not gently either. Grant sprawled on his back, his jeans and underwear tangled around his work boots. Hank straddled him, still stroking his dick while he laughed. Then he went down to his own knees and lifted Grant's legs. He yanked on Grant's pants and ripped his underwear as he pulled it over Grant's work boots. Grant felt his thighs spreading as he drew them against his chest. His asshole, suddenly exposed to the air, twitched expectantly.

"Nice ass," Hank remarked. "White and hairless and smooth, just how I like 'em! Very fuckable. Can you take a big dick like mine up there?" Hank leered and stared down at the spread ass in front of him. Before Grant could reply, Hank jammed a blunt finger-tip into his asshole.

Grant howled. He felt impaled by Hank's brutal invasion. "Chew on this. It'll keep you quiet!" Hank huffed, shoving the glove from his left hand into Grant's gaping mouth. Grant tasted leather and wood dust and felt the finger driving deeper into his ass.

"I'll spit on it good, don't worry," Hank offered. "I'll get you nice and stretched out before I feed you my hard dick!" His murmuring voice was husky with passion. As he became absorbed in the task of stretching Grant's bunghole to accommodate his horse dick, his eyes sparkled. He spit into Grant's crack, rubbing the goo into the center of it. Then he used two fingers of his other hand to loosen Grant's butt ring. So he was able to ease another finger into the throbbing slot. Grant tried to temper his breathing and to relax into the approaching fuck.

Hank spat again, landing a huge gob of saliva directly on Grant's loosening pucker. Then he added a third finger to the pair he'd already managed to wedge into Grant. Grant howled into the glove filling his mouth, tossed his head about, and squirmed madly. He'd taken three fat fingers up his ass in less than a minute. And Hank shoved and twisted, probing deeper, without mercy.

"Open up that tight little cunt," Hank growled. "Something even bigger is going up there, and I know you want it, for all your carrying on. You been wanting it for months, wiggling your nice plump buns in front of me day after day, brushing up against me, grinning at me and commenting on my muscles. You want to get fucked, and you're sure as shit going to get fucked."

As Hank spoke, he spat several more times, working the gobs far up Hank's straining hole with his three prying fingers. He was thoroughly enjoying his work.

Grant gazed up at the burly foreman. It was growing dark—only the utility light from partially finished hallway illuminated the two of them. The floor was strewn with lumber, dirt and dust, discarded wires, and long strips of plastic sheeting. A big, hot, hairy man was shoving three fingers up his butthole, while he lay begging for it amid the debris of a construction site. It was a wet dream come true.

With that thought, Grant's asshole opened right up. He wanted Hank to fuck him, to violate him, to fill his asshole and dominate him totally.

Hank felt Grant's butthole relent to his assault, and he laughed out loud. "I think you're ready for my dick, don't you?" he said with a chortle. All in the same broad gesture, he pulled the filthy glove out of Grant's mouth and slipped his fingers out of Grant's limber asshole.

Grant felt bereft, empty, his asshole slack and dripping spit. "Are you ready?" Hank repeated, shoving his hips forward and placing the head of his rocket directly in the center of Grant's slippery ass rim.

Grant felt it there, the big thing poised to fuck him. He was shaking all over, his heart galloping like a racehorse in his chest. He shouted, "YES! FUCK ME!"

"That's the spirit!" Hank said with a hearty laugh. "Now, what do you want?" Hank's his dick head nudged Grant's swollen, sensitive ass lips.

"Fuck me!" Grant pleaded. "Stick your big dick up my butthole. Fill me with cock, shove it in me. I want you so bad. Please, Hank, fuck me!"

Hank began to enter him, slowly stretching Grant's violated ass rim. He hawked another good amount of spit over his disappearing dick head, then repeated the procedure to help ease the next couple of inches into Grant's quivering hole.

Grant lay back and let his body go limp. Hank mounted him, his naked thighs pressed into Grant's ass cheeks, his hands grasping Grant's shoulders as he held him firmly. Hank's dick head was beyond the ring of asshole muscle and began to slide into the channel just past that. It was exquisitely huge, stretching Grant wide open, throbbing in time to Hank's heartbeat.

Grant's pain became a powerful ache, a maddening itch that only Hank's prodigious prong could reach. Grant lunged upward with his hips and impaled himself on the giant dick above him. Half of it slid inside him.

They both shouted. Grant nearly fainted as another wave of heat rushed through his already burning body. Hank rammed deeper, plunging until his balls slapped against Grant's backside. "I'm in you," he said, panting. " I'm in your beautiful ass. Now I'm gonna fuck you good!"

Grant flung his arms around Hank's shoulders and held on for dear life. Locked in this steamy embrace, they felt like one person. Grant's thighs pressed against his chest as Hank, his trusts accelerating, leaned in to suck on Grant's tongue. Hank's giant dick was buried to the hilt, wrapped in heated ass flesh. The two of them became one beast.

Hank began to fuck Grant hard. At first he slid his shaft only an inch or two out of Grant's tight orifice, just enough so he could feel Grant's quivering ass rim and pulsing prostate. Then the foreman began to pull farther out, before plunging deep and withdrawing again. Slowly at first, then faster, he built a feverish rhythm, until he was pulling right out to the tip of his dick head before plunging until his balls slapped loudly against Grant's spit-soaked ass cheeks. They both moaned loudly at first. They began to huff and gasp as Hank picked up the pace.

"I think you're ready for it now," Hank groaned in Grant's ear. "Your hole is ready and wide open. You're a hot cunt for my hard dick, aren't you?"

"Yeah, yeah, yeah! Fuck my hole good, I can take it!" Grant replied, astonished to hear his own voice saying the words.

Hank reared up and drove his rod home. "Take it!" He shouted. He began to fuck in earnest, ramming into Grant, shoving his ass all over the floor, clutching Grant's shoulders fiercely as he ploughed him like a workhorse. Grant blubbered, moaned, and squirmed under the weight of the massive fucking machine on top of him. His prostate throbbed, his balls roiled, his own dick strummed with need between their heaving bellies. He felt like one huge open hole, a maw to be filled with hot fat meat. Then he came. He bellowed like an animal as come spurted across his stomach, ran down to his balls, and mixed with the spit and ass juices dribbling from his battered fuck hole.

"Yeah, that's so sweet, I'm fucking the come right out of you, right out of your hard dick!" Hank shouted when he felt the spray of sticky jizz erupting from Grant's prick. His fucking grew wild and he lifted Grant's ass to hold it steady as he pounded away like a pile driver.

Grant floated in a postorgasmic blur. By then his asshole was just a gaping cavern, wet and open and conquered. His body was bathed in sweat—both his and Hank's—and his own jizz. He smelled sweat, sex, and the dirty floor.

"I'm coming up your poor butthole!" Hank bellowed. A river of warm love juice filled Grant's ass. He heard his own blubbering moans and Hank's choked gasps of orgasm.

But it was not over. Hank pulled his spewing dick from Grant's weary asshole. He released the fucked-over young man and quickly tore off his jeans, which still bunched around his ankles. Then, come still spurted from the purple end of his glistening knob, Hank squatted over Grant's face.

"One more thing," Hank panted. "I gotta feel your tongue up my asshole, and I gotta feel the insides of your sticky butt while you eat my ass."

The words didn't quite register on Grant's sex-fogged consciousness, but the hairy butt that descended to cover his face certainly did. Ass funk filled his nostrils. He opened his mouth and jabbed with his tongue, searching for and finding the parted crevice and the hair-ringed slot. He whimpered with delighted when his tongue entered that small knotted passage. Heated butt cheeks smothered him, covering his face with hard man-flesh.

Then he felt familiar fingers—at least four of them—invading his freshly fucked hole. They dug into him, searching, twisting, and frigging. He could barely hear Hank's voice through the hairy thighs clamped against his ears. "What a sweet, jizzy pussy hole you have," Hank said, with relish. "Yeah, I gotta finger it deep and feel my own come up there. Eat my ass while I finger you till you come again."

Grant understood what was required of him. His flagging dick began to grow stiff again, even though he had come only moments earlier. The taste of Hank's scrumptious asshole and the feel of his roughly probing fingers provided the stimulation he needed to get back in the game. He writhed beneath the hairy beast squatting on his face, thrusting his hips up into the four fingers ravaging his slack butthole.

In a blur of appreciative words, Hank said he loved Grant's squishy fuck hole, he loved Grant's tongue wedged into his own fluttering pucker. He promised Grant he would force another load of come out of him. Grant barely heard any of it. He was concentrating on the beautiful manly rump perched on his face. He squeezed the hefty cheeks, pulling them apart so he could ram his tongue deeper into Hank's tight ass channel, licking the swollen butt lips, then sucking on the twitching hole.

Grant didn't know how long the scene lasted. He could have stayed there all night, covered by a hard, hairy man and filled with a wad of thick knuckles and probing fingertips. But his own body betrayed him: His cock suddenly throbbed and shot another load over Hank's hairy belly.

They lay together for some time afterward, their hands lazily exploring each other's sweaty bodies, which had become caked with the filth of the jobsite. Far below them the city buzzed in the night, and cool air caressed their naked backs and asses.

After half an hour of lazy fondling brought them back to a state of hard, oozing dicks and eager anuses, Hank whispered in Grant's ear. "I'm gonna fuck you again," he said. "This time with my asshole. I'm gonna fuck your dick with my tight asshole until you fill my guts with your come."

Grant did not object. Heck, he wouldn't have objected if Hank had told him he was going to shove a 2-by-4 up his ass. But having his dick up the hunky foreman's sweet bunghole—that was yet another dream come true. You can bet he wasn't going to object.

It was all he could do to hold back a new body-ripping ejaculation when that hairy, tight ass ring enveloped his aching dick for the first time. The next hour was agony. And it was the best overtime of his life.

Cock Pit

Karl Taggart

A lex calls me a heathen when I tell him I worship his butt. I've
got my face down there, playing around his rim. I squeeze his
cheeks in response.

"Amen," I say, admiring his little rosebud pucker.

"All that promise," I tell him. He knows what I mean because
I've said it before, and I'll say it again. It's my own personal mantra.
For me, it's all about what's in there, down inside: soft pink flesh, so
innocent until you pull it open to reveal that little candy center.
That's where I go; that's where I live. I think about this as I push his
cheeks together. I knead him, working my fingers into his taut little
behind, then slowly relent, letting the crack widen: promise. My dick
twitches in anticipation.

Alex squirms beneath my ministrations. He's got a hand on
himself, holding on to try to keep himself from firing. When he
starts to beg, I give in. I pull him open, and there it is.

"Do it," he pleads. I go in again with my tongue—farther this
time, breaking the surface to get at his taste.

I always mount him from behind because, for me, there is no
other way. All I want is ass. I'm on my knees in supplication as I roll
a condom on. Then I get into position and hover at his rim. I'm
holding him open, and he's winking at me, clenching his muscle in
invitation.

"Do it," he says again.

I tell him, "With pleasure," and push in.

I hold him by his hips as I thrust. My thumbs prod his cheeks, and I watch my cock disappear into his hole. And then the word comes back to me like it always does: cock pit. I laughed like hell when somebody said it at a party, but it's totally accurate because no matter how pink and sweet and pristine a butt looks, it's really a dirty little pit. I grind myself into Alex to emphasize the point, as if we're carrying on a conversation when we're really communing with ass and dick. He rides me now, wriggling back on my cock. How I love a working ass. He's voracious, like he wants the whole goddamned world to get in there.

He starts coming and makes it known, letting out a stream of words as well as spunk, which spurs me on. Seconds later, as I'm unloading into him, I visualize big squirts going up into his bowels. He's part of me at that point; I own this ass.

I pound him, ramming home until I'm empty, but even then I don't let go. We gradually subside, everything slow now, easy. When I slide out of him, his hole gapes at me, red and wet. I'm finishing up and thinking about starting in again.

Alex is good about not talking a whole hell of a lot. Beyond his climax chatter he stays quiet, happy to be of service. He follows my lead, does what I ask—the perfect bottom in more ways than one.

When he comes back from a trip to the bathroom he puts on a little show for me. Naked, he moves about the room, examines himself in the mirror, playing with his cock while giving me a view of his juicy rear. He runs a hand back onto his butt, and I suck in an audible breath because I know where he's going. He spreads his legs, continues to play around, then one finger creeps over to his crack and runs the length of it. He moans as if it's a surprise, as if my fingers are back there instead of his. Then he prods, squirms, and pushes into his hole. He leans forward against the dresser and finger-fucks himself, and my dick wakes from its nap and starts to fill. I get a hand on it, working myself slowly as I watch the show.

When Alex gets a second finger into himself, it's all I can do not to jump up and take over, but I lie there, my dick stiff now, dripping precome, while he works himself into his own brand of frenzy.

He squirms as if something foreign is snaking into him, as if he's trying to accommodate a foot-long dick. I picture my own dick going up into his gut, a blind mole navigating the steamy tunnel.

"Come here," I finally say, and he pulls out his fingers, holding his cheeks apart, and then clenches and squirms. He moves to the bed and awaits instructions.

"Get me a rubber," I say.

He does so, then rolls it down my cock and adds lube.

"Get on," I tell him, and he grins and squats over me. "Turn around," I command, because I want his ass, not his face. He does an about-face, and there it is: the ever-rosy pucker, ready to receive.

"Now," I tell him, and he begins his descent, easing down until my cock head pokes his rim. He hovers a second, then drops in one swift motion, driving me up into his rectum in a single thrust that pushes a moan of deep pleasure out of him. He sits anchored there, and I feel his butt muscles contract. He's sucking dick with his ass, trying to fuck himself.

"Ride me," I say, because I need him to get moving. I need a full-out fuck, not his ass play. I watch him lift up, his thigh muscles tightening. Then he begins a steady bounce, taking me to the root with each stroke. He's a master at this. He doesn't bother with his own cock; he knows mine is the priority. I know that he's perfectly happy taking dick—and that he'll possibly get off unaided during the ride.

We settle into a steady rhythm that I know is going to last. The second round is always the best for me. All I want is to stay inside his little cock pit.

We go at it for what seems like hours. Twice Alex gets off and adds more grease. By the time I come, we're awash in hot, runny lube. I grab his hips as I go over, and he holds still as I ram up into him. He lets out grunts with each thrust, as if I've gotten up where nothing's been before. My load is incredible, coming out in long pulses that send shudders through my ass and down into my legs.

When I leave Alex he's still in the bed, still naked. He doesn't want me to go, but knows to keep quiet. There are other priorities now. He's on his side, curled so his pink butt faces me. I think about getting into it again—about that singular taste, that juicy feel—but hold myself in check. I tell him I'll call him. He smiles because he knows I will.

It's late when I hit the street, but I'm not headed home. There is one more stop I need to make. I drive two miles to Ron's house and ring the bell. He answers quickly; he's used to these late-night visits.

He's wearing only briefs when he answers the door. "Hey there," he says as I come inside. He's a big bear of a man, with his furry barrel-chest, and is ruggedly handsome in a way I crave.

We don't say much; we don't have to. He leads me to the bedroom where I undress and crawl onto the bed. Ron stands to one side, the bulge already prominent in his shorts. When he drops them I'm treated to the sight of his big cock on the rise.

There are no prelims with Ron. He gets onto the bed, rolls me over, pulls my ass up, and dives in, issuing a low growl as he licks my rim. When his tongue goes into my hole, my own tongue stirs, as if Alex is still under me. Frenzied, I squirm at both ends. Ron eases off, leaving me wet and ready. I squeeze my muscle, silently begging. He chuckles, then shoves a well-lubed finger into me. I let out a cry and clamp down on him, He obliges with a second digit. I want to get a hand on my dick but am too dizzy to grab hold.

I wish Ron were the talkative type. I think of what he'd say with that low rumble of a voice, how he'd tell me what he was going to do: stick his big cock up my ass and fuck the shit out of me. But he's the silent type—into action, not words.

I'm riding his palm, pushing back as he works my chute. He knows I'm about to come because I'm moaning nonstop. He withdraws, leaving me gaping as he pulls on a rubber. When he sticks his big animal-dick in me, I shoot my load into the sheets, letting him know he's driving the juice out of me. I buck back into him as I squirt, but he just keeps on fucking.

I relax now, relishing the sensation of his big meat up my ass. My thoughts drift back to Alex, to my dick inside him. Half the pleasure of fucking Alex comes from knowing Ron is going to fuck me afterward.

But Ron doesn't care about any of that. He's a fuck machine—all he knows is I've got a willing ass. I discovered long ago that worshiping another butt wasn't enough. I want to worship my own, want to get a cock up there to enjoy things from the inside.

Ron pumps me with the force of a real bear, and I consider that: He's an animal who will devour any creature that happens to cross his path. I revel in the pounding, my ass cheeks tingling as his big body slams into me. I think about what it would be like to have my dick up Alex's ass at this point, how we'd be one long fuck-train. I'd get the best of it: taking a cock up my ass while meat is buried in another sweet bottom. I dream about orchestrating such a scene some day. But for now all I've got is this one-after-the-other scenario: Fuck Alex, then go and get fucked by Ron.

As if to clear my head of such thoughts, Ron leans forward, flattens me, gets prone atop my back, wraps his arms around my chest, and begins to give me a full-body screw. He's grunting with each stroke, and it feels like his cock is blazing a trail up there, pushing into uncharted territory.

It takes him a while to empty himself—no surprise, considering the size of his balls. When he's finally done, he pulls out and heads for the bathroom. I'm left alone in his bed. I rise, look in the mirror, and turn around to view myself from the rear. My butt cheeks are flushed a bright red. I run my hand over them and squeeze, then pull them open to view the center. There's a dribble at the rim, still gaping from the ride and tingling in fond remembrance of Ron's big dick. I think about it again: cock pit, the center of the universe. Ron comes back into the room and catches me inspecting myself.

"Whatcha doin'?" he growls. I'm almost embarrassed, but I don't let my embarrassment stop me. I poke a finger at my hole, and he says, "Want some more, do you?"

He's not gentle, and I love it. He positions me at the dresser with my ass thrust out at him, then shoves a couple fingers up me and starts working my chute again. He strokes his big bear-dick at the same time. I watch us in the mirror, this big furry creature behind me, getting ready to ream me all over again. He fucks his cock into his palm, and I know he's almost ready. I ride his fingers, eager for him to give me his slab of meat.

He pulls his fingers out, gets a rubber, readies himself, and opens my cheeks. He shoves himself into me with a long single stroke. I let out a grateful moan; this is what I live for. My recollections of fucking Alex are vague now. A cock up my ass reduces everything else to insignificance. Now Ron is riding me, holding me at the waist and pounding me while I grip the dresser and watch the show.

"Live porn," he says as he screws his meat into me. He grinds and growls until I start to come. Cream shoots all over the front of his dresser. I howl, and he emits a half-growl, half-laugh. His big thighs are taut as he shoves his man-meat up my rectum.

The fuck is a long one; I'm so dazed I can barely stand. Ron has an iron grip and holds me firm as he spears me over and over. When he finally announces he's there, I picture his big prick spewing streams of come. I feel the power of his orgasm flooding my bowels.

Afterward he pulls out and hurries to the bathroom. Once again I'm left alone. I stagger to the bed and fall into the sheets, struggling to regain my breath. As my ass tingles in its own post-fuck euphoria, I hope Ron will go for a third helping—maybe even a fourth, if I'm lucky. I squeeze my sphincter muscle, knowing my cock pit will never get enough. And I think of sweet little Alex, with whom, right now, I feel a special kinship.

Hit-and-Run

Sean Wolfe

"That's it, man. Shove it up my ass. Deeper. Harder. I can take it."

Those were the words that pushed me over the edge, past the point of no return.

I'd been inside the dark closet-size stall for nearly 15 minutes. I was just about to give up and leave when I heard the flimsy door of the stall to my left open and then quickly swing shut. By the time I leaned down to look through the large hole in the middle of the wall. it was too late. I couldn't see what the guy on the other side looked like.

Not that it really mattered. There were only seven or eight other guys in the entire bathhouse, and none of them was a complete troll. After walking aimlessly through the dark mazes and past empty hot tubs for almost two hours, I decided to just slip into one of the glory hole stalls and wait. I was so horny I would have gladly sucked or been fucked by any of the other patrons in the rambling, almost empty building.

I dropped to my knees and was just about to rub my fingers against the edge of the glory hole, signaling for the guy on the other side to shove his cock through so I could swallow it deep into my throat. I love sucking big, fat, anonymous cocks through glory holes more than just about anything.

But it didn't go that way this time. This time the guy on the other side of the wall beat me to the punch and rubbed his fingers along the curved edge of the glory hole. I tried to move his fingers away and trace my own circle around the oval opening, but he pushed my hand aside and stuck his tongue through the hole insistently.

"Let me suck your cock, man," he said huskily. "I wanna get it all hard and wet so you can shove it up my ass and fuck my brains out."

I shook my head dazedly, but stood up and leaned into the hole anyway. My cock was barely through the smooth opening before his tongue reached out and touched it. He lapped at the head for a few seconds, then wrapped his lips tightly around the shaft as he sucked the rest of my eight-inch prick into his warm, hungry mouth.

I moaned as my cock got rock-hard and I began to pump in and out of the unseen flesh hole on the other side of the wall. I'd always prided myself on being a great cocksucker—and had been assured on more than one occasion that I was not mistaken in my assessment. But if I was even half as good as the guy who was swallowing *my* cock, then I should have won several awards by now.

My knees began to buckle, and I found it difficult to breathe. My shaved low-hanging ball sac drew closer to the base of my throbbing cock. Against the darkness of the room, little red dots flashed before my eyes as the familiar tingle welled deep in my groin.

Before I could pull my cock away from the demanding mouth, an orgasm overtook me. My body went limp as I shot seven or eight thick jets of come down the stranger's throat. He swallowed all of them and continued sucking on my dick, milking it of every last drop.

"Fuck, man, that was great," the husky voice whispered. "Can you keep it up for some more? I really want to feel that fat cock in my ass."

Normally, I'm finished after my first load, but hearing this desperate man pleading for me to fuck him was more than I was used to. My cock bounced excitedly and remained fully hard and ready.

Within seconds, the hot wet mouth on the other side of the wall was replaced with two smooth, hard butt cheeks. The stranger pushed his ass against the glory hole and ground it against my cock, begging me to take control.

So I did just that. I reached through the broad hole in the wall and grabbed his ass with both hands. Then I pulled it up against the wall and held it steady as I knelt in front of the hole. I stuck my tongue out and licked his ass crack vigorously, making sure to use as much saliva as I could muster. His moans of approval were all I needed to motivate me. I snaked my tongue into the hot hole in the center of his muscular ass and pushed forward until I was all the way inside.

"Oh, yeah, dude, that's it. That feels great. But I want the real thing. I want your big dick up inside my ass."

I immediately withdrew my tongue and rose to my feet. All of the glory hole stalls were supplied with condoms, and I fumbled around in the dark until I found the small tray that held them. I ripped the corner off one of the cellophane packets and rolled the pre-lubed rubber down my hard shaft.

"Come on, man. Give it to me."

Damn, this guy is pushy, I thought. I grabbed my cock by the base and shoved it back through the hole in the wall. It didn't take long for me to find his hot asshole, and I pushed all the way into it with one quick thrust.

I expected him to cry out in protest, or to whimper and try to pull himself off my spearing cock. Instead, his hot ass muscles gripped my throbbing rod and squeezed it like they were milking an overburdened udder. The guy on the other side of the wall grunted in enjoyment and worked his tight, muscular ass up and down the length of my dick. I felt his internal muscles envelope my cock as he rode it with wild abandon. The thin wall separating us creaked in protest as his body repeatedly slammed against it.

"Fuck me, dude. Fuck my tight ass harder."

Up to this point I hadn't really needed to be the aggressor because he'd pretty much done all the work. But now I was determined to give him the fuck of his life. I withdrew my long cock until only the fat head remained inside his ass, then slammed it back in ferociously. I repeated the movement over and over again, thinking I was really showing this guy who was who. I counted to 10 in my mind and tried to think of anything that would keep me from shooting too soon.

"More," he cried out. "I want more!"

More? My head began to spin as pinpoints of light flashed before my eyes for the second time that night. Because he was on the other side of the flimsy wall and I couldn't grab him by the waist, I hooked my hands over the top of the wall and held on tight as I rammed my cock into his ass harder and faster. Once I was buried inside him, I twisted my waist so that my cock slid along the inside walls of his clutching chute.

"Oh, yeah, that's it. That's what I want. Fuck me harder."

Sweat poured down my face and chest as I thrust myself into him with every ounce of strength I had. My knees began to shake from the force of my fucking. I knew it wouldn't be too long before I'd be unable to hold back my load. I tried to slow down a little, but his tight ass grasped my cock even tighter, locking me deep inside him, refusing to let me out. His ass muscles massaged my cock like tiny fingers and tickled the head as it pushed up against the deepest part of his insides.

"That's it, man. Shove it up my ass. Deeper. Harder. I can take it."

"Oh, fuck, man, I'm gonna come," I almost yelled.

In an instant he pulled himself off my rock-hard cock, and I felt a brush of cool air surround the base of my dick and balls.

"Pull off the rubber," he panted. "I want you to shoot on my face."

"It's too late," I moaned. "I'm com—"

His hands reached through the hole, grabbed my cock, and ripped the condom off just as the first spurt of come shot up my shaft and out the head.

My body convulsed as wave after wave of spunk spewed from my cock. My knees gave out after a few seconds, and I had to lean against the wall for support. At the same time I heard the guy on the other side moaning loudly. His moans became more guttural—more animal—with each fresh splash of hot come across his face.

When I was completely spent, I felt his tongue lap at my cock. He eagerly licked up every drop of jism lingering on my prick head. Then, a couple of seconds later, as I was still trying to catch my breath, I heard the door on his side of the wall squeak open and shut again. His footsteps faded down the hall before I could open my door and get a look at him.

Clean Shorts

S. Flitman

It was 5 P.M. on a Sunday evening, and I was faced with a situation. I hadn't done laundry in forever and had no clean clothes to wear to work. More important, I had no clean underwear. I could get over wearing a pair of jeans or a pullover a couple or three times, but I had to have clean shorts. So, I threw on an old pair of sweats and a T-shirt, then began stuffing dirty clothes into a big plastic bag.

The smell of detergent and bleach greeted me when I walked into the Laundromat about half an hour later. I made my way through the sitting area and rows of folding tables to two empty washers in a corner. I separated my wash, dumped in some powder, set the dials, threw in some quarters and was in business.

I plunked my ass down on one of the seats and picked up the sports page from a discarded newspaper. Just as I was getting settled, the door opened with a whooshing sound. I glanced over the top of the paper in time to see a woman in a leather jacket stride through. And trudging behind her, arms laden with a basketful of laundry, was one of the sexiest men I'd ever seen.

I felt my jaw drop as my eyes widened. I realized I was staring and raised the paper, hoping to regain my composure. A second later I lowered the newspaper to sneak another peek.

He was at least 6 foot 1 or 6 foot 2, and in his late 20s or early 30s. His face was almost unbelievably handsome: short dark hair, strong cheekbones, ice-blue eyes, a square jaw, and a neatly trimmed mustache.

This dude had the body to match. He set the basket of laundry on top of the empty washer next to mine, giving me a good view of his physique, including a hard, square ass showcased in a well-worn pair of blue jeans. He wore shit-kicker construction boots on his big feet and sported an old ball cap that bore the logo of our local pro-football team.

As I listened to the woman in the leather jacket bark orders at him, it became clear he was pussy-whipped. Proof of just how much power she wielded over him glinted on his left hand in the form of a gold wedding ring.

Using the paper as cover, I observed him as he lugged in two more big baskets of wash. As the wife fired commands at him in a soft and pretty but firm voice, the scowl on his hard square jaw deepened. Yet he complied, never once daring to contradict her.

"No!" she snapped. "You're using too much powder! Make sure you separate the colors—and put your work clothes in by themselves. I don't want your stuff mixed in with mine."

He growled something under his breath but did as he was told. The woman in the leather jacket checked her manicured nails before retrieving car keys from her purse.

"I'll be back in a few hours," she said, and with that she exited—no hug, no kiss, no nothing.

The hunk grunted a response while stuffing dirty sweat socks into one washer and lingerie into another. I figured that he—like me—wanted to be anywhere but washing clothes on a Sunday night. Home watching sports with the remote in one hand and a cold beer in the other would probably be his first choice. I couldn't help thinking this probably wasn't the only thing that wasn't going his way. The wife was probably only giving it up to him twice a year—once on his birthday, the other on their anniversary—leaving him to jack off to magazines the rest of the time.

"Sad," I huffed aloud. I realized I'd said it a bit too loud when the man at the washer shot a look in my direction. A jolt of adrenaline pulsed through me. Thinking on my feet and playing it cool, I shook the sports page, indicating the baseball scores. "You believe this shit?"

His face broke into a slight grin. He didn't say anything, though, and for the moment the crossing of our paths ended there. With four washers filled and more laundry waiting, the hunk popped a cigarette into his mouth and strutted outside, leaving me alone mere yards from a basket of whites—his whites.

My heart began to beat faster at the sight of his underwear. I though of how it hugged his hairy nuts all day long and held his cock snugly. It probably had a wonderfully manly scent, and all that was about to be washed down the drain.

Before I could stop myself I swiped a pair of underwear from the top of the basket and jammed them in the pocket of my sweats, rubbing them against my boner nervously. The hunk walked back in, oblivious to my theft, and threw another load into a washer.

About half an hour later, while I transferred my clothes to a dryer, I watched him load the last of his wife's shit into an empty washer. And as he did so, I caught the handsome fucker doing the same thing I planned to do to his shorts once I got home. While stuffing her panties into the machine, he bunched up a pair, brought them to his nose and sniffed deeply. Just as I noticed the bulge of a boner beginning to pop up between his legs, he noticed me looking. He shoved the panties into the washer, closed the lid, and headed toward the door of the Laundromat, fumbling with his pack of cigarettes on the way out.

I don't know how long I sat paralyzed, aware that my own cock had stiffened noticeably in my sweats from seeing him get aroused. Nor do I know what possessed me to follow him—other than the fact that I was hoping to see even more of him in his excited state.

It was already dark outside, and my hunk was nowhere to be seen—at least not near the entrance. A trace of cigarette smoke led me to toward the right side of the Laundromat and, with lumps in both my throat and my pants, I forced myself to go around the corner of the building.

What the fuck are you doing? I asked myself. By the time I got the answer I was there, staring at an alleyway bound by a chain-link fence and some trees on one side, the building wall on the other. Down that alley, under an overhang, stood the hunk.

It was hard to see much in the poorly lit alley, but I could make out that he had one foot against the wall with his legs slightly spread—and his fly was open. His right hand was nestled inside the well-packed tent of his crisp white briefs. The other held a lit cigarette. I wasn't sure if he saw me at first, but something crunched beneath one of my shoes as I stepped closer, alerting him to my presence. He looked up and realized I'd again caught him in the middle of doing something intensely private.

"What the fuck?" he growled in a deep manly voice.

A wicked grin crossed my face. I knew that I'd shocked him. I also knew that he was as hard as a rock in those shorts.

"I just wanted to bum a cigarette off you, dude," I said coolly. "But after seeing that," I tipped my head toward his crotch, "I'd rather wrap my lips around your cock."

He mumbled something profane and tossed his lit smoke before fumbling with his pants, trying to get them closed. "Get the fuck out of here."

I couldn't believe what I was saying, or how bold I was with him. But it was just the two of us alone in the dark, and he was hurting. I knew it, and so did he.

"I mean it," I said. "You need some attention, don't you? I'll give it to you."

I heard his zipper rise. Then, to both my shock and excitement, he lowered it again—slowly, hesitantly at first. I peered through the shadows to see the hand he'd been pumping himself with clamped around the lump in his underwear. I moved to within a yard of him. When he didn't protest, I shuffled even closer, reaching toward his tented underwear. My fingertips brushed the back of his hand, which slipped aside to expose his open fly. I reached in, gripped the moist, warm protrusion, and gave it a firm squeeze to seal our understanding. He wanted his dick sucked, and I intended to suck it. So down I went.

I sank to my knees on the pavement and felt the shock of the hard cement through the material of my sweats. I pressed my face into his package, smelling the clean, manly odor.

"Yeah," he groaned, gripping the back of my head with one of those strong, bear paw–like hands.

I took another whiff of his musk, then tugged his pants down, taking his tightie-whities with them. His hard, thick cock snapped up in my face. It curved upward and was ready to be sucked. Beneath it dangled two meaty low-hangers, loose despite a sudden rush of cool air across his sac.

I extended my tongue and brushed it against the straining head of his cock. I caught a taste of salty moisture from his pee hole. I licked around the ridge of his tool and down the veined, bumpy underside until his seven bone-hard inches thumped against my forehead, and I had a face full of straight-dude nuts.

"Ungh," he grunted. He slid his free hand back onto his cock and stroked it while I licked the manly sweat off his hairy, meaty balls. He took his dick by its hairy root and patted the side of my face a few times, enough to draw my mouth back to the helmet of his dick head. I gulped his cock between my lips and gave it several hard sucks.

The straight hunk moaned a deep "Fuck!" and urged me to keep going. "Suck that dick. Show me how much you want my cock!"

I opened even wider and took as much of his shaft as I could. He obviously appreciated my deep-throating technique. The way he was reacting, I figured his woman hadn't given it to him like this in a long time—if ever. I had no way of knowing if he'd ever let another guy do this to him before, but I sure as fuck planned to make the experience unforgettable.

I came up for air, then plunged down on his tool again, all the way to his patch of musky-smelling pubes. I grabbed hold of his nuts and squeezed them. With my free hand I stroked his solid, hairy legs.

I continued like that for several minutes. His feral grunts grew louder and deeper the longer I sucked, and the coating of his nut juice on my tongue grew thicker.

I knew he was close. He had to be. I'd come dangerously close to blowing a load in my own shorts—and I hadn't even touched my own boner! When I took my hand off his hairy quads and reached into my sweats to squeeze my dick, my fingers found a puddle of precome.

I moaned, then resumed sucking his cock. I barely broke stride and settled into stroking my dick in my sweats. I was so into it that I almost didn't hear him grunt, "You ready for my load, cocksucker?"

The lava in my nuts bubbled closer to eruption. I skidded up his cock and back down it, burying my nostrils in his bush.

"Here it comes!"

The next slide up his pole did it. A blast of hot spunk spewed violently onto my tongue. I did my best to hold it in my mouth and managed to catch the successive squirts he dumped down my throat. When he was finished, I hastily pulled my hand out of my sweats.

With his head thrown back, the hunk didn't see me spit his wad onto my palm and reach back into my sweats. Using his still-warm jizz, I lubed up my cock and, after several strokes, dumped a desperately needed load of my own.

I staggered back into the Laundromat with stains on both of my knees and stale come on my lips and in my sweats. I quickly grabbed my clean, dry clothes and drove home, still dazed by the events of the day.

Back at my place I stripped off my sweats and headed to the shower, tossing my nasty clothes in a pile on the floor. The underwear I'd swiped from my handsome stranger fell out the pocket of my sweats. Picking it up, I brought it to my nose and inhaled deeply. I knew I'd have to go back to the Laundromat in a week or so, but I probably wouldn't take that pair of shorts with me. I liked them just the way they were.

Rendezvous
at Sunset

Thom Wolf

On the second week of my vacation, I settled into a loose routine. I got up around midday, tired and hung over, but generally feeling pretty chipper. I was determined to get some sun on my skin and return home with a stunning tan. I usually managed to wake myself up with a long shower and make it to the beach by 12:30 or one o'clock. After smearing myself with sunscreen, I crashed on a sun bed for three or four hours, catching up on sleep while working on my tan.

Most days I made it back to the apartment around six, crashed on top of the bed for a couple of hours before getting ready to go out. It sounds like I did nothing but sleep, but on an island like Ibiza, a boy needs to save his energy for the night. I usually got something to eat in one of the local bars. Then I'd head into town around midnight. None of the bars really got going until around 11:30. Two-thirty to three in the morning was time to hit the nightclubs. Around six, depending on my mood, I would either head back to the apartment or walk up onto the ramparts of the old town. Cruising on the ramparts really got going between six and eight.

Most mornings I didn't bother. I rarely had the energy. The nightclub Anfora gets packed with some of the hottest guys in Europe: Spanish, English, German—they all flocked to Ibiza to party and get laid. If I didn't manage to bag a guy on the dance floor, the top floor of Anfora boasted a large, well-populated dark room.

As soon as I got to the club I would grab a drink from one of the drag queens at the bar then head up to the dark room for half an hour. I'd suck a couple of cocks then let some guys suck me in return, all to the soundtrack of guttural groans, slurps, and slapping skin. The place reeked of sweat, come, and poppers.

It was compulsively sleazy.

Once I'd shot my load, getting all that raw energy out of my system, I would hit the dance floor. European dance music is the best—uplifting and euphoric. Once I started dancing, it was difficult to stop. Off went my shirt and with it my inhibitions.

Anfora was set within the ancient walls of the old town, and the dance floor is actually a large cave. It was hot and intimate, packed with sweaty guys, most of them shirtless and having a great time. I usually managed to pick up a cute Spanish boy or a horny Englishman to finish off the night.

It had been a sexually eventful vacation. So far the highlight had been a gorgeous British couple in their late 20s, whom I met during my first week. I went back to their apartment and didn't surface for 36 hours. We fucked ourselves into a stupor. That was the only day I didn't make it to the beach. I met them again a few nights later for a drink, but they had since returned to England. A shame, that: I would have loved to see them again. We exchanged contacts before they left, and I had an invitation to visit them in the U.K. before returning to the states.

Halfway through my second week, another day was beginning at noon. I'd gotten in early in the morning around five. I was exhausted. The constant partying, all the sex, and the excessive drinking were all starting to catch up with me. I needed a rest. I wished I'd had the guts and the cash to visit Ibiza when I was a teenager. At 18, full of energy and spunk, I would have maintained the pace effortlessly. At 25 I was starting to struggle.

I got to the beach later than usual. The heat was scorching. I managed to get a sun bed in my usual space, with its magnificent view of the Mediterranean Sea and the gorgeous guys who frolicked in it. I smiled and nodded at the man to my left. Just like me, he chose the same spot every day. We always smiled at each other, though it was friendly rather than cruisy. He was good-looking with blond hair and spectacular muscles. He looked to be in his 30s, and I assumed he was German. He was a handsome bastard, all right, just not my type.

I spread out my towel and crashed on my back. On my headphones I had a CD of mellow dance tunes. I read for a while, admired the view (tight Latin bodies in tiny trunks), but eventually I began to dose.

I woke around five. The sun had dipped slightly in the clear blue sky, but it was still fierce. I glanced around. There was still plenty of flesh to admire, but my German friend had packed up for the day. I wondered whether I should fuck him before the end of the holiday. Like I said, he wasn't my type, but that didn't matter too much. I had a feeling that sex with him would be fantastic.

I decided to gather my stuff and leave. I'd had enough of the beach. I tossed everything into my bag—towel, books, sunscreen, and CD player—and headed onto the promenade. The bars along the front were all busy: still more gorgeous guys in tight trunks, drinking beer and sangria. Walking along the promenade was akin to a catwalk: lots of turning heads and meaningful glances.

The notion of a cold beer in this intense heat suddenly seemed appealing. I was already planning on a quiet night tonight (a self-imposed three A.M. curfew and no nightclubs), so there was no harm in having an afternoon drink.

I wandered along to DJ's, my favorite bar, which was run by a couple of British guys and had an open-air terrace. The sound of Kylie Minogue drifted along the road as I drew nearer. The bar didn't over look the beach directly, so it tended to be a little quieter than the ones right on the promenade. The up side of this was that it was exclusively gay; the beachfront bars had a tendency to attract stray straights.

There were around a dozen men sitting on the terrace, the

majority of them English. I smiled at a couple on my way in. A large electric fan slowly turned at the edge of the bar, but the heat inside was almost unbearable. I ordered a large glass of beer and carried it back to the terrace.

The tables were all occupied. I was about to sit down on the low wall when I noticed a young Spanish guy sitting alone and sipping a beer. There were three empty chairs around his table. I looked at the guy. Wow! The view from DJ's terrace was impressive enough, but this boy improved the natural landscape a hundred times more.

"Excuse me," I said, wishing I'd persevered with the Spanish lessons back home. "Is this seat free?"

He smiled. "Yes," he said as he motioned for me to sit down.

I tossed my bag on the floor and climbed onto the high chair. Over a heavy synthesized beat, Kylie was singing about her love-sick fever. Stealing glances at my Latin companion, I knew what she meant.

He was wearing a pair of baggy red shorts and sandals. He was tall with a great body, lean and taut. I guessed that he was younger than I, maybe 21 or 22. He had a handsome face with a wide mouth and clean jawline. His hair was thick and wavy, tucked behind his ears.

I pulled out a packet of cigarettes, offered it to him.

"*Gracias,*" he said, thrusting the cigarette between his plump lips.

I lit my own and passed him the lighter. Our hands brushed lightly when he gave it back. He held out his hand.

"Mikos," he said.

"*Hola,*" I said shaking his hand. "My name is Thom."

We started chatting. Although Mikos spoke with a strong accent, his English was first-rate. I professed my shame over knowing no foreign languages and vowed to take up Spanish lessons again. Mikos was from Madrid, in Ibiza for a short holiday. Like me, he was here on his own.

In no time our beers were finished and the packet of cigarettes was almost empty. Mikos went to the bar, returning with two more large beers. I had a hard-on. Sitting here on a sun-drenched terrace while drinking beer in the afternoon with a gorgeous guy was the stuff of wet dreams. I already knew that Mikos was hard. When he returned with the drinks, his red shorts concealed nothing. He was sporting a meaty piece of cock.

I was about to ask if he would like to come back to my apartment when he beat me to it.

"My hotel," he said, pronouncing it *O-tel,* "It has a good view of the sea. It is very nice to watch the sun setting."

I nodded, smiling.

"Would you like to see?" he asked.

"Yes," I said. "I'd love that."

His hotel was only a block away from my apartment. He had a spacious room on the fourth floor. He was right about the view: His balcony overlooked the bay, and the panoramic scene was breathtaking. I leaned over the edge and gazed out. The beach was almost empty now, since everyone had headed back to hotels and apartments to prepare for the evening. The sky was changing color from blue to a rich shade of violet streaked with orange.

Mikos put on a CD and joined me on the balcony with two cold bottles of beer. He had kicked off his sandals.

"Do you like it here?" he asked.

"I like it a lot. The view from here is better than my own apartment."

We looked at each other, eyes connecting. We put down our beers and started kissing. Suddenly, we were hungry, mouths open, tongues thrusting. I devoured his lips and the sexy flavor of beer and smoke. His arms were around my back, one hand pulling up my T-shirt, the other grabbing my ass. I shuffled around until Mikos was leaning against the balcony, then I broke free of his kisses.

I dropped to the floor. His large package throbbed in his shorts. I rubbed my face against his groin, feeling his heat and hardness through the rough material. He groaned, murmuring words I didn't understand. I got the meaning, though. I mouthed his cock through his shorts. Mikos was probably no longer than I was, a decent seven inches, but he was thicker—a lot thicker. He throbbed against my open lips.

He put his hand on my head, moving me back slightly, and shoved down the front of his shorts. His fat cock almost hit me in the face. He was so stiff that his foreskin had already slid behind his cock head of its own accord. I dragged his shorts over his hairy brown thighs and down to his ankles. Mikos raised one leg at a time and eased them all the way off.

I fell onto his cock, mouth open, determined to deep-throat him on the first attempt. His big fat shaft slid down my throat, stretching and filling me. He muttered more words in Spanish. I turned my head from side to side with his cock buried deep, inhaling the meaty odor of his pubes. He had a rich, manly scent. My jaw was already starting to ache.

With my face impaled on his cock, my hands moved round to his ass, grasping two tight little mounds. He had one of those impossibly high, gravity-defying butts. I squeezed his flesh, working my fingers into the tight crack. I dug into the hairy cleft, targeting his hole. As I fingered the brown bud, Mikos gasped and his cock throbbed.

As much as I loved sucking cock, I was an ass man at heart. I withdrew his cock from my mouth and looked up into his tender brown eyes.

"Turn around," I whispered.

With a flash of his attractive smile, he offered me his beautiful ass. It was smooth and creamy, the color of a rich latte, and adorned with a dusting of soft brown hair. I grabbed it in both hands and kissed each cheek in turn, rolling my tongue across his skin. He rested his elbows on the balcony and bent over, giving up more of his butt. His cheeks widened as he stayed in that position, and I spread them farther apart. His asshole was a small pouting pucker surrounded by a swirl of damp hair. I felt his body shiver when I brushed my tongue down the full length of the crack, skimming lightly over his anus.

The scent and the flavor of his hot cleft were intoxicating. I buried my face in his butt, kissing, licking, and breathing him in. I heard him gasp when I used the tip of my tongue to open him, moving softly inside.

I sucked my index finger, getting it good and wet. Then I used it to trace his puckered ass rim. His anus put up no resistance when I entered him, slowly moving deeper. He took a second finger effortlessly. With my left hand flat against his butt, holding him open, I used two fingers on my right hand to explore his passage, soothing and relaxing the robust muscle.

"I want to fuck you," I said, kissing the base of his spine, where he had a small patch of fussy brown hair.

"Yes," he replied, his asshole fluttering around my fingers.

I had a safe-sex kit with me in my beach bag. I handed Mikos a sachet of lube. He tore it open and greased his ass while I lost my clothes. I love watching a guy stick his own fingers up his butt. My eyes fixed on his hand, watching his fingers slip in and out of his hole. I barely looked at my own cock while I rubbered up. I was so adept at putting on a condom that I could do it in pitch darkness. When Mikos was finished with the lube, I used the remainder in the sachet to coat my dick.

He kept his position, leaning against the balcony. I stood behind him, sliding one hand around him and holding his flat belly. I used my other hand to guide my cock into his ass. I pressed my head against his hole. He pressed back. His asshole unfolded around my cock at first, before it offered a slight resistance. He gave a gentle sigh, then I was in. We both groaned as I pushed all the way into him, my hips pressed against the firm curve of his ass.

I stood still, holding him, enjoying the warmth and tightness on my cock. I kissed the back of his neck and ran my lips over his hair. Mikos relaxed and, as he gripped the rail, began to gently rock his pelvis. "Yes," he whispered, "I am ready."

I moved with him, finding his rhythm. My cock tingled with infinite sensations, sensations that only a man's ass can induce. I held his tiny waist, kissed his neck. He turned his head, wanting me to kiss his lips, tongue thrusting. His ass gripped my cock tighter, and

I fucked him harder, pulling back further, slamming deeper. Mikos's cock bobbed against his stomach. I grabbed hold of it, squeezing him tight. Precome leaked over my fingers. His cock fucked my hand with every thrust I gave his ass.

His ass tightened around my dick and, with a guttural moan, Mikos came. His come blasted in spurts against the balcony wall. His ass was now so tight that I could barely move. With two more thrusts I began to blow. I clenched my teeth and filled the condom with an orgasm that seemed to last for hours.

When I withdrew, his ass was so tight that the come-heavy tip of the rubber remained inside him. I released it with a firm tug and tied it off.

We reached for our beers and quenched our thirst, laughing.

"Come," Mikos said, holding my hand.

He led me into the bedroom where two single beds had been shoved together to make a double. We lay on top of the white sheets. He climbed on top of me, kissing all the while. We kissed and caressed each other, stroking our cocks, which had only softened slightly. Pretty quickly, we were hard again. We rolled over—I was on top. Mikos's hands stroked my back and my ass.

This intimacy was almost unheard of. Most of the guys I had met on holiday couldn't wait to say goodbye in the wake of orgasm. With the exception of the English couple, there was seldom any kissing and caressing afterward. I love holding a man like this, kissing. Why does it always have to stop after one orgasm?

Mikos rolled me onto my back again. With a grin, he raised my knees to my chest. "It's my turn," he said, moving toward my upturned ass.

His mouth bypassed my cock and balls and moved straight into my butt. He tongued my crack, finding my asshole and darting into it. I groaned, lifting my hips higher. The lip service he lavished on my ass worked me into a stupor. My head was spinning around. I was half crazed with pleasure.

"I want to be fucked," I gasped.

Moments later he was kneeling between my legs, his fat Latin dick rubbered up and shining with lube. I gripped the back of my thighs and pulled them tight to my chest, giving him an unrestricted shot at my hole. I trembled with anticipation, moaning as the blunt head nudged my ring. He pushed inside. My asshole was already relaxed from the attention he had paid it with his mouth. I opened up to his cock effortlessly. It was the thickest cock I'd had during my entire holiday, and I took it easily. Slowly, Mikos pushed all the way in, filling me with his meat. I felt his balls press against my ass. I reached around and grabbed his butt, pulling him further in. He leaned forward. I lifted my head, mouth open, and we kissed.

He began to thrust, and I moved with him, rocking my body. I wrapped myself around him: my legs around his waist, arms around his shoulders. I never stopped kissing him. There was no hurry— we settled into a deep lingering fuck. As Mikos's strokes became longer, his cock slid out of my ass and slipped back in smoothly. His breath came faster, and a determined look brightened his eyes. He was coming. With a loud grunt, he buried his warm head against my shoulder and emptied his balls into my ass.

When he was done, his cock still inside me, we rolled over. I sat on top of him, high on his cock, and began to jerk my own. I came all over him, coating his chest and stomach with a torrent of sticky white cream.

Finally, spent and content, we fell asleep on top of the covers.

It was almost ten when we woke up, still holding each other.

"I am going home to Madrid tomorrow afternoon," he explained.

I nodded, kissing his smooth brow.

"I would like to spend my last night with you," he said. "It's not too late to go to dinner if you want to. Most restaurants are open until two."

"Yeah," I laughed. "I get hungry after sex."

Mikos toyed with my soft dick. "Then I think I should order a large breakfast for the morning. We will both be hungry after tonight."

I couldn't keep my eyes off him over dinner. We went to a tapas bar with a terrace overlooking the sea and ordered calamari and grilled prawns. The food was excellent, but I was thinking about a different kind of nourishment. Mikos wore a red shirt and dark blue jeans. I couldn't help watching the tightness of his sleeves around his biceps and the curve of his ass when he got up to go to the bathroom. He looked as good in his clothes as he did out of them.

We drank two bottles of red wine with the meal and were both giggly and unsteady by the time we left the restaurant. We fell against each other on the steps outside. Mikos suggested a walk to clear our heads.

"Good idea," I said, taking his hand and guiding him down to the beach. A large moon reflected on the placid water. The salty air helped to clear my head. I inhaled deeply. "What shall we do now?" It was after 11. If we walked into the old town, the bars would just be warming up.

"I don't mind," Mikos said.

"It's your last night," I told him. "You should make the most of it."

"I already have." He squeezed my hand and directed me toward the rocky shore.

He pressed me against a large rock, and I felt him slide around me in the darkness. His tongue went inside my mouth while his hands started on my body. My shirt slipped away. The sea air was surprisingly warm on my skin. His kiss went deeper, probing further. He leaned his body into me, pressing his thick Spanish cock against my stomach. I rose, letting him feel my own hardness against his thigh.

Mikos did not speak. He lifted me up and turned me around, pulling down my pants before leaning me over the rock. His fingers brushed my ass. I waited, listening to the soft whisper of his clothes as he shed them. He leaned over me, careful not to crush me. His mouth moved down the back of my neck. I shivered. His fingers were in my crack, playing with my hole. I was still relaxed and sensitive from our earlier fuck. He caressed the swollen bud, probing kindly.

"Fuck me again, baby," I said encouragingly.

"Are you sure?"

"Yeah. Your cock makes my ass feel good."

He suited up and spread a sachet of lube over my asshole. He massaged the sticky fluid into my orifice, working it in. I spread my legs wide, pushing back from the clammy rock. His blunt cock head began to press, stretching my already loosened hole. His tongue tickled the back of my neck as he pushed all the way in. My guts ached with a deep satisfaction.

"Is this OK?" he whispered.

I reassured him with a firm backward thrust that brought his warm hips right up against my buttocks. As his confidence grew, he began to thrust his fat member back and forth feverishly. I urged him on, begged him to fuck me harder and faster. He gripped my hips, steadying himself and getting better leverage. His hips slapped noisily against my ass.

"That's how I want it," I growled.

"I'll fuck you harder," he said, squashing himself farther into my wet ass.

I sucked at his dick with my ass, and the most incredible sensations traveled through my bones. Mikos moaned as I made it tighter for him. He spat onto his fingers and reached for my cock, palming the head and sending waves of ecstasy through me. Moments later, I felt his body tense. His breath hissed in my ear. I felt the spasms of his cock, the start of his orgasm. He gripped my body, blowing off inside me. He rode it out, grinding his hips in an erratic rhythm. My dick swelled in his hand, and I shot a massive wad of cream all over the rock. My knees were weak.

Mikos withdrew and tugged off the condom. He embraced me and we started kissing again. Our moist, softening dicks pressed against each other. He stroked my ass as he kissed me.

"You should get to bed," I said. "Long journey home tomorrow."

He laughed, looking around for his clothes. "I didn't come to Ibiza to sleep. It's not even midnight."

"I like your attitude."

"Come on. Let's get a drink. There is so much more I want to do before this night is over."

I pulled up my pants and followed him.

Human Sex Toys
Christopher Pierce

Eleven at night. Time for all good slave boys to go to sleep.

At least all of my good slave boys.

I'd been so engrossed in my research I hadn't noticed the time. I was sitting in my office in my underwear, surfing the Web to prepare for my next big project at work. Last time I looked at the clock it had been 9:30, now it was already eleven.

I had five slave boys. Yes, five. I tell you, I'm not very popular in certain circles of the leather community—mostly with masters who can't manage to train and keep one slave boy, to say nothing of more than one. I wasn't aware I had any special touch or "magic." Slave boys just seemed to come to me, and if they were still around after my (admittedly tough) training sessions, I claimed them as my property.

So five isn't all that many, considering the sheer number of boys that came to me to be trained.

I had trained my slave boys to help each other and to get themselves ready for bed at the appropriate hour. Only a few things required my attention by the time I began to make my rounds at eleven, checking to be sure everyone had been safely prepared for sleep, according to my instructions. I'd tuck them in—finish them off, so to speak.

And now another day was over and it was time for bed again. I went to the bathroom and got a handful of small hand towels, then started my rounds.

First, off to the living room.

There was Jeremy, all nice and tucked away in his sleep sack on the floor. The leather bag completely encased his body, leaving only his head sticking out of the top. But I knew what the leather concealed—long, floppy auburn hair, handsome face, good body, probably 5 foot 10 and 170 pounds.

The sack was almost completely laced up, but his cock and balls were poking out, hard, as usual.

I knelt on the floor next to him. He knew I was there without even opening his eyes.

"Master," he whispered.

"I'm here, Jeremy," I answered softly. "Master's here." I gently took his cock in my hand and started stroking it. With my other hand I carefully brushed away some hair that had fallen down over his eyes. He murmured with pleasure as I jerked him harder, using my free hand to caress his balls. Then I lay the first hand towel on top of the sleep sack, just beyond my slave's genitals, and I jacked even harder. With a soft yelp of bliss, Jeremy came, shooting a nice big burst of cream and making his whole body quiver inside its bondage. His spunk landed harmlessly on the hand towel, which I had put there for just that purpose. It wouldn't do to have a stain on the floor or on the leather.

Jeremy was already asleep when I tucked his cock and balls back inside his sack and finished tying him up in it.

One down, four to go.

Next stop, the dungeon. We'd converted the second bedroom into a playroom of sorts: It was painted black and contained most of our large bondage equipment and furniture. It was also the home of a large metal puppy cage, where I found my next boy.

"Jake!" I said excitedly. He was awake, his tongue hanging out and his naked butt waving back and forth, just like a real dog greeting his master.

"Woof! Woof!" he said, delighted, as always, to see me. He was small and cute, just like a puppy dog (or puppy boy) should be. Bright blue eyes, short brown hair, nicely toned body, he was a delight to the eye at about 5 foot 6 and 140 pounds.

There was enough room in the cage for him to be up on his hands and knees and lay down comfortably, but not enough to stand up or turn around. I stuck my hand into the cage and Jake licked my fingers happily, then pushed the top of his head into my hand so I could pet him and scratch behind his ears.

"Have you been a good dog, Jake?" I asked with mock seriousness.

"Ruff! Ruff!" was his answer.

"Good dog, good dog. You're my good dog," I said.

"Ruff."

"I know what my puppy boy wants," I said, unbuckling my jeans. "He wants his nightly feeding!"

"WOOF!" Jake said, going absolutely crazy in his cage, banging against the walls and wagging his butt so hard that it looked like he actually had a tail. I got down on my knees and pulled my cock out, then gently moved closer to the metal so my stiff meat slid between the bars and into the cage.

Jake licked my dick a few times with excitement, then started sucking it. It was wonderful to feel my puppy boy suckling me as if I imparted his life blood. I dropped another one of the hand towels into the cage, and Jake knew what to do with it. Without turning his attention from my cock, he arranged the towel under his groin and started jerking himself off.

Seconds later he whined and moaned with such desperation that I laughed and said, "Good dog, go ahead." His eyes lit up, and he clenched his cock tightly in his hand. Seconds later a big healthy dose of puppy come squirted out of him and landed on the towel. Jake moaned and groaned in such loud ecstasy that I had to put my finger to my lips.

"Good dog," I said softly. "You're my good dog. Settle down now. Good dog, settle down." As I spoke, I softened my voice until it was just a whisper. I petted him, making the strokes increasingly gentle, just like my voice. As always, Jake became sleepy when I did this and finally curled up on his side and closed his eyes. "Good puppy boy," I said as I reached into the cage to retrieve the towel. Then I gently pulled my cock and my hand out of the cage.

If my puppy boy had a tail, it would've wagged one last time before he was asleep. I turned off the light in the dungeon and closed the door behind me as I walked out.

Now my rounds took me down the hallway to the large master bedroom. A small mountain of muscle and steel lay in the doorway, blocking the entrance to the room.

It was my slave Jeff.

(You may have noticed by now that all my slaves have names starting with *j*. It's too crazy to be a coincidence, of course. The explanation is quite simple. I love names starting with *j,* so when I train a boy and he makes the grade, I give him a "slave name"— that is, I give him a name that starts with *j*. His real name is still on all his paperwork and legal documents. The *j*-name is just what I call him in the context of our relationship.)

"Jeff," I said. "Assume the position."

"Yes, sir!" he said, standing up. And up and up. Jeff was 6 foot 4 (outdistancing me by four inches) and a prize-winning body-builder: as I said, a mountain of muscle and steel. The steel, of course, referred the custom-made collar that encircled his neck, marking him as my slave, and the long chain attached to it that served as a leash. The leash was securely fastened to the wall.

He was naked, just as Jake had been. I like them that way. It reminds them that they're objects that I own, that they're my slave meat. Not that there's ever any doubt. But with a house full of red-blooded American men, all coming from upbringings that prized their self-determination, it is important always to remind them who owns their flesh and who runs the show.

That was why this enormous bodybuilder obeyed me and assumed the position he had been taught: feet apart, shoulders back, hands behind his back, head bowed respectfully, his enormous cock hard and erect at my presence.

"How long have you been my slave, Jeff?" I asked.

"Two and a half years, sir," he answered.

"How long would you like to remain in my possession?"

"For the rest of my life, sir!" he said, as if shocked that I'd ask.

"And how would you rate your performance as my slave so far?"

"Uh," he started, clearly not expecting this question either. "Satisfactory, sir?"

"Wrong!" I said and his face fell. *What have I done poorly?* As amusing as it was, I didn't want to torture him for too long.

"Your performance has not been satisfactory," I said, and he closed his eyes in anticipation of the coming blow. "Your performance has been exemplary."

After a second of confusion, he understood I had been teasing him and got a big grin on his face as he let out a relieved sigh.

"Thank you, sir," he said.

"I love you very much, Jeff," I said.

"Thank you, sir. I love you too."

"Now show me what a good boy you are and come in ten seconds."

I took his penis in one hand and started jerking him. As always he thrilled to my touch, his eyes rolling back as he closed them.

"One...Two...Three...You're my slave boy, Jeff—you belong to me, remember that—always!"

The bodybuilder moaned with passion as I jerked him.

"Four...Five...Six...Seven..."

Sweat broke out on his forehead in concentration.

"Eight..."

I held out the towel in the place I predicted his boy juice would squirt.

"Nine...come for me in the towel, boy. Ten! Come for your master!"

Jeff groaned as I pumped him one last time. His surge of come shot out of his penis and landed squarely on the towel.

"Good boy!"

"Thank you, Master," he said breathlessly.

"Now go to sleep," I said, reaching up to tousle his hair playfully. He obeyed, dropping back down to his favorite place—guarding the door to my bedroom. He stretched out on the floor, looking like a lion on the savanna. He was a powerful boy, and I had tamed him: I'd harnessed his tremendous strength into a tool I could use at will. The clinking and clanking of his chain stopped when he found a comfortable position and settled in for the night.

I looked down at him lovingly. He was mine, all mine.

They all were.

I stepped over Jeff and headed into my private sanctuary: my bedroom, the place where I enjoyed my most intimate moments.

There were two more boys waiting for me on my bed. These last two rounded out my slave boy stable of five. I called them my "bed-boys," because they were the ones I chose to actually sleep with. The other boys had their chance to share my bed once in a while, but they were happy where they were. In fact, they'd be happy wherever I put them.

Jason, a bleach-blond skater I'd found on the beach, lay on the left side of the bed, nicely tied up and gagged. He made a handsome and humpy piece of merchandise. Of course, I knew how valuable he was because I owned him! He was probably 5 foot 11, lanky yet graceful. His hands were bound together on his chest, and his feet were tied at the ankles. A padlock chain hung around his neck.

Joel reclined on the other side of the bed, and he had a big wide smile waiting for me. He was a nice-looking, clean-cut, wholesome American boy next door.

A boy next door who was also an expertly trained piece of slave meat owned by me, that is.

In any case, Joel was beautiful in his simplicity. All his needs and wants were clear to me. There were no hidden agendas of any kind, and his emotions were all right there on the surface, in his face and in his body language.

He was naked, of course, with a custom-made leather collar around his neck. No chain was attached to his collar: His bond to me was invisible, but strong as steel.

Three down, two to go.

"Get on your hands and knees and give your brother some attention," I said.

"Yes, sir," Joel said obediently, straddling Jason and taking his cock into his mouth. Jason shuddered as pleasure rippled through him. Joel gently sucked his slave brother's dick as I looked on.

But as enticing as this scene was to watch, I had something else to do.

Joel's delicious naked butt was right in front of me, and I could never resist that ass, of all my slave boys' asses. I put my face between his butt cheeks and rimmed him, stimulating and caressing his asshole with my lips and tongue. My boy moaned in bliss as he continued to suck Jason's cock.

"I'm going to come, Master," Jason said, his words distorted by the gag.

"That's good, boy," I said reassuringly. "Go ahead whenever you're ready. Your brother's right here, and he'll drink it all down. Just go ahead."

Jason yelped in ecstasy, and I knew he was shooting his load down Joel's throat, the perfect place to do so. Joel swallowed a few times, gulping it all down before letting his brother's penis slide out of his mouth. He started to back up, as if to get up off Jason, but I said: "No. Stay right where you are, Joel. I like you there."

"Yes, Master," he said, staying straddled on his hands and knees over Jason.

"Put this towel on your brother under your cock," I said, handing the last one to him. He obeyed silently.

Now we were ready.

I stepped out of my shorts and slipped a condom over my cock, then spat into my hand and used the moisture to lubricate myself.

I grabbed Joel's hips and pulled him closer to the edge of the bed. He stuck his butt out, wiggling it a little, to show me how badly he wanted it. I nosed my cock between his ass cheeks, prodding his butthole with my hard, stiff tool. Then I started to push it in, slowly and gently at first, then harder as my cock head slid all the way inside him.

Finally, the fucking began.

As always, fucking one of my slave boys was spectacular. To screw another man was a deliciously dominant and possessive experience in itself. But when you added the knowledge that the man being fucked, being penetrated, was a slave boy who had turned his will and his life over to another man—me—the fuck became one of the hottest, most erotic experiences in the world.

With thoughts like this running through my mind, it didn't take long for me to come. I shot my load into the condom buried deep in Joel's guts, and I heard and felt him sigh in bliss as he jerked himself to orgasm.

It was over.

I pulled out threw away the condom, then told Joel to get Jason and himself under the covers. I would be there in a second. I tossed all the soiled hand towels into a laundry bag in the bathroom.

Then I got into bed and pulled my two bed-boys close. My arms were around just the two of them, but the grasp of my love and mastery extended to all the boys who shared my home: our home.

"Good night, my slave boys." I whispered as I turned out the light.

Brain Fever

Bob Vickery

I lift off the top of the large white box on the table in front of me and look inside, my heart pounding like a wrecking ball. There, nestled among the folds of tissue paper, lie the black square of the mortarboard and, under it, the smooth, cool silk of the graduation gown. I run my hands slowly, reverently, through the gown's folds, feeling the softness of the fabric, the hairs on the back of my hands and wrists erect with static electricity. That's not the only thing on me erect. My dick gives a sharp, hard throb as my fingertips touch the black silk.

I take the gown and mortarboard out of the box and arrange them carefully on my bed. By force of habit, I glance at the pile of porn magazines lying on my bedside table and scan their titles: *Brainy Boys, Gay Geniuses, Nude Professors.* Like a kid reluctant to put away old toys, I pick up the top magazine and open it to the centerfold. It's one of my favorites: a nude model bearing an uncanny resemblance to Albert Einstein lies sprawled on a laboratory bench, a dreamy, come-hither look in his mournful brown eyes. Sweet Jesus, the loads I've squirted over that picture... My hard-on gives another throb, but I resist the temptation to whip it out and wank off. *I'm saving my wad for something better tonight,* I think.

I quickly strip and slip on the graduation gown, leaving it unbuttoned in the front. Its smooth silkiness, crackling with electricity, slithers over my skin caressingly. I adjust the mortarboard on my head, letting the tassel fall to the right side, tickling the upper curve of my ear. I swing open the closet door and stare at my reflection in the full-length mirror. The flared, red head of my dick pokes out between the folds of the gown like some animal peering out of its burrow. "I question the basic premises of your hypothesis," I growl at my reflection, as I wrap my hand around my cock and stroke it slowly. My strokes become faster, my balls swinging in a fleshy blur. "It's clear you're operating from outmoded paradigms"—I gasp at my reflection, pulling my eyebrows down in a frown of concentration. I stop just before squirting. *There's no doubt about it,* I think excitedly. *I look as intelligent as hell! Baby, am I going to score tonight!* If I had any doubts, all I have to do is look at the list of final grades that came in the mail today for my last semester at U.C. Berkeley. *4.0 GPA!* I crow to myself. *Solid A's! What a fuckin' stud I am!*

I think about how I've worked my ass off for the past three years to get where I am tonight, exercising my brain five times a week, rigorously following a strict academic workout routine. Given the way the gay community obsesses on intelligence, it's what you have to do to get laid around here. And now, tonight, I know I'm ready for the final big leap: going in full black silk drag to one of Folsom Street's cap-and-gown bars.

This is a fantasy I've never shared with anyone. I hang out with a pretty vanilla crowd, guys who dis the cap-and-gowners as "a bunch of queens who beneath all their intellectual pretensions have the minds of cretins." Fuckin' hypocrites. Are they any better, parading down Castro Street on a Sunday afternoon, their pastel calculators dangling from their key chains, wearing their Lacoste shirts with $E=MC^2$ neatly stitched above their right pectorals? Or making the rounds at the circuit parties, engaged in Socratic dialogues on the nature of the archetypal forms of the Good, the True, and the Beautiful while buzzing on ecstasy and Special K? *Fuck 'em,* I think, as I clip on the Phi Beta Kappa keys that I bought in a downtown porno shop. I look at myself one last time in the mirror, squeeze my crotch and wink at my reflection before turning out the light and heading out the door.

When I get off my bus at Folsom and 10th, I know exactly where

I want to go: Plato's Cave, one of the most raunchy, sex-sweaty, academically-advanced bars in town. The bartender (who goes by the hokey name Gray Matter), is a Stanford Ph.D. physics candidate and one of gay filmdom's hottest porno stars. I've seen Gray's latest video, set in a mock-up of the Lawrence-Livermore cyclotron. The final orgy scene, when all the studs begin shooting their loads while hydrogen ions are being broken down into their component quarks by gamma-ray bombardment, is the talk of the gay community. Plato's Cave is packed.

I cautiously walk into the dimly lit bar, mentally feeling my ground. Black-silk bars have this whole code of behavior, all these dark mating rituals that have to be followed meticulously. Those who don't are contemptuously dismissed as "dilettantes" and promptly ignored. Occasionally, in groups of two or three but mostly solo, young men in their graduation drag line the walls or crowd around the bar. Over the sound system, Madonna is sexily sobbing the periodic table to a driving disco beat.

I push through the crowd as I make my way to the bar. Above the blare of the music, snatches of bar clichés float to my ears. "Haven't I seen you at a Mensa meeting?" "Do you matriculate often?"

"Vanadium," Madonna croons, "chromium, manganese, iron…"

All around me all these courting rites are taking place; the active cruisers are flexing their intellect in front of their desired targets. "Alexander Pope's *The Dunciad* is probably the most lacerating example of Augustan Age mock-epic verse form to be found," a burly tattooed man in shabby black robes whispers pleadingly to a young bored-looking academician. The young man rolls his eyes and walks away.

"Thallium," Madonna husks, "lead, bismuth, polonium…"

Two men on my left are arguing heatedly. Suddenly, one of them in piercing tones exclaims, "Jesus! This queen thinks she knows partial derivatives when she can't even get the Pythagorean theorem straight!"

"Oh, really?" the other hisses. "And just who is it who claims she read *Moby Dick* three times, when the closest she ever got to Herman

Melville was Classic Comics?" The two men glare at each other.

"Uranium," Madonna sighs, "neptunium, plutonium, americium…"

Behind the bar, Gray is spellbinding the crowd with the hypothesis that gravitational forces may eventually be discovered to be the products of "gravitons," a so-far merely hypothetical subatomic particle. He reeks of sex, and when he starts talking about how the graviton's existence may eventually turn out to be the missing link to proving Einstein's proposed unified field theory, I can cut with a knife the lust emanating from the crowd. I feel it too and shrug at my reaction. *Fuck it. If I'm just another shallow gay boy who puts brains above everything else, so be it. At least I'm honest about it.*

Gray tears himself away from his admiring audience long enough to give me a beer. I fight through the crowd again, achieve a relatively isolated corner, and gulp it meditatively. For once, this attitude isn't a pose; I'm genuinely contemplating my next move. I look around carefully, hunting for a subject on which to ply my lines.

Yet I'm vaguely dissatisfied with what I'm about to do. I'm being too sedate about all this, too guarded, too *routine.* Hell, I'm acting like it's another Saturday night on the Castro, where, after throwing a few lines of Nietzsche out at someone, you take him home and fuck his brains out. This is a night to indulge in fantasy all the way: the first time I've ever gone to a black-silk bar in full cap-and-gown drag. I know what my next move should be.

I nervously shift my eyes toward the back of the bar. Through the smoky haze I can dimly make out a doorless opening leading into a dark hallway. I know from stories I've heard that this is the way to Plato's Cave's well-trafficked backroom. I lick my lips uncertainly; I'm not sure if I'm ready for that kind of scene. As if on cue, the sound system erupts with an old Village People hit. "Brainy, brainy man!" they shout. "I want to be a brainy man." I smile at the timeliness of the song. I square my shoulders. If I back down now, I might as well stick to quoting Monarch Notes synopses of "great books" to the dummies who hang out in the tackier bars on lower Polk Street.

Taking one last swig from my bottle, I push myself away from the sheltering wall and into the crowd. "I'm dean's list material, I'm dean's list material…" I keep repeating to myself as I thread my way across the room. I feel my throat constricting and my heart hammering, and I have to stop and wait until my breathing is better. *I have to be coolheaded,* I think. *My thinking has to be clear. That's crucial.*

I finally make it to the opening and walk down the short hall, trailing my fingers along the wall to guide me in the darkness. There's a sharp 90-degree turn, and suddenly I'm in my first orgy room. Pools of light feebly spill out from reading lamps haphazardly strung out along the upper wall. In varying degrees of darkness, shadowy figures merge and part. Barely coherent murmurs and moans float in the air, snatches of Hobbes, Shakespeare, Descartes. Someone suddenly comes, gasping out lines from Kant's *Critique of Pure Reason*. The air is hot and fetid, and I feel rivulets of sweat trickling down my back and under my armpits. I've got a roaring hard-on.

As my eyes adjust to the gloom, my attention focuses on a solitary figure standing directly under one of the lights. He's dressed in the full scarlet robes of a Cambridge don, and while some men might have looked hopelessly pretentious in such an outfit, the stranger is able to wear it with a free and natural confidence that radiates pure intelligence. He has a high, in fact lofty forehead; always the size queen, I'm guessing that the man's hat size must be at least an 8½. The guy's calmly reading a copy of Plato's *The Republic* in the original Greek, seemingly oblivious to the activity around him.

My center of consciousness suddenly drops 2½ feet, and my prick assumes full control. With a boldness found only in the inexperienced and the desperate, I stride across the room, stop next to the stranger, and place my hand upon his left pectoral. He raises his eyes and coolly looks at me but makes no other movement. Emboldened by this, I unbutton the front of the scarlet robe and slip my hands under the silk, stroking the furred chest beneath. "I'm Harry," I say, as I squeeze the man's nipples. "What's your name?"

The stranger looks at me silently. "Rocco," he finally growls. His nipples are fully erect now under my fingertips. He continues staring at me, waiting.

Time to start flexing the brain muscle, I think. "I see you're reading *The Republic,* Rocco," I say, "where Plato traces the journey of the soul into a spiritual immersion in the Eternal One." My hands descend slowly down Rocco's hard, furry abs.

Rocco keeps his level gaze aimed at me. When my fingers are a couple of inches above the bulge of his cock, Rocco's hand darts out and grasps my wrist. "Fuckin' A," he growls. "Of course, Plato's model of a purely ascending creative force was eventually adopted by Saint Thomas Aquinas to describe God as the Unmoved Mover."

I smile at the easy trap Rocco has set for me. "I believe you're mistaken," I say calmly. "Aquinas's Unmoved Mover was inspired by Aristotle, not Plato." I free his hand and wrap my fingers around Rocco's fat cock. I start stroking it slowly, pulling the silky foreskin up and down the thick shaft. I pull out my own dick and wrap my hand around both our cocks, stroking the twin dick shafts together. Rocco leans back and closes his eyes as I murmur, "Aristotle envisioned a purely ascendant God, but Plato's Ultimate Good also embraces the descent into the manifest."

I feel a hand slide down my back and squeeze my ass. I turn to see a young street punk standing next to me, his black silk gown falling open to reveal a smooth, tightly muscled torso and a heavy horse-dick swinging half-hard between his thighs. His eyebrows and left nostril are pierced, and he sports a tattoo on his bulging left biceps that reads BORN TO STUDY. "Yeah," the punk growls. "But Plato was fuckin' ripping off Parmenides, who first came up with the model of an Ultimate Good that descends into the realm of the manifest a full century before Plato ever did." Before I can respond, the punk drops to his knees and takes my cock in his mouth.

I sigh as I feel the warm, wet mouth expertly work my dick. I being pumping my hips, fucking the punk's face with long, slow strokes. Rocco's hands are working my body now, tugging on the smooth, hard flesh. I pull Rocco to me and kiss him fiercely, my tongue pushing deep into his mouth, as the young punk sucks and slobbers over first my dick and then Rocco's and then back to mine again. The punk opens his mouth wide and swallows my fleshy balls, rolling his tongue around them. I look down, and the punk meets my gaze, his mouth full of my ball sac. "Yeah, fuckin' suck those balls," I growl as I slap my dick across his upturned face. "You might be right about Parmenides," I add, "but big fuckin' deal. The Buddhist sage Nagarajuna came up with the concept of the divine in the manifest world centuries before any of the Greeks."

"Not to mention the teachings in the Bhagavad Gita," Rocco adds, his voice low and guttural. "And, before that, the Hindu Upanishads. They all were making the same fuckin' point." I'm still stroking Rocco's massive dong, fast enough to make his balls bounce heavily, and Rocco's eyes burn with a feverish light. It's so fucking hot to watch him leaning against the wall, his hips thrust out, the light from the reading lamp spilling onto his hairy, muscular torso.

"Bullshit!" the punk growls as he slides his tongue up the length of my wanker and rolls it around the purple flared head. "You can't compare the Greeks to the Buddhist philosophers. The Buddhists were preaching dependent origination, where no object in the universe exists by itself." He slides his hands down my ass cheeks, squeezing them, running his fingers over the smooth skin. "Whereas the Greeks believed that every object could be traced back to an ideal form." His hands work their way up my torso again, and he gives each nipple a hard squeeze.

"OK, OK," I gasp, as the punk burrows his head down between my legs. I feel my ass cheeks being parted, and the punk massages my asshole as resumes licking my ball sac. "Damn!" I groan, distracted. With an effort, I collect my thoughts. "So what if Plato didn't fuckin' *originate* the concept of the divine in the manifest? It was how he developed the concept that mattered."

"Yeah," Rocco grunts. He pulls his massive boner down and releases it, letting it slap against his hairy belly. His heavy ball sac swings from side to side, like ripe fruit on a windblown tree branch. "Plato set the prototype model of the One Source and

Ground for all the other Western philosophers, from Plotinus right up to Spinoza and Hegel. So fuckin' lay off him, OK?" With a quick shrug, he slips his scarlet robes off his shoulders and lets them fall to the floor. He stands before me buck naked, his ponderous dong bobbing heavily between his beefy thighs, begging to be sucked. It's an offer I can't refuse, and I bend down and take Rocco's engorged cock in my mouth and greedily suck it as the punk continues to play with my asshole.

I can't get enough of Rocco's fat dick, and I feed on it voraciously, first circling my tongue around the bulbous red head and then sliding my lips down the shaft until my nose is pressed hard against Rocco's black, crinkly pubes. The punk is now corkscrewing a finger up my ass, inch by slow inch, as he strokes my dick with his other hand. I close my eyes and let the sensations sweep over me: Rocco's hard dick shoved deep down my throat, the punk's finger working my ass while he's stroking my dick. The air in the room seems to close in on us, and I feel streams of sweat trickle down my body and splash onto the floor below. Others in the room watch the show we're putting on with hard, feverish eyes, beating off to the sight, offering counterarguments between fondles or collaborative evidence accented with stroking and heavy sucking.

A huge bearded giant of a man breaks free from the crowd and approaches us, his monstrous, condomed dong swinging heavily between his massive thighs. He pushes the punk aside, spits on his dick, and proceeds to slowly impale my ass. "Of course, Freud was a Neoplatonist," he growls, as he slowly skewers me. "The two major forces in the human psyche that Freud identified as Eros and Thanatos are just other names for Plato's ascending and descending spirits."

I pull Rocco's cock out of my mouth and turn my head toward the giant. "That's horse shit," I gasp, relaxing my ass muscles and breathing deep to accommodate his huge prick. "Freud's forces of the psyche never ascend into the transpersonal realm like Plato's, and thus they cancel each other out rather than reinforce each other. That's why Plato was an optimist and Freud essentially a pessimist." I begin pumping my hips, meeting the giant's thrusting cock, stroke for stroke. I squeeze my ass muscles tight as the giant pulls his dong out, and he gasps with pleasure. "Yeah," Rocco grunts, as he crams his dick back down my throat again. "Freud was a classic reductionist, keeping all forces of the psyche confined to the prepersonal realms. What an asshole." He reaches over and squeezes the giant's left nipple, twisting it hard.

The giant glares at him with hard, bright eyes. "Of course, Jung committed the opposite fallacy," he grunts, his face bathed in sweat, "by elevating all psychic forces to the transpersonal realm." He thrusts his ramrod dick full in me, slapping his balls against my ass, and then slowly grinds his hips.

I give a mighty groan and take Rocco's cock out of my mouth once again. "I hear you, man," I gasp. "All those archetypes Jung was talking about deal with states of consciousness that take place before the development of the ego. Jung had his head up his ass when he called them transpersonal." The giant has his arms wrapped tightly around my torso in a bear hug, and I feel the weight of his body press down on me as he drives his fleshy piston in. I go back to gobbling on Rocco's pulsating dick meat.

I feel the dicks of the two studs impale me from both ends, Rocco's pushing down my throat while the giant's is shoved deep up my ass. It's like being spitted by one giant cock that runs through the entire length of my body, and I close my eyes and sink into that thought. Rocco and the giant keep on plowing my orifices as they continue their discourse. Meanwhile, the punk has crawled down under me and is dragging his tongue over my stiff, fat cock and balls. I'm immersed in sensation, dicks and mouths and hands exploring every inch of my body, quotes from Hobbes and Hegel faintly buzzing in my ears.

The giant is increasingly punctuating his arguments with low groans and trailing whimpers. He gives one final hard thrust of his dick up my ass, and I feel his legs tremble against me. "Shit, I'm coming!" he cries out. He gives a mighty groan as his body spasms, and his dick pulses deep inside me, pumping his jizz into the condom up my ass in one spurt after another. With one final deep sigh, the giant pulls out and collapses to the floor, mumbling something about Retro-Romantics and the pre/trans fallacy.

Rocco's thrusts are coming deeper and faster, and I'm having a hard time accommodating his huge dong full down my throat. I start sucking on his low-hanging balls, rolling them around with my tongue, as I stroke his spit-slicked man-root. Rocco looks down at me with glazed eyes, sweat pouring down his face, his mouth open. "Yeah, you sexy, brainy stud," he growls. "Wash those balls. Stroke that dick. Make me come." I pump my hand up and down Rocco's humongous tube of meat a few more times, and then he groans loudly as his body trembles against me. "Oh, shit, I'm coming!" he cries out. His dick throbs in my hand, and the first volley of spunk arcs out and splatters hard against my face, followed by another and then another. By the time Rocco's done shooting, my face is drenched with his dick-slime. I feel it drip sluggishly down my cheeks and chin, mingling with my sweat. Rocco bends down and slowly laps it up, like some thirsty jungle cat.

The punk is working my dick hard with his mouth, and I fuck his face energetically, meeting him thrust for thrust. He's a skillful cocksucker, and I feel my load being slowly pulled out of me. "Talk dirty to me," I growl to Rocco.

Rocco bends over and whispers Heisenberg's uncertainty principle in my ear as the punk continues to work my dick. That does the trick for me, and I feel myself slip over the edge into the orgasm. "Fuckin' A!" I groan, as I shoot my load deep down the punk's throat. He drinks it thirstily, sucking on it like a baby on its mother's tit, feeding on my spermy cream. Rocco plants his mouth over mine and kisses me hard as my body spasms. I collapse on the floor with the other men, ours arms and limbs intertwined together, our sweaty bodies pressed together. I close my eyes, lost in post-sex catatonia, listening to someone across the room slowly chanting the three laws of thermodynamics. Minutes pass, and I begin to feel chilly as the sweat evaporates off my back. I slowly get up and pull my soiled and crumpled graduation gown back on. The other men recover their gowns too.

Rocco and I walk out of the bar together, leaving the others in the orgy room. Neither of us talk, silently realizing that any further conversation could only be anticlimactic. I smile wanly at the pun. When we reach the street corner, Rocco pulls me to him and kisses me one last time. "You fucking genius," he growls in my ear. "You fucking intelligent stud." Then he turns and walks away.

I stand quietly on the corner for a few seconds, watching Rocco's receding back. Then, numb to the bone with fatigue and joy, I strike out in the opposite direction. I begin to sing softly. "Brainy, brainy man. I want to be a brainy man."

Zoran's Big Meet
Duane Williams

As soon as the list was posted, I checked to see if Zoran had made the team. My name was on the list, of course. This was my third year as team captain and my last before graduating from Lister. My goal was to make the varsity team at university and, eventually, the Olympics. Zoran's name was on the list, written just under mine. Zoran Vujnokovic. I went home after school and jacked off to the thought of wrestling Zoran in the nude.

Our first practice was the next day. I changed and was leaving the locker room when Zoran came barreling through the door, crashing into me head-on. "Sorry," he said. He was out of breath, and his black hair was hanging in his eyes. "Hey, buddy. I'm late for the practice. Tell Mr. Sanger I'll be a few minutes."

During the practice, Zoran came up and apologized again. "Hey, don't worry about it," I said. I wasn't exactly upset about Zoran running into me. He looked even hotter than I'd expected in his singlet, which he packed full in the crotch. The other guys were checking him out too. It was hard not to notice. "Congratulations on making the team," I said. "I'm team captain, so if you need any help with the training, let me know."

We trained every day after school through the fall. Because we were so closely matched, Zoran and I were always paired up during practice. Zoran couldn't beat me, and that burned his ass. He came close a few times, but his technique wasn't nearly as slick as mine. He had power, but I had flexibility and speed.

"Think you'll ever win?" I asked Zoran one day at practice. I had him in a killer gut wrench on the mat. The other guys were standing around watching, cheering me on. Zoran was hurting bad, I could tell, but he was showing no sign of giving up.

"Fuck. For sure," he said. He was grunting the words through his teeth. "You're a horse-meat fucker." Zoran was from Yugoslavia. His English was good, but not always correct. Sometimes he said things that didn't make much sense.

"In your fucking dreams, loser!" I laughed and let Zoran go, giving him a shove off the mat.

"Fuck yourself," he said, getting up on his feet. The veins in his forehead were popping, either from my wicked hold, or from his being totally pissed off.

"I guess somebody has to beat me someday."

"You're a fuckhead asshole," he said. He took off out of the gym, and the door slammed behind him.

After the coach finished bawling me out for laughing at Zoran, I went into the locker room to apologize. My timing was perfect. Zoran was just getting out of the shower. I pretended to be squeezing a zit in the mirror, but I was watching him out of the corner of my eye. He had a dark, thick bush. His cock and balls looked heavy. I stopped looking because I was getting hard in my singlet, which makes a woody very obvious. When he stepped out of the shower, I acted like I was surprised he was there.

"Hey, Zoran…How's it going?" He looked at me but didn't say anything.

"Sorry for calling you a loser, man. I was just joking around, you know."

He still didn't say anything as he toweled off. It was hard to keep my eyes off his cock. He was uncut, which was unusual in the showers at Lister. He dried off from the bottom up, starting with his big, muscular feet. He looked at me as he lifted his balls and dried between his legs. "What is the fuck with you? Are you jealous of me?" he said, looking at me with blue eyes. He threw the towel on the bench and stood there with his hands on his hips.

"Hey, I've got nothing to be jealous about," I said. "Let's not forget who's been captain for three years."

"Ah, fuck you!" he said, blowing me off with a flip of his hand. He grabbed the towel and walked away naked. His ass was as perfect as the rest of him.

Next practice, Mr. Sanger matched Zoran and me together, as always. Zoran looked pissed-off as we stepped on the mat. Mr. Sanger blew the whistle, and I was quickest on the draw. I grabbed Zoran through the legs and dumped him on the mat, squeezing up his balls against my arm. I got a good grip around his waist, but Zoran was a strong mother. He kicked his legs up over his head and broke out. When he flipped back, his face landed in my crotch, which was on the swell.

"OK, guys," Mr. Sanger hollered. "Warm-up's over. Five minutes on suplex, belly to belly."

"I'm ready now," Zoran said. He grabbed his singlet by the straps and twisted it back into position, rearranging his bulge. Zoran didn't wear deodorant. His ripe pits were turning me on. Mr. Sanger blew the whistle and we grabbed each other by the shoulders.

"You want my dick in your face again?"

"It is so small to notice," he said. I threw him over—my best flap jack—and pinned his shoulders to the mat.

"You'll notice it when you're sucking on it."

The final meet of the season was the provincial finals in Toronto. We had to stay overnight at a hotel, and Mr. Sanger put Zoran and me together in the same room. He was always trying to get us to like each other, or something. "Neither one of you will win if you're fighting each other off the mat," he said. "Great athletes learn from their competitors."

From the balcony of our hotel room, we could see the CN Tower and the Skydome. We arrived the night before the meet, but the coach said, no, we couldn't go check out the prostitutes on Yonge Street. "You're both only 18. You probably wouldn't know what to do with one anyhow," Mr. Sanger said. "Unpack your bags and get some sleep. We didn't train all fall so you two could blow your wad on some pussy."

Zoran and I got unpacked and changed into sweats. Zoran wore his without a jockstrap, and the sight of his big cock bouncing around inside was making me horny. We stood on the balcony and looked out over the city. "Cool, eh? All the lights look so cool. Far fucking cry from Lister, that's for sure."

"Yeah…it is beautiful. Not like Sarajevo. The war destroyed my city," he said, leaning out over the railing. He was staring down at the street, not saying anything more.

"What war's that?" I asked after a while.

"The people look like bugs," he said, looking down at the street. I asked him again about the war, but he didn't want to talk about it, so we went inside the room to see if there was any alcohol in the bar fridge. It was empty, but I had some juice packs in my gym bag so we drank those instead. We discovered a porn channel on the TV, but neither one of us had the cash to pay for it. Just the idea of watching porn with Zoran was making me hard.

"Nervous about tomorrow?"

"Not too much," he said.

"Well, I guess you've already sized up the competition." We were one another's only real competition. Except for some guy from Sudbury, there was nobody in our weight division who was anywhere close to being a threat. "But I'm still planning to whip your ass," I said.

Zoran pretended to laugh hysterically. "A fat fucking chance," he said.

"Fuck you. You don't stand a chance," I said, twisting his arm in a wringer. He quickly broke the hold and pushed me on the bed. He jumped on me, and we wrestled around for a bit, fighting but not fighting.

"You want to suck my cock, buddy."

"You're the cocksucker," I answered. Zoran was on top of me, holding me down with the full weight of his body. "At least I have a dick." I could feel his cock pushing against my back.

Zoran was hard. "Yeah, you don't have a cock like me," he said. He was grinding his dick against my back. His pits were hot and musky, and I took a deep breath. I tried to flip him back over so I was on top but only ended up turning myself over. He was sitting on my chest now, holding my arms down. His cock was pitching an enormous tent in his sweats. Zoran leaned forward so his crotch was pushed up against my face. I turned my face to the side and pretended to fight him off.

"Get the hell off me," I said.

"You want my cock," he said. "I seen you many times looking down there."

"Whatever," I said, "Now get the fuck off, gay boy." Zoran reached into his sweats and pulled it out. It was the biggest cock I'd ever seen, muscled and leaking jizz as he slapped it around on my face.

"Maybe I'll let you win tomorrow," he said. "If you suck my cock."

My dick was about to explode. His crotch was musky, like the rest of his body, but hotter and more intense. I turned my head and did it. I reached out with my tongue and took his cock. "Oh, yeah...fuck, that is good," he moaned, pulling out of my mouth after a few minutes He was getting close. He let my arms go and braced his hand against the headboard. With the other hand, he held his cock at the base and pumped my mouth slowly. He was groaning so loud that I thought the guys in the next room might hear. He gave my mouth one deep pump, then pulled out again, his whole body flexing as he sprayed a load on the sheets.

When Mr. Sanger came by to see if we were in our room and asleep, Zoran answered the door without his shirt on.

"You guys aren't fighting in here, I hope."

I was sitting on the floor in my sweats, stretching out my quads. Zoran looked at me and rolled his eyes.

"Come on, guys, it's time to get some sleep," Mr. Sanger said. "Do

I have to remind you that tomorrow's the biggest meet of the year?"

"It is mine for sure," Zoran said.

"I wouldn't be too sure about that," I said. "You haven't beat me once yet. Face it, man…you're a loser."

"You two are perfectly matched," Mr. Sanger said. "You both have swollen heads. Make sure one of you wins, OK? Now get to sleep. I'm not kidding." He left our room, and Zoran locked the door.

Zoran walked over to where I was sitting on the floor. "You're an asshole," he said. He pulled down his sweats and pushed my face in his crotch. "You haven't won nothing yet," he said.

Riding the Train

Dale Chase

I saw him through the window, running toward the train as the doors began to close. It was a desperate sprint. But I saw exuberance in it too. I guessed he enjoyed cutting things close.

He leaped into the car just as the doors shut, and he stood grinning for a moment, obviously pleased with himself. I wondered what had delayed him and how far he'd run.

It was near midnight, so the car wasn't crowded. I was headed back across San Francisco Bay to Berkeley after an evening in the city. I was all alone and very horny.

He glanced up and down the car with an expectant look on his face, as if he expected applause. When none came, his gaze caught mine and he lingered on me for a moment. Then he took a seat at the other end of the car.

I let the sparks from our brief connection course through me as he settled in. He faced me, riding backward and looking out the window, even though we were still underground. Our moment had electrified me, and I relished its lingering charge.

He had fair skin but dark, curly hair—a mop of it—and boyish features. He looked a year or so younger than me: around 20, maybe. He had clothed his slim physique in a yellow windbreaker and a pair of jeans. He seemed very at ease with himself. I watched him lounge in his seat as if he was in front of a television. I pictured us there together.

I dreaded each stop the train made, growing increasingly

anxious that his would be the next one. We passed through San Francisco, then into the tube under the bay, then up above ground in West Oakland. I kept him in my sights the whole time.

How many times did I look at him directly? Enough to let him know? Had I piqued his curiosity? Was he indifferent to my attention? He fidgeted in his seat, propped an elbow against the window for a while, and finally settled down again. Three more stops and I would have to leave him. Or maybe I wouldn't. Maybe he'd get off with me. Maybe he was a student. Maybe he was on his way to his dorm.

He rose suddenly, moved toward the door, and plopped down into the seat across from mine. He grinned at me, and I smiled. He chuckled, as if he did this all the time. For a second I hated that possibility, but he stood as the conductor announced my stop: Rockridge. I found myself standing beside him, though I couldn't remember leaving my seat. An erection crowded my jeans.

The cool air on the outdoor platform refreshed me. Only then did I realize how hot I was. The guy ambled along, and I fell in beside him, matching his stride. He said nothing. I *couldn't* say anything. I wasn't deft at casual pickups. My attractions never felt casual, and I invariably clammed up just when I most wanted to be open.

We share a step on the escalator, descending to the plaza and always-bustling College Avenue. I liked coming back to the cozy neighborhood and often lingered amid the crowds, caught up in the sights, smells, and comforting din of the lively community. Now, however, I found the hubbub intrusive. I wanted quiet; I wanted to be in my own little world and to take this guy with me.

I was pretty sure he sensed my desire for him as we walked along; he didn't alter his pace or turn his gaze to any of the many distractions that might have caught his eye. He looked straight ahead, and I spent a few blissful blocks believing he was following me home—until I began to wonder whether he wanted me to follow *him* home. How could I ask for clarification without betraying myself as a complete dolt?

As if on cue, he asked, "So where do you live?"

"Next block," I told him. When he just nodded, I added, "Want to come up for coffee?"

"Yeah, sure."

That was it. He asked nothing more and, as much as I wanted to begin a conversation, I kept quiet. When we reached my apartment, I couldn't even get my key into the lock. The physics of the maneuver was just too much to handle.

"Take it easy," he said, and I laughed and turned the key. *Easy,* I thought. This kind of thing was never easy for me.

Once we were inside, I discovered he was way ahead of me; I need not have worried whether we were both feeling the same thing. He tossed his jacket aside, undid his jeans, and pushed them to his knees. His cock was short, thick, and already wet. He reached down to his balls and played with them while his cock bobbed up and down—beckoning me. I stared at him so long he laughed.

"So?" he asked, and I almost apologized for my fugue.

Instead of heeding my impulse to fall to my knees and suck him madly, I moved slowly. Fully dressed, I pressed myself against him and trapped his cock between us while I kneaded his butt cheeks. I looked into his eyes and thought to kiss him, but hesitated. He grinned, then opened his mouth in invitation. As I went in— tongue first—he began to undo my pants. As our kissing heated up, he wedged a hand into my jeans and onto my prick. He began to pull. We went at it like that for several minutes before he pulled back and asked, "You got a bed?"

His question made me feel clumsy and inexperienced. He was leading me along when I wanted to be the one with the moves. I let those useless thoughts scatter as I took him to the bedroom, where he stripped. After watching him, I did the same.

He rolled onto the bed with such nonchalance, I knew he'd done this hundreds of times. He was experienced and proud of it. He lay on his back and raised his knees. His dark hole winked at me.

"Well, c'mon," he urged gently as I stood there, naked and transfixed by the sight of his ass. "It's all yours."

I fetched a condom and some lube from my night table and suited up. Then I crawled onto the bed and got down between his legs. I pushed a gob of lube into him with a finger. He squirmed and said, "Gimme two." I added a second finger and more lube, and began to work him a bit as he stroked his stiffening dick. After a minute or two, he said, "For Chrissakes, fuck me, will you, dude?"

I slathered my swollen prong, guided it to his hole, and pushed in.

"Yeah," he moaned as his sphincter muscle clamped onto me. When I settled into an easy stroke, he asked for more. "C'mon, give it to me. Ride my ass."

As turned on as I was, something held me back. Maybe it was the swiftness of it all. I wanted to come in the worst way, but more than that, I wanted to connect a bit—even though I knew this was pretty much a fuck-and-run scenario.

"C'mon," he pleaded again, pushing against me until he got me where he wanted: pounding him steadily and forceful. "That's it," he coached. "Ream my ass good."

At that point I let myself go and forgot about any connection other than my dick screwing his butt. I pulled out and let my wet cock slide up between us, then speared him again. He let out a cry, and I saw how gone he was—totally into getting done.

I grabbed his feet and pushed them up toward his ears to angle for maximum torque as I gave him his fuck. As my load started rising, I slammed into him, growling with each massive thrust. He began to pull his dick frantically. Seconds before I let go, he shot an impressive wad onto his stomach. He kept pumping himself as I unleashed my own torrent deep inside him.

Exhausted by the fuck, I slumped forward onto him, then slid out. He wrapped his arms around me—loosely, as if the embrace were a token gesture.

"Some fuck," he said as he worked his way out from under me.

I didn't get up. I watched him dress and fought the urge to ask him to stay; I knew that wasn't his thing. I could feel it. He was headed elsewhere—either back onto the train or to a club or the baths. Wherever there was fresh cock.

"See you around," he said from the foot of the bed.

"Yeah, sure," I replied, and he was gone. I rolled over and reminded myself he'd been just what I needed. Soon I was fast asleep.

About a week later I found myself on a late-night train again. I'd met friends in San Francisco for a show, and I'd just managed to catch the last train home. It was sparsely peopled, and the end car I entered was empty—or so I thought. We were in the Transbay Tube before I realized there was another guy onboard.

Amid the low railroad rumble, I heard the unmistakable sound of a hand working on a cock. Knowing that lowlifes occasionally frequented the cars, I hesitated. But when my dick began to get hard, I decided to take a chance and look.

He was sprawled in an area where two seats faced each other, with his feet up on the seat opposite him. His coat was open, his jeans were undone, and his sizable cock was wet with spit and precome. His eyes were closed, and he seemed perfectly content to work over his meat in this very public place. As I appraised him, I guessed him to be about 19. He had long dark lashes, olive skin, short medium-brown hair, and an uncut cock that looked intensely inviting. I slipped in beside his feet.

He sensed my presence and opened his eyes. He boldly met my stare. "You're not taking me off this train till I'm done," he said.

"I'm not a cop," I assured him, "just an interested bystander." He took a long look at me and apparently liked what he saw.

"Want a taste?" he asked.

I got up and leaned toward his crotch, and he let go of himself.

"Suck my dick," he murmured as I hovered over him. I reached down to his dark bush and grasped the base of his shaft, then closed my mouth over him. "Oh, yeah," he moaned, pushing up at me.

The train made a stop at West Oakland. Fortunately, nobody got on. The doors closed, and we started moving. I kept him in my mouth the whole time, playing with his delicious foreskin, tonguing his piss slit, caressing his sweet, sensitive underside. Then I sucked him into my throat.

The train arrived at the 12th Street station in Oakland. Again, no one entered the car. It was a good thing because he was getting vocal. He told me what he was going to give me—and that he was going to give it to me more than once.

I sucked him dry, then sat back with my hand still on his cock.

"Now me," I said as I pulled open my khakis. He got down between my legs and fished out my swollen, throbbing prick.

When the car was back above ground, I glanced out the window as bits of Oakland flashed by. I relished the sensation of a good blow job. The experience was even more titillating for the public venue—never mind that nobody was actually there to see us. The doors opened and closed with each stop, but I made no move toward cover myself; this guy was good, and I was about to let go. I told him when I was about to unload, but he held on. When my jizz started to erupt, he kept gobbling. Even when I was done he still sucked.

We were through the Berkeley Hills Tunnel when we sat back and really looked at each other.

"Where you headed?" he asked me.

"Actually, we passed my stop. How about you?"

"Concord. I was at this party in the Mission, but it was a bust. There was one really hot guy and a bunch of losers, and the hottie took off with someone else. I got so turned on thinking about him that I couldn't wait till I got home."

"I'm glad you couldn't. You know, I ride the train all the time, but I've never done anything like this."

He stroked his cock, and I watched it start to fill again. "How about we do a little more?" he asked. When he handed me a condom I understood what he had in mind. I rolled it over his rigid prick, and he said, "Climb on."

He lubed himself with spit while I pushed my pants down. He spread his legs and eased me into his lap and onto his dick. As it inched into my rectum, I looked out the window. For a while we rode along quietly anchored, as I sucked him with my muscle and he gave me just the slightest thrust. Silence filled the car. When he started to ram his cock up into me, everything else disappeared.

He dug his fingers into my hips and held me while he thrust his big dick up my chute. The familiar, squishy sound of a skin-on-skin fuck-slap filled the car. I jerked my cock furiously, knowing he was about to drive the come out of me.

When we reached Walnut Creek, he relented. I settled down onto him as doors opened and closed. Again, nobody entered the car. It was unlikely we'd have company now; we were deep into suburbia. Here, everyone was already securely tucked in for the night.

When the train resumed its pace, so did we. As we sped toward the stop before Concord, he reached a frantic pace, obviously ready to blow.

"Oh, man," he said with a grunt. I knew he was shooting cream inside of me, and that knowledge took me over the edge as well. I pumped myself and watched my juice shoot onto the seat beside him.

It was a long climax, considering what we'd already done. When I finally dismounted and slumped into the opposite seat, my ass tingling and my pants at my ankles, I saw he was still hard. He pulled off the rubber, tossed it under the seat, and fingered the residue of spunk on his cock head.

"Why don't you come with me?" he asked. I didn't respond immediately; I just sat there looking at him and that dick. "I've got a whole lot more," he added, "and you look like you could handle it."

The conductor called the Concord station. I watched him stuff his erection into his pants. After only a moment's hesitation, I quickly dressed and followed him out. In the parking lot he unlocked the doors to a late-model sedan and climbed into the backseat.

"Here?" I asked.

"Yeah, I can't take you home. I'm still crashing with my parents." He was already out of his pants. I knew I could get what I needed; here in the emptiness of the deserted lot, I could really let go. I unzipped and climbed in.

"You've got one sweet ass," he said as he ran a finger up my crack. He got my pants off and positioned me on my knees, facing out the back window. He moved behind me and worked two fingers into my hole. He prodded until I began to beg for it, then he suited up and shoved his cock into me again.

As he began to thrust in earnest, I heard a train pull into the station. In a dim corner of my mind I recalled that the suburban trains stopped running at midnight. I banished the thought; at that point, nothing else mattered. All I wanted was a good fuck. I squeezed my sphincter muscle and heard an appreciative moan behind me, then the sound of the departing train. I hoped I'd missed the last one.

Beautiful Inside

Thom Wolf

"Do you serve food here?"

He sits at a table on the pavement, looking up at me with almond-shaped eyes. His irises are huge and blue. I recognize him from Cruise but decide not to let on. He is by himself.

"Just cold snacks," I say. "Sandwiches." I give him the menu and can't help noticing how big his hands are. He is big all over: one of those guys who spend five days out of seven in the gym. I wonder where he goes, not having seen him working out myself. His forearms are massive.

He studies the menu a moment. "I'll have a sandwich," he decides. "Chicken on whole wheat bread. Hold the mayo. And a glass of milk. Skim."

I scribble on my pad, but I'm watching him rather than writing. I reckon he's about 22, though it's not always easy to put an age on a muscle queen. His hair is brown, streaked with blond. It hangs across his forehead, brushed to the right. His lips are full. He's pouting. I imagine those lips stuffed with cock. He's not wearing much: two honey-brown nipples peak out the side of a tight muscle vest. His chest is shaved, of course.

I smile and take his order inside, wondering whether he's worth pursuing. Although the package is appealing, more often than not I find myself disappointed with muscle boys. They take it for granted that their body is reward enough. I've yet to find one with more to offer than just brute strength.

Mario is having a cigarette on the sly in the yard. He jumps guiltily.

"Customer," I say, giving him the order.

Mario grimaces. It's late afternoon and business is winding down. We're waiting for the evening shift to arrive so we can go home. There's about 20 minutes to go.

"No mayo," I warn, pouring a large glass of skim milk. From the window in the kitchen door I can see straight through the café to the tables outside. Muscle Boy is the only customer. He rearranges his balls as I watch him. He's wearing baggy shorts. I doubt he has anything on underneath. As I watch I see the front of his shorts twitch and tent slightly. I hadn't expected him to be big down there too. Fuck. Some guys really do have all the luck.

Mario makes the sandwich, and I take it out with the glass of milk. Muscle Boy crosses his huge thighs as I approach, hiding that monster meat. I smile, looking straight into those baby blues. His lip curls at one side.

"This heat won't quit," I say, shielding my eyes from the sun.

"Shouldn't complain," he says, taking a bite out of his sandwich.

"I guess not. Might even catch a couple of hours of work on my tan when I get off."

"You go to Cruise," he says wiping his mouth on the back of his hand. "I've seen you there on the weekend."

"Never miss it."

His name is Michael. I think he might be younger than I had first assumed. There's a naïveté to his conversation—a boyishness beneath all that masculine muscle. I like him, so I tell him I'm nearly finished. I tell him about the roof of my apartment and how it catches the best of the day's sun in the late afternoon. It's perfect for getting an all-over tan.

"I'm meeting someone in half an hour," he says.

Shit! I hate making a fool of myself over men like this. "No problem," I say, giving him my couldn't-give-a-shit smile. "I had better cash up before the next shift arrives." Then I step back.

"It's my friend," he says. "Her fiancé just left her. I promised I'd go out with her tonight."

"You don't have to explain to me."

"I'll be at Cruise this Saturday," he says. "Will I see you there?" He uncrosses his legs again, and I can see the shape of a monster head tenting his shorts.

"Like I said, I never miss it."

Like most guys, I don't handle rejection well. I can't stop thinking about him. I'm in a mood. Not even two hours of nude sunbathing on the roof of my building can relax me. I've got a damn hard-on that won't go down. Though I try to ignore it, I find my hand wandering down to give it a few slow tugs. I roll onto my stomach, but that's no better. I grind the throbbing organ into my towel.

Why has Michael affected me like this? He's not the kind of guy I would usually go for. I do like a man in good shape, but when they're obsessed with working out to the exclusion of everything else, I find it a turn off. I can't stop thinking of his eyes, looking at me beneath those straight brows. I imagine looking into them while he's fucking me, wrapping my legs around his waist and my arms around his broad shoulders, and looking into his eyes with his dick deep in my ass.

I haven't been fucked for a while. All the guys I've hooked up with lately have been bottom boys; no sooner have I got their pants off than they're lying on their backs with their ankles in the air. Not that I mind—I'm a versatile guy—but it's nice to fucked for a change. I wonder about Michael. You can't always tell from the look of a guy what he's into. Some of the biggest men I've ever had have been real princesses in the bedroom. Married guys are the worst; all they ever want is to get fucked.

I think about the dick I glimpsed today. It was only an outline in his shorts, but it promised so much. It would be a waste for that monster not to go in my ass.

I roll back over so I can get a good handle on my cock. No one ever comes up here. I get a good action going, concentrating on the shaft and the ultrasensitive area just below the head. I'm already spitting precome on my stomach. I whack it harder, tugging at my nuts. My ball sac is loose from the heat. I think about slobbering over those big nipples, and suddenly I'm coming, squirting a healthy dose over my chest and stomach. My come smells good, so I scoop some up on my fingertips, which I then shove into my mouth. My spunk is still warm when it drizzles down my throat.

I look for Michael on Saturday night. Cruise is packed. He usually hangs out on the second-level dance floor. I get a drink and go in search of him. I'm looking good. I've been to the gym after work to get myself pumped for tonight. I'm wearing a tight T-shirt to show off my chest and shoulders. I'll probably take it off soon and shove it down the back of my jeans. My jeans hang low enough on my hips to show that I'm not wearing any underwear.

There are a lot of familiar faces here tonight. I've had most of them. I should really find a new place to go. It's getting tired here. I need a fresh scene. Maybe after tonight I'll find one. Fucking Michael can be my farewell gesture to Cruise.

He's on the dance floor, alone. Like most of the muscle boys, he's not wearing a shirt. He has a thick waist and a hard stomach. I've always found that little potbelly that bodybuilders have totally hot. There's not a scrap of fat there: It's all muscle. He's dancing to Kylie. He hasn't seen me. I watch him for a while, as I nurse my drink. I wonder whether he's on something, not that I mind.

After I've killed enough time, I move onto the floor. He won't reject me this time. I tap him on the shoulder. He turns and smiles. His eyes are even bigger than I remember. "Hi," I shout. "How's your friend?"

"She's fine," he shouts back. "She's gone to her parents' for the weekend."

"You here on your own?"

He nods. We end up dancing to four records in succession. My shirt comes off during the second song. My jeans dip lower on my waist, revealing the hard line from my hip to my groin. I grind my pelvis and stroke my abs as I dance. Michael's nipples are hard, pointing straight at me. I resist the urge to chew on them right there.

"Want a drink?" he asks.

We move over to the bar, where we both have vodka mixed with diet tonic. Michael leans one elbow on the counter. His hips lean toward me, almost touching mine. There's a bulge in the front of his jeans. I'm surprised to see a tuft of hair peaking over the low waist. I assumed he would shave everywhere.

He smiles, then looks down into his drink. He's shy. I find that endearing. I lean in to his ear. "What's the matter?"

"Nothing," he says. "Nothing at all. Quite the opposite."

"Good." I put my hand on his waist and move closer. He's rock-hard. He smells of spicy cologne and light sweat. "I could do with a big boy's cock in my ass. It's been a while."

When he laughs two dimples frame his full mouth. "You know what you want."

"I usually get what I want too."

I run my hand from his waist to his dick. I'm not disappointed: It's long and fat. It pulses strongly as I squeeze. He looks nervous. A group of guys is watching us. I recognize one of them from last month. Dean, I think his name is—big mouth, total bottom, wanted me to fuck him in front of a mirror. I move my hand back to Michael's waist and lead him away from the bar.

"Where are we going?" he asks.

"Bathroom," I say. I haven't got time to take him home. I have to have him now. We're lucky. There's a free stall. Michael goes in ahead of me. I shove the door closed with my butt and slide the lock home. I kiss his mouth, my hands already working on his fly. His monster cock thwacks into my hand. His tongue is inside my mouth. I pull away and drop down. His cock head is sticky and moist. I give it a slow stroke, just under the head, moving up to the slit. He throbs and more fluid dribbles onto my tongue. I open my mouth and slide him inside. I look up as I start sucking. His eyes are open, watching me, his lips in a pout. I go deeper. He's too big for me to deep-throat, but I take what I can, stuffing his meat to the back of my mouth. My jaw aches.

I get a hand on his balls, still surprised at their hairiness. He has a low-hanging sac. I roll my thumb around his ample nuts. I move my other hand to his thighs, which are thick and hard, then slide it around his body to get a feel of his ass. It's solid and smooth. I can't even get a finger into the crack. Even though my face is stuffed full of his cock, I manage a smile; I've found the top I've been looking for.

His hands grip my head, holding me still while he begins to thrust. He shoves it deeper. I love the feel of him sliding across my tongue. He grunts with each thrust.

"Damn, that's a good suck," he groans.

I concentrate on taking him, managing to go deeper than I expected. I'm already thinking about how this monster is going to feel in my ass. I can't wait for this boy to fuck the shit out of me—I'll do anything he wants me to. He's breathing faster. He lets go of my head and pulls back. He's got his cock in both hands now, jerking fast. His thighs tense, and he squirts a massive load right in my face. I close my eyes and savor the warm fluid gushing over my forehead, my eyelids, and my cheeks. I can feel a rope of spunk hanging off my chin. Michael rubs his cock over my face. I open my eyes, and he's smiling.

We clean up with toilet paper, and Michael fastens his jeans. He's got a huge grin on his face. "That was awesome," he says, patting my ass as we leave the stall.

"Let's have one more drink, then get out of here."

"I'm buying," he laughs. "I owe you big time."

I find a place to sit on one of the huge leather couches, while Michael goes back to the bar. He returns a few minutes later with two vodka martinis. He's still smiling. I find his enthusiasm endearing; most guys want to zip up and run after a blow job, not share drinks and chat.

"How come you're always here on your own?" I ask him.

"I don't have any gay friends," he says. "And my straight friends aren't ready for a place like this."

"I guess not."

His thigh presses against mine. The legs of his jeans are stretched tight over massive muscle. I'm already thinking about what he is going to do to me. What I want him to do to me. "Come on," I say, finishing my drink. "Let's make a move."

We go to his place because it's nearer. He shares an apartment with a guy called James. As we enter we hear James banging a girl in his bedroom. Michael motions me into his own room and shuts the door. It's small but nice, pretty much what I had expected—movie posters on the wall, huge video and DVD collection. There's an obligatory set of weights on a stand in the corner.

Michael turns on some music, just loud enough to drown out the noises from the next room. He chooses Janet Jackson's "Velvet Rope" album. Good soundtrack for the scene we have in mind. He grabs me, shoving me against the door. He takes my face in his hands and starts kissing me. His body feels so much bigger and muscular than my own. With our lips locked, each of us struggles with the other's clothes, tearing at buttons and zippers, tossing them in any direction. When we are naked, I feel a brief sense of inadequacy. I work out, and I'm in good shape—lean all over—but my body seems so slight in comparison to his huge bulk. While his dick is bigger than mine, what I'm lacking in inches I more than make up for in hardness. My dick is so rigidly stiff that it's all but stuck to my stomach.

"Damn," Michael says, fondling my cock. "You're beautiful."

I believe him and suck harder on his tongue. He grabs my waist with both hands and picks me up. I wrap my legs around him and hold on tight. His dick bounces into the open cleft of my ass. I can't get enough of his kisses. Spit is drooling down both our faces.

He carries me over to his bed and drops down on top of me. He crawls over me, moving down my body. I realize he wants to eat my ass. I hitch my hips upward and pull my knees into my chest to accommodate him. His mouth latches on to my butthole and licks it until it's tender. I writhe and moan, which encourages him to greater intensity. He's got a good circular action going with his tongue, which really works for me. My hole surrenders to him.

"Aw, fuck," I say as he plunges into the tight ring. I love it. There aren't enough guys in my experience willing to get their mouth working down there. Michael knows how to make a boy happy. His big blue eyes watch me while he's eating. The underside of my balls rests on the bridge of his nose. I moan loudly.

He stays down there for ages, taking ownership of my asshole. If a guy is willing to rim me for 10 or 15 minutes, I don't give a fuck what else he has in mind. He can do whatever the hell he wants to me.

Michael moves back over my body, paying special attention to my balls and the shaft of my cock. His chin glistens with spit. He moves higher, tugging at my navel ring with his teeth, twisting gently. He reaches my nipples, sucking and chewing with just the right amount of pressure. My legs are around his waist again and his cock rubs against my butthole. I want it in there.

Michael lubes up the head of his dick before sliding a rubber over the big shaft. He lubes up the outside with a slow, determined hand. I watch with wide eyes. He nudges my thighs farther apart and lubes up my ass, shoving it in. Even his fingers are big. I lie back and he climbs over me, moving his cock into position. I wrap my arms around his shoulders. I'm so ready for this. He eases himself in slowly and pauses for a few seconds once the head is in there. "Give me more," I growl in his ear.

He moves his hands beneath me, holding my ass and pushing his cock in farther. It's a strain, but I want it. I bear down on him, determined to take it. I lock my legs around him and pull him in, taking everything.

"Damn," he cries, "this is tight."

I sigh and take deep breaths. It's in me now, all the way. We lie there for a while, motionless. I can feel the pulse of him inside me. I start to play with my sphincter, tightening and easing. "OK, I'm ready now," I tell him.

Michael digs his knees into the bed and starts to fuck me, building up a rhythm when he's sure he isn't hurting me. I grab at his body, caressing his muscles, smearing his sweat across his skin.

He digs his fingers into my ass and fucks me harder. "Yeah. Fuck me hard. Fuck me real hard," I moan. There is no such thing as too hard.

He pulls out and rolls me onto my side, lifting one leg onto his shoulder. He pushes back in. The change in position brings with it a whole new set of sensations. I watch the contraction of his abs with each thrust. I feel a strong sense of safety with this big boy fucking me. He's slamming his cock into me so hard now that the force is bouncing me across the bed. Michael's huge hands grab my waist and haul me back toward him where he can fuck me some more.

He changes position again, flipping me onto my hands and knees. He applies more lube to his cock, grabs both cheeks of my ass and drives back inside. I spread my legs wider on the bed and steady myself against the pounding he's giving me. The mattress bounces beneath us. He's pumping furiously. I demand more. I can feel sweat pouring down my face, stinging my eyes. All I care about is this boy fucking me.

"How's does my cock feel inside you?" he asks.

"Fucking beautiful," I cry. "Your cock feels beautiful inside me."

Our skin slaps together loudly—a hard sound that echoes above the music. I twist my head to watch him. There's a determined expression on his face. I'm certain he could fuck like this all night, if he set his mind to it. But I'm nearly done. The constant jab of his cock against my prostate means I'm going to come soon, and I tell him so.

"Want me to come inside you?" he asks.

"Fuck yes. Bury your load in my ass."

His strokes become shallow and fast. He's fucking like a rabbit. He groans and rams it in to the hilt. I feel the pulse of his cock blowing off inside me. That's all I need to feel. I take my right hand from the mattress and fasten it around my dick. All it takes is a couple of strokes. The first shot blasts the underside of my chin. The rest of my load hits my stomach and the bedcovers beneath me. My asshole has gone into spasms around Michael's meaty cock.

He pulls out of me. My asshole tightens after coming, and the tip of the condom gets stuck. He gives a little tug to free it. I expect him to tie off the rubber and throw it in the bin, but he empties it over my raised buttocks and rubs his come into my skin. I love the warm trickle of it dribbling over my ass. Once Michael has massaged his load into my skin, he gives my butt a little pat and we lie down.

I'm totally satisfied. We lie there, kissing and cuddling. I feel his cock against my leg: He's still hard. I love the way he looks at me. It sounds like the action in the next room has finished.

"Will they have heard us?" I ask.

"I don't care. He keeps me up every weekend with that noise. About time he heard what it's like on the other side." It's getting late: after three in the morning. "You can stay, if you like," he offers.

We get down under the covers, our arms around each other. It's rare to have this kind of closeness after sex. I make the most of it, falling into an easy sleep. The CD is still playing.

When I wake up later, it's quiet. It's still dark outside. I can't have been asleep long. Michael's fingers are inside my ass, wriggling around. I turn toward him. His eyes glisten in the dark. He presses more insistently, pushing deep. It feels like he's got two or three fingers in there. I roll over, against his huge chest. He's finger-fucking me with a fluid, circular motion.

"Want to do it again?" I ask, brushing my cheek against his face.

"I wouldn't wake you without a good reason." He reaches for the tube of lube, coats his fingers, and shoves them back inside me. I'm still pretty loose. I sit on top of him, reaching for a rubber. When it's in place, he squeezes a blob of lube onto his cock head, and I rub it over the shaft for him. He's most sensitive on his underside, moaning when I pay attention to that area.

I straddle his waist, pushing my ass down over his cock. I'm sore from our earlier fuck and need him to go easy on me. This position is perfect. I ease him back into me, pausing when it feels like too much, giving myself a moment before dropping farther down. Michael moans. When I feel his balls press against my ass, I know

I've done it. He puts his hands around my waist and holds me there. After another moment, he twitches his cock. I gasp.

"Is that OK?" he asks.

"Just take it easy."

He lets me do the work; I rock my pelvis slowly when I'm ready. I put my hands on his mammoth chest, bracing myself, and shove my ass right down on his hard meat. The burning in my rectum has almost gone. He twitches again, a small motion that seems to fill me right up. I pick up the pace, squeezing his chest and riding his cock. I move higher, managing a longer stroke. My own dick is slapping against my stomach, leaving a silvery trail around my navel. My ass is feeling juicy, and I can take him really deep now. I grind my balls into his pubes. Michael's hands dig into my flesh, moving my ass on his cock faster and deeper. I jerk myself while I ride. I can't last long in this position. Neither can he.

"I'm gonna come," he cries. There's a helpless sound to his voice that gets me harder. I'm ready to come too. We give in together. Michael comes inside me, tearing up inside my ass, still fucking me hard. I shoot high. The first spurt hits the hollow in the base of his throat. The rest gushes over his abdomen. I fall on top of him. Two hearts thunder against one another.

When I wake up again, it's morning. Michael is on the floor doing push-ups. I prop myself up on the pillows and watch him. He counts breathlessly to 60. When he's finished he pushes back onto his knees. His face is red. He's got a hard-on.

"I was gonna run out and get us some breakfast," he says. "You can stay for breakfast, can't you?"

I nod, smiling. My ass is still sore, and I'm not up to a morning fuck. But as I watch Michael's ass stepping into a pair of shorts, I'm already thinking of getting in there. I just hope he shares my appreciation for versatility.

Dogboy Chews Stranger's Meat

Christopher Pierce

When Mitch first came to stay with us, I knew he would have to have me before he left. And he did.

Mitch was one of my Master's oldest friends. They had known each other in New York when they were both starting their own businesses. When Master got the news that his buddy was coming to L.A. for a visit, he insisted that Mitch stay with us.

I had seen photos of Mitch so I knew he was handsome, but I wasn't prepared for the sight of the hunky stud I saw when Master opened the door.

He was about 5 foot 11, with gray-blond hair and a nice clean-shaven face. His eyes were bright blue, looking almost silver in the late-afternoon sun. The polo shirt he wore gripped his torso tight, showing off nicely shaped pecs and a washboard stomach that looked hard as a rock.

Mitch had a big athletic bag over his shoulder, so I could see one of his arms flexing nicely. The bulge in his arm was almost as big as the bulge in his pants. From my perspective, on all fours on the floor, it was right in my line of sight.

I must have stared at his crotch longer than was appropriate because my Master kicked me lightly with his booted foot.

"Get out of the way, boy," he said. "Give Mitch room to walk in here."

Snapping back to my senses, I crawled out of the way and watched the man walk into my Master's apartment. The two men exchanged handshakes and hugs, smiling and laughing like the old buddies they were. Mitch set his bag down and I couldn't help sniffing it. It smelled great, the hot manly smell of gym clothes. He must have been traveling all day.

"This is my dog-slave," Master said. "Say hello to Mitch, boy."

"Woof!" I said enthusiastically, wagging my naked butt back and forth like a tail. The men laughed as Mitch hunkered down to one knee to be on the same level with me. He put a hand on my head and scratched me as he would a dog. I figured he must know what Master was into, because he didn't seem surprised that I was naked except for a leather collar around my neck.

"How you doin', boy?" he asked.

"Great, sir." I answered. I can speak English if addressed directly. Otherwise, I know Master prefers dog-speak. "I've been looking forward to your stay with us."

He grinned at me, and the sight of his flashing white teeth got my doggy-cock hard. Mitch saw it and reached between my legs, gripping it lightly in his hand. His touch was wonderful, strong and masculine, so like Master and yet different.

"He's a horny one, ain't he?" he asked my Master.

"Yep," he answered. "He's always ready to get plowed."

"Is that right, boy?" Mitch asked me. I howled, and they laughed again as he stood up and walked into the living room with Master.

I got beers for them and they sat down to talk. While I was making them dinner, I noticed Mitch watching me, his eyes roaming up and down my body.

"You always keep him that way?" he asked Master.

"Damn right. Naked and collared is how slave boys should always be."

"Amen," Mitch said.

I heard them clink their beer bottles together in a toast.

"He's one fine-looking boy," the visitor said. My cheeks turned red. Master doesn't usually compliment me because he doesn't want me getting full of myself, so the unexpected praise brought a blush to my skin.

"That he is," Master agreed. I kept my mind on my work, trying not to let their conversation distract me. When dinner was ready, I served it to them at the table before returning to the kitchen for my own meal. As always, I ate it out of my dog bowl with no hands. When I was done, I cleared off the table and cleaned the dishes.

After dinner I was allowed to curl up at Master's feet while he and Mitch smoked cigars and talked about old times. It was wonderful to lie there knowing I was the personal property of my Master. Earlier, he had scratched me behind the ears and told me how proud he was of me, so I was a very happy boy. I was so content lying at their feet that I fell asleep right there on the floor.

It was pretty late when Master woke me up and said it was time for him to get to bed. Mitch said he was going to stay up and watch some TV before hitting the sack himself.

Master ordered me to fix up the guest room for Mitch before reporting back to him in his bedroom. I scurried to obey, getting clean sheets for the guest bed and making the room nice and comfortable for him. Carrying Mitch's bag to the room in my mouth, I even got to smell his delicious man-odor some more.

When the room was ready, I reported as ordered to my Master in his bedroom. He was already nearly asleep. I sat obediently at the side of his bed, sniffing his arm like the curious dog I was.

His hand reached out to scratch behind my ears. Mmmm, I loved it when he did that. It made my puppy-dick hard whenever he touched me with such affection.

"Boy," he said, "Mitch's one of my best friends. He doesn't have a boy of his own right now, and he's really aching to work a hot piece of meat over. I want you to go out there and offer yourself to him. He's a good man. We can trust him." He gestured to a large drawstring sack next to the bed on the floor. "Take that to him. Tell him he can use anything in it." I was looking at the sack, imagining what was making it so plump and full. Master gently took my chin in his hand and brought me back to looking at him. "And, you," he said, "serve him like you would me."

"Yes, sir!" I whispered enthusiastically, wagging my butt.

"Good dog," he said, settling back against his pillows. He'd be asleep in seconds, I knew, so I was careful not to make any noise as I leaned over and picked up the sack in my mouth. It was heavy, almost as heavy as Mitch's athletic bag had been. But I could handle it.

I padded out of the room and all fours, taking care to quietly nuzzle Master's bedroom door shut on the way out. The apartment was dark. The only light came from the ghostly reflections on the walls created by the TV in the main room.

Squaring my shoulders, I crawled down the hallway toward the light, toward Mitch. As the TV came into view, I could see that it was no late-night talk show our houseguest was watching. Two gorgeous stud-pups filled the screen, humping each other and stroking each other's cocks. Mitch had discovered Master's collection of porn tapes.

Coming around the edge of the couch where he was sitting, I saw that Mitch was far from sleepy. His eyes were wide open, and he had pulled his dick out of his pants and begun to jerk off. It was a beautiful cock, not really long but wide and firm, the foreskin gone to reveal the powerful head to the world. Shining with lubrication, his erect penis looked like a glowing talisman in the dark.

Mitch glanced over at me with a surprised look on his face.

"Hey, boy," he said. "You scared me for a second. C'mere." I dropped the sack and crawled over him, rubbing my head against his leg affectionately. "Thought everyone was asleep. What did you bring?" he gestured with one hand at the sack while he petted me with the other.

"Master told me to offer myself to you, sir." Out of the corner of my eye, I could see his cock flex at the words. He got a big smile on his handsome face.

"Is that right?" he said.

"Yes, sir." I reached over and pulled the sack close, picking it up in my mouth and holding it out for him. He took it, holding it on his lap. "He said to tell you that you can use anything in that sack on me, and that I'm yours for the night. I'm to serve you as I do him."

Mitch leaned back, the smile on his face getting bigger and bigger. I could tell my news pleased him greatly.

"Well now," he said. "This is what I call hospitality. Let's see what we've got here."

He opened the sack to look inside and the grin on his face got even bigger. I could read his expression as clear as day: `

Then he put the sack aside and leaned back, pushing his body further down on the couch. His cock jutted up, looking magical in the strange light of the TV. It made me salivate just seeing it.

"You can start by serving my dick, puppy boy." Mitch said.

"Oh, thank you, sir," I whispered as I maneuvered myself between his legs, my mouth enveloping his gorgeous cock-head. I forced myself to savor it, to stay there and just enjoy the feel of that bulb of hot man-meat. Stroking it with my tongue, it seemed as if it came alive in my mouth, growing and pulsing with pleasure and excitement.

"Mmmmm," Mitch murmured, putting his hands behind his head in a gesture of utter satisfaction and contentment.

Little drops of precome started to ooze out of his piss slit, and I lovingly slurped them up. He tasted so fucking good—again, like Master, but also very different. My doggy-dick was standing straight out, hard as a rock from the incredible intensity of serving this hot man.

I couldn't hold back anymore and started to slide my mouth down over his shaft, letting the head penetrate farther and farther until it hit the back of my throat. Still hungry, I tried to get even more of him inside me. I managed to almost reach down to his pubic hair. His dick was so intense, like a throbbing hot iron in my mouth, except that it didn't burn with fire: It burned me with passion.

Mitch put his hand in my hair and, gently grabbing a fistful of it, he guided my head into a wonderful up-and-down motion, not too fast, not too slow, but just how he wanted it. I obeyed his non-verbal command, imitating the action and speed so precisely that he let go of me and put his hands behind his head again.

I sucked his cock slowly and deliberately, cherishing each stroke down toward his crotch and every stroke back up toward the head. I felt full and complete because. I was a thing being used by this totally hot stud: used like the dog-slave I was, used to bring pleasure. I couldn't imagine what could possibly be more fulfilling than this.

As my sucking continued, Mitch sat up and pulled off his polo shirt, letting it fall to the couch. Although my angle was not the best, what I did see of his torso made my knees weak. My earlier guess had been right: That tight shirt concealed a physique of utter perfection, sculpted and molded as if carved from stone.

He reached into the sack and pulled something out. I couldn't tell what it was in the darkness until he leaned forward over my shoulder. His strong, powerful hands found their way to my crotch and took hold of my balls. They felt utterly trapped in his grip. I felt completely in his power because I knew he could crush my balls in a heartbeat. I would do anything for him. And I *wanted* to do anything for him. I had my orders.

But even if I hadn't, serving this man was second nature to me. I was a born slave, and knew that I had been born to worship men such as Mitch and my Master.

Then both of his hands were in my crotch, pulling something tight around my extended balls. He had pulled my ball sac away from my body, and now wrapped whatever it was around the newly exposed base. I realized what it was, then, and reveled in the feeling of the leather thong binding me. Tightly he knotted the thong, keeping my balls stretched far from my body. My cock bulged in ecstasy, its tip already slick with precome.

Mitch left the end of the thong long, trailing, and loose. He wrapped a few inches of this leash around his fingers and sat back. Now he had me by the balls, and could pull and stretch them at his whim. As if I hadn't already been completely in his control, I was now bound and leashed. One yank of that thong, and I would drown in a sea of pain. As always, I found it intoxicating to know that I was helpless and that another man had total power over me.

"Oh, yeah," he moaned as I sucked his dick harder. The pain in my crotch as he pulled on the thong made me steadily more aroused.

Suddenly, he slid forward, dropping off the couch and onto his knees in front of me. Then he slid his cock out of my mouth. A long trailing tentacle of saliva connected us until it snapped apart. Now Mitch's chest was right in front of my face, and his powerful muscled arms wrapped around me, squeezing me tight.

"Good boy," he whispered. "Good dog. You make me feel so good."

I wagged my butt in happiness, and I heard him chuckle. Then he dropped the thong and, taking my head in his hands, kissed me hard, fast, and firm on the mouth. Instantly, his tongue was inside, probing, searching, and dominating me from the inside out.

Wanting to be totally open to him, I willed my throat to open even further, to show him that my whole body, my whole soul, was his to explore and to use however he saw fit. His kiss was passionate, wonderful: forceful and yet tender, both rough and sensual.

Then his mouth moved away from my lips and and trailed down my neck and onto my chest, sucking and biting all the way before finally settling on my left nipple. Little yelps of pain and pleasure escaped from me as he worked my tits, alternating quickly between biting and caressing. His tongue swirled around the sensitive skin, then he was chewing me, gnawing on the nubs of flesh as if they were tasty treats. He squeezed me again, very tightly.

"Good dog," he whispered in my ear. "Good boy."

I whimpered in response. Human speech was no longer adequate to express how I felt. The smells of him—sweat, musk, day-old deodorant, and cologne—were spellbinding, electrifying my mind just as much as his touch did my body.

Then he moved upward. I closed my eyes and put my face forward, connecting to his body with my mouth. My lips and tongue left a trail of saliva on him as he stood up to his full height. Our houseguest wiggled out of his pants and let them and his boxers fall to the carpet.

Looking up at him, I beheld his magnificent cock, which stood straight out from his body. It cast a huge shadow on the wall. The stud-pups on the TV had outlived their usefulness for Mitch. He picked up the remote and clicked off the TV and VCR.

"Time to hit the hay, boy." he said.

He reached down toward me and with one hand gripped me around the wrist. Pulling me up to my feet, he slung me over his shoulder like I was just a sack of laundry. He used one arm to anchor me in place while he reached down with the other hand to pick up Master's sack. Tossing the sack over his other shoulder, Mitch headed for the guest room.

Even with my cock and balls tied off and painfully smashed against the man's shoulder, I was totally turned on. I love getting carried by guys—it's so primitive and possessive. My puppy-cock was raging by now.

Mitch carried me into the guest room and shut the door behind us. Then he set me down on the bed that I had so nicely made a few minutes before.

"I've had my eye on you since I first showed up," he said, reaching into the sack and pulling out a leather penis-shaped gag. "Don't want to wake up your Master," he said as he slowly stuck it inside my mouth. I stared up into his beautiful eyes as he did it. It was so intense, he pushed the gag into my mouth with the same sensuality and animal heat I knew he would use when he eventually pushed his cock into my ass.

I hoped I wouldn't have to wait long for that.

He tightened the straps around my head and fastened the gag securely tight. Now even if I did make noise, it wouldn't be loud enough for anyone to hear. Next Mitch pulled a pair of handcuffs out of the Master's sack. Expertly, he fastened my wrists together in front of me.

Mitch pushed my hands over my head so my armpits were open to the ceiling. Now I was vulnerable and helpless.

"Just keep those hands out of my way, boy," he said.

I moaned obediently into the gag, and the muffled sound brought a smile to my user's face. What he did next surprised the hell out of me. Somehow that made it even hotter than if I had known it was coming.

The hot stud leaned over and took my hard puppy-cock in his mouth and started sucking me like a pro! Now I was trained the old-fashioned way, in which only slaves and bottoms sucked dick. Tops acted and bottoms got acted on, so in all the time Master had owned me, I had never gotten a blow job.

But there was one rule I learned that was more important than any of the others, and that rule is the reason I didn't freak out completely when Mitch, a consummate top, starting slurping on my tool. I was a slave, and slaves are made to serve, and serve however their Master sees fit. I had been ordered to give myself to this man, and if this was how he wanted to use me, that was his option.

And besides, it felt unbelievably good.

Man, his mouth was wonderful, smooth and hot like electric satin on my desperate dick. The sucking didn't last long. More than anything else, it was simply a tease. But for the seconds Mitch blew me I was in pig-boy heaven.

Mitch pulled off my cock and put his hands on me. He explored my abs and chest, probing and searching, like a blind man whose only way to experience me was tactilely. His hands moved over every inch of me, passing over my erect nipples and making them shiver.

"Mmmm," he murmured, as if savoring a fine wine. "I haven't had a slave to work over in a long time." It was almost like he was talking to himself. I was overjoyed to be there for him, to be available for whatever he wanted to do to me.

Then he climbed on top of me and lay down. He wasn't as heavy as my Master, but feeling all that solid muscle on me was wonderful. I felt trapped, held down, confined. I knew these were things that frightened and disturbed many people, but I totally got off on them.

Mitch started moving, grinding his big top-cock against my pecker. His mouth was on my face, kissing my eyelids, his tongue flicking in and out like a snake's tongue, every touch of it like a brush dipped in fire. The man gripped one of my wrists in each of his hands, pinning them to the bed. As if I was going anywhere! But this added restriction got me even more turned on. I was hungry for his abuse.

Humping me harder now, every stroke burned against me as our rigid cocks slammed together. His panting breath was in my ear. I could hear him getting steadily more excited.

Suddenly, he grabbed me by the waist and flipped me over onto my stomach. I promptly stuck my ass up in the air. I wanted him to see how much I wanted to serve him, how open I was to his every whim. If I hadn't been gagged, I would have been whining and crying like a bitch in heat, dying for him to screw the shit out of me.

But the houseguest had other ideas, as I could see when he reached into the sack again, this time pulling out a rolled flogger. He unfurled it, and the leather thongs hung down like 20 rattails.

Mitch planted his dick between my butt cheeks, resting it on top of my ass. This, of course, was maddening, and I pushed up and back, as if I could somehow get him inside me on my own. He chuckled quietly and played with the flogger, dragging the tails across my back and down the trail between my shoulder blades. Every stroke drove me deeper and deeper into sexual hysteria, silently crying out, *Please whip me! Please fuck me! Please use me!*

The cock on my ass heated up, moving slowly back and forth without entering me. I whined and moaned into the gag. Then the flogger began to hit me, lightly at first, then harder and harder.

Smack!

Smack!

Smack!

Mitch hit me with the flogger and tortured my ass with consummate skill. I could feel his body moving rhythmically. If the stud was moving to music, it was a song for his ears only.

The blows on my butt and back began to hurt, like little bursts of fire, flashing brightly and fading quickly, to be replaced by more seconds later.

"You know what, slave boy?" Mitch asked suddenly.

I made a questioning noise through the gag.

"I don't think you're ready for this yet," he said. Then he pulled his pulsing cock away from my ass. Shaking my head violently, I made desperate, pleading noises, by which I hoped to say, *No, please, no! I am ready! I AM ready!* It was absolute torture to feel him pull away from me. He stopped flogging me, and I collapsed on the bed, breathing heavily.

Still on my stomach, I couldn't see what Mitch was doing behind me, but I did hear him rummaging around in the sack I'd brought him. A moment later I heard the sound of a lube bottle being squeezed. Something new was between my butt-cheeks now, and I realized it was a dildo: a big one.

"Yeah, this is better," the stud growled. "You weren't quite ready for my stud-man's cock, were you?"

"Yes, sir!" I tried to say through the gag. "I'm ready for your stud-man's cock!"

But Mitch had made his mind up, and nothing was going to change it. He worked the dildo up and down my ass-crack, teasing me. As if I weren't already excited enough! What would it take to please my horny houseguest?

I moved my ass around, moaning and crying, trying desperately to communicate, to let him know I was ready, that I needed to be taken. I needed to be penetrated!

Please, sir. I'll do anything. Just please take me!

Mitch yanked at the thong that held my balls in its tight grip and pain seared through me. I must have been making too much noise, because the stud on top of me said, "Shut up, dogboy. Quit whining and crying like a she-bitch, or I'll leave you right where you are, and you can just think about what you've done while I get some sleep. You can just sit there, all open and empty, waiting for a cock that won't come. And you'll have plenty to answer for when I tell your Master how I disappointed I am with you. Then you'll be shit out of luck, won't you?"

I nodded slowly.

"Now, you gonna behave? Gonna be my nice, hungry, quiet dogboy?" he asked as he yanked the thong again. I swallowed the yelp of pain and nodded again.

"Excellent," Mitch said. "Now we can get back to the good stuff." He released my balls and picked up the dildo again. I heard him slather more lube on it and felt him resume using it on my butt.

This time the strokes were more direct, less teasing. I flexed my ass muscles, trying to open myself as much as possible. I wanted to provide the easiest access I could for my welcome intruder. When Mitch was ready for injection, I was as prepared as any boy could be.

The dildo's sculpted head nosed its way inside me, easily popping past my sphincter and into my most private of places. My houseguest pushed, and the simulated penis moved farther into me. He pushed more, and soon enough I had the entire dildo inside me, with just its base sticking out.

Mitch's low, heavy breathing was wonderful to hear. It sounded like he was getting off on this as much as I was. My own forgotten cock rubbed against me, trapped between the bed and my groin. Then he began to fuck me with the dildo, pulling it out, then pushing it back in. My ass made delicious slurping noises as it gripped the plastic penis.

"Turn over, boy," he said from somewhere above me. "But keep the dildo inside you." He pushed it until its entire length was in me, to make his order a little easier to carry out.

Holding my breath, I clamped my muscles around the invading dildo. Then I began to turn myself over, from resting on my stomach to resting on my back. Mitch maintained his grip on the tool he was using to fuck me, and it was sweet bliss feeling it stay in place while my body rotated around it. When I had turned over completely, my hard dick was exposed and dripped pearly drops of fluid onto my abdomen.

"That's what I like to see," Mitch said as he yanked my dick away from my body and let it smack back painfully. "Now I can see your face. I can see your eyes." This seemed particularly important to him but I didn't know why.

He ran a hand down my arms, where my muscles strained in the cuffs that held them above my head. His hand found my nipples and tweaked each one in turn. All the while he continued to fuck me with the dildo. This went on for what seemed like a long time, every torturous second piling up.

It was wonderful to be used and stimulated like that, but I hoped it was only a prelude to the real fucking that was coming.

Finally, Mitch seemed to tire of the game. He put the dildo aside and went into the sack one more time. I immediately recognized the packet he fished out—the shiny square of a condom package was unmistakable.

Mitch removed the wrapper and unrolled the condom over the shaft of his nice big pecker. The whole time, his eyes never left mine. He avoided breaking out eye contact at any cost.

No time like the present. The big man grabbed my legs and tossed them up over his shoulders. With a clear shot at my quivering hole, he shoved himself forward. The muscles of my rectum greeted his cock with enthusiasm, tightening up not to keep it out, but to keep it inside me.

He fucked me: deep, hard, and strong. Beads of sweat formed on his forehead and dripped down onto my face. I hungrily licked up the ones I could reach with my tongue.

It was heaven to be used this way, by Master's friend, just to be there for him to manhandle however he wanted. I was just another piece of Master's property that he could loan out to a friend, like a valuable book or a car.

Before I knew it, Mitch's body began to tense up, and I knew he was shooting off inside me, the condom catching all his spunk and holding it prisoner, just as Mitch was holding me prisoner.

I was his, I realized. I belonged to Mitch.

Even if only for a short time, I belonged to this man, even if only for a second, a heartbeat was all he needed to completely and utterly own me in every possible way.

And in that instant, with his eyes boring into mine, he grabbed my cock in his fist and jerked me—once, twice, three times—and I came. Intense ecstasy flowed through me as jizz flooded out of my rod, landing thick and milky on my chest. The man attached to the dick inside me sighed long and hard, caught his breath, then gently pulled out. Moments later, with the condom and its contents flushed safely down the toilet, Mitch climbed back in bed with me.

"That was just perfect," he said. "Just fucking perfect." He reached between my legs and carefully untied the cord that encircled my balls. Relief coursed through me, and I experienced intense prickly pain as blood flowed back into my balls.

Grinning, Mitch took the gag out of my mouth. "You won't be making any more noise tonight, boy," he whispered, and I nodded submissively. He left the cuffs on my hands and pulled himself into the circle of my arms. Now we were literally bound together. It was absolute heaven having this hunky stud snuggle in close to me, but I was fading fast. As I drifted away I heard him whisper, "Go to sleep, my boy, go to sleep…"

I slept the deep slumber of contentment, satisfied that I had performed as ordered.

Mitch left the next day, after giving a full report to my owner. Master beamed with pride as he hugged his friend and wished him well.

"You're welcome to stay here any time!" he said.

"I'll be back!" Mitch replied as he threw his bag over his shoulder. "You can count on it!"

After he was gone, Master scratched me behind the ears.

"Come on, boy!" he said. "Time for your reward!"

Circuit Party Sex

Jay Starre

The promoters had aptly named the party "Inferno." It was hot as hell on the packed dance floor. I'd lost my shirt at least an hour earlier in the frenzy of the pounding music and writhing male bodies. This way my first gay circuit party, and I was getting happily carried away by the sweat, the beat, and the sexy men all around. That's my excuse for what happened to me that night.

My friends appeared and disappeared amid the other dancing men. Strangers rubbed up against me as though we were lovers. The floor became even more crowded. There had to have been over 500 gay men jammed into the seething mass. My eyes sought the gaze of others. I smiled and nodded. I ignored and was ignored. Cruised and was not cruised. I loved it, dancing as if it was the only thing I wanted to do in the world. And it was! The party continued for hours, and I wished it would never end. I never wanted to leave that heavenly mass of male flesh.

Just past midnight, the intensity of the party suddenly increased. The half-naked bodies writhed more abandon, the beat pulsed louder and more powerfully. Men crowded even closer. Many were entwined in couples or groups as they danced and shouted together. I lost sight of everyone I knew. Total strangers surrounded me. That was probably the reason for my suddenly uninhibited behavior. No one knew me. I could be anyone.

Just then I felt hands reach from behind and unbutton the fly of my jeans. With men's bodies pressing in on me from all sides, I could not turn around to see whom the hands belonged to. Not panicked in the least, I merely rode the beat and swayed along with the mass of other male bodies. The hands at my crotch were big, tan,

333

and hot. A hard, equally hot body pressed against me from behind. My new best friend slowly unbuttoned my fly as he humped against my back and ass. I felt another hard body part, unmistakably a stiff cock, pressing into me as well.

For one brief moment my head cleared and I rebelled. I grabbed the hands at my waist to resist as they inserted themselves into my underwear and groped my turgid bone intimately.

"Relax, go with it! It'll feel good," a hot whisper tickled my earlobe.

I twisted my head and stared into half-lidded eyes set into a classically good-looking, square-jawed face. My new pal responded to my prudish protests with a crooked grin and a lewd wink. His stiff poker pressed against one of my plump butt cheeks.

Overcome by this hot stud and the energy of the party, I surrendered. I thought it was just for that moment, just to allow those burning hands to caress and massage my stiffening meat. I inhaled sharply: The odor of male sweat and the scent of delicious cologne combined in a heady aroma that sent my head swimming.

I reeled. The bodies around me held me up. I focused my attention on the hands in my shorts. One hand kneaded my cock into an aching erection while the other tugged steadily on my roiling nut sac. I gasped when those hands shoved down my underwear to unleash my hard cock. I was exposed, my stiff boner waving in the open in front of hundreds of men.

Of course, the bodies were pressed together so tightly that only the half-dozen men immediately around me could actually see my embarrassing boner. I glanced around and realized some of them were staring at me with hungry interest, while others were lost in their own orgiastic dancing frenzy. Once again, I gave in to the situation. The massaging hands did not let up. Instead, they began to pump my cock. The body behind me moved up and down in time to the music, and the hard cock attached to it rubbed insistently along my ass and crack. Tantalizing sensations rocked my guts as those big hands stroked my bone, slowly at first, then more rapidly. The hands tickled and teased my cock head and gently played with my balls.

I closed my eyes for one delicious moment to appreciate the feeling of those fingers on my cock and balls. That was when my anonymous paramour decided to yank down my jeans. In one swift movement, I was bare-assed! I gasped from the shock.

"Nice butt, very nice," that throaty whisper teased my ear again. I shuddered as I felt the rough material of his jeans rasp against my naked butt cheeks. One hand returned to my cock to resume pumping. The other hand groped my butt. Coarse fingers grazed my naked flesh with tantalizing strokes. They roamed over one cheek, then moved to the other. I shivered with electric desire when those fingers traveled between my cheeks and began to explore my tensed crack.

"Relax, take it easy, open up that sweet butt," the whispering man said, sending chills down my spine.

I had not opened my eyes. I was afraid to. But when the stranger's fingers began to tickle the rim of my puckered butthole, they flew open. The men around me stomped and shouted to the pulse of the pounding music. Most of them ignored us. The few whose eyes were riveted on us leered with feral lust. I shuddered again and felt myself spread my thighs, as far apart as my tangled jeans and underwear would allow. What had come over me?

A tongue suddenly began to lick my earlobe and then my neck. Wet lips dragged across my shoulders. I quivered and bent over, leaning into the bare chest of the men in front of me. He and his companions laughed, but otherwise ignored me. Fingers began to probe my asshole: teasing the rim and tickling the fluttering butt blossom. I flushed when I considered what was happening to me. I was getting fingered right there for anyone to see!

But I could not stop it. I did not want to stop it. I wanted more.

"Stick your fingers up my ass," I heard myself say in a low, guttural moan.

He heard me. He returned his mouth to my ear and licked there for a moment before he whispered again. "You want my fingers inside you? Do you?"

"Yes!" I grunted back.

The fingers tapping my butt pit were suddenly gone. I moaned and thrust backward with my hips, longing to find them again. I ached to have them inside me! I felt the man's rough jeans and stiff cock rubbing my left ass cheek. With his other hand he continued to squeeze my dripping knob. I felt a frenzy of frustrated desire overtaking me. I needed those fingers in my ass!

Finally, I felt them return. This time they were slick with lube! They strummed my fluttering asshole like it was a fine violin. I clenched and released the muscles of my anal rim, intent on getting those slippery fingers inside my ravenous hole. Another teasing moment passed before two of them poked into the lubed center of my crack. I let out a long, grateful moan as they slammed past my snapping ass rim.

"You like that? You like those greased fingers up your tight ass?" The whisper in my ear became a deep growl.

I murmured my answer—a groaning "Yes"—but it was lost in the cacophony of the music and howling men. I was lost in that sea of flesh as well, bent over, my hands on my knees, with two fingers digging deep into my lubed asshole while other fingers played with my twitching cock. I found myself wiggling my ass to ride those digging fingers, in time to the pulse of the music that moved through the mass of flesh like a living being.

Fingers worked my ass. Then two became three. The growl in my ear was feral, as hungry as the ache in my bottomless bottom. Those three fingers plunging inside me then lifted me up by the rim of my hole, almost off my feet. I couldn't believe what was happening. I'd become a slobbering, moaning hole, right there on the jammed dance floor.

The stranger's fingers were still buried to the hilt, when I suddenly felt two hands tugging on my naked nipples. Digit and thumb tweaked them and pulled on them. The electric sensation coursed through my body in ripples of lust. I looked up into the eyes of a leering muscle daddy. He was half-naked, his huge hairless chest sported twin tit-rings. He laughed as he pinched and pulled on my nipples. My mouth was open in a moaning "Oh…" of appreciation when the three fingers plowing my asshole suddenly slid out.

I leaned into the muscle daddy, who was pinching my taut nipples. My other buddy's hands continued to massage my cock with agonizing intensity. My ass was exposed, greased, and freshly fingered. I did not know what to expect next. Behind me, the hard body pressing against mine was suddenly naked. I felt hairy hips and a big throbbing boner, which slid up and down my crack.

"Don't worry, it's wrapped!" the throaty snarl in my ear assured me.

He had put a condom on his cock. There was only one reason for that. His hard bone slid up and down my parted crack for just a brief tantalizing interlude, then slammed into me.

"Nice, tight ass!" he shouted out in my ear.

I gurgled from the shock of his assault. I felt as if a torpedo had been fired up my ass. The huge thing tore into me. I was already lubed and stretched by his fingers. But the depth and swiftness of that plunge nearly knocked me off me feet. The fingers on my chest held me up, tugging at my burning nipples while that big meat reamed me from behind.

He fucked like an animal. I spread my legs as far apart as I could, bent down, and took it—every inch of it. I reveled in the slamming sensation rocking my prostate. The music pounded to a crescendo and continued at a feverish tempo for what seemed like hours. I was fucked and fucked and fucked. His pounding hips lifted me off the floor. I floated in a sea of sweating male flesh. Hands reached out and groped me all over. I felt them on my ass, pulling my cheeks farther apart for that cock to pound even harder and deeper. At one point I was actually off my feet while that cock slammed my poor butthole in a burning frenzy.

Suddenly, I shot my load. Somehow jizz just boiled up out of me. I'd had no warning. I was in a fog of ecstasy, my ass a torrid tunnel of aching pleasure, when suddenly my cock just blew. I screamed, but no one heard. I was off my feet and still getting fucked. That big fuck stick continued to bang into me mercilessly. My spunk leaked out of my boner and dribbled over the fingers stroking it.

I was granted no reprieve. My anonymous fuck buddy did not relent. If anything, he picked up his pace. Countless pairs of hands held me in the air while his thrusting accelerated. The muscle daddy lifted my head and covered my mouth with his, slobbering wetly over my lips and jamming his tongue deep into my throat. I could not speak. I could not think.

Suddenly, the music came to a crashing end. The cock behind me slammed in to the hilt but then remained immobile. I knew he was shooting. He was shooting his jizz in my ass. He loved my hot ass so much it had made him come. I felt a strange sense of power course through me. My anal muscles responded. Slack and accepting, they suddenly convulsed and danced around his throbbing boner, milking it of every drop of man juice.

"Oh, man…oh, man! That is the best ass I've ever had!" he proclaimed, his voice carrying over the shouts of the crowd.

It seemed the dance was over. Muscle daddy's tongue was still lodged in my throat, however. Then I heard it begin again. A heavy bass beat pounded through the air. The men around me began to writhe and stomp again. The cock up my ass slid out. My asshole gaped and quivered. Then I felt fingers sliding back inside it.

"I have to feel it. I have to feel that sweet hole I just fucked so hard," my buddy crooned in my ear, leaning over me and once again tickling my earlobe with his wet tongue.

With muscle-daddy tonguing my throat, I still could not speak. The stranger continued tonguing my ear. And his fingers burrowed deep into my stretched, hungry asshole. They belonged there, to fill a void that had momentarily left me feeling bereft.

That's how the night ended. Three fingers worked my gaping hole until the music eventually ended. I grew stiff again and shot twice more. Come splattered me from all sides as guys got themselves off while watching the violation of my ass. I was a circuit party slut. I was in paradise.

Stop and Go
R.J. March

Clay steps out of the steam of the shower and wraps himself in a towel, shy suddenly, not at all as comfortable with his nakedness as Bingham, who loiters nude at the bank of lockers, his body dripping still, his towel nowhere in sight.

"Forgot it," he says, grinning. "Borrow yours?" And in a moment Clay finds himself uncovered again, digging through his gym bag for fresh underwear and trying to be oblivious to the luxurious drag of his towel across Bingham's chest. He tries to ignore the rough ball of it between Bingham's legs, realizing he'd be once again in possession of that towel and that it would become, he's decided, infinitely more valuable. He steps into boxers, finds his deodorant, glances at the white cheeks of Bingham's ass, tightly muscled and flexing like coy winks.

"You look hung over," Bingham says, and Clay blinks himself back into consciousness, having taken a little visual side trip, wandering through the thick brush around Bingham's balls.

"What?" he says, dumbly as he feels himself blushing.

"You're like a fucking retard," Bingham says, throwing the towel at his friend. It lands around Clay's face and he freezes, his dick wobbling. He quickly grabs the soggy towel, sniffing and smelling nothing but his own soap, but imagining something else, and it's like an aphrodisiac, and he has to hurry into his jeans, pulling them up before his excitement shows, fumbling with the buttons, a breeze from nowhere fluttering across his nipples.

Bingham, naked still, turns toward the mirror at the other end of the locker room. "Fucking shoulders, man" he says as he examines himself in the mirror. "Where the fuck do they go?"

"They haven't gone anywhere," Clay mutters, examining things just as closely. Someone's going to come in, he thinks, and he doesn't even care. Clay watches Bingham's ass, the smooth white flesh, the dark split, the squat backs of his thighs, the pale behinds of his knees and his overmuscled calves. Clay elbows into his shirt, retrieves his dropped towel and sprays cologne on himself, ignoring the fact that his cock has become engorged, thick as a brick. Bingham leaves his reflection and comes back to their shared bench, his dick fattened and unacknowledged, but not by Clay, who watches the slow ascent until it is tucked away in Structure briefs, an arrested semi that Bingham smooths out before he steps into his jeans. Clay gets a shudder of chills.

"What are you doing tonight?" Bingham asks.

Clay shrugs. He shoulders his gym bag.

"Give me a call," Bingham says. He's still in his briefs. They are dark blue and cling mid thigh. His shaved smooth belly rises up from the waistband, and his navel is perpetually popped out like a sweet roll. He is stalled, stalling. He goes through his bag but pulls nothing from it. He glances in the mirror again and then down at his own pecs. Then he looks at Clay.

"OK," Clay says, and Bingham just stares at him.

Clay is at the mall in the men's room on the lower level near the garage. There's a note written on the inside of the stall door, saying the shit goes down at four, and Clay is waiting. He sits on the toilet, listening to the pound of his heart. The rest room door opens, hinges screaming, and Clay's eyes go wide. He freezes. He listens to the footsteps and to the sounds this man is making, his breathing and noises, the drag of his zipper, his breath held now and the long wait for piss to splash in the toilet.

And in the waiting, Clay goes hard. He pulls himself out of his jeans and pinches the head of his cock, thumbing the slit that oozes, and he tugs quietly on the head, again and again and again, waiting for anything to happen, not sure how these things go. The man—Clay can see the side of one of his Adidas athletic shoes—doesn't pee and he doesn't move, but he's breathing again, and his leather coat pulls loudly, and still there's nothing.

Clay is pulling harder on himself while picturing Bingham's shower scene earlier that afternoon at the gym. In his mind's eye Clay sees Bingham turning into his spray of water, twisting his body, his stomach tightening into neatly sectioned muscle, the hair there turning into a black ribbon that unfurls down to his thick stubby cock, curling around it and spreading down over his big pink balls. Clay licks his thumb and forefinger and works them over his cock head. He wedges his fingers into his jeans to search for his balls, bringing them out, rubbing them with his left hand. They are big balls, bigger than Bingham's, only not as hairy, and he strokes them through the easy give of the sac. Taking himself in a fist, he leans over and drops a gob of spit on his palm, not caring about the obvious noise this produces.

The sneakered foot remains unmoving, its trio of black stripes going nowhere. In Clay's fantasy Bingham is showering, spitting, squinting through the spray, legs spread, water falling from his dick like piss, the expression on his face unreadable. He looks at Clay. Who knows what he sees? Clay squeezes up on his shaft. Behind his closed eyes he sees Bingham's hand, soaped, between ass cheeks, making his hole clean.

Clay's nylon sleeve is loud and telltale, each swish clearly defining the action of his arm, each stroke of his prick. He doesn't care because the man at the urinal has come over to the stall door and is peering through the crack, watching Clay jacking off. He is an eye and some shoes and then a voice telling Clay to stand up, to take down his jeans. Clay pushes his jeans down his thighs, the air cool on his skin, and his cock is electric—harder, he thinks, than it's ever been, but he can't touch it, because it's already humming, dribbling, twitching with pulse and want. The voice tells him to lift up his shirt, and he does, offering his belly, his pink nipples that are tight as spring peas and just as small. The eye darts up and down. Then the voice commands him to turn around, and Clay turns and bends over. He holds on to the seat of the toilet, and he smells the rim heady with the scent of many men, and he swears he can feel the eye on his tight little hole. His head reels from the smell of old piss, from the sight of curling dropped hairs of men and boys before him. He pushes his cock and balls between his thighs because the voice tells him.

"I'm coming," Clay says in a perfectly normal voice, and the voice that belongs to the eye, still whispering, tells him to turn around. Clay turns and sprays the walls of the stall. He comes until he begins to think he will never stop coming. He hears the man's harsh breathing and sees light glinting off the eye that never blinks until the end, when the man holds his breath and comes between the door crack, his semen thick and yellow and dripping, adding to the mess of the rest room floor.

Bingham's flannel shirt is undone. He's wearing a wife beater underneath it with a dragged-out neck and a hole under his right arm. His shirt has slipped off one shoulder, revealing the hard-balled deltoids. Clay wants to know where they're going, but it doesn't really matter. He's not sure what matters anymore. He used to think it was baseball and girls and PlayStation 2 and a fake I.D. to get beer on the weekend and maybe getting promoted at the paper mill, maybe going to college someday. They're heading toward Glens Falls, and then they get off at the South Glens Falls exit and get back on the Northway, heading south again. Winter is over, but it's still cold and there's still snow, though not much, and Clay is not cold, but he settles into his coat, and Bingham lifts his arm to slip his shirt back where it belongs. They pull into a rest stop, and Bingham cuts the engine. He looks through the windshield at the trees at the edge of the grass.

"It's all fenced in now," he says, "but you used to be able to come here and walk the trails back there." He turns to Clay. "Mad shit, back there on those trails, man," he says, smiling.

Clay understands. It's like the mall rest room, and it's like the county park after dark. Men with their hands shoved deep in their pockets staring holes through you. He starts the car again.

Neither one talks. Clay watches his breath when he gets out of Bingham's car. The driveway is empty; Bingham's parents have gone to Vermont for the weekend. Bingham was supposed to work today, but he called in to take the day off.

In his bedroom, Bingham takes off his flannel shirt. Clay sits at the desk, going through Bingham's CDs, but he watches his friend flex his biceps as though he can't help himself. There are sketches— Bingham's tattoo designs—on scraps of paper littering the desk. Among them are tribal bands, barbed wire, and entwined Celtic intricacies. He's staring at Clay, and Clay quickly realizes that there won't be any talk, any discussion. There's no need for words now. Bingham has a hand over his fly, gently strumming the front of his jeans. Talk would define, and definition would bring a false sense of meaning to what can only be, for Bingham, a meaningless act. Clay can see it in Bingham's expression. He can read already the raw need with nothing more behind it. It's the eye again—and its hunger.

Clay stands and touches the front of his own jeans. He's hard, has been hard for some time. His cock is hot and flat against his belly, hidden beneath layers of clothing. Bingham's is much more obvi- ous—it presses up to the left of his fly and makes a widening wet spot. He steps backward and sits down on his bed, leaning back on his elbows, his white tank riding up his belly, baring his navel and the dark trail of hair there. He doesn't have to say anything to make Clay walk over to him and touch the damp stiffness, swirling his finger against the leaking head beneath. At this, Bingham exhales— it is almost a moan. His eyes close, and his head tilts back, and Clay leans in to put his lips on the boy's throat, just over his Adam's apple, and Bingham groans and pushes up with his hips against Clay's hand and forearm. Clay tongues the soft skin under his bristly chin and accepts the hand that grabs the back of his head, moving it gently but insistently down. His lips press against the dampened jeans, and Bingham's hips arc upward to meet his embrace.

Clay struggles with button and fly and then the tangle of underwear until he actually touches the firm hot flesh of Bingham's pole, the humid bush. Wetness is everywhere. Clay wrestles the jeans off Bingham's hips, baring his cock. It is thick and hovering, a slimy drip leaking from the pale end, its deep slit. Clay tastes him then, and Bingham writhes beneath him, pressing toward Clay's eager maw.

Bingham's cock hits the back of Clay's mouth, and Bingham lets out a pained grunt. He grips Clay's head tightly and fucks his thick shaft into the boy's mouth. Clay snorts and chokes but stays on the prick, his lips stretched, kissing curling pubes with each beat. His fingers roam Bingham's torso finally, the plaited belly, the slabs of his pecs. He tears at the wife beater and it comes apart easily, making Bingham groan again.

"Holy shit," he whispers roughly, jacking his hips. He rolls over, never breaking contact with Clay's mouth, and gets him on his back and continues to fuck his face. He gropes the front of Clay's jeans: the bone-hard covered stump. He squeezes it tightly, repeating the motion ever more quickly until Clay is moaning. Clay is close to release, swallowing the salty leak of Bingham's dick, his jaw aching but still hungry. His back arches, and his throat constricts, and his cock blows in his pants under Bingham's heavy grip. Bingham shudders above him and drags his prick from Clay's throat and tries to hold off, clutching each breath, his balls tucking upward, and he blows his load across Clay's face, leaving clotted chugs of warm white on his cheeks and nose and lips.

This will happen again or maybe not. It's up to Bingham to make it happen. Clay lingers on the bed. He has wiped his face clean with a towel. He holds the towel over his crotch, watching Bingham walk over to the window and look out through the blinds, his cock still hard and shining. Clay watches and waits. He has all the time in the world.

In the Dark

Michael Stamp

I licked my lips, savoring the tang of salsa and the sour aftertaste of come. Jeff's plane had left over an hour ago, but I could still distinguish both flavors in my mouth. The salsa we munched on the way to the airport had been both hot and spicy. Jeff's flesh had been just as hot when I touched it, as if the salsa had gone straight from his stomach to his cock.

Jeff was running late, so we didn't have time for a proper good-bye at home. But at the airport I gave him a fond farewell in the front seat of the car. Luckily, the underground parking garage was deserted. If we'd had more time, I would have let Jeff fuck me. Since his plane was leaving in half an hour, I sucked him off instead: my going-away present to him.

Even though he protested, I know it turned Jeff on to be naked in a public place. Usually, I have to stroke him hard, but his cock started to stiffen the moment I touched it. I knelt on the cold garage floor and put my head in his lap. Then I took his rigid seven inches down my throat.

I worked fast, and in no time Jeff was moaning, and his body squirmed against the leather seat. His right hand gripped the seat-belt strap while his left hand tangled in my short dark hair, urging my head forward until his wiry pubes tickled my nose. Soon I felt Jeff's legs stiffen under me. Knowing he was close, I worked my hand down the back of his shorts and fingered his asshole. Even though I never fuck Jeff, he likes it when I play with his asshole.

That's because I have very talented fingers. I hit his prostate dead on, which always makes him come. And he did, sending his blistering load into my mouth after only a couple minutes of sucking.

The moment his cock slipped out of my mouth, Jeff pulled me up to him for a long, deep kiss. With his tongue he explored the place where his cock had been. I thrust a gob of his come back into his mouth. I was glad I was able to send Jeff off on his trip so satisfied. It made me feel less guilty about where I was going, and what I wanted to happen once I got there.

I only cruise the leather bars when I know Jeff's going to be away for a week or more. It gives the bruises time to fade. I don't know what I'd do if Jeff ever saw me right after. He'd be so angry I know he'd leave me. It's not that I don't love him. It's just that every once in a while I need something Jeff can't give me—won't give me, even though I've told him how much I really want it.

Jeff and I did have rough sex once. At least I thought of it that way. He was all torn up about it later because he was afraid he'd hurt me. Anyway, it wasn't something either of us planned.

He'd had a really bad day at work and had started drinking the minute he came home. I said something that pissed him off. I don't remember what. Suddenly, he was all over me, demanding sex. When I said no, he grabbed me and forced me down onto the bed. I fought him, and he went nuts. Jeff outweighs me, so it wasn't much of a contest. He climbed on top of me and held me down while he fucked me hard and fast, pushing my face into the pillow to keep me quiet. It was the first time I came just from Jeff being inside me.

Afterward, Jeff was really frightened by what he'd done. He held me close, saying he didn't know what had come over him. I told him it was all right, that he hadn't hurt me. That seemed to calm him down. Then I told him I'd found it kind of exciting.

Jeff was horrified. He said, "You're only saying that to make me feel better."

"No, Jeff," I said truthfully, "I really mean it."

"No you don't," he insisted. "You must hate me for what I did to you. I'd understand if you couldn't ever forgive me."

"I don't hate you, Jeff," I told him. "I love you. And there's nothing to forgive." I know I should have left it at that, but I couldn't help myself. I told him I'd really enjoyed the sex and wouldn't mind if it happened again.

I never forgot how I felt when Jeff held me down and forced his way inside me. Or how much I wanted to feel that way again.

At first I was able to satisfy my craving just by fantasizing during sex. While Jeff was fucking me, I'd pretend I was the bottom of some faceless leatherman, some muscle-bound stud who'd tie me facedown on the bed and shove a pillow under my ass to raise it. I'd imagine him using his belt to turn my ass cheeks a bright shade of red, then fucking me hard and pinning me to the mattress with his huge cock.

That worked for a little while, but soon pretending wasn't enough. I had to have the real thing. That's when I started using Jeff's business trips as my chance to explore the side of me I couldn't share with him.

I never go to the same bar twice, even though there have been some guys I wouldn't have minded seeing two or even three times. But I was afraid to tempt fate by going to the same place more than once. There's always the chance someone will recognize me when Jeff and I are out together and say something to me in front of him. So I always pick somewhere new. The more out of the way, the better.

Sometimes I'd just fall into a scene, stumble upon on it through nothing but dumb luck. That's how I wound up at the Beacon after I left the airport. I pulled the car over when I saw a group of men on the street disappearing into a dark doorway—hot-looking men, some going in alone, others in pairs. So I drove a few blocks away, parked the car on the street, and walked back.

The combination of smells assaulted me when I walked in the door: sweat, piss, beer, and leather all mixed together in an aroma I would stand in line to buy if somebody bottled it. Heads turned when I came in wearing my khakis and crewneck sweater. The expression on every face told me I didn't belong there. But I did, at least for the night.

I made my way to the bar, sandwiched myself between the bodies, and ordered a beer. I liked to guess how long it I would have to wait for someone to speak to me. It was a little game I played with myself. Sometimes I waited an hour to get what I wanted, but that wasn't going to happen this time. I could tell that right away.

He stood by the pool table, a cue stick in one hand and a bottle of beer in the other. He was tall—well over six feet—and big. Sparse patches of beard covered his ruddy face, but he wasn't making a fashion statement. He just hadn't shaved in a few days.

He put down the pool cue and ambled toward the bar. He raised his beer to his lips and took a long swallow, then wiped his mouth with the back of his hand. "Are you in the wrong place?" he asked with a sneer.

"I don't think so, sir," I replied.

He was surprised I knew to address him with the proper respect. He took another swig of beer and asked, "You didn't make a wrong turn on your way to a different bar?"

"No, sir," I said, stressing his title. "I'm not looking for conversation."

"What *are* you looking for?"

For a minute, I was afraid it wasn't going to go any further. But then he made his move, extending his bottle toward me, putting the long neck under my sweater and lifting it up to expose my tits. My chest is completely hairless, and while my pecs are well-defined, I'm far from muscular. I do have nice nipples, though: small and extremely sensitive. When he used the mouth of his bottle to flick my left nipple, it hardened immediately.

"Well, looky here," he said to the men around us. "Looks like we've got someone whose nipples are in need of some attention. Is that right? Do your tits need some instruction?"

He put his bottle down on the bar and reached out, took one of my nipples in each hand, and rolled them between his heavily callused fingers. It felt like he was rubbing my nipples with sandpaper. They grew bigger and harder under his severe coaching. "You like that?" he asked.

I wasn't wearing underwear under my khakis, so everyone in the bar knew just how much I was liking the nipple play. "Very much," I moaned.

His rolling soon became squeezing, then savage twisting. "How about now?" he asked.

"Yes, sir," I gasped, biting down on my bottom lip. "Thank you, sir."

He was impressed by my willingness to take so much abuse without telling him to stop. "You got nice tits, but I'll bet you have an even nicer ass."

"I was hoping you'd want to find out, sir."

The minute the words were out of my mouth I knew I'd made a mistake. My purpose was to please him, not myself; even though I'd derive pleasure from our encounter, that pleasure would be irrelevant to him. I'd been so excited by the prospect of this man using me that I'd forgotten my place. I waited with my eyes downcast, sure I'd ruined my chances with him.

But he only laughed. "Kind of forward, aren't you, son?" he asked.

I let out the breath I'd been holding. "Yes, sir," I said.

"Well, I don't mind you showing some initiative."

"I'm glad, sir."

"Now let's see just how shy you are in public." He reached out, unzipped my pants, and pulled them down to my ankles. Freed from the confines of my khakis, my erection sprang out in front of me. I'm cut and not very thick, a respectable eight inches when I'm hard. But he had no interest in my cock. He turned me around to face the bar and ran his hand down over my ass cheeks. "Very nice indeed."

"Thank you, sir."

I suddenly felt like a prize thoroughbred at an auction. At least a dozen hands stroked my ass cheeks, spread them, and poked their fingers up inside me till they had me on my toes. I was treated to a chorus of "nice ass," "hot ass" and other assorted terms of endearment before I heard the one I had been waiting for.

"But it's too pale, Bill," someone said. "I've never seen you fuck an ass that pale."

The word "stop" sounded in my brain, but I was able to swallow it before it could leave my mouth. There had always been some kind of a back room before. Twice I'd gone home with men who had chosen me. But I'd never done anything with other men watching.

My heart began to race as I heard the sound of his belt sliding through the loops on his jeans. Just knowing he was going to whip me there in front of everyone made my cock grow. I felt a drop of precome leak from my piss slit.

I leaned over the bar, stuck out my ass, and braced myself for the first stroke. It landed with a loud *crack* on my left ass cheek. I gasped and stiffened at the burn, but held my position. There had been a lot of force behind the blow. It was obvious he didn't believe in starting off slow and working up to his full potential. I took a deep breath and waited for the second stroke. It came, harder than the first, landing on my right cheek with such a bite I couldn't hold back my cry. I know he heard me, but he didn't reproach me. My reprimand came from his belt. The next stroke was still harder and a little lower, catching the back of my thighs. I gritted my teeth, but stayed quiet. He picked up the pace and kept it. The leather sharply bit first one cheek, then the other, each stroke finding its target perfectly and each landing with greater force than the last.

I lost track of the time. I tried to click the minutes off in my head as his blows continued to fall, but I couldn't concentrate. Tears blurred my vision. I wanted to scream, but I kept it in.

My ass was a quivering mass of burning pain when he finally stopped. Actually, I didn't realize my punishment had ended until someone pressed a beer bottle against one of my ass cheeks. The shock of the ice-cold glass made me yelp and elicited laughter from the men around me.

I turned around and saw he had opened his jeans to reveal his engorged cock—the thickest I'd ever seen. For a split second I panicked at the thought of him ripping me open as he tried to enter me, and I contemplated making a run for it. But the two men who had held me down were still at their posts. I knew I'd never make it to the door.

He held out a condom, which I meekly accepted. I ripped open the cellophane and rolled the rubber down over his erection. Then, without a word, I resumed my position on the bar.

Again many hands groped me. They played with my flaccid cock and slapped my balls, but these attentions didn't provide enough distraction to take my mind off the battering ram that was working its way inside me. Sour sweat ran down my face and into my mouth. His cock grew longer and thicker inside me, stretching me wider than I thought possible. I held onto the bar tighter and bore down. My asshole blossomed, welcoming his invasion.

My cock started to fill again. I caught myself holding my breath, releasing it only when I reminded myself to breathe.

Just when I didn't think I could take any more punishment, my muscles yielded, and his thick column of flesh filled my greedy ass. I felt light-headed and gripped the bar for support.

He did his fucking at full tilt, like his whipping My knees hit the bar with the force of each thrust. His form wasn't great, but he made up for that shortcoming with enthusiasm: a lot of fast pumping accompanied by a lot of loud grunting. Even with his lackluster style, he still managed to hit my prostate every few strokes. He kept his hands on my hips while he pumped, withdrawing halfway, then pulling me back against him so he could impale me on his cock.

My cock was rock-hard and dripping, my need to come almost unendurable. I was afraid of what would happen if I came without his permission, so I forced myself to hold back. What I didn't figure on was a lone, spit-lubed hand reaching under my belly to encircle my cock and slowly jerk me off. "Please!" I begged, but the hand continued, and without warning I exploded like a shaken can of beer on a hot summer day. My sphincter clamped down on his cock, he cried out, and his cock shot as wildly as my own. He came so long I didn't think the rubber would hold all his spunk. When he finished, his bulk came down heavily on top of me. His breathing was labored, his breath foul.

The phone was ringing as I put my key into the lock on our front door. I knew it was Jeff, calling from California. He's such a romantic. He always calls to say good night when he's away. I quickly let myself into the apartment and picked up the phone on the fourth ring.

"Hi, lover," he said. "Thanks for the wonderful send-off tonight. I was so relaxed, I fell asleep on the plane. They had to wake me when we touched down at LAX."

"You're welcome," I answered. I let out an involuntary gasp when my ass touched the sofa cushions.

"Is something wrong?" Jeff asked. I could hear the concern in his voice.

"No, everything's fine. I just bumped my knee on the coffee table. So how long do you think you'll have to stay out there?"

"At least a week, maybe more. Will you miss me?" he teased.

"Of course I will," I said, opening my pants and sliding my hand down over my burning ass cheeks. "You know I'm lost without you."

"Good night, babe," Jeff said. "I love you."

"I love you too, Jeff," I told him, smiling as I felt the heat rise from the welts on my ass. "Hurry home."

Contributor Biographies

A native Californian, **Bearmuffin** lives in San Diego with two leather bears in a stimulating ménage à trois. He has written gay erotica for *Mandate, Honcho, Torso, Manscape,* and *Hot Shots.*

Dale Chase has been writing erotica for four years and has had over 60 stories published in *Men, Freshmen, In Touch,* and *Indulge.* His work has appeared in four of the Friction series anthologies as well as *Twink, Bearotica, Full Body Contact,* and *The Best of Friction.* One of Dale's stories has been acquired by independent filmmaker Edgar Bravo and will eventually reach the big screen. Chase lives near San Francisco.

M. Christian's stories have appeared in such anthologies as *Best American Erotica, Best Gay Erotica, Best Lesbian Erotica, Best Transgendered Erotica, Best Fetish Erotica, Best of Friction, Of the Flesh,* and over 150 other books, magazines and Web sites. He's the editor of over 12 anthologies, including *Rough Stuff* (with Simon Sheppard) and the upcoming *Roughed Up* (also with Sheppard), *Best S/M Erotica, The Burning Pen, Guilty Pleasures,* and many others. His first collection, *Dirty Words,* was nominated for a Lambda Literary Award—and his second collection, *Speaking Parts,* is currently available from Alyson Books. For more information, check out his Web site at www.mchristian.com.

Cage Crawford is the pseudonym for a freelance writer who currently lives in Los Angeles, Calif., where he writes for several local and national publications. His erotic fiction has appeared in *First Hand, Guys, Straight Man Tales,* and *Men* magazine as well as the upcoming Alyson compilation *Full Body Contact.* He is also at work adapting several of his stories into screenplays for adult films.

Wendy Fries writes and publishes male-male erotica with startling regularity. She has also created a sweet little religion around jelly beans. If you want to know what Alan Currier in "One Wish" looks like, go to any video store and rent *Passion in the Dessert.* Take a gander at Ben Daniels. After you're through licking the TV screen, you can E-mail her your thanks at w_fries@excite.com.

Duncan Frost grew up in the Midwest and attended a small liberal arts college in Ohio. After he received his doctorate in Art History, he taught for a few years, then decided the type of men he wanted to meet were more likely to hang around a construction site than a faculty tea. Duncan traded his mortarboard for a hard hat and is now a master carpenter who pounds nails during the day and raunchy men at night.

Todd Gregory is a born-and-bred Southern boy who now makes his home in the French Quarter of New Orleans, where even stranger things than "Angels Don't Fall in Love" occur. This is his first published story, and he is currently working on an erotic suspense novel called *Sunburn.* He has neither an MFA nor an undergraduate college degree, but he works out five times a week and is always on the lookout for a new ways to express himself—on the page, sexually, or both!

T. Hitman has written features for several national magazines and newspapers as well as short fiction, several novels and nonfiction books, and a few television episodes, of which he hopes to do more. In his spare time (spare being a rare and relative term), he freely admits to watching professional sports like baseball, hockey, football, and extreme sports in the way that most men watch porn. "Clean Shorts" and "The Ice-cream Man Cometh" are his third entries in the Friction series.

Lars-Peter Ingemann describes himself as a "typically unfocused blond." His professional writing encompasses erotic magazines, music journals, history texts, retail Web sites, computer games, puppet videos, and greeting cards. However, none of these reflects his actual day job, which remains a mystery. The little trouble-maker currently resides in Hollywood.

R.J. March wrote his first erotic story in the sixth grade. Since then, he has won wide acclaim as one of the most talented and prolific writers of gay erotic fiction. His collection of erotica, *Looking for Trouble,* was a national best-seller, and his work appears regularly in erotic magazines such as *Men, Freshmen,* and *Unzipped.*

Jay Maxwell calls Canada his home, where he loves to write in his spare time, pounding out one-handed tales about some of his sexual conquests.

The erotic fiction of **Christopher Pierce** has been published in *Advocate Classifieds, Bound & Gagged, Care & Training of the Male Slave, Cuir, Daddy, Eagle, Firsthand, Honcho, Inches, In Touch, Indulge, International Leatherman, Mandate, Manifest Reader, Manscape, Mantalk, Powerplay, Super MR, Torso,* and *Urge.* Write to him at chris@christopherpierceerotica.com and visit his Web site at www.ChristopherPierceErotica.com. He lives with his partner of nine years in South Florida.

A New York–based writer, poet, and now author, **L.M.Ross** has published work in various media, and his erotica has graced the steamy pages of many popular magazines and anthologies. "A Duplicitous Summer Night" is an excerpt from his acclaimed first novel, *The Long Blue Moan,* recently published by Alyson and now available on Amazon.com and in stores nationwide.

Simon Sheppard is the author of *Hotter Than Hell and Other Stories* and the forthcoming nonfiction book *Kinkorama.* With M. Christian, he's coeditor of *Rough Stuff* and its sequel, *Roughed Up: More Tales of Gay Men, Sex, and Power.* His work has appeared in three previous editions of *Friction* as well as *Best Gay Erotica, The Best American Erotica,* and over 60 other anthologies. His second short-story collection, *In Deep,* will be published by Alyson Books in 2004. He lives in San Francisco, believes firmly in the pleasures of queer love and desire, and loiters shamelessly at www.simonsheppard.com.

Danny Smith enjoys writing gay tales—and poking gay tails in his spare time. He is one of many horny gay writers living on the rainy coast of British Columbia, Canada.

Mel Smith's stories have appeared in *In Touch* and *Indulge* magazines, online at *Velvet Mafia,* and in the anthologies, *Best Gay Erotica, Friction 5,* and *The Best of Friction.* Mel had wanted to be a writer since the fifth grade but got sidetracked by a stint as a firefighter and 13 years in law enforcement, where the men were plentiful and easy.

Michael Stamp's earliest influences were the novels of Gordon Merrick and John Preston, so it's not surprising that all the New Jersey–based author's own gay erotic stories, including his S/M tales, have a decidedly romantic bent. Stamp's erotica can be found in the anthologies *Best American Erotica 2002, Best Gay Erotica 2001* and *2002, Best S/M Erotica, Casting Couch Confessions, Sex Toy Tales,* and *Strange Bedfellows,* the E-book *Y2Kinky,* and publications such as *Inches* and *In Touch.*

A first runner up in the Mr. B.C. Leather 2002 contest, **Jay Starre** resides in Vancouver, British Columbia. He has written for numerous gay magazines including *Men, Honcho, Mandate, Playguy,* and

Bear and anthologies such as *Friction 4* and 5 and *Buttmen 1* and 2.

Karl Taggart is relatively new to the erotica scene, with a few stories published in *Men* and one in *Friction 5*. He works for a suburban San Francisco insurance company. His coworkers have no idea a porn writer lurks in their midst.

Stories by **Bob Vickery** (www.bobvickery.com) can be found in his three anthologies, *Cocksure, Cock Tales,* and *Skin Deep,* and within numerous other anthologies, including the Friction series, *Best American Erotica* (1997 and 2000), *Best Gay Erotica* (1998 and 2000), *Best Bisexual Erotica* (1999 and 2001), and *Queer Dharma*. He is also a regular contributor to *Men* and *Freshmen* magazines.

David Wayne ("Entangled States") and his lover of eight years live in upstate New York. He does not, in general, give relationship advice (even when people ask), for fear of jinxing a good thing. That being said, "Entangled States" holds most of his answers.

Duane Williams lives in Canada. His short fiction has appeared widely in anthologies, including *Queeries, Quickies, Queer View Mirror, Blithe House, Contra/Diction, Velvet Mafia, Suspect Thoughts, Buttmen 2, Harrington Gay Men's Literary Quarterly,* and *Full Body Contact.*

Novelist, playwright, and critic, **Thom Wolf** lives in E__ and with his partner of seven years. He is the author of the erot__ vel *Words Made Flesh,* and his short fiction has appeared in F__ 3 and __ *Bearotica, Twink, In Touch, Indulge, Men, Fresh__nd Incl__* Thom loves Liam Neeson, vodka, and Kylie Min__ He dis__ getting old. By the time you read this, he'll be 29__

Sean Wolfe has been writing gay erotica for fo__ __b-lished over 40 stories in *Men, Freshmen, Playg__ F__* and *Honcho* magazines. His stories have a__ and 5 as well as *The Best of Friction, Twink, My First Time Volume 3,* and *Three the Hard Way.* He has also penned the monthly video review column RUSHES for *Torso* magazine. Sean lives in Denver with the love of his life and partner of 12 years, Gustavo, and their pug, Spanky, and cat, Comet. He is currently in the last phase of writing his first nonerotic gay novella, *Braden's Heart,* a vampire tele to be released by Kensington Books the summer of 2003. He also has nearly completed two additional nonerotic gay novels.

Publication Information

Bear ("Construction Hank") can be contacted at P.O. Box 237, Lewisberry, PA 17339.

Bound and Gagged ("Dogboy Chews Stranger's Meat") can be contacted at (212) 736-6869.

Cherryboys ("Sweet Country Butt") can be contacted at Sportomatic Ltd., P.O. Box 392, White Plains, NY 10602.

Freshmen ("Riding the Train," "Money") can be contacted at (800) 757-7069.

Honcho ("The Craving," "Human Sex Toys") can be contacted at (888) 664-7827.

Inches ("In the Dark") can be contacted at (888) 664-7827.

Indulge ("One Wish," "Teammates," "Anything He Wants," "Flawless," "Fantasies of Hoss") can be contacted at (818) 764-2288.

In Touch ("Rendezvous at Sunset," "Beautiful Inside," "Pretty Little Pup") can be contacted at (800) 637-0101.

Mandate ("Circuit Party Sex") can be contacted at (888) 664-7827.

Men ("Entangled States," "Hit-and-run," "Cock Pit," "Touché," "Late Night, Summer, Behind the Garage," "Escorts") can be contacted at (800) 757-7069.

Playguy ("Pump It, Punk") can be contacted at (888) 664-7827.

Torso ("Tag-team Muscle Studs") can be contacted at (888) 664-7827.